THE LIGHTBODY LEGACY

Carolyn Ruffles

Carolyn Ruffles

Cover designed by Rob Ruffles & Derek Jackson.

This book is a work of fiction. Names, characters, places, and incidents either are products of the author's imagination or are used fictitiously. Any resemblance to actual persons, living or dead, events, or locales is entirely coincidental.

Carolyn Ruffles
Visit the website at https://carolynrufflesauthor.com.

First Printing: September 2023
Publisher: Carolyn Ruffles

ISBN 13: 978-1-9163913-5-2 The Lightbody Legacy

For Teresa, Rosy & Cam.

And for all my wonderful family and friends who have helped me through the past year.

Thank you.

Carolyn Ruffles

AUTHOR'S NOTE

This is a work of fiction. Real places in Suffolk and Norfolk are an integral backdrop to the narrative but I have added imaginary locations of my own, including the village of Wickthorpe. The legend of the Wickthorpe Witch is entirely fictional. Likewise, the characters in *The Lightbody Legacy*, are creations from my imagination and bear no resemblance to anyone, living or dead.

Eagle-eyed readers from Suffolk may spot some similarities between Wickthorpe and the beautiful village of Woolpit – my childhood home. Woolpit was originally intended as the location for *The Lightbody Mystery* series but, as the story evolved, I realised I was taking far too many liberties, both historical and geographical, for that to be credible. Therefore, although I could not resist keeping some of Woolpit's features, the village name was changed to Wickthorpe.

Indeed, Woolpit has its own fascinating legend, *The Green Children of Woolpit,* which is well worth researching.

"Tolerance implies no lack of commitment to one's own beliefs. Rather it condemns the oppression or persecution of others."

– John F. Kennedy

PROLOGUE

Martha
13th August, 1645

Never had Martha known terror such as this.

Her arms were secured behind her back and a piece of cloth tied roughly around her head, covering her mouth. It smelt of rotten meat. Nausea washed over her, mingling with the fear and despair. There seemed no hope of escape.

Two thugs gripped her arms, pulling her between them. Her bare heels dragged into the earth but the men were too strong for such feeble resistance. She cast her head around, desperately searching for help. If only Malachi Smith were to appear ... but even he would not dare to take on such a large group. There were many, both forward and aft of the two hauling her through Wickthorpe. She shuddered at what lay ahead.

At the end of the street, they turned right. A rough, rutted track. Beyond lay a large wood and, in its midst, a shaded lake, commonly known as Dark Water. Martha knew it well, having spent many hours collecting plants and herbs from there. It was a place she had grown to love but now it loomed before her. Black and menacing. A place of terror. She had no doubt what the men intended. *Trial by drowning.*

Water held no fear for her. She was a strong swimmer. But her limbs were tied. And even if she did, by some miracle, manage to swim free, she would be captured and branded a witch, her fate sealed. As she was marched along, her brain churned, trying to summon a solution, although she knew in her heart it was hopeless. All she could do was trust to the mercy of God, and the men surrounding her, that she would be dragged from the water before she drowned.

Within minutes, they reached the wood. The path through was narrow and difficult. One of the men was forced to release her arm. Could she break free? Make a run for it? She dismissed the notion. With her hands tied behind her back, she stood no chance. There were too many of them. Brambles tore at her nightgown as she was bundled roughly through the undergrowth. Her heart thudded a terrified gallop and she desperately wriggled numb fingers. The rope cut tightly into her wrists; the knot was secure.

'Tie her to the chair,' Holley ordered when they reached the water's edge. *Roger Holley – her nemesis.* She knew he was enjoying his chance for revenge. One of the men stood aside and she was muscled onto a solid, wooden seat, carried there for the purpose of the trial. The rope securing her hands was untied and she pulled her arms forward, rubbing blood back into useless limbs. But the respite was short-lived. Her wrists were once again yanked behind and, this time, knotted at the back of the chair.

Holley stood before her, a self-appointed judge. 'This is your final chance to spare yourself from trial by water. Confess your sins; admit you are a witch; then this will go no further.' The filthy gag was removed from her mouth, ready for her response.

Martha turned contemptuous eyes upon the assembled crowd of men. 'What you plan is a travesty in the minds of all good Christian folk.' Her voice rang out, clear and loud in the early morning air. 'I am no more a witch than any of you, or your wives, or daughters. Your heads have been filled with superstitious nonsense.'

'Are those your final words on the matter?' Satisfaction gleamed in Holley's eyes.

'No.' She regarded them all with as much dignity as she could muster while furtively testing the strength of her bonds. They were looser. Maybe there was a chance after all.

'What is it you wish to say?' Holley twitched with impatience.

'I repeat, I am innocent of that which you accuse me. I am *not* a witch.' Silence greeted her words. She saw doubt in men's faces but knew she was a long way from convincing them. There would be no final reprieve. Hatred for the man responsible filled her heart and she rushed on, her tone bitter and angry. 'But, if I were, I would put a spell on *you*, Roger Holley. I well know your true motive for this treachery.'

More mutterings from the throng. 'What does she mean, Roger?' asked one of the men, his face pale and apprehensive in the half-light.

'Talk of spells is proof enough of her guilt,' Holley declared, eager to move the proceedings along. 'Such utterances can only be those of a witch. We will discover soon enough if she is as innocent as she claims. Lift her into the water.'

'Hear this,' Martha cried, struggling on the chair as the men closed around her, desperation in her voice. 'Roger Holley is …' A rough hand was clamped against her mouth.

'Gag her! Ouch!' Holley shouted. 'She bit me!'

'If I die, know this. I curse you, Roger Holley, and any man who stands with you.' She could speak no more. The loathsome cloth bit into her mouth and was pulled tight. A few men stepped back, fidgeting with uneasiness.

'I will have no part in this,' declared one, turning away, anxious for others to follow his lead.

'Aye, nor me.'

Holley's lips curled with disdain. 'Cowards. Afraid to do what is right.' He spat on the ground. 'We don't need you. Abel and I will suffice.' Abel Packer, Holley's right-hand man, jerked at the sound of his name but was pinned by a harsh glare. 'You are in my debt, Abel. You know it. You will not shrink from my order.'

The man nodded, his face resigned. He took up his designated position on the other side of Martha. With a grunt, the two men hoisted the chair between them. She uttered a final, silent plea to God as, trembling with terror, she was carried above the inky depths of the lake.

Silence, apart from the slosh of liquid against thighs and the heavy breathing of the men bearing her weight. Even the birds ceased their dawn chorus, seemingly hushed by the horror they were about to witness. Martha closed her eyes, trying to prepare for what lay ahead, praying for strength and courage.

'I reckon here is deep enough.' Holley's voice sounded the death knell. 'On three, throw the chair forward. One, two, three ...'

She sucked in a deep breath as she was launched through the air. Blood rushed in her ears. Toppling over frontwards, she hit the water face down. It smashed her skin; a cold slap. Then the weight of the chair forced her down through the blackness and, thrashing helplessly against her bonds, she sank like a boulder to the bottom.

CHAPTER 1

Present day

Wickthorpe's oldest residents preferred to avoid Hundred Acre Wood, a sprawling mix of oak, ash, beech and silver birch, which lay at the northernmost tip of the Suffolk village. The reason for their aversion sat at the heart of it. Dark Water Lake – the site of many unexplained deaths throughout Wickthorpe's wretched history. They claimed the lake was cursed. In the seventeenth century, a witch had been drowned in its dark depths; but her wicked oath, promising vengeance against the village, lived on. Younger generations and recently-arrived inhabitants scoffed at such far-fetched opinions, enjoying the dappled walk which skirted the lake's edges. They scorned the ancient curse and mocked those who warned them of its dangers.

Whatever the truth, at just after nine o'clock on a drizzly Monday morning, the air was eerie with a sense of foreboding. Dark Water Lake, patiently pulsing to the rhythm of the raindrops rippling its Stygian surface, prepared to offer up its latest victim.

The iron-grey sky hung low with heavy cloud as Rob Richards sauntered along Thatcher's Lane and through the entrance to the wood. Underfoot, the earth was saturated after a deluge the day before and mud squelched beneath his boots. The forecast had said it would brighten up later but no sign of it yet. Still early though. As always, Rob stopped beside the board, displaying walks and indigenous wildlife, to unclip his dog's lead. Jet, his seven-year-old mongrel, waited patiently.

The small clearing also served as a car park. Looking up, Rob noticed a green Renault Clio. He did not remember seeing it there before. The area was a favourite of dog walkers from the neighbourhood, especially an older woman who brought two unruly Weimaraners. Rob liked to steer clear of them if he could. Jet was uneasy around big dogs and easily upset. He did not think the car belonged to her but would watch out, just in case.

As Jet bounded through the undergrowth ahead of him, nose to the ground, Rob followed at a more leisurely stroll. It was good to be out, even if it was miserable weather-wise. The day before had been a wash-out, and his beloved dog had been forced to make do with just a couple of short outings down the road from the terraced, ex-council house which he and his wife, Georgia, rented. He would make it up to Jet today though. There was plenty of time before his shift began at 2 p.m.

Since he and Georgia had moved to Wickthorpe, eighteen months ago, he had worked as a driver for a taxi company in Bury. It was fine, as jobs went, but he was growing weary of the long, unsociable hours. Same for most driving jobs though, and the idea of retraining to do something else made him nervous. He had never found learning easy. Still, the job had its benefits. It gave him leisurely mornings spent walking with Jet, away from the house and arguments about money. It was a struggle to pay for everything they needed, on top of the extortionate rent they had to fork out each month, and now Georgia was pregnant, things were going to get harder. When she gave up work as a teaching assistant, there would be only maternity pay topping up his wage. Even tougher to manage then. And a baby was expensive. No wonder Georgia was nagging him to get a better-paid job.

Shrugging his problems aside, he stopped and stood, just listening. The sounds of the wood were soothing. Today it was the drip of water against leaves, tiny pops and splats. As he tuned those out, he detected the whistle of a nuthatch from somewhere above him. Craning his neck to see, he pulled a small pair of binoculars from his pocket. After a few minutes spent honing in on the sound, he thought he caught a flash of its golden breast but could not be sure. He loved bird-watching. When he was a lad, he had spent hours with his dad, binoculars glued to his face, waiting for a sighting of some rare visitor or another. He sighed, pocketed the binoculars, and moved on. Life was simpler then.

The path grew narrower and he took the right-hand, less worn path which skirted the murky expanse of Dark Water Lake. Not many came this way. Some silly village superstition about a witch's curse, or something like that, put people off. That kind of thing never bothered him. For that matter, he quite enjoyed the type of gory horror film which terrified Georgia. In his mind, you only needed to fear things which were real, not made up or unproven. She told him he lacked imagination but, if that was what made her jump at shadows, he was glad he did.

Jet sprinted towards a massive oak tree and the suddenness of the movement made him start. A squirrel most likely. Yes, there it was, scampering to the safety of higher branches. 'Too slow, old girl,' he murmured, scratching the top of her head before moving on again.

It was muddier now and the earth sucked at his wellies. Bracken brushed his legs, leaving damp patches around his thighs, as he picked his way carefully through the wettest parts of the route. At last, the rain seemed to have stopped completely but the sky remained a sombre shroud. According to the forecast, it could be another hour before the promised sunshine broke through. The path wound through the trees, sometimes veering to the very edge of the lake, and sometimes concealing it from view. He was walking in a clockwise direction around its three-mile circumference. By his calculation, he had passed the furthest point from the car park and was now heading homewards. The thought did not bring him joy. The best part of his day would soon be over.

Ahead of him, Jet's tail was the only part of her visible as she darted in and out of the bushes. Wagging furiously, it was like the fluctuating needle on a confused compass, constantly changing direction as the dog's nose sought the best scents. Hers was such an uncomplicated life: enough food; a comfortable home; people who doted on her; at least one good walk a day; no worries keeping her awake at night. He could not help feeling envious.

They ploughed on, now in the darkest part of the wood, where branches formed a canopy overhead, shutting out daylight. He could see why superstitious villagers avoided this area. An over-active imagination might well conjure evil spirits, lying in wait for unwary visitors. Even he, blessed with a more prosaic type of mind, found himself quickening his step. It was the weather, he consoled himself, and the leaden sky. Normally, it seemed much less forbidding. Still, he experienced a flicker of relief when they emerged from the twilight zone into the final section of the walk, alongside the lake where the path widened, leading back to the car park.

The first strange thing he noticed was the flattening of the undergrowth. Someone had chosen to stomp all over it rather than suffer the inconvenience of muddy boots from the wet footpath. As he walked, he could clearly see the trampled trail and muttered an expletive under his breath. Some people had no respect. Easier to destroy the precious plants lining the walkway than to have the inconvenience of cleaning footwear. Didn't they know this was a conservation area with many protected woodland plant species?

The second thing was Jet. She stopped dead, head up, sniffing at the air, emitting a low growl. He looked around, his hand on her neck to console her. 'It's OK, Jet,' he soothed. 'Nothing to worry about. Come on, old girl.' He stepped forward, expecting her to follow, but she remained where she was, looking out across the water, her growl now an urgent rumble in her gullet. 'Jet, come on!' he called, continuing onwards. After a few strides, he turned. She still refused to move.

Huffing with impatience, he strode back to where she stood, hackles up, snarling at something in the lake. 'What is it?' He crouched on his haunches beside her and, from the lower angle, glimpsed something brown in the water, caught in rushes a little way out. 'What on earth is that?' Frowning, he stood and stepped closer until he was right at the water's edge. A gust of wind caught the object, causing it to billow briefly, before it once more flattened against the surface of the water. Strange. Not a piece of wood, his first thought. And Jet's reaction was weird, to say the least. He had never seen her so spooked.

Stirrings of unease fidgeted in his stomach. Something was amiss. He pulled out the binoculars and put them to his eyes with an unsteady hand. The vision was blurry and he realised the lenses were still wet from his earlier attempt to spot the elusive nuthatch. Taking a deep breath, he gave them a wipe and brought them back to his eyes, training them in the direction of the mystery object.

'Oh God!' he muttered. It was an item of clothing – a sweater of some description, maybe a jacket or a hoodie. But there was more. Like a film scape of mounting horror, the shapes revealed themselves: a head; long hair; the pale hue of a hand trailing, limp and lifeless. *A body. Drowned.*

With a strangled gasp, he reached for his phone.

CHAPTER 2

Three months earlier

Taking a deep breath, Deborah Ryecroft steered her Mercedes off the A14 towards the beautiful, historic village of Wickthorpe in Suffolk, her childhood home. So long since she had been here – over thirty years – but she still felt the suffocating dread of old, starting as an ache in the pit of her stomach and climbing the trachea until it scorched her throat. What was there to fear? Her parents were gone and she was a very different person from the girl who had last visited, terrified and alone, aged seventeen. Then, she had vowed never to return. Yet, here she was, and this time not a fleeting visitor either.

Deborah slowed the car as she approached the thirty mile-an-hour sign heralding her entrance into Wickthorpe. The village had changed. Busier; wider roads; industrial units. Jaunty daffodils waved their heads in the cold March sunshine as she headed along Hay Road past a cricket ground. The familiar church spire came into view and ugly memories flooded back before she could suppress them. Passing the village school brought a fresh wave of recollections. There had been a time when the building, and the people in it, had been her sanctuary. But, aged twelve, she had been despatched to boarding school and villagers viewed her differently after that. An outsider. And, after the tragedy, she became a target of blame and hatred. 'The Wickthorpe Witch,' they called her. Mostly, behind her back, but sometimes kids, hunting in packs, would surround and taunt her. *Wickthorpe Witch.*

Wickthorpe Witch. She fancied the breeze still carried the strains of their relentless chanting and cruel laughter.

She turned right, into Green Road. Just a few hundred yards later, her childhood home, Greenways Farm, came into view, large and forbidding in grey-flint. A long, gravel drive snaked between paddocks. Deborah noticed two horses, swaddled in striped rugs, in the meadow closest the road. She knew they belonged to her neighbour's daughter, who rented the grazing. The house and grounds were all which remained of the property, the farmland having been sold long ago. Not that she cared.

Deborah parked her car outside the front door, switched off the engine and took another breath. *Home sweet home.* Her lips twisted at the irony. The designer, to whom she had paid a small fortune, had been given a blank canvas to refurbish the place, and her personal assistant, Agneta Kent, had overseen the project. Deborah's only involvement had been her instructions to 'change it completely' and 'make it light and bright.' Eradicate those dark childhood memories which wormed into her adult dreams. Her parents would certainly have disapproved at the ruthless removal of their Puritan legacy. It was a satisfying thought.

There were just two cases to take inside. Most of her belongings had been efficiently moved and relocated by a company specialising in such services, under the personal supervision of Agneta, whilst some possessions would remain at her house in London. Greenways Farm had already been minimally furnished by an interior design company. Everything should be ready for her arrival – even down to food supplies in the cupboards and fridge. If not, someone would feel the sharp edge of her tongue. She had learnt, at an early age, failure was not to be tolerated. The overall cost had been eye-watering but well worth it if she was to endure a whole year living there.

That was the crux of it; the terms of her mother's will; the stipulation of her inheritance.

Her first instinct, when she learned of the draconian conditions, was to walk away. She needed neither the house nor the money. Old resentments burned as fiercely as ever and this was yet another searing blow. Obviously, her parents had never forgiven her defiance and wanted to drag her back to a village she hated as a final, twisted act of revenge. She would not give them that satisfaction. After a week, though, she began to consider things differently. The house was rightfully hers; why shouldn't she claim it? Could she really allow their Machiavellian spite to triumph? She would grit her teeth, hold her head high, live at Greenways Farm for the allotted time, and sell the wretched place when the year was up.

From the outside, the old farmhouse already looked different from the mausoleum she remembered. Keys in hand, she set down her cases and stood at the front door – no longer centuries-old solid oak, stiff and heavy to open, but sleek and modern, with tall, glass panels framed in dark grey aluminium on either side. All the windows had been replaced, creating a lighter aspect to the flinty exterior. The ivy, which had clawed into crevices over the whole frontage, had been painstakingly removed. The difference was incredible and lifted Deborah's spirits. She could do this.

The key slid smoothly into the lock and the front door opened inwards to the accompaniment of insistent beeping. The alarm. She swiftly located the panel and disarmed it. Only then did she allow herself a first look around, sucking in her breath in tense anticipation and releasing it in a whoosh of relief. It was so different. The entrance hallway felt spacious where it had once been dark and claustrophobic. Gleaming, light grey tile had replaced threadbare, brown-patterned carpet. A wall lined with heavy-framed pictures had vanished, and light flooded in through a ceiling-to-floor window at the far end of the hall. Deborah walked slowly towards the huge, open plan kitchen/dining area. This space had once been a plethora of tiny rooms: cramped kitchen; laundry room; back lobby; Father's study; formal dining room with mahogany furniture and hard, high-backed chairs. It was almost impossible to picture it now. Large, glass double doors opened out onto the garden beyond and she frowned. She had not thought to consider the outdoor space which currently looked messy and overgrown – a mental note to do something about that, sooner rather than later. Untamed nature jibed at her need for order and a sense of control, the mantras by which her life was governed.

She turned back to the hallway and opened the door on the left-hand side. This had always been the front room where her parents had entertained friends from their church. She remembered loud, domineering men and mousy, silent women. When she was little, she had been locked in her bedroom when guests arrived. As she grew older, she was expected to sit quietly, on a wooden seat in the far corner, listening but not speaking unless spoken to first. The room still felt slightly formal, with patterned wallpaper and a dark green sofa with matching armchairs. However, there the similarity ended. Gone were the worn carpet, the dusty brocade curtains, the grey netting obscuring light, the bookcases heaving with old tomes. It felt larger – friendly and comfortable. And there was a massive television screen on one of the walls. Her parents would be turning in their graves!

She spun on her heel and returned to the hallway before opening the door opposite. This had been used as an additional study, with more bookcases and a desk at which she had been expected to sit, night after night, after school, doing first her schoolwork and then her bible studies. Hours of loneliness, where her childish imagination had dreamt of escape. Now it was a modern office space, something she needed to run her London-based business from Suffolk. She glanced briefly at the large desk, the computer monitors, the storage spaces. It would do. She planned to make regular commutes to London for meetings and her staff were well-trained and reliable. They did not last long in her company if they failed to meet her exacting standards.

Deborah returned to the kitchen to check out the remaining downstairs area. A small extension had been added to provide a utility room, toilet, separate shower room and downstairs gym, necessary for the daily workout which kept her in shape. She nodded approval. Adequate.

The old staircase leading up from the hall had been replaced by light-oak railings and luxurious beige carpeting. As a child, she had never crossed the threshold to the main bedroom, so she took deliberate pleasure in throwing open the door. A wall had been removed, this time to replace a bedroom next door with an en-suite bathroom and dressing room. The whole effect was sleek, modern, and impersonal, with an emphasis on quality and comfort. The designer had done well. There were two additional bedrooms and a family bathroom to inspect before Deborah could finally relax. The echoes of the past had been obliterated from the fabric of the house. Now, she just needed to erase them from her mind. Easier said than done.

The shrill of the doorbell made her jump. It seemed an anachronism in this house. Previously, there had been a brass knocker on the front door. As Deborah descended the stairs, she wondered at her visitor. Most likely a delivery. Something Agneta had overlooked. Or something extra to impress her. Flowers, perhaps, from Rupert? Their relationship had cooled of late, certainly from her side, and he had not taken it well when she suggested, because of her enforced sojourn in Suffolk, it would be a good idea to break things off between them. In the end, she had relented a little, certain in her heart that distance would do the job for her. Perhaps she had underestimated his persistence. She peered through the glass just as a male outline lowered his head to check inside, causing her to jerk away, despite knowing the caller would be unable to see anything through the one-way window film applied to the glass. Hmph! Someone had seen her arrival and wanted to pry. A nosy neighbour. She pursed her lips. Village life never changed.

Not best pleased, she flung the door open and raised her eyebrows at the man standing in front of her. 'Yes?' she asked coolly. 'Can I help you?'

He was tall and muscular, broad-shouldered, dressed in shirt sleeves and a gilet, despite the chilly nip to the air. Unruly dark hair, streaked with grey, framed a lean, lightly-tanned face. He smiled and looked younger, blue eyes crinkling as his gaze met hers, and Deborah suppressed an inconvenient flutter of her pulse.

'Hello.' His voice was deep and her heartrate skidded faster. 'I'm your neighbour, Tom Oldridge. We farm next door.' He held out a hand and she was forced to reciprocate. His skin felt warm and work-roughened. The contact was disturbing and she pulled away.

'Deborah Ryecroft,' she replied curtly.

'I know.' His smile widened. 'I vaguely remember you from years ago when you were just a kid. Well, I was too, but a few years older than you.' A fuzzy recollection of a stringy lad with tousled brown, curly hair teased the edges of her memory. Tom Oldridge - son of John and Alice who lived next door but whom she rarely saw. Her cheeks flushed. He would be aware of her history in the village. She scanned his face for traces of scorn or disgust but saw neither. 'It's been a long time.'

'Yes.' Her tone remained brusque and she refused to smile back.

'You've had a lot of work done here. The old place looks good.'

'Yes.' Her discomfort grew and she wondered what he wanted.

'I thought I'd just stop by and see if you needed anything.'

'That's kind but I'm fine thanks.'

He took a step back. 'Good. Well, I can see you're busy so I'll leave you to it. Don't hesitate to call if you want help at all. Would you like my mobile number, just in case?'

'I guess so. Thank you.' She pulled her phone from her pocket and obediently tapped in the digits as he said them. 'Thanks for stopping by, Tom.' Her lips curved momentarily in a cool, professional farewell.

'Oh, I almost forgot!' He clapped a hand to his forehead. 'My daughter, Emma – those are her horses in the field, by the way – asked me to invite you round tomorrow evening for a drink. Six p.m. Nothing fancy. Just to say hello.'

She was taken aback. 'I don't think ...'

'I'm sure you can spare an hour,' he said smoothly. 'Emma will be very disappointed if I say you've turned her down. We live in the same old farmhouse, just down the road.' He gestured left as he turned away. 'See you then.'

'But ...' She was too late. He was already halfway down her drive, his long-legged stride taking him swiftly out of earshot. Dammit. She would have to think of an excuse and ring him later. Annoying.

***

Tom Oldridge was intrigued. He had not known what to expect from his new neighbour, although the village had been humming with gossip about her for months, most of it damning. *A cold, hard bitch. Trouble. And worse.* He was all for an easy life and would have steered clear of her, but that was not possible. When he saw her car pull into the drive, he had allowed her a little time to settle in, and then had gone straight round. Direct approach. That was his way. Get it over with.

Initial impressions, though, were confused and he felt drawn to her without knowing why. She had been suspicious and clearly viewed his visit as an intrusion. He had expected that. But she also looked anxious – lost and vulnerable – stirring his protective instincts. And she was stunning to look at: blonde; eyes like sapphires; full lips; slim-hipped; long legs. Yes, he found her attractive. A complication, but not an unpleasant one. He grinned to himself.

'What are you smiling about?' His daughter, Emma, interrupted his errant thoughts. Since completing her degree at Writtle Agricultural College four years ago, she had worked alongside him on the farm. 'Nick is here to look at the John Deere. I've told him I think the clutch needs replacing.'

'Right. Good.'

'And did you call on Deborah Ryecroft?'

'I did.'

'What did you think?'

What *did* he think? Too soon to make judgements. He grinned. 'I knew it was her straight away. Long, black hair, pointy hat, broomstick, cauldron bubbling in the kitchen ...'

'Dad!' Emma shot him a look of exasperation. 'You know I've got no time for the rubbish people are saying. I just wondered what she was like ... if she'll be a good neighbour, stuff like that. Did you invite her round tomorrow?'

'I did.' He saw her raised eyebrows but said no more. Teasing his daughter was as habitual as breathing.

'Dad!' She stretched the word into three syllables. 'Is she coming?'

'Not sure.'

'What's that supposed to mean?'

He shrugged. 'We left it that she's coming ...'

'Well, that's alright then.'

'But I wouldn't be surprised if she calls off.'

She snorted. 'Don't let her. You're good at that. Refuse to take no for an answer. Make sure she doesn't change her mind. She's going to need some friends around here, and I've already invited a few people.'

'And would one of those people be Rick Billington, by any chance?'

She blushed. 'Might be. I've invited all the neighbours, if you must know.'

'Oh heck. I'm not sure Deborah will appreciate *that*!' The protective feeling resurfaced as he imagined his new neighbour being pushed, centre-stage, into the village spotlight. 'That seems a bit much, Em.'

'It'll be fine,' she replied breezily. 'Deborah Ryecroft runs a multi-million-pound business. I'm sure she can cope with drinks with a few villagers. You're underestimating her.'

'OK.' He held up his hands. 'You know best.'

'I do. *And* I bet I'm right about the clutch on the tractor.'

CHAPTER 3

'You've heard she's back?' Enid Green reclined on her throne, a well-padded armchair in the corner of the village post office, regaling all customers with the same question as they crossed the threshold.

'Who?' came the inevitable response.

'That woman ... Hannah Ryecroft's daughter ... the Wickthorpe Witch.'

'Mum,' Ava protested from behind the counter, 'leave the customers be. I'm sure Honoraria is busy.' She smiled apologetically at the auburn-haired woman squeezed into a scarlet, woollen coat.

'I'm not surprised,' Enid continued as if her daughter had not spoken. 'People like her ... it's all about the money. Couldn't be bothered to put in an appearance when her poor, old mum needed her. Oh no!' She folded her arms over her sagging bosom and leaned confidingly towards Honoraria Simpson-Fairchild, secure in the knowledge she had found a willing ear for gossip. 'Didn't *even* come back for the funeral, you know. Or for her father's when he passed, God rest his soul. I was there on both occasions to pay my respects. It was the least I could do. But that daughter ... not a sign of her! It was a disgrace.'

Honoraria's pale blue eyes widened. 'She sounds like a nasty piece of work.'

'That she is,' Enid concurred, jowls quivering in readiness to impart her next nugget. 'You heard what happened when she was just a young girl ... why people call her a witch?'

'Yes.' Honoraria straightened with a smug smile and patted her hair. 'It was before I lived here but I know all about it. The history of the village, including the curse, has become somewhat of a speciality of mine. We have discussed it before, if you remember, Enid, at History Society meetings.'

They were interrupted by the entrance of a tall, smartly-dressed woman who also stopped to hover by Enid's chair.

'Can I help you, Mrs Hampton-Brown?' Ava called, anxious to intercept the latest customer before her mother repeated her diatribe. 'Only I'm expecting a stock order any minute.'

'Oh, alright.' The customer turned reluctantly to the counter. 'I've come to collect my pension.'

Ava nodded. Thursday – pension day. Many villagers still preferred to collect their pension in cash, rather than have it paid directly into their bank account. It was her busiest day. Her mother was all too aware of it. She was invariably entrenched, ready to waylay customers, every Thursday, salivating at the prospect of a good natter. And Deborah Ryecroft's return to Wickthorpe had given her plenty of new material. At nine o'clock, having eaten her preferred breakfast of toast and marmalade, served to her by her daughter, she hobbled through on her stick from her ground-floor bedroom, moaning loudly so anyone within the vicinity could hear how she suffered,

'Mum, please stop haranguing the customers,' Ava said for the third time when they were alone once more.

'Hmph, I can't help it if they're interested in what I have to say, unlike *some* people,' Enid retorted with a snort.

'Mum, you don't know anything about Deborah Ryecroft. Not really.'

Another snort. 'I know enough. That woman's got a nerve, swanning back here after all these years. I bet she thinks we've forgotten what she did.'

Ava rolled her eyes. There was no point arguing with her mother. Enid was always right. Fortunately, the delivery driver was knocking on the back door and she could make her escape. As she ticked off boxes on her checklist, she thought about her invitation for drinks at the Oldridges' house to welcome Deborah Ryecroft to the neighbourhood. The anticipation of a night out was like a warm hug. It would make a lovely change from her usual routine, even if it was just for an hour or two. And it was kind of Emma to invite her.

Ava remembered Deborah Ryecroft from her childhood years. Deborah had been a few years older and went to a different school, so she never really knew her, but she certainly knew *of* her, especially after the tragic accident. Ava was eleven at the time and her brother, Andrew, the apple of Enid's eye, had been five. All the schoolkids had been agog with the terrible drama of it. Still, it was a long time ago. And she never really knew the details – just her mother's account of events and *that*, she knew from experience, was a highly coloured, prejudiced version. She decided not to tell Enid where she was going tomorrow evening. That way, she would be spared the inevitable interrogation afterwards. It was not easy living with her mother.

The tinkling of the bell on the counter interrupted her thoughts and, setting aside her clipboard, she scurried back into the shop. Jane Holley, part-time pharmacist and wife of the heartthrob village GP, Dr Seb Holley, was leaning towards Enid and speaking in a hushed whisper.

'I thought as much,' Enid was nodding. 'There will be many folks not pleased to see her back, I can tell you that much. I hear the work she's had done at Greenways Farm cost an absolute fortune. No expense spared. Mabel Littlebody saw a whole load of gym equipment being delivered. Top of the range, she said it was.'

'Mum, are you sure you're not imagining things?' Ava could not help her exasperated outburst. Her mother really was beyond the pale. 'I can't think someone like Mabel would be spreading gossip. Anyway, how would Mabel know it was top of the range? She's in her nineties and has terrible arthritis. I'm not sure she would recognise an exercise bike or a rowing machine, especially when it's still in its packaging. It might not even have been gym equipment.'

'That's where you're wrong,' Enid glared back. 'The delivery van had a sign saying "First for Fitness" or something like that. That was hardly going to be bringing a washing machine, was it?'

'There's been a never-ending stream of goods vehicles going past our house,' Jane Holley announced. She was a slight, pale wraith of a woman in her late forties with a heavy fringe of iron-grey hair and an air of worn-out martyrdom. 'It's been very disruptive. I'm hoping she'll soon get bored of living back here. The way she treated her poor parents was unforgiveable, in my opinion.'

'Yes,' Enid nodded, scratching the wart on her chin and sniffing her own disapproval. 'Not like *you*, Jane. I know you made a lot of sacrifices, you and

that nice husband of yours, to move back here when *your* mum needed you.'
She shot a venomous glance at her long-suffering daughter. 'Some girls
can't do enough for their mothers.'

'Well, I just did what most people would have done,' Jane interjected,
oblivious to the tension between the other two women. 'I know I had to give
up a lot, moving back here and giving up my career for a while when Mother
could no longer cope. She refused to go into a home, you see, and it seemed
the only thing to do. Of course, not everyone feels that way about caring for
a parent. Deborah Ryecroft for one. She always thought she was better than
the rest of us. That's what happens when you go to one of those posh
boarding schools.'

'Didn't *your* boys go to a private school?' Ava asked mildly.

'Well yes, but they didn't board. And they would have attended the local
school but it had such a poor reputation. Drugs and all sorts. You'd expect it
in the cities but not in *Surrey*. To tell you the truth, we didn't want our boys
mixing with the types who went there so we had no choice. Fortunately, they
turned out alright. Not like Deborah Ryecroft. You mark my words ... there
will be trouble now she's back.'

'That's just what I said!' Enid's chins wobbled vigorously in agreement.
'Wicked, that's what she is. A curse upon the village. The Wickthorpe Witch
has returned and I've barely slept a wink these past few nights from the
worry of it. I won't rest easy in my bed until I know she's gone.'

Ava refrained from mentioning the regular, nightly trumpeting from
Enid's room which disproved that statement. Instead, she asked Jane how
she could help and took the money for stamps. The knives were certainly out
for Deborah Ryecroft and she had her sympathy. Ava regarded the village
curse as nonsense and current talk about the newcomer as pure spite. In her
opinion, if witches existed in Wickthorpe, they were right there in that very
room.

CHAPTER 4

The water is deep and cold, so cold. I swim as fast as I can, front crawl, smooth, steady strokes, but it isn't enough. Panic and fear clog my throat, making it hard to breathe. The water feels like treacle, tugging at my arms and legs, holding me back. The others have gone for help but it will be too late. It's down to me.

When I'm three quarters of the way across, I lift my head. The roaring in my ears ceases and the air holds its breath. I see nothing. Head above the water now, eyes searching, I swim on. The trees at the far side stand peacefully, benign where they seemed so full of menace just a few minutes earlier. I head for the oak with the low-hanging branch, the one which viciously swept across the water's surface, propelled by a sudden gust of wind, just as Ayesha popped up. Where is she?

I'm close enough now to see the detail of the leaves, dark green, starting to crinkle at the edges. The cloud, cloaking the lake in a grey mantle, shifts and a shaft of sunlight hits the water. I stop swimming, treading water, catching my breath, desperately looking for my friend. She isn't here. She must have scrambled into the undergrowth. 'Ayesha!' I call. 'Ayesha, where are you? Are you hurt?'

Then, I catch a glimpse of white – a pale limb. No! I refuse to believe it. Urgent strokes take me closer. A frail, skinny, lifeless torso in a sagging green swimsuit; face down; long, dark hair fanning out like a halo. 'No!' I cry again ...

The sound of her own voice woke her, confusion and disorientation fogging her senses. Not her room ... not her London house ... Wickthorpe ... her parents' old room.

Deborah pushed back the duvet, wishing she could shrug off the past as easily. Greenways might be unrecognisable from her childhood home but the old nightmare was all too familiar. Steeling herself for the day ahead, she padded barefoot over the thick pile. It felt reassuringly new. In the bathroom, she stepped straight into the shower. First night back, she reasoned, as the comforting spray of hot water engulfed her body. No wonder the nightmare returned. Forget it.

Downstairs, she switched on her new coffee machine and headed to her home office, mobile in hand. Work would help erase the ghosts. 'Agneta,' she barked into her phone as she waited for her computer screen to come to life. 'Are you in the office?' She glanced at her watch. 7:45 a.m.

'Good morning, Deborah. Yes, I've just got in. Is everything alright with the house?' The PA's voice sounded calm and unruffled, as always, despite the early call. Nothing fazed her. She had worked for Ryecroft PLC for more than ten years and Deborah relied upon her more than she cared to admit. Agneta made sure her life ran smoothly, managing all the small details generated by Deborah's busy schedule. Reassuringly dependable.

'Yes, the house is fine. Very good. I'm pleased with the work. Thank you,' she added belatedly. She *did* appreciate her assistant, but gave praise sparingly. Another product of her childhood. Many called it a fault. 'You did a good job.'

'Thank you, Deborah. Did you find the boxes of your mother's personal effects? There were two, in the cupboard in the smallest of the spare rooms.'

'Yes, I saw them.'

'And the letter? The handwritten letter addressed to you? I put it at the top of one of the boxes.'

'Yes.' She had seen it. She had opened the boxes and found the pale lilac envelope with her name on the front, written in blue ink in her mother's careful, neat writing. That was as far as she had got, tossing it back into the box and shutting the cupboard door. She was tempted to burn the lot. 'Is Paul in yet?'

'Not yet. Do you want him to call you when he gets in? I thought you were taking a week or so off to get settled in.'

'Mm.' She had said that. The truth was there was nothing for her to do. Not really. After unpacking the day before, she made herself a simple pasta meal, drank a glass of chilled Chablis, and had an early night. The reality of a week not working stretched ahead of her like a barren wasteland. Her to-do list read 'Find a cleaner and a gardener' – that was it. *Go through Mother's boxes. Read her letter. Get it done.* She pushed the whisper aside. Work was a preferable distraction. 'Yes, I'm taking a bit of time,' she said in response to Agneta's question, 'but I'm still available. Tell Paul that, and that I checked in, but otherwise there's no need for him to ring unless he needs me.' She ended the call. That would be enough to keep him on his toes, she thought.

Paul Williamson had been with her since the early days: mid-forties, ambitious, director of finance and her second-in-command. The two other directors of her company were women. Lainey Lewis was an American she had poached seven years ago from a competitor – bright, single, ruthless and sharp. The company had almost doubled in size since she had taken the helm of its strategic direction. Lainey was still in her thirties, and Deborah was aware that the ambition, which had proved so beneficial for Ryecroft PLC, may come back to bite her at some point in the future. It paid to keep a close eye on what Lainey was up to. The head of personnel matters, Gill Leatherstock, brought experience and pragmatism to the team. She was older and had worked in Human Resources all her life, across various businesses. Solid and dependable; capable of dealing with any personnel crisis which arose; just the kind of staff member Deborah needed. Managing people well was something she found difficult. Her skills in judging a person's true character had proved lacking in the past. Generally, her approach was to think the worst, and be pleasantly surprised if proved wrong. That way, no one ever let you down.

She wandered back to the kitchen and poured herself a coffee. The sight of the garden wilderness through the long window irked her. Finding a gardener really was the top priority. The image of Tom Oldridge popped unbidden into her head. He would perhaps know who had worked for her mother. She should give him a call, which would also provide an opportunity to back out of his invitation that evening. Grabbing her phone, she found his name in her contacts. He answered almost immediately.

'Morning, Deborah.' The lazy warmth of his deep voice made her skin tense. 'I'm glad you've called. You've saved me the bother of coming round to see you.'

Bother? The word grated. 'Oh, yes?' she queried, her voice cool.

'Yes.' He sighed. 'I just wanted to give you the heads up about drinks this evening. When I spoke to Emma, my daughter, she admitted she had also asked a few of the neighbours to come along and meet you. I think I may have given you the impression it would be just us. Of course,' he continued smoothly, 'I know a crowd will not bother a woman such as yourself. You must be used to being the centre of attention. But, forewarned is forearmed and all that. I didn't want you to think I'd misled you on purpose.' There was a brief pause and she could hear the rumble of machinery in the background. 'Anyway, now I've got that off my chest, why were you phoning?'

'Can you tell me who my mother used for the garden? I want to see if he or she is available for some regular work.' Irritation sharpened her tone. His little speech had effectively thwarted her plan to make her apologies for the evening. To call off now would look churlish or cowardly, and put the daughter to the additional trouble of cancelling the other guests.

'Ah.' Another pause. 'Actually, it was me. At least, I cut her grass when it needed doing. When Elijah died, Hannah asked if I'd mind doing hers when I did my own. I didn't like to say no, so I've done it ever since. However, I am happy to relinquish that responsibility. It's not that I don't want to do it – just I don't really have a lot of spare time …'

'Naturally, I wouldn't want to put you to any trouble,' Deborah interrupted, 'and I need a gardener as soon as possible. Do you happen to know of anyone who would be interested?'

'I'll have to have a think and get back to you, I'm afraid. No one springs to mind. Remind me to let you have a copy of the parish magazine. It's full of ads for that sort of thing. Anyway, I'll look forward to seeing you later. Six o'clock. See you then.' He rang off, leaving her frowning at her phone, and with the horrible feeling that, on this occasion, she had been outmanoeuvred. She wouldn't let it happen again.

***

Deborah's restlessness continued throughout the morning. A break from work, in the ordinary scheme of things, would mean a holiday somewhere, but the terms of her mother's will precluded that. Three hundred and sixty-five consecutive nights at Greenways Farm, or everything went to the Church. No time limit; no date by which the year needed to be completed. This morning, it felt like a prison sentence hanging over her, especially as old memories refused to stay silent.

Her father accused her of being 'a constant disappointment' – flighty, worthless, unfit to be his daughter. She craved his love, but received harsh treatment in return. 'Spare the rod and spoil the child' was a favourite saying, but his verbal barbs stung far more than the frequent beatings from the willow cane he kept in his study. However hard she tried, she could never please him. *Useless; waste of space; good for nothing;* she heard those epithets so often she started to believe them.

One time, when she was ten, her teacher entered her short story in a competition. To her elation, she won. She returned home from school, bursting with pride, her prize – an anthology containing her story, and a framed certificate – clutched in her hand. Her father barely listened to her excited explanation. Without a word, he opened the book and scanned the first few lines. Then, with a contemptuous flick of his wrist, he tossed it on the fire. As she watched the flames shrivelling the still-open pages, he turned back to the Bible on his desk, muttering about the sin of vanity. The taste of triumph curdled in her mouth; silent tears coursed her cheeks. Her mother had not even seen it, and now it was gone. The achievement was never mentioned again. Most of the time, her father chose to ignore her completely, and her mother wore a face of constant disappointment.

There had been no point trying to please them and, when she started at the local Secondary School, she stopped. Defiantly, she refused to do her chores, answered back, and stayed out well beyond her curfew. When beatings had no effect on her attitude, she was locked in her room. She climbed out of the window, shimmying down the ivy clinging to the outside wall, but lost her hold and fell. A broken ankle was the result. Her father blamed the left-wing, nurturing influence of the comprehensive school system and she was shipped off to a hard-line boarding school, paid for with funds, she now knew, he could ill-afford. Subsequently, she spent little time back in the family home, only returning during school holidays. The village kids, some of whom had always found her solitary nature standoffish, decided she was 'too good' for them, and even the few whom she had considered friends now avoided her. Her only ally was Ayesha Khan, the daughter of immigrants from Pakistan who ran a small newsagent and general-purpose shop in the village.

Ayesha was a loner too, an outsider, bullied because of her different heritage and skin colour. They met, aged nine, when the Khans moved to Wickthorpe, and each recognised a kindred spirit in the other. Ayesha was desolate when Deborah went to boarding school, she knew, from the letters they exchanged. Journeys on the school bus became torture for her, sitting always on her own, taunted and abused, sometimes physically. Kids could be incredibly cruel and the bullying pack-mentality thrived. Deborah sympathised but had her hands full with her own problems. Settling into life at an all-girl boarding school was not easy. The first term was tricky but she kept her head down and tried not to upset anyone. After that, she found a niche with the less popular girls who were academically-minded, and eventually thought of the school as a haven from life in Wickthorpe. She was still in touch with a few of the friends she had made there, and recently met up with them at a school reunion. Packing her off to boarding school was the one good thing her parents had done for her.

Things did not improve for Ayesha though and, on her sixteenth birthday, she confided to Deborah there were times when she considered taking her own life. Deborah was horrified. 'Promise me, you won't!' she pleaded, grasping her friend's hand. 'I couldn't bear to be here without you.'

Ayesha regarded her sadly with huge eyes of liquid caramel. 'But you're only here for a few weeks, and then you go off again. I endure it all the time. It's too much.'

'But what about your parents? Have you talked to them about it – the bullying and stuff?'

Ayesha nodded, a long curtain of black hair falling across her face. 'Of course. They hate it, but there's nothing they can do. It happens to them too. There are many who resent us. My parents work hard in the shop and for very long hours. They are doing well and people don't like it. I've heard customers telling them to "go back where they came from". They turn the other cheek and advise me to do the same.' She sighed. 'But it's hard.'

'Oh Ayesha, please tell me you won't ... you know ... It's only for a few more years and then you'll be off to uni.'

She bit her lip. 'Maybe ...'

The conversation then turned back to Deborah. After O levels, she wanted to do English, Sociology and History A levels. Her father flatly refused. 'I'm not paying for you to study useless subjects like those. If you want to stay at that fancy school for two more years, you'll do what I say. Sciences or nothing,' he proclaimed.

'But I'm not good at science,' she replied meekly. 'They won't accept me on those courses.'

'Maths, then. You're good at maths,' he said. It was the only time he ever said she was good at anything.

Deborah had been forced to compromise, and her troubled friend patiently listened to her complaints about her father's unreasonable behaviour.

And, less than four weeks later, Ayesha was dead.

CHAPTER 5

Martha's diary
11th October, 1644

My beloved husband, John, bought me this diary as a wedding gift. I had oft spoke of my longing for such a book and yesterday he asked if I had written in it. I had to confess I had not, and resolved to remedy the matter forthwith. But where to begin? There is much to impart ...

We arrived in Wickthorpe – John, baby Josiah and I – one month hence. Tis a friendly place and we are quite content in our small cottage. When John found employment at Jed Finch's farm, I felt settled at last. Mr Finch is a gentleman of a kind disposition, I am pleased to say, and we were fortunate a farmworker had moved on, leaving a cottage for our use. I dare hope our move to Wickthorpe may prove a blessing.

Tis strange though to be so far from my childhood home and out in the country where tis so quiet. I confess I miss my family in King's Lynn. Oft when John is working and Josiah deep in slumber, I catch myself daydreaming – silly, childhood memories: playing with my brothers and sisters by the water; watching the boats head out, sails billowing, growing ever smaller; imagining ourselves aboard, set 'pon a great adventure; the men laughing at my puny efforts to help Father load the carts (the sacks were so heavy I could scarce move them). Those times, though, are long gone. I am now a wife and mother and most happy to be so although I wish I was not so far from my family.

I can blame naught but myself for our current situation. We were most comfortable in Grimston – not far from King's Lynn – but, newly arrived in that place, I was foolishly eager to share my knowledge of herbs and healing, hoping thereby to gain favour and comradeship with other women. To my dismay, my words were met with great distrust. I later discovered there had been talk of witches living among us, practising dark arts 'gainst good Christian folk. A man named Matthew Hopkins, the son of a Puritan vicar, yet travels south of here, seeking out such witches and bringing them to justice. In a place called Manningtree, tis said Mr Hopkins overheard a group of women discussing their meetings with the devil! I discovered this from my husband, who was told to warn me. In this strange time of fear and suspicion, people in the village questioned my 'powers' and believed I too was a witch, come amongst them to do harm, not good. Despite my protestations, they refused to believe my innocence and John was discharged from his employment.

Twas a difficult time. With our few belongings, we fled Grimston and journeyed south. I was unable even to get word to my family, such was the abruptness of our departure. For many weeks, we travelled, til John found work in Wickthorpe. Talk of witches is rife in this part of the world also. No one is safe. Just yesterday, I heard tell of an elderly vicar, incarcerated in Framlingham Castle, accused of sending imps to sink a ship at Harwich. Whate'er next? A vicar of all people! A man of the church!

In Wickthorpe, we have found naught but goodwill. Those I have met have shown kindness to both John and myself, but I remain aware of the need for care. My immodesty proved my downfall afore, a mistake I am most eager to avoid repeating. John cautioned me against collecting herbs and I heeded his words ... until last week when Josiah was sick with a fever. Fortunately, I found an abundance of oxeye daisy, mugwort and, at the edge of a wood, some herb–robert. Josiah soon recovered and, I confess, I have since been out foraging again, just as I always did. Tis in my blood. On Mother's side, I come from a family of healers: her mother; her mother afore her; and so on. A wealth of knowledge has passed, generation to generation. How can I allow it to be lost? How can I stand by, do nothing, when I have the means to help, to heal? But I am vigilant. When I venture out, baby Josiah in a sling I have fashioned, I inform those I meet that my bounty is for the cooking pot. My impulsive nature makes such restraint difficult, however. Yesterday, a young woman I befriended, whose husband also labours for Jed Finch and who has recently discovered she is with child, asked to accompany me. It would have been churlish to refuse. Prudence Harkness is her name and she proved a most eager companion, asking so many questions I quite had to bite my tongue, lest I reveal too much. On our trip to the nearby wood, we stumbled across some horse mushroom, parsley, ginger root and hedge garlic. I am proud to say I informed Prudence of the culinary uses for such ingredients and kept blessedly silent about their powers to heal. If I continue to employ such caution, surely John and I can live most peaceably in Wickthorpe? I pray twill be so. I cannot bear the thought of being uprooted once more.

News of the war comes seldom to these parts and I continue to pray for our King and his loyal supporters. I fear Mr Cromwell and his Roundheads are gaining the upper hand. Tis most distressing. I can scarce believe tis now more than a year hence since King's Lynn was taken. As a thriving port, King's Lynn was a prize to be sought. In August, Sir Hamon LeStrange had declared the town, quite rightly, for the King. When he learnt of this, Father predicted there would be danger afoot and he was soon proved right. Parliamentarians laid siege to the town with as many as eighteen thousand troops. Twas the most fearful of times, with cannons fired across the river, causing much devastation. One cannonball crashed through a window of St Margaret's Church during a service! In circumstances such as those, the good people of the town were quickly forced to surrender and King's Lynn became surrounded by walls and ramparts, built by Mr Cromwell's men, to protect their bounty. At least now tis more peaceful for my family living there but I am loath to consider what may happen next. I pray the King's troops will soon overcome the usurper and no more lives will be lost in this abominable war.

John thinks we should guard our tongues on this matter also. Tis quite beyond my comprehension that there may be those who would wish us harm for our loyalty to the King but I know he speaks the truth. These are troubled times, such as we have ne'er seen afore. I will do as he says and speak with others only of the weather and matters concerning family and household. Truly, I am becoming a most obedient wife ... if not in everything, at least regarding this instruction!

CHAPTER 6

Dusk was setting purple hues across the fields when Deborah stepped out that evening. The short walk along Green Road to Orchard Farm, where Tom Oldridge lived, was not as she remembered. When she was a girl, an apple orchard skirted the road, rows of squat trees laden with glossy fruit. Village children reached over the fence with sticks to get to the apples, giggling with that heady combination of excitement and apprehension. John Oldridge, Tom's father, an irritable man at the best of times, would roar threats from his yard when he saw them, scowling as they scarpered like rabbits. However, the field was now bare of trees. Instead, a green expanse of young wheat plants stretched along the road. *Shame.* The taste of those crisp, shiny, red apples – sharp, tangy, always juicy – was still the standard by which she judged varieties available in the supermarket. But now they were gone. Progress, she supposed. The pursuit of profit. She could not imagine old man Oldridge tearing out his beloved trees. It must have been Tom. For the first time, she wondered if John was still alive. Unlikely. He was an old man when she was a child. His wife was younger by a good fifteen years and bore him three girls before Tom, the long-awaited, expected son and heir. If only her own mother had been able to have a son. Her life might have turned out very differently.

Orchard Farm house was a sprawling, two-storey, L- shaped edifice, built in the white bricks produced in Wickthorpe from the seventeenth century until the Second World War. Externally, it had not changed much. Deborah always thought it looked a friendlier, more inviting house than Greenways Farm but did not remember ever going inside. A first time for everything.

She had just lifted her hand to ring the bell when the front door swung open, revealing a tall, young woman with a freckled face, a wide smile, and bright amber curls tumbling over her shoulders. She was dressed casually in jeans and a pink shirt, and Deborah was relieved she had set aside formal attire when selecting her own outfit of trousers, boots and an emerald, woollen jacket.

'Hi, you must be Deborah. I'm Emma. Come on in. Everyone else is already here. Let me take your jacket.' A friendly voice. Brisk. No-nonsense.

'Hello Emma. It's kind of you to invite me round.' She handed over a bottle of wine and shrugged off her outer layer.

'Thanks. Not at all. We've all been dying to meet you. You're quite a celebrity around these parts.' Emma's face flooded with colour. 'Sorry ... I didn't mean ... I was talking about your career ... not ... you know ... gosh, this feels so soft. What a beautiful jacket. Sorry, I'm rambling. Let's go and meet everyone.'

Contrite blue eyes, flecked with hazel, begged understanding and Deborah warmed to her. On impulse, she touched the younger woman's arm. 'Please don't worry. I realise what some people may have been saying and I appreciate this invitation.' As she said the words, she realised she meant them, and the Oldridges, father and daughter, notched up in her estimation.

She followed Emma through a narrow hallway into a large kitchen with a huge Aga. Several curious faces turned her way as she approached and she spotted more people gathered beyond a brick arch. Tom Oldridge stepped forward. 'Glad you could make it,' he said with a grin. 'Let me get you a drink before I introduce you to everyone. What will you have?'

'A glass of white wine would be lovely, thank you.'

'Coming right up.' Tom reached across and picked up a half empty bottle as a tall man, with sandy-coloured hair and the bluest eyes Deborah had ever seen, stepped forward.

'I have to say the photos don't do you justice. Hello, I'm Seb Holley. Live just down the road from you. Welcome to the village.' He held out a hand and Deborah took it. It felt strong and warm and she felt slightly mesmerised by those eyes, allowing her hand to rest there a shade too long. His stare held the watchfulness of a lion stalking an antelope.

'Hello Seb. Deborah Ryecroft.' Disturbed, she snatched her hand away. Had she imagined the frisson between them? Not attraction – something else. 'Have we met before? There's something familiar about you but, I'm sorry, I can't quite place you.'

'Sadly not. I would *definitely* remember.' His hypnotic eyes caressed her face and she found it hard to look away.

It was a relief when Tom claimed her attention once more by handing her a glass. 'Seb's a doctor, a GP here in Wickthorpe. A relative newcomer to the village, although his wife was born and raised here,' he said. 'You might know her. Jane. Ah, here she is.'

Deborah was pinned by gimlet, grey eyes as the doctor's wife slipped a proprietorial arm through his. 'Hello Deborah. It's been a long time. Of course, you were Debbie, then, and we were just young girls.'

Deborah's heart sank. Someone who knew her before. One of her peers. That did not bode well. She searched the taciturn face for clues. 'Jane?' she asked lightly.

'Yes. I'm not surprised you don't remember me. We weren't friends, and it was a long time ago.'

That told her! There was malice in the cold eyes and an unmistakeable warning in the grim line of her mouth. *Jane Hodrick.* Of all the people she least wanted to see again, Jane and her best friend, Melissa Shipman, were top of the list. It had not taken long for the past to catch up with her. She hid her long-buried resentment and gave the woman a cool smile. 'Not at all. Lovely to see you again, Jane,' she lied. 'Are you still in contact with Melissa? I remember you were almost joined at the hip when we were younger.'

The dislike intensified. 'I was. You're right, we were very close. Sadly, Melissa is no longer with us. She was only twenty-seven when she died.'

'Oh, I'm sorry.' The shock was real, as was the sympathy. Melissa Shipman had been so vibrant and such a forceful character. A leader. Confident, bright, attractive. It was difficult to imagine her life snuffed out at such a young age. Uncomfortable now, she changed the topic of conversation. 'You decided to stay in Wickthorpe then?'

'No, I only moved back three years ago. Seb and I lived in Surrey for many years, along with our two boys. My mother needed looking after so ...' she paused for a martyred shrug, 'we relocated here. Then I could give her the care she needed.' Jane let the statement hang in the air, the contemptuous look she gave Deborah underlining the subtext. She knew she was addressing someone who, given similar circumstances, had failed to do her filial duty. To emphasise the point further, she added, 'I have to say, Seb was marvellous with *your* mother before she had to go into the hospice. Nothing was too much trouble.'

'Thank you, Seb,' Deborah said quietly. With a degree of reluctance, she turned to meet the intense, blue gaze of the handsome doctor. 'I'm sure she was very grateful.'

'You're more than welcome, as was she.'

He sketched a self-mocking bow and she shivered as a second blast of recognition hit her. *They must have met before.* The air thickened with tension. It was as if they were the only two people in the room.

Tom filled the awkward silence by taking her arm. 'Sorry Deborah, but I feel I should move you on. Emma has charged me with introducing you to everyone so brace yourself.' With an apologetic smile, he steered her away from the Holleys and towards a nearby group of younger people which included his daughter. 'You've already met Emma. She works with me on the farm. This is Rick Billington and his sister, Freya. Rick's a vet; Freya has just finished university and is currently getting some work experience at the doctors' surgery.'

Rick was a tall, athletic-looking individual with a genial face and a mop of tousled, fair hair. His sister was a stunner: tall and slim like a model; long, silky, blonde hair; an exquisite face with bright, blue eyes; flawless skin; pert nose; and a perfectly-shaped, full-lipped mouth. Freya smiled shyly at Deborah before sliding her gaze back towards Seb and Jane Holley. 'Dr Holley and Jane have been very kind,' she said. 'They're friends of my parents, who send their apologies, by the way, but they're both working tonight.'

'Rick and Freya's parents run *The Lamb Inn*, the village pub,' Tom explained. 'We should have a drink there sometime soon so you can meet them. Any excuse for a decent pint.' Before Deborah could voice any objection, he moved on, indicating the fourth member of the group, a young girl with glossy, black hair, almond-shaped eyes and smooth, brown skin. 'This is Amelie Charles. She's also just finished uni, I believe.'

Amelie turned eager eyes towards Deborah. 'Yes. My degree was in marketing. I'm a huge fan, Ms Ryecroft.'

'Really?' Deborah gave a self-conscious laugh. 'You make me sound like a rock star!'

'You *are* ... in the business world,' Amelie responded. 'I'd love to work for you. I'd learn so much. I don't suppose ...?'

Deborah sighed inwardly. She was used to unsolicited requests for jobs, work experience, help, money ... Ordinarily, she would give the girl the brush-off but this was a bit awkward. She didn't want to embarrass her in front of her friends.

Her hesitation was noticed. 'I'd work my socks off for you,' Amelie continued, brown eyes beseeching. 'You wouldn't regret it.'

'I can vouch for that!' Rick added. 'Amelie would be an amazing asset to your company.'

Deborah felt slightly broadsided by his fervour, and the way his face shone as he spoke. 'I'm sure,' she said politely. She turned to Amelie. 'It never hurts to send your CV to companies, even when they're not advertising. I'm sure my personnel manager, Gill Leatherstock, would be interested to hear from you, but I'm afraid I can't make any promises.'

'Oh, thank you! I'll do that.' Amelie laid her small hand on Rick's and gave it a squeeze. 'And thanks, Rick, for the endorsement.'

'Any time,' he replied warmly.

As Tom steered Deborah through the brick arch and out of the kitchen area, she saw him give his daughter a consoling pat on the shoulder. Before she could think anything of it, they were in a large, grey-tiled room furnished with a dining table and cushioned bench seating under a bay window. Her face was already aching from the effort of keeping her smile in place. She never enjoyed this kind of social engagement. In business, it was the part of the job she avoided if possible. Superficial banter always eluded her but, over the years, she had learnt to hide her insecurities behind a cool, composed, brusque exterior. Hence her media tag, the 'Ice Queen' of the business world. She was grateful Tom was by her side, making introductions and smoothing her path through Wickthorpe's inquisitors.

Ava Green from the Post Office was amongst the next clique, a bright-eyed, birdlike woman with mouse-brown curls and a kind face. Deborah would not have recognised her. The girl she remembered from childhood was a few years younger than she – small, dark, watching the world with serious eyes, lonely like her. Ava used to help her widowed mother in the Post Office. Enid Green. Deborah recalled *her* all too vividly. A piece of work – judgmental, sharp-tongued, full of nasty gossip, never a kind word for her daughter. Deborah always felt sorry for the browbeaten child.

A good-looking, fair-haired man lounged beside her, pale blue eyes skittering around the room. Tom introduced him as Andrew Green, Ava's younger brother. 'Sorry my wife, Julie, couldn't make it. Afraid we couldn't get a sitter for the kids. But it's my absolute pleasure to meet you,' Andrew said as he shook her hand. His palm felt smooth and the intent way he stared into her eyes reminded her of many men she had met. A charmer and a chancer, she decided – a man who knew he had charisma and liked to use it.

'I remember you playing on the floor of the Post Office,' she said. 'A little boy with blond curls ... face of an angel.' She smiled, leaving unsaid her other recollection of Andrew: the disposition of the devil, renowned for epic temper tantrums conducted regularly in the shop in front of the customers.

'I like to think I look a little more manly these days,' he quipped. 'I seem to remember Mother liked my curls and refused to get them cut. There are lots of photos where, quite frankly, I look like a girl.' He chuckled and raised a hand to his slick, gelled hair, inviting a response.

Instead, Deborah turned back to his quiet sister. There was something about Andrew which made her skin crawl, even though his manner was perfectly amiable. 'Are you still at the Post Office, Ava?' she asked. 'I remember you too, of course.' She gave her a warm smile.

'Afraid so. I never managed to escape,' Ava replied grimly.

There was a story there, behind the sad eyes. Deborah would have liked to continue the conversation but a large, buxom woman in purple, velvet trousers thrust herself forward. 'Honoraria Simpson-Fairchild, president and founding member of the village History Society. A pleasure to meet you Ms Ryecroft.'

'Oh please, call me Deborah.' She raised her eyebrows as Honoraria stepped closer, in front of Ava, ensuring she had the guest-of-honour's full attention. Not that it would have been easy to overlook the sparkly, voluminous blouse and limp, silver bow which shuddered on the shelf of Honoraria's copious bosom like a floundering fish.

'When I moved here twenty-seven years ago, I couldn't believe Wickthorpe didn't have one. A History Society, that is. Nothing for it but to start my own,' Honoraria bellowed. 'We meet on a Wednesday, once a month, at seven o'clock. Perhaps you'll join us?' Deborah was spared from answering as she continued. 'I've tried to persuade Tom to come along for years, both him and his wife, but to no avail.'

Tom's wife? Deborah gave him a quick glance but his face remained impassive.

'You would enjoy it, Tom.' Honoraria laid a bejewelled hand on his arm. 'I could understand that Belinda wasn't interested but *you* were born and raised in the village. I'm sure you'd find it all completely fascinating.'

'I'm sure I would,' Tom agreed, 'but I just don't have the time.'

'That's a poor excuse,' Honoraria scoffed. 'You farmers work so hard. You deserve some time off. I've tried to lure him out of his lair with the promise of my speciality, steak and kidney pudding.' She directed this at Deborah, squeezing her large frame slightly to the left, closer to the man in question. 'But, so far, he's resisted the temptation. He's a stronger man than Edgar ... my husband ... died nine years ago. He loved his food. They say the way to a man's heart is through his stomach. Can you cook, Ms Ryecroft?'

Deborah had begun to tune out and was startled by the abrupt change of conversation. 'Er ... not very well. I get by.'

'I see.' She shot Tom a look of triumph. 'Just like Belinda. That was where things went wrong. Many a man can be swayed by a little culinary expertise. That's what I told your Emma. If she really wants to impress a young man, she needs to master the art of pastry. I have offered to help her in that department but she's as stubborn as her father.' She paused to glance at him fondly. 'You both need a good woman to take care of you.'

'I'm sure you're right, Honoraria,' Tom said mildly. 'Now, please excuse us. I need to make sure I introduce Deborah to everyone.' As he ushered her away, he muttered under his breath, 'Sorry about that. Honoraria is hard to stop once she builds up a head of steam.'

Deborah chuckled. 'I can imagine.' She snuck a glance at him. 'Who's Belinda?'

'My ex-wife. Divorced several years ago.' A couple were waiting expectantly for their approach and Tom greeted them with enthusiasm. 'Ah, hello Felix ... Jules ... looking gorgeous as ever.' He kissed the silver-haired woman, a striking figure in a well-cut black dress.

'Thanks Tom. I do my best,' the man grinned. He winked at Deborah as he extended his hand, the buttons of his checked shirt straining across his chest.

'Not you, you idiot!' Tom turned to Deborah. 'These are my good friends and neighbours on my other side, Jules and Felix.'

'Pleased to meet you,' Deborah smiled politely. *Lord, how her face ached!*

'And we're so happy to meet *you*,' Jules said warmly, her smoky, grey eyes glowing. 'You've been quite a mystery woman. The whole village has been agog at the news of your arrival! Felix has lived here all his life, but it's been hopeless asking *him* questions about you. I think he's a bit older so I guess your paths didn't cross much when you lived here as a child.'

'I remember seeing you walking to school, I think,' Felix interjected. 'Our parents didn't socialise, sadly, so ...' He shrugged. 'Anyway, it's a pleasure to meet you properly. Hopefully, we'll see lots of you, now you're back in the village.'

'That would be nice,' Deborah inclined her head. 'I'm afraid I don't really remember you either. My parents were never ones for attending village events.'

'And the two of us, Tom and I, were either helping out on the land, feeding or milking cows, or up to who knows what,' Felix returned. 'We were at school and college together. I tried to keep him out of trouble but ...'

'You were lucky you had me to keep *you* on the straight and narrow!' Tom retorted. 'You'd have been clueless without me.'

'True enough,' Felix nodded, eyes gleaming with mischief. 'Like that time when one of us fell in the cesspit and the other had to come to the rescue ... Oh, wait a minute, that was *me* doing the rescuing and *you* in the smelly stuff. I fear *you* were the clueless one, my friend.'

'If I remember correctly, that was hardly my fault. *Someone* had failed to put the cover on ... *you*, Felix.' Tom held out his hands. 'I rest my case.'

Deborah chuckled, enjoying the easy camaraderie between the long-standing friends. 'Do you still farm, Felix?' she asked.

'Afraid so. Just arable now. Like Tom.'

'And you, Jules?'

'I'm a teacher – at a primary in Bury. Apart from breaks when the children were small, I've been teaching for over twenty-five years. Love the job but I *am* thinking of retiring. It would be nice to be able to do what I want when I want. I have lots of plans.' Jules directed a meaningful glance at her husband.

'That's what I'm afraid of!' he groaned.

'What plans?' Deborah inquired, happy to keep the conversation away from herself.

'Oh, don't get her started!' Felix exclaimed. 'Doing up the house, travelling ... lots of expense.'

'He's such a cheapskate!' Jules said. She turned to Deborah. 'I'd love to see what you've done to your farmhouse, if you didn't mind, to get some ideas. Sorry, I'm hopelessly nosy, as you've probably realised! Our house is pretty much still as it was when Felix's parents lived there. With the kids, the farm, my work ... it never seemed to be a priority.'

'Of course. You'd be very welcome, although I'm afraid I had nothing to do with the renovations. The ideas were from an interior designer.'

'Oh.' Jules gave a rueful smile. 'Somehow, I can't imagine Felix agreeing to splash out on a designer so it'll me making all the decisions ... and probably doing all the work too. Still, I won't mind,' she added cheerfully. 'It'll be lovely to do something entirely different and the house really does need modernising. I can't imagine how I've put up with it for so long.'

'The house is fine, isn't it, Tom?' Felix argued.

'Er ... I think we'd best move on.' Tom gave his friend an apologetic grin. 'Catch up with you both later.' He steered Deborah towards a final group of guests, talking as he did so. 'Right, over there is Wendy Robinson, the rector. Next to her is her husband, Ralph. They're talking to Valerie and John Hampton-Brown.' He gave her a smile. 'It's a nightmare trying to get everyone's names right. Emma and I always refer to the Hampton-Browns as the HBs. I had to ask her what HB stood for this evening.'

'You're doing a good job. I appreciate the trouble you and Emma have gone to on my behalf.' She smiled back and was surprised to see his cheeks colour.

'No problem,' he murmured and launched into the next round of introductions. Immediately, Deborah was aware of hostility bristling from the HBs.

'I was a very good friend of your mother,' Valerie announced in clipped tones. 'Poor Hannah. She needed her friends around her, especially at the end. I made a point of visiting her every day.' There was an uncomfortable silence.

'I expect you've found Wickthorpe has changed a great deal?' Wendy Robinson addressed her question to Deborah, glossing over the awkwardness with a friendly smile. 'I've been the rector here for nearly five years and there have been plenty of changes just in that, relatively short, space of time.'

'Definitely,' she replied. 'Lots of building work.'

'Yes ... at Greenways Farm too,' Valerie Hampton-Brown said pointedly. 'I'm sure Hannah would have been grateful for some improvements to the house while she was still alive to reap the benefits.'

'I wouldn't know,' Deborah returned coolly. She turned to Ralph Robinson, a stout, bald man in his fifties. 'Tom said Wendy was the rector, but he didn't mention what you do, Ralph.'

'I'm an accountant. Semi-retired now. Just work for myself and do the accounts for some local businesses.' Ralph's voice was deep and sonorous, redolent of a Shakespearian actor. 'I help at church a bit too. Wendy always finds things to keep me busy.'

His wife grinned. 'I like to keep you on your toes, true enough. And the Lord's work is never done.'

'You do lots for charity too, don't you, Ralph?' Valerie inserted herself back into the conversation. 'Both Ralph and John did their first triathlon last summer. For the British Heart Foundation.'

'First and last,' Ralph grimaced. 'The swimming was OK. Even the biking wasn't too bad. But the running ...' He shook his head and patted his stomach. 'This body is not built for pounding the streets in trainers. My next charity endeavour will be something which involves no physical activity. I'm thinking of sponsored beer drinking, or something along those lines.'

'Sponsored beer drinking sounds good to me. Count me in, Ralph,' Tom laughed.

'In your dreams, boys,' Wendy admonished with mock severity.

'Luckily for you both, Valerie is organising a summer ball to raise money this year. No pain involved, except to your pocket.' John Hampton-Brown spoke for the first time. He reminded Deborah of a retired colonel, dressed in tweeds and sporting a grey handlebar moustache. His whole demeanour bristled superiority – a man used to respect from lesser mortals.

'Indeed. Perhaps your company would be generous enough to sponsor it, Deborah? It's for a very good cause. The British Heart Foundation. I don't know if you're aware your mother suffered from heart trouble?' Valerie glittered with malevolence.

'I'm sure that would be possible.' Deborah ignored the second part of the question. 'We have a budget for deserving charitable causes. Please email me the details.' She handed Valerie a business card from her bag and turned back to Tom. Time to call a halt to the proceedings. She had been there long enough. 'Thank you for a lovely evening but I'm afraid I must be going. I'm expecting a business call at eight.' This was true but only because she had asked Agneta to phone at that time.

'Oh …' Tom was taken aback. He looked at his watch. 'In that case, I'd better announce your departure. Everyone …' he raised his voice and the room quietened, 'I'm afraid Deborah has to leave us now but I'm sure you'll agree it's been a pleasure meeting her – and, for some of you, having the chance to become reacquainted.'

A ripple of assent and a few snorts of disagreement greeted his announcement. All eyes turned in her direction. 'Such a shame you have to leave so early but it was a delight to meet you, Deborah,' a male voice called out.

She turned to meet the blue eyes of Seb Holley and his piercing gaze disturbed her anew. Giving herself a mental shake, she addressed the crowd. 'Business, I'm afraid. Lovely to meet all of you. I appreciate you taking the trouble to welcome me to the village, especially Tom and Emma. Thank you.' With a parting smile and nods of farewell, she headed towards the door, Tom following in her wake. Seb Holley stood in her path, now alongside the younger group of Emma's friends, his wife nowhere to be seen.

'I hope we'll soon meet again, Deborah. I'm sure Jane will be in touch, with you being old school chums. You'll have to come round for supper.' His penetrating gaze caused her cheeks to flush, and his smile widened at the edges.

'Thank you.' She inclined her head and turned away as Emma materialised by her side, holding her jacket.

'It's such a shame you have to leave so soon,' the younger woman said, handing it over.

'I'm sorry to cut the evening short. It was very kind of you to want to do all this for me.'

'Oh,' Emma looked surprised. 'The idea was Dad's.' Deborah raised her eyebrows. 'He thought it would be a neighbourly thing to do. But any excuse for a bit of a party, I say. Not everyone could make it, though,' Emma continued. 'It's a shame you didn't get to meet Kai and Phil, who live in the house next to Mabel Littlebody's bungalow – the one with the fabulous garden. They're always a great laugh.'

'Mabel Littlebody ...' Deborah said slowly. 'Gosh, I remember her. She's still alive?'

'Yes,' Tom interspersed. 'Very much so. Mind as sharp as a tack, although she must be over ninety. Sadly, she's crippled with arthritis but never complains. She loves visitors as she doesn't get out much.'

'I'll have to call round.' She flicked her wrist and glanced pointedly at her watch. 'Sorry, but I really must be off. Thank you again, both of you. It's been ...' She struggled for an apt word.

'An ordeal,' Tom said with a grin. 'Sorry about that. We thought we'd better invite all the neighbours – it's so easy to offend people otherwise – but some of them are easier to get along with than others!'

She gave both Oldridges a wry smile as she waved them farewell. 'I noticed.'

Deborah walked away, feeling the tension in her body ease. *Thank goodness that was over!* And it could have been worse. Not everyone had been hostile, and most guests had been welcoming and friendly. Perhaps life in Wickthorpe would be bearable.

Even as optimism surfaced, the irksome contradiction of Emma's final statement returned to disturb her equilibrium. Emma said the invitation for drinks was Tom's idea. When Tom came round, he definitely told her the idea came from his daughter. One of them was lying, and Deborah suspected Tom. Why, though? What would be his motive?

Just a small thing, but annoying! She had a feeling it was a question which would keep her puzzling long into the night.

CHAPTER 7

Honoraria Simpson-Fairchild was buzzing in the afterglow from the drinks party. It was so nice to be invited out. She was accustomed to holding soirees herself, in her small, sixteenth-century, oak-beamed cottage, but had recently been disappointed by the turn-outs. People seemed too busy these days to spend an evening enjoying high-brow conversation over a gin and tonic. And she rarely received invitations in return. Last night had been a real treat. She had spent some while talking to Jane Holley, who had known Deborah Ryecroft when they were both young girls, and it had been fascinating to learn what she thought of Wickthorpe's most recent newcomer. Jane did not like her – that was very clear – but had been reluctant to say why. Probably something to do with the awful death of that young girl back in 1988. Terrible, that was.

Humming to herself, she squeezed into her red, woollen coat, grabbed her handbag and headed towards the village centre. It was a pleasant walk along Green Lane. About half a mile took her past an old village pump and across the road to the Post Office, disappointingly devoid of customers this Friday morning. In fact, no sign of anyone, not even Enid Green in her customary chair. She always liked a gossip and Honoraria had hoped to fill her in on last night's events. After ringing the bell on the counter with a firm hand, it seemed to take Ava forever to appear.

'I'm so sorry to keep you waiting, Honoraria,' the younger woman said.

Poor Ava. She really needed to do something about her appearance. She could be quite pretty with a bit of make-up, a good haircut, and highlights to liven up that dull brown. As for her dress sense ...

'What can I do for you today?' Ava's prompt interrupted her thoughts.

'Six first-class stamps, please. Sorry we missed the chance to chat last night, Ava. You had left before I could get around to you. What did you think of Ms Ryecroft?'

'Seemed pleasant enough. We only exchanged a few words. Was there anything else?'

That was the trouble with Ava. Always too busy to chat. 'No, that's all, thank you.' As Honoraria fumbled for her purse, she tried again. 'She wasn't at all what I was expecting. Quite ordinary really.'

Ava merely smiled as she handed over her change. 'Enjoy your day, Honoraria. Sorry, but I'm in the middle of something out back. You'll have to excuse me.' And, with that, she disappeared.

Well, really! Her charitable view of Ava took a nosedive. The woman always rejected her overtures of friendship. Abrupt to the point of rudeness, actually. She did not deserve the offer of help to 'take her in hand' which fluttered as a possibility in Honoraria's head. *Her loss.* Carefully, she counted her change and deposited it in her purse. Then, she cast a discerning eye around the small shop. Ava was not the only one needing a makeover. Those displays had been the same forever: a tired collection of greetings cards; postcards of local views on a revolving stand; a few books about Wickthorpe high up on a shelf; a stationery section; a display of small gifts and village mementoes. She shook her head and clucked her tongue. The whole place reflected Ava's personality, tired and boring. It would take only a fraction of her own flair to transform both the woman and the shop. *Such a shame.*

Her auburn curls were still shaking as she opened the door and almost bumped into Valerie Hampton-Brown. Now, *there* was a woman who knew how to take care of herself. Honoraria cast envious eyes over the navy cashmere jacket and matching bag in the softest Italian leather, wishing she had that kind of money. 'Oh, hello, Valerie,' she said. 'You're looking very glamorous. Are you going anywhere nice?'

'Just into Bury.' Valerie cast a quick glance at Honoraria's coat and failed to return the compliment. However, the habitual, disparaging set of her features was, today, unusually animated. 'Tell me, what did *you* think of last night?'

'How do you mean?' Best find out what Valerie thought before she committed.

'Well ...' Valerie lowered her voice. 'It's started already. Did you see the way *that woman* flirted with the men, trying to weave her spells? Tom Oldridge is already a lost cause by the looks of things, judging by the way he trailed after her like an acolyte. And poor Jane Holley was quite upset at the way she deliberately set out to attract her husband. There will be trouble, that's for sure.'

'Really?' Honoraria exclaimed. 'I'm afraid I didn't ...' She cast her mind back to the previous evening, revisiting her view of events in the light of Valerie's keen observations. 'Oh, I *do* remember seeing her chat to him again on the way out ... but you don't think ...?' A frown from Valerie instantly dispatched the contradictory words forming in her mind. Instead, she muttered, 'Goodness, poor Jane! Not that *Dr Holley* would do anything amiss, I'm sure, but how ...' she struggled for an appropriate word, '*brazen*!'

'Mm.' Valerie pursed her thin lips. 'The curse of the village is back. The Wickthorpe Witch. I could sense her evil as soon as she walked in. The whole atmosphere in the room changed. Did you notice? It felt as if we were all assembled last night like a cast of potential victims in an Agatha Christie novel.' She shuddered.

'You don't *really* believe she's a witch, do you?' Honoraria was on safer ground now, itching to display her expertise on the matter. 'You know the history behind the legend of the Wickthorpe Witch, I assume?'

'Of course.' Valerie snapped. 'I've lived here a lot longer than *you*, Honoraria! It stems from the sixteen hundreds when the witch cursed the village before she was drowned in Dark Water Lake.'

'Mm, not quite,' replied Honoraria, smug with superior knowledge. 'In 1645, Martha Lightbody was *accused* of witchcraft and subjected to trial by drowning. She was tied to a chair and thrown into the lake. In her last words, she cursed the village and its descendants.'

'Yes, I know.' Valerie was impatient. 'That's what I said.'

'*But* there was no proof the woman *drowned*. The legend says her body was never found. The villagers believed she survived and therefore really *was* a witch. *That* was what gave the curse credence. And then, the following year, the wife of one of the men involved was found dead in the lake. The death was even recorded as "drowned at the hands of a witch." After that, any tragic or unexplained events in the village were blamed on the Wickthorpe Witch and the legend was born. When that tragedy happened in 1988 ...'

Valerie's face was pale and set in grim lines. 'You do not need to tell me all this Honoraria. I was living here in 1988. I am very aware of what went on. And Ayesha Khan was not the witch's only victim.' There was a brief pause and Honoraria wondered what she meant. *Not the only victim?* She was about to ask when Valerie launched her parting volley. 'Listen to me, that woman will cause grief. I just pray there are no more deaths. The sooner she sells up and leaves, the better ... and safer ... for us all. John and I intend to steer well clear of her. I would advise you to do the same. Now, I had best get on. John is waiting for me in the car.'

'Oh, right, of course. Have a lovely day in Bury.' Honoraria stepped outside and spotted John sitting staunchly behind the wheel of his green Range Rover. She gave him a cheery wave, considering crossing the road to have a brief chat, but decided against it. He was on the phone. Busy people; busy lives. She was like that once. As she headed further along the street, around the corner towards the independently-owned grocery store, Latimer's, she reminded herself she had no regrets. She had given up her career as a history teacher over ten years ago to care for Edgar when he was diagnosed with leukaemia, and had never gone back. As the years went by, she found other things to fill her days: two mornings a week she volunteered at a charity shop in nearby Stowmarket; she hosted coffee mornings in aid of Cancer Research; she was an active member of various village organisations; and she had founded the History Society, which was her passion. Recently, she had been doing further research into witchcraft in East Anglia in the seventeenth century and had lined up a speaker who was a renowned expert on the subject. It would make for a *particularly* relevant discussion at the next meeting.

In Latimer's grocery store, she discovered Ralph Robinson, the rector's husband, at the coffee section, deliberating between an expensive jar of *AllGold* and a much cheaper *BudgetBuy* alternative. Gently, she prised the offensive *BudgetBuy* from his podgy fingers. 'Now, now, Ralph. You don't want to be buying that. Trust me! False economy. There's nothing worse than cut-price coffee. Tastes like dishwasher, honestly! Wendy won't thank you for saving a few pennies on that, I can assure you. If you want something a little less pricy but still with lots of flavour, you could try this.' She handed him a jar of *CafeAuTaste*.

'Oh, right. Thank you.' Timidly, Ralph put it in his wire basket, alongside a packet of *BudgetBuy* chocolate wafers. Honoraria was about to tell him about the *Kit-Choc* ones she had recently discovered when he diverted her with a question, asking how she had enjoyed the previous evening.

'It was lovely, thank you, Ralph. Always a treat to be invited out. And interesting to meet Ms Ryecroft.'

'Indeed,' he beamed back. 'Charming woman. Obviously, very clever too, to be so successful.'

Or ruthless, or even worse, Honoraria thought, unconsciously mirroring Valerie Hampton-Brown's opinion. Not that she would say that out loud, especially to Ralph, who was goodwill personified. 'Absolutely,' she said instead. 'Quite a celebrity.'

'And I thought Tom Oldridge seemed quite smitten by her. She must have made quite an impression for him to host a drinks party. Tom's never been one for that kind of social event.' He chuckled, his brown eyes twinkling.

'Hm.' Honoraria pressed her lips together in a smile which concealed a pang of jealousy. She had noticed that too, and was quite content to dislike Deborah Ryecroft for that reason alone. Whilst she herself was older than Tom Oldridge by a good seven or eight years, she harboured a secret passion for him, repeatedly making her feelings clear to the man in question, to no avail. She had consoled herself with the belief that his apparent indifference to her womanly charms could not be sustained forever. But now the very attractive Deborah Ryecroft was in the picture, and she *had* noticed Tom toting her around last night, never far from her side. Ever the optimist, she hoped Tom was being nothing more than the perfect host to a village newcomer, but first Valerie, and now Ralph, were reading more into it. *Irritating.*

'Yes,' Ralph continued. 'I wouldn't be surprised to see a romance developing there. I said as much to Wendy when we got home last night. That would be lovely, don't you think?'

'Mm, what did Wendy say?'

'She told me I'm a hopeless, romantic, old fool and not to get carried away.' He grinned. 'I know it. But that doesn't stop me keeping my fingers crossed for Tom.' He gave her a parting wink and disappeared behind a stack of toilet rolls.

Honoraria remained deep in thought as she wandered slowly through the shop, picking up the few items she needed. Ralph's talk of romance reminded her of her own date that evening. Jack Jones. She wondered if that was his real name. Fifty-three. Single. Delivery driver. She felt her cheeks turn pink as she handed the cashier her card. How fortunate that others couldn't read your thoughts! Hers were X-rated, currently envisioning Jack's hands exploring her secret places ...

For Honoraria, the worst thing about being a widow had been the lack of sex. Nothing for an achingly long while after dear Edgar passed on. They had lived happily together for twenty-seven years until he got sick. Her grief, when he died, was real and all-consuming. She was bereft. But, as time passed and her sadness faded, familiar urges reclaimed her private thoughts. She and Edgar had enjoyed a very active and, many would say, adventurous sex life. Her collection of lingerie, role-play outfits and toys languished in her chest of drawers, and she mourned that part of her life which was gone forever. Night-time fantasies, previously with Edgar as the male lead, began to feature the eligible men of her acquaintance. Tom Oldridge was a regular visitor to her dreams. In real life he may never have favoured her with anything more than polite interest. But, at night, when she lay alone in her king-sized bed, he became a passionate and demanding lover. After a while, her imagination was unleashed sufficiently to include other Wickthorpe males. She giggled to herself as she recalled a recent scenario starring John Hampton-Brown – she in her favourite dominatrix role, dressed in a black leather corset and high heels, slapping his bound, surprisingly-muscled, spread-eagled body with a paddle.

As she wandered home, pausing only to exchange the time of day with a young woman pushing a child's buggy, she wore a secret smile. Those thoughts set every pore itching in readiness for the night ahead. Fantasies were all very well, but they could not match the real thing.

Two years ago, she had fronted up to her dilemma. How could a woman of a certain age advertise the fact that she was available for sex? A well-known internet dating site had proved frustratingly restrictive. Endless, boring evenings with strait-laced professors and dull-as-ditch-water bank clerks were all very well if they led to something else, but none of her dates had shown an inclination to take things beyond companionship. And they seemed obsessed with talking about themselves, their strange hobbies, or their ex-wives. It was a problem.

Then, after reading a particularly racy novel, she embarked upon a brazen plan. She created an alias for herself – Madam H – and, having researched acronyms on the internet, placed an advert in the personal column of a regional newspaper:

Sexy widow 54 wltm single man for SWS Box no 1456AJ

SWS – sex without strings. Who would have thought? Responses flooded in and she corresponded with potential candidates, weeding out weird ones and those who objected to her insistence upon several email communications prior to meeting. That was a master stroke, the email chat; it was like delectable foreplay – lots of lovely teasing and promises as to what they could each expect. Often, that part of it proved better than the actual meeting!

She was careful. Anonymity was crucial. She would have been mortified if details of her private life became known locally. The horror if ex-colleagues or pupils were to find out, to say nothing of her friends! Meetings were arranged in discreet, out-of-the way hotels where rooms could be booked should both parties be mutually agreeable. She prided herself on her judgement of character and was confident in her ability to detect any sinister shenanigans.

The first time was unbelievably exhilarating and nerve-racking. She drove to the outskirts of Cambridge to meet a car mechanic called Ken. He had described himself as divorced and in his early sixties. Upon meeting, she suspected he was nearer seventy but then she had not been entirely honest about her age either. His additional claim to be 'well-endowed' had proved gloriously true. They had a very unmemorable meal followed by a most satisfactory bout of frolicking upstairs, possibly enhanced by her long-enforced abstinence. He asked to see her again and she had toyed with the idea but, to be honest, she could do better. There were plenty more fish in the sea, and the prospect of meeting other men, perhaps younger, held more allure. After Ken, there had been many such escapades and, frustratingly, more than a few disappointments. Still, she was an eternal optimist and there was always the next one.

Jack Jones. Fifty-three. Single. Delivery driver.

The photo he had sent promised a good-looking chap with twinkly eyes and good teeth. His emails had tantalised with increasing explicit detail. *Delicious!* Honoraria Simpson-Fairchild, village matriarch and President of the Wickthorpe History Society, trembled with moist anticipation.

CHAPTER 8

Work failed to distract her. Deborah read emails, scanned reports, and checked markets. When she phoned Agneta, she was quietly reminded she was supposed to be taking time off. Nevertheless, she stayed at her desk, determined to lose herself in the world of facts, figures and spreadsheets, even whilst questions about the previous evening continued to niggle. Emma's revelation, that the drinks party had been Tom's idea, had unsettled her. Something was going on and it felt disquieting. She was used to being in charge, calling the shots. Here, in Wickthorpe, she already felt like a player in other people's games.

Tom's behaviour last night was equally puzzling. The undercurrent of hostility from certain quarters had not surprised her; she had expected it. People had long memories where scandal and tragedy were concerned. Yet Tom had subtly tried to shield her from it. That was curious. What was his motive? Was he trying to impress her? For her money? Her father had been forced to sell his farmland. Was the Oldridge outfit in similar difficulties? Did he see her as a cash cow who could, with a bit of wooing, save his livelihood? If so, he was out of luck. She made a note for Agneta to make enquiries about his farming company. There were ways to find out these things. If he was trying to charm her out of her fortune, he would soon discover his mistake. The thought was strangely depressing. Despite her reservations, she liked Tom Oldridge.

Seeing Jane Hodrick again – Jane Holley, as she now was – had also disturbed her. Not once had she considered the possibility that either Jane or Melissa would remain in Wickthorpe. She gave herself a mental shake. So what? Jane had more to fear than she from any future encounter. Then there was Seb Holley and his casual promise to invite her to supper. Something was off-kilter about him too, something which made her recoil without knowing why. Probably, the fact he was married to her nemesis.

Meanwhile, the box of her mother's effects, along with the letter left for her daughter, sat like a time bomb upstairs. Deborah was a decisive person, always had been. So why the squeamish reluctance to look through it? One reason for her return had been her desire for closure. Rid herself of childhood demons, once and for all. And she could simply dispose of the box. Refuse to read her mother's final words to her. That would be the ultimate revenge. Her mother deserved nothing from her. No further chance to berate her ... nor to beg for forgiveness, if guilt on her deathbed had prompted such a desire, which she doubted. But she could not bring herself to do it. She still wanted answers. And, if she was being completely honest, the existence of the letter had lit the tiniest, residual spark of childish hope that her mother had loved her. Added to the terms of the will, which gave her Greenways Farm with such strange strings attached, it confused her. Why had her mother not simply left the house to the Church? And why the special conditions? None of it made any sense and perhaps the letter would explain it. But she could not stomach the thought of opening it. Soon.

Restless and irritated with herself, she decided to get out of the house. A drive to the nearby town of Bury St Edmunds, she decided. The empty walls in her newly-renovated farmhouse were already grating on her. In London, she was surrounded by much-loved, handpicked artwork. She missed the presence of her things around her, pieces she had chosen. It was all very well resolving to stay detached from Greenways Farm when she was in London; living in it threatened to be a soulless experience if she wasn't surrounded by beautiful objects she had selected personally.

Decision made. Purpose and direction – qualities which kept her sane and successful. A few paintings by a local artist would be a start. In London, dealers knew her tastes. They could be relied upon to contact her when they had something they thought she might like. Here, she was starting from scratch. A spark of excitement ignited within her. Art galleries. Were there any in Bury? Surely there were. Check the internet first. No point idly wandering the streets, browsing. She did not have time to waste like that ...

Except now you do. The thought was an unpleasant jolt, a reminder she had cut herself adrift from almost everything she knew. Her life in London was conducted at an orchestrated, hectic pace. Even leisure time was carefully planned and filled. She had thought she could return to Wickthorpe for a year, commute as necessary to London, continue to run her business, and remain untouched by the whole experience. Already, she realised that was not possible. For starters, it would drive her mad to cocoon herself in this place. And she was not prepared to hide herself away, like the lonely child she had been all those years before. She would live exactly as she had always done since she was nineteen – on her own terms. She would get to know her neighbours and others in the village, and choose friends wisely. And, once and for all, she would eradicate the taint of the village curse and the Wickthorpe Witch.

Previous stirrings of panic receded as she scrolled through search results for art galleries on her phone. A problem recognised was halfway to being solved. She had never shirked from problems, she reminded herself. Always met them head-on. A tough and uncompromising business resolve was applied in equally ruthless measure to her own life.

Your mother's letter, the mocking voice whispered in her head. *Not so tough and full of resolve there!*

When I'm ready, her inner self retorted angrily.

***

Deborah was charmed by the beautiful, historic town of Bury St Edmunds. As a child, she recalled excursions to the supermarket there, and grim, half-yearly check-ups at the dentist, but very little else. Now, through adult eyes, she appreciated the stunning architecture, artisan shops and abundant greenery. Whilst her purpose was to visit the plethora of small art galleries, she promised herself she would return soon to explore the town properly. The thought of it lifted her spirits. She enjoyed meandering through each of the galleries, but found nothing to her taste and returned home two hours later, empty-handed but feeling more positive. The outing had done her good.

On impulse, after parking her car, she walked back down the drive and knocked at the door of the bungalow opposite. She had recalled Tom's mention of Mabel Littlebody. Mabel had been a rare shining light throughout Deborah's early years, someone who always treated her with love and compassion. Tom had intimated she was now unable to get out much and Deborah felt she needed to repay her kindness. Standing on the doorstep reminded her of another time, long ago, a sultry summer evening filled with sounds of lawnmowers and laughter, when Deborah's world had fallen apart and Mabel was the only person to whom she could turn ...

'Come in. The door is open,' a thin, reedy voice beckoned. Deborah turned the handle and stepped inside. 'I'm in the sitting room.'

The narrow hallway was stuffily warm and Deborah removed her shoes and coat, before heading through the first door on the right. The room was tiny and filled with objects: books, piles of opened mail, ornaments, photographs. In one corner, covered with a rug and with glasses perched precariously on the edge of a long, pointed nose, Mabel Littlebody sat peering at her with open curiosity. She had shrunk from the woman of Deborah's memory, shrivelled like an old plum, but her eyes shone with the same blue brightness and her smile was full of warmth.

'How lovely to receive a visitor! Come and sit by me, my dear.' The old woman gestured to a nearby stool, covered in a stack of magazines and journals. 'I'm afraid my eyesight lets me down these days, so you'll have to remind me who you are.'

'Deborah Ryecroft. You probably don't remember ...'

'Oh, Deborah! I heard you were back. How lovely! Don't be silly; I remember very well. My body may well be decrepit but there is nothing wrong with my mind – not that I'm admitting in any case.' Her small, impish face twinkled with delight. 'Come and sit down. I've been so excited, hearing people talk about your return and the procession of delivery vehicles this past week. Jane Holley kept me well-informed – such a kind girl – visits me often and always has lots of news about everyone. Now, I want to hear all *your* news. I hear you have done very well for yourself. You always were such a clever thing.'

Deborah smiled and did as she was told. Just like old times. Mabel was the one adult in whom the young Deborah felt she could confide without judgment, who would make her feel good about herself. In turn, Mabel would tell her stories of her life and missionary work in Africa, in Malawi – tales of hardship, endurance and always, at the heart of them, her beacon of belief in God's love. As a child, Deborah had clung to the force of Mabel's faith like a lifeline, but it had frayed, eroded and finally been ripped apart by subsequent events in her teenage experience. How could God exist where there was so much evil in the world and so much heartache? Now, though, she could feel the strength of Mabel's religious conviction radiating through her inherent goodness. She had been feeling sorry for the older woman, thinking she must be lonely and frustrated with the lack of independence imposed upon her by her failing body. Not a bit of it. Her spirit remained undimmed and as optimistic as ever. Briefly, she gave Mabel an outline of her business and her current life in London.

'How exciting to live in London!' Mabel exclaimed. 'Always busy, always lots going on. Are you happy there, dear?'

'Very happy. The life there suits me.'

'So why have you returned to Wickthorpe? Is it just to sell the house? That would be a shame, but I can understand why you've moved on. An important business woman like you probably couldn't live in a village like Wickthorpe, even if you wanted to. Although, we are very close to the A14, and I'm told we now have people who commute daily to the city.' She grimaced. 'Not something I would ever choose, but I've always been lucky. Everything I need and want is right here.' Painfully, she lifted a gnarled hand and clasped it to her heart.

Deborah was grateful that Mabel's speech gave her time to compose a response to her questions. She had always told her the truth as a child, but that was a long time ago. Maintaining her privacy had since become an integral part of her being, not something she was prepared to give up lightly, even for Mabel. But she could not tell a lie – not to this woman. 'The house needed a lot of work,' she began carefully, 'and, having done all the refurbishment, I am going to live here for a while. I'll have to commute as well, but not every day. With technology these days, I can work mostly at home. Meetings can take place online. I'm very fortunate to have that choice.'

Mabel gave her a beatific smile. 'Oh, that's wonderful! I'll get to see something of you. That makes me very happy.'

Deborah thought it best to change the subject. 'How are you, Miss Littlebody? Tom … Oldridge … mentioned you suffered from arthritis.'

'Oh, call me, Mabel. You can, now you're all grown up. I'm very well, dear. Yes, I have arthritis, but that is a small price to pay for the privilege of reaching the ripe, old age of ninety-two. It means I need a wheelchair to get out and about. And some kind person to push me. I used to have a scooter but my body won't work well enough to manage it unaided anymore. I'm very lucky, though. Many people help me and bring me meals, so I manage well enough. And I receive lots of visitors. I really am blessed.'

'Would you like to take a walk around the village now? Deborah asked. 'It's a lovely day.'

'That's very kind of you, dear, but I usually have a bit of a nap around now, if that's alright with you.'

'Oh.' Deborah leapt to her feet. She could take a hint. 'Of course. I won't keep you up any longer then. Do you need help getting to bed?'

'No, thank you, dear. I just nap here, in my chair. Look, it reclines.' With difficulty, the misshapen, bony fingers located the switch. 'I'll be fine. You can see yourself out … and Deborah, I really am delighted to see you back in Wickthorpe, after all this time. I'm so happy you're strong enough to take on the past, and show the people who doubted you that they were mistaken.'

Deborah hesitated, feeling such a generous statement deserved a response, but Mabel's eyes were already closed. 'Thank you,' she murmured softly. 'I'll be back to see you soon.'

Closing the front door gently behind her, she felt somewhat like the prodigal child, welcomed back into the fold, despite years of absence. Seeing Mabel Littlebody again had been a humbling experience. Her life had made her self-sufficient, independent and necessarily selfish, and her view of others was coloured likewise. But not everyone thought only of themselves. Mabel was the living proof.

'Hello. You must be Deborah Ryecroft.' A male voice assailed her from the neighbouring garden as she walked down the path. She swivelled towards the sound and saw a man in his thirties, wearing skinny jeans, a burgundy gilet and jaunty cap, strolling towards her. His smooth, handsome face beamed at her across the fence.

She smiled in return. 'And you are ...?' She struggled to recall the names of Mabel's neighbours.

'Kai ... Kai Melandri. I'm just about to stop for a coffee. Would you care to join me? I can offer you a slice of carrot cake. Freshly-baked but, I confess, not by these hands. By the lovely ladies in *The Pastry Parlour.*'

'That's kind of you.' Deborah warmed immediately to Kai's friendly manner. He reminded her of Rafe, an art-dealer friend in London. She made her way along the road to where Kai was waiting at his gate, peeling off gardening gloves and brushing dirt fastidiously from denim-clad legs.

'Sorry I wasn't able to meet you last night at Tom's,' he grinned. 'I hear you were a hit.'

'Really?' She pulled a face. 'I can't say I got that impression.' She wondered at the source of his information. Not Jane Holley, nor the Hampton-Browns, that was for sure.

'Yes well ...' He gave her a wry look. 'You can't please everyone ... at least, that's what Phil and I have found. Phil's my partner. He's in Germany at the moment. But you impressed the people who matter and that's what counts. Otherwise, I wouldn't have been keen to invite you in, although I *was* bursting with curiosity. This way. We'll go around the back, if you don't mind, so I can take off these boots.'

She followed him along the path through neat borders already peppered with early spring colour from daffodils, narcissi and primroses. 'Your garden is beautiful,' she said.

'Thank you. It's my pride and joy. That and ...' A bundle of black hair shot out of the door, wagging a long, silky plume of a tail and licking at Kai's hands. 'Jez ... short for Jezebel because she's shameless when she wants her own way. Jez meet Deborah. No jumping up.' He watched the spaniel with the adoring eyes of a parent as she sniffed at Deborah's legs.

'She's beautiful,' Deborah said, running a hand along the dog's glossy back and being rewarded by a swift lick.

'She is,' Kai replied fondly, 'and doesn't she know it! She'll settle down in a minute. Come through this way.' He led her through to an immaculate, white-tiled kitchen with a large central island unit. A variety of houseplants were artistically positioned around the space, giving it the feel of an oasis.

'Have a seat.' He gestured at the tall bar stools tucked around the island. 'Milk? Sugar?'

'Black, please. This is lovely. Have you lived here long?'

'Two years, more or less. Long enough to upset the homophobic percentage of the neighbourhood.' He grimaced. 'You may well have met a few of them last night. Mind you, that's not why I wasn't there. I had a deadline I had to meet. All done, now.' He chuckled. 'That's why I've given myself the day off.'

'What do you do?' she asked politely.

'Engineering design. I won't bore you with the details. It means I can work from home most of the time, which is handy with Jez here, especially when Phil is away. And get out in the garden when I need a break. There you go.' He handed her a mug with the slogan *Witch's brew* and gave her a wink. 'Sorry. Couldn't resist! Hope you're not offended. Here's cake to make up for it.' He gave her a boyish grin which didn't look apologetic in the least. His brown eyes danced with humour as he awaited her response.

'How apt!' she said, her voice dry. 'Beware lest I turn you into a frog! This cake had better be good!' She forked a piece into her mouth and nodded approval. 'Lucky for you, it is. Delicious, in fact.' She looked him in the eye. 'Obviously, my reputation has preceded me.'

'Too right! It's all the village have been talking about for months. Ever since it was rumoured you were returning to Wickthorpe. Enid Green at the post office has been beside herself, telling stories about you. Phil and I have been quite jealous. You've managed to replace us as her favourite topic of conversation. I hope you're going to do your worst while you're back. I'm happy to be the lovely assistant in your devilish plans.'

She chuckled. 'I'm sure I have robes which will fit you, although you might have to provide your own broomstick.'

'Done.' His grin widened. 'When do we start?'

'Ready when you are. From memory, I suspect Enid Green would make a good candidate for frog material.'

'Definitely.' He rubbed his hands together. 'Although that might be too good for her. And too harmless. She's more of a viper, I'd say. Another slice of cake?'

'Thank you but no, tasty as it was.' She took another sip of her coffee, eying him thoughtfully. 'So ... Enid Green has been reawakening old rumours and stirring everyone up about the village curse?'

'Yes. It's very exciting. We had no idea when we moved here that Wickthorpe had its own witch ... and curse.'

'Mm.' Her brain was whirring. Was that why Tom Oldridge had hosted a drinks party? To rubbish the nonsense being discussed in the village?

'Nobody takes any notice of Enid, of course.' Kai was speaking again, his eyes sympathetic this time. 'We've had a good laugh about how ridiculous it all is. Nothing to get bothered about.'

'I'm not bothered,' she replied. It wasn't true though. Her teenage hurt and sense of injustice had, for years, festered in her chest, and her return to Wickthorpe had peeled away her protective sticking plaster, exposing old wounds. She gave him a bright smile. Time to change the subject. 'Do you have help in your garden? I'm looking for a gardener. Perhaps you know of someone?'

'No and no. I do it all myself so I can't recommend anyone. I'm far too possessive of my garden to let anyone else loose in it. Even Phil. Not that he has shown any inclination to get his hands on my secateurs. There might be a copy of the village magazine around here somewhere.' He slipped off his stool and began rifling through a drawer. 'Here you are. Lots of local tradespeople advertise in there.'

'Thanks.' She took the proffered booklet, the image of Tom Oldridge jolting, unbidden, into her thoughts. He had also suggested the village magazine. 'I guess I'd best get going.' She stood. 'Thanks very much for the cake and coffee.'

'No problem. It's been a pleasure to meet you.'

'Likewise.'

He led her out into the garden and she paused. 'I love what you've done with this space. Are you *sure* you're not available for a bit of gardening work on the side?'

'I wish. I'd love to take up garden design full time. Tell you what, I'm happy to come and cast my eye over your garden to see what needs doing. I'd love that ... and see if I can come up with a few ideas. Then you can take it from there.'

'That would be great, Kai. If you're sure you don't mind?'

'No problem.' He gave her a parting wave. 'I'll pop round later this afternoon if you're going to be at home?'

She nodded. 'See you then. Thanks again, Kai.'

Deborah walked towards Greenways Farm, her earlier feeling of malaise forgotten. In addition to an enjoyable trip to the local town, she had renewed an old acquaintance and made a new friend. Kai was her kind of person – relaxed, undemanding, good-humoured, fun to be with. She needed allies in Wickthorpe and already she felt Kai would have her back. Things were looking up.

CHAPTER 9

In a cramped room adjoining the pharmacy at Wickthorpe Health Centre, Freya Billington endured a sunless Friday afternoon dreaming of the weekend ahead. Their first mini-break! Her fingers trembled with anticipation as she counted pills into bottles whilst watching minutes tick by on the old-fashioned, round wall clock. Concentration was impossible. More than once, she'd had to start over.

'Haven't you finished that yet, Freya?' Jane Holley's irritating voice interrupted her reverie. She looked over her shoulder to see the pharmacist behind her, hands on hips, eyebrows raised in disapproval.

'Almost, Jane, sorry. I'll be there in a minute.'

'We're getting behind. At this rate, you'll find yourself working late.'

Not likely! There was barely enough time to rush home, shower and get to the station for the 17.57 from Bury to Cambridge as it was. Grimly, she upped her pace. *Focus, Freya!* 'Sorry,' she said again as she completed the bottle and glanced up. 'I kept miscounting.'

Jane sighed, disappointment clear, and bustled with brisk efficiency to the desk to hand over a prescription. 'There you are, Mr Godfrey. One tablet, three times a day, to be taken with meals.'

After fidgeting the tiny pills into the bottle, Freya began her next task. Honestly, there seemed to be no end to the list of mindless jobs Jane Holley could find for her! After uni, when her dream job in the pharmaceuticals industry had failed to materialise, getting some work experience in the local surgery had seemed like a good idea. But she'd had enough. And other plans were now on her horizon ...

Seconds ticked by with painful slowness as excitement roiled in her stomach. A whole weekend with him all to herself, after all those snatched moments and brief, secret meetings. She still struggled to believe someone like him had even noticed her, let alone fallen for her. He was so fantastic, so perfect. And the sex, that one time, even rushed and urgent in his car, had been amazing. *Paroxysms of ecstasy; a million lingering starbursts of sensation.* She had thought of it endlessly, describing it to herself in a heavily romanticised narrative, ever since. God, all those other times with her ex-boyfriend, Craig, were nothing by comparison. And, unbelievably, he had been so sweet afterwards, stroking her hair and apologising that she drove him so crazy he had been unable to control himself. She wanted to tell him how incredible he was, but was too shy and in awe of him, and it was too soon. Instead, she listened as he promised, next time, they would take it slowly. He would explore every inch of her ... Quivering, she glanced back at the clock. The hands hovered just before quarter past four. Fifteen more minutes. How could she stand it?

***

Emma Oldridge had been in a bad mood all day and Tom suspected he knew why. Something to do with the previous evening and a certain, young vet. Tom sighed. Poor Emma. She was crazy about Rick Billington, but the relationship was sadly one-sided, and such a slow burn it was permanently in danger of petering out. Still, Emma persisted, using any excuse to engineer social interaction between them. Usually, they met in group contexts, but had been on a date once, just the two of them. A couple of months ago, Emma had booked two tickets to go and see *The Jokers*, Rick's favourite band. She pretended a friend had let her down and asked if he wanted to use the spare, already-paid-for ticket. Rick jumped at the chance and Emma had hoped things might develop from there. They hadn't, and last night he was all over Amelie Charles. Tom thought that young woman pushy, asking Deborah Ryecroft for a job like that, but young Rick was clearly smitten. *Oh dear.* Tom hoped Emma would move on at long last. If the lad preferred *that* young girl to his fabulous daughter, then he clearly did not deserve her.

His thoughts shifted back to Deborah Ryecroft. He was still unsure what to make of her. Cool, well-groomed, very attractive – he had been expecting that. But beneath that tough, polished exterior, he also sensed warmth and humour. She did not match her hard-bitten media image; nor did she fit the profile, bandied about by many village residents, of a wicked 'witch' who had committed a heinous crime. He shook his head, mulling it over. It was hard to believe, now he had met her, that she could ignore the illness, death and funeral of her mother, Hannah. He guessed there was history there but it was still difficult to understand. Hannah had been a sweet soul. He had liked her. The father, Elijah, was a different story. Tom had met him barely a few times but that was enough. There was a man with a chip on his shoulder! Tom could quite believe the young Deborah had a tough time. Little wonder she stayed away when he was alive, but afterwards ... Tom shrugged. Deborah obviously had her reasons, and he no longer believed her to be the hard-hearted woman he had imagined. He had felt her vulnerability as he paraded her in front of all the neighbours, and felt sorry for her as she parried questions and thinly-veiled animosity. He wondered what she had made of it. But there, soon she would no longer be his problem. A drink at *The Lamb Inn* one evening and he would consider his obligation fulfilled. The thought made him frown. In truth, he was looking forward to seeing her again. As he replaced the points on his cultivator, he remembered it was Friday, his usual pub night with Felix and Jules. It couldn't hurt to invite Deborah along. As soon as he finished his current task, he would give her a ring. Pleased with himself, he whistled along to the radio blaring in the workshop.

***

Enid Green was furious. 'You went to a party for *that* woman? How *could* you? You know what I think of her! And you thought you could hide it from me? I'm ashamed to call you my daughter! Were you *trying* to make a fool of me?'

Ava sighed. She was used to Enid's temper, but living with it did not get any easier. 'I'm sorry it's upset you, Mother,' she said quietly. 'Emma Oldridge invited me for a drink with the neighbours and, yes, Deborah

Ryecroft happened to be there. I hardly spoke to her. It was just nice to be invited out.'

'Yes!' Enid spat. 'It would have been nice to have been invited. How come she asked you and not me?'

'I think I just happened to be there, at the doctors' surgery, when she was asking Jane Holley. I was picking up your prescription on Wednesday, if you remember. I overheard and I think young Emma felt sorry for me. She's such a kind girl.'

'Well, you could've told me and I could've gone with you. I can't believe how sneaky and underhand you are!'

'But you wouldn't have gone, Mother. You said so yourself. But yes, I should've mentioned where I was going. I'm sorry.'

'Hmph.' Enid folded her arms and simmered in silence for a few moments while Ava continued to stir the chicken dish she was making for tea. 'So, what was she like?' she asked eventually, curiosity getting the better of indignation.

That was a tricky one! It would be a red rag to a bull to confess she had found Deborah Ryecroft pleasant and likeable. She was predisposed towards her anyway, given the vitriol her mother was spouting about her. It gave them a common bond. 'Didn't you hear all about her from Jane Holley?' she hedged. Jane had appeared into the post office on her way home from work and, when Enid wasn't in her usual chair, asked if she could pop along to see her in her sitting-room. Ava had guessed why. Jane Holley shared her mother's views. Hence, she was ready for the eruption when she had closed the shop and ventured through to their living quarters.

'Poor Jane,' Enid was saying. 'She was too upset to say much. The guilt she has endured over the years because of Deborah Ryecroft and what happened when she was a teenager! Still scarred from it, she is, even all this time later. And, by all accounts, the woman was swanning about last night as if she had done nothing wrong. The whole thing made her sick.'

'I wonder why she went, then,' Ava mused.

Enid shot her a look, suspecting an undertone of sarcasm, but her daughter's face was guileless. 'I think the poor girl was hoping to find some closure. She thought there might be an apology, at the very least, for all the suffering that woman has caused. But no! Apparently, she looked down her nose at Jane, as if she was something unpleasant she might have scraped off her shoe, and then proceeded to flirt with Jane's husband! Completely shameless! She always was Miss High-and-Mighty; thought she was better than others in the village.'

Ava said nothing. Best way. There had been a few people wanting to put the knife in when Deborah left the previous evening, but many guests thought her charming. They agreed with her that the legendary village curse was nonsense. She had been a child when the tragedy happened, and much of the gossip at the time had passed her by. Eventually, it all died down. Without a physical target for their hatred, the village scandalmongers moved on to other matters. Sixteen-year-old Deborah had done the right thing in leaving the village. *Good riddance*, her enemies had cheered at the time. Since then, her success in business had not gone unnoticed and some had complained about that too. *She didn't deserve to do well – probably put a curse on anyone who stood in her way.* When she had failed to return throughout both parents' terminal illnesses and funerals, that too was wrong. According to her critics, it proved what kind of a person she was. Ava had to admit, she was as surprised as anyone when Deborah finally arrived in person. There had been rumours of her return, especially whilst Greenways Farm was being refurbished, but nobody really believed them. The collective view pegged her as a money-grabber who would sell the house. That Deborah should choose to return to live there sent shockwaves through Wickthorpe and plenty of nervous excitement too. Everyone wanted to meet her, or find out what she was like. It was the most gruesomely thrilling thing to happen to the village in most people's memories!

Now she had met Deborah again, Ava was rooting for her. It was not going to be easy for her living in Wickthorpe and Ava admired her courage. She had encountered old Mr Ryecroft on several occasions while he was alive, and the experience was never pleasant. He was what the village folk called, "a man's man" and he had been either blunt, rude or downright cruel. Ava always felt sorry for his wife, a downtrodden woman if ever there was one. The young Deborah could not have had a happy childhood. And then, after the tragedy, the whole village turned against her. Good for her, coming back here and showing them all they could no longer touch her! That's what she thought. She wasn't going to admit that to Enid, though!

***

The March night-time chill could not cool Deborah's warm, wine-induced glow as she walked back to Greenways Farm alongside the tall figure of Tom Oldridge. It had been a fun evening, at *The Lamb Inn,* spent with Jules and Felix Goode. There had been a few people hanging round the bar area whom Deborah recognised from the drinks party at Tom's: Rick Billington, Amelie Charles, and Andrew Green, again minus his wife. They all gave her friendly nods. Kai Melandri and his partner, Phil Abbott, also showed up and had them all in stitches as Kai described his attempts to put up a shelf a month ago when Phil was last away.

'Phil always does all the DIY stuff,' he chuckled. 'That's how we are – we each have our areas of responsibility. I do the cooking and gardening and he does cleaning, bins ... that sort of thing.'

'Yeah, all the fun stuff,' Phil put in drily.

'And any DIY jobs. Obviously, I'm the creative one in the relationship,' Kai added, shooting his partner a cheeky wink.

'And I'm the one who picks up all the pieces.'

Kai grinned. 'Anyway, he was scoffing the other day that I couldn't even put up a shelf. So, I thought I'd show him. I watched a couple of YouTube videos and found his drill. Well, that was the first problem. His drill is so complicated ... so many bits and pieces ... I wasn't sure which to use. Anyway, I marked where the holes were going. Checked that they were in line using a spirit level. All good. Got the drill going. Made the first hole. Perfect. Trouble was, the hole was too big for the screws. Googled that. Needed wall plugs. Hadn't got any. Had to drive to B & Q. Spent quite a bit of time chatting to an assistant with a lovely, pert bottom ... it was a job to concentrate on what he was telling me! Came home. Needed a coffee before I could face the shelf again. Loaded with cappuccino and armed with the drill, I attempted the second hole and that was when it all went wrong.' He threw up his hands theatrically.

'Oh no, I think I can guess where this is going!' Felix grimaced and looked across at Tom.

'Me too,' Tom nodded. 'Was there something important you'd forgotten?'

'Maybe.' Kai's grin was infectious and Deborah couldn't help giggling.

'Don't tell me you drilled into a water pipe!' she spluttered. 'Oh no! You did!'

Kai shrugged. 'It wasn't my fault. I blame YouTube. Although, in fairness, the videos might have mentioned something about that. I fast forwarded the boring bits.'

'Thank God you didn't drill into an electrical cable!' Felix remarked.

'I know! That's what Phil said when he came home and I had to confess what happened. Fortunately, he's hidden his drill so I can't do any more damage.'

'Yes, I should stick to what you're good at.' Tom took a sip of his pint and turned to Deborah, who was sitting next to him on a corner table in the main bar. 'What are you good at, Deborah? Apart from business, of course.'

She raised her eyebrows, toying with the stem of her wine glass. 'Not DIY, cooking or gardening, that's for sure, although Kai gave me some very helpful pointers when he came round this afternoon to look at my overgrown jungle.' All around the table exploded with laughter at her unintentional double-entendre and it was some while before she could continue. 'I may be tempted to give gardening a go. I think some of Kai's enthusiasm has rubbed off.'

'Yes, but what do you enjoy doing?' Tom persisted. 'In your spare time.'

She pulled a face. 'I'm afraid I don't have a lot of spare time. Going to the theatre … and I like art, books, that sort of thing.' God, she was making herself sound so boring! Probably, because she was.

'Me too!' Jules jumped in. 'I do envy people who live in London, or any of the cities for that matter, having all that culture on their doorstep. All I get is farm or school chat. Not that I would change things,' she added hastily with a quick smile at her husband. 'I love living in the country, I really do. But I was brought up in Manchester, and I do miss some of that city lifestyle.'

'What are you going to do with yourself now you're stuck here with us?' Felix asked.

'There is a book club in the village … and an art club. I belong to the book club and you would be very welcome to join us,' Jules chipped in.

'And not forgetting the history club. Honoraria was keen to get a plug in last night,' Tom reminded her.

'We'll see,' Deborah hedged. 'I will still be very busy with work. I'm not planning on commuting every day – two or three times a week – but otherwise, I'll be working remotely.'

Kai frowned. 'Oh, I'd got the impression you were retiring here. Why else would you move so far away from your work?'

There was an awkward pause while Deborah decided how to answer. Before she could speak, though, Tom came to her rescue. 'I think that's Deborah's business,' he said to Kai. He turned back to Deborah. 'We're a nosy lot. Feel free to ignore all the personal questions. Who's up for another drink?'

And a few more drinks later, Deborah found herself being escorted home by Tom, chatting amicably about the recent history of *The Lamb Inn*.

'The Billingtons moved in about five years ago and completely renovated the place. Before that, it was pretty grim. They work very hard and, I'm pleased to say, it's doing very well,' Tom told her.

'That's good.' Both Gerald and Sally Billington were amiable landlords – relaxed but efficient, and genuinely interested in the customers. He was tall, thickset and liked a joke. His laugh rumbled around the bar as he greeted people and took their orders. Sally was fair; striking-looking. Deborah could see the resemblance with her stunning daughter, Freya. She was quieter but equally smiley and welcoming. All in all, Deborah counted herself lucky to have met so many friendly people in such a short space of time since arriving in Wickthorpe. It was very different from what she had expected.

Now, she walked alongside Tom Oldridge in companiable silence. Stars glittered overhead in a clear sky and Deborah hugged the image to her, storing it away for when she was back in the city and vast, starlit canvasses were just a memory. She was inordinately conscious of the man at her side and wondered what he was thinking. Tom Oldridge had been growing on her and, fuelled by alcohol and the romance of the beautiful night-time walk, her awareness of him as a man and potential lover was burgeoning into fantasy. It was the kind of night when a woman wanted to be held and kissed and caressed and ...

'Would you like me to walk up the drive with you?' His voice cut into her errant thoughts and she realised they had reached the gateway leading to Greenways Farm.

Lord, she was tempted. 'No, no, I'll be fine, thanks. It's been a lovely evening. Thanks for inviting me along.'

'You're welcome.'

Involuntarily, she leaned towards him, sensing he was about to kiss her. And she wanted him to, she realised. More than a little ...

Instead, he took a step back. 'Goodnight then.' His voice sounded formal and distant in the darkness, and something slipped inside her.

'Night.'

Alone, she wandered, slightly unsteadily, up the drive towards the lights of the house. She could not remember the last time she had consumed three glasses of wine. It had clearly affected her judgement. Stifling her disappointment, she opened the front door.

She did not see it straight away. After kicking off her shoes and removing her outer layer, she padded through to the kitchen to fetch a glass of water. It was only when she returned, to head up the stairs, she saw the envelope lying on the mat. Picking it up, she realised it was blank. *Strange.* Wearily, she tore it open, extracted the single sheet of paper and drew in a sharp breath. Handwritten, in black ink, were the words:

Witches are not welcome here. Leave before you get what you deserve.

CHAPTER 10

Three weeks on, public interest in Deborah Ryecroft and the Wickthorpe Witch legend had not diminished. In fact, it had escalated, Honoraria reflected with great satisfaction as she surveyed the best-ever turnout at a History Society meeting. Having booked the Village Institute, as she always did whenever she had a guest speaker, she prayed she would not be embarrassed by a poor attendance, but she need not have worried. Bodies were jammed in the upstairs room like sausages in a supermarket packet. The regulars were all in attendance – Ava and Enid Green, Jane Holley, old Gretchen Cooper (who was only there for the biscuits and usually slept through the talk) and the rector, Wendy Robinson. But today the number had swelled considerably. Even John and Valerie Hampton-Brown had put in an appearance! However, the biggest coup was Tom Oldridge, who had turned up with his daughter, Emma. Honoraria had wondered, rather anxiously, if Deborah Ryecroft would show up but, thankfully, there was as yet no sign of her. That would have been awkward as tonight's topic was witchcraft in East Anglia. The guest speaker was local historian, Dorothy Fairbanks, whose book, *Witches and Witch-Hunters Through the Centuries*, had topped the local non-fiction charts when it was released back in 2010 and was currently undergoing a resurgence in popularity. Several of the assembled throng had brought copies for the author to sign. Honoraria checked her watch. 7 p.m.

exactly. With a discreet cough, she made her way to the front of the room where Dorothy was already seated.

'Good evening, ladies and gentlemen,' she boomed. 'Welcome to the Wickthorpe History Society. It's wonderful to see so many of you here tonight.' She cast an assured eye over the audience, checking she had their full attention. Yes, even old Gretchen's eyes were wide open. 'It gives me great pleasure to tell you that, in a short while, the esteemed author and local historian, Dorothy Fairbanks, will be giving us a talk on the history of witchcraft in this region, but first I would like to give you a brief introduction about our village and how the legend of *The Wickthorpe Witch* was born.' Was that a groan from the back of the room? Honoraria narrowed her eyes, attempting to locate the source of the sound, but only blank faces stared back at her. She must have been mistaken.

Smile back in place, she launched into her well-practised account. 'In 1645, a young woman called Martha Lightbody was accused of witchcraft. She was a relative newcomer to the village and had fallen under suspicion, like many others at that time, because of her knowledge of herbs and their uses in treating the sick. She was subjected to trial by drowning – tied to a chair and thrown into Dark Water Lake. If she drowned, she would be declared innocent; not much of a consolation.' She chuckled, receiving nods and wry smiles in response. 'If she floated, that was seen as proof she was a witch and she would be sent for trial at Bury St Edmunds, where she would be convicted and hung. You may not know that the reasoning behind this barbaric practice was that witches had renounced the Christian faith and thereby the baptism symbolising that faith. Therefore, water would reject them and they would float. This was a time of absolute terror for women like Martha. The son of a puritan vicar, a young man called Matthew Hopkins, appointed himself Witchfinder General and scoured East Anglia for likely candidates. In 1645 alone, eighteen people were hanged for witchcraft in Bury St Edmunds. Anyway, back to Martha. Before she was thrown into the lake, legend has it that she cursed the whole village and its descendants ...'

A pause for effect. She really did have them all in the palm of her hand! It reminded her of teaching days, when she was imparting something particularly ghoulish to her students and their rapt faces were engrossed in her every word. That heady power was rarely experienced these days and she wanted to savour the moment, enjoy it, before continuing. Dorothy Fairbanks' deliberate cough shattered the magic and she hastened back to her speech.

'Martha was never seen again. The chair surfaced, but empty, and there was no sign of her. Most villagers believed she escaped and swam to freedom. Some thought she drowned although her body was never found. Martha's husband and young child left Wickthorpe shortly after the incident. No one knows what became of them. And therein lies the mystery. What had happened to Martha Lightbody? We still don't know to this day. But, back to the curse. For a while, villagers fretted over it but, as days and weeks passed, that fear eased … until the following year when a woman was found drowned in that very same lake, Dark Water. The dead woman's husband was one of the ringleaders behind Martha's arrest so the whole village believed the curse was responsible. And the legend was born, passing down through subsequent centuries. Now, before you all panic and put your houses on the market …' Another pause for polite laughter. 'Historians suspect the legend of the curse may have been fuelled by foul play. Any villager wanting rid of someone, for whatever reason, could drown their victim and dump the body in the lake, thereby absolving themselves of culpability. Statistics show Wickthorpe has recorded a much higher number of deaths by drowning than other, similar villages in the east of England. Over time, as the legend grew, villagers believed the witch would perpetrate murderous deeds by inhabiting the body of a woman in Wickthorpe. Hence, many women in the village found themselves termed the Wickthorpe Witch. As recently as 1903, a Wickthorpe woman, Blanche Dent, was tried and hung for the murder of Harriet Jones. Much of the evidence cited against her at that time was that she was known to practise witchcraft. Interestingly, Harold Jones, the widower of the victim, inherited a substantial sum of money from his late wife's estate, and then went on to wed a young woman forty years his junior less than a year later. You can make up your own minds as to what you think about that. Personally, I suspect there have been many cases of wrongful accusation at the hands of the village legend. After the war, for example, in 1946, an attempt was made to re-open Wickthorpe's brickworks. Unfortunately, a workman inadvertently hit a spring with his pickaxe, flooding the site and rendering it unusable. There was talk then that the witch must be back in the village, and one poor woman was sorely persecuted until she and her family moved away. In 1988, as some of you here will recall, a young girl, only sixteen years old, drowned in the lake. The coroner's verdict was accidental death by drowning, but another girl, supposedly the victim's friend, was deemed responsible and has since been known as the Wickthorpe Witch. That girl is now a successful businesswoman and has returned to the village. Many here still believe in the legend and are fearful, convinced it may be only a matter of time before the Witch claims her next victim.' Honoraria hesitated. The audience held its breath. 'I suppose only time will tell ... but certainly our special guest tonight, Dorothy Fairbanks, will be able to shed light on the whole concept of witchcraft. Perhaps she will alleviate these fears ... or not. Ladies and gentlemen, please welcome ... Dorothy Fairbanks.'

A round of applause broke out and, as the new speaker stood, Honoraria sat, pleased with the impact of her introduction. Unlike many of the audience, who had purchased Dorothy's book recently, she had read it when it first came out, and reread it in preparation for the meeting, so she had a good idea of many of the things Dorothy was about to say. Still, she sat back on her chair, listening attentively, while the author introduced herself and cited her impressive credentials: Cambridge History Professor; Curator of St Edmundsbury Museum; Director of the Museum of Witchcraft and Magic; author of several papers on the history of witchcraft worldwide and best-selling author of *Witches and Witch-Hunters Through the Centuries*. Dorothy had a deep, engaging, almost hypnotic tone to her voice and was dressed all in black, in a long skirt and knee-length black jacket. Honoraria suspected those sartorial choices were deliberate. Physically, she also looked the part, with a short, squat body, long, grey hair twisted in a plait hanging down her back, and even a large wart on the right-hand side of her chin. Dorothy was confident in her subject and delivered her talk without the aid of notes.

'My fascination with witches and witch-hunters began when I became a volunteer at St Edmundsbury Museum back in the 1990s,' she said. 'I had been a history professor for many years but I lived in Bury and had been involved with the museum services, in both Suffolk and Cambridgeshire, in an informal, advisory capacity. It was then that I decided to take a step back from teaching and focus on research. At the museum, there was a display of witchcraft – dead cats, shoes, witch bottles, all sorts of things which had been discovered bricked up behind the walls of houses to ward off evil spirits. People did all manner of strange things to protect themselves. When witches were tried in Bury in the seventeenth century, they were subjected to having locks of hair or nails removed. These were then stored in jars, the theory being that, if the witch was not whole at the time of her death, then she could not return in the next life as a whole witch. Fascinating stuff!' She gave the audience a wide smile. 'Of course, I say *she*, but not all the accused were women. Far from it. Men were also tried and convicted. There was even a vicar, the Reverend John Lowes of Brandeston, hanged for witchcraft. Honoraria mentioned Matthew Hopkins' crusade against witches in the 1640s. He was responsible for around one fifth of the executions in England at this time. John Lowes was one of his targets. Possibly, the Reverend Lowes was considered too 'High Church'. This was a Puritan age, you have to remember. The eighty-year-old vicar was accused in 1642. He was 'swum' – the process Honoraria has already described – in the moat of Framlingham Castle and declared guilty when he floated to the surface. As was his habit, Hopkins tried to extract a confession as well – the safest way to secure a conviction. He kept the old man awake for many nights and had him running back and forth in his cell until so exhausted he scarcely knew what he was saying. Accounts state that Lowes eventually admitted to sending imps to sink a ship near Harwich and that was that. His fate was sealed. But I digress. Across Europe, approximately six thousand men, ten to fifteen per cent of the total, were executed for practising witchcraft. Another surprising fact is that, in England, most of the accusers against witches were women. Now, let me give you a little bit of background and context to all of this.'

The room remained hushed as Dorothy described the sixteenth and seventeenth centuries as a time of religious upheaval and division where both Catholics and Protestants were suspicious of each other's practices. Against this backdrop, she said, concerns about witchcraft and magic grew. As she detailed the Acts against witchcraft, the audience began to grow restless. They were not there for a boring history lesson. Honoraria sensed the mood and fidgeted in her chair. Get back to the interesting stuff, she urged silently.

'As a capital offence, witch trials were held before a judge and jury,' Dorothy droned on. 'The evidence was then presented. Some court records detail extraordinary eyewitness accounts, cited as evidence, of the accused flying on a broomstick or cavorting with imps. It may surprise you to learn that the verdict of these trials was by no means a foregone conclusion. Only about a quarter were found guilty and executed. That was why Hopkins worked so hard to get confessions from his victims, to ensure their convictions.' She paused as a hand was raised. 'Yes?'

'What was his motivation?' Wendy Robinson, the village rector, asked. 'Was he a religious zealot?'

'That's a matter for conjecture,' came the reply. 'He was from a Puritan family but chose not to follow his father and brothers into the clergy which, some might say, proves his main motivation was not religion. Certainly, he was very well-paid for his efforts and the driving force behind his persecutions may well have been money. Historical accounts from the time focus more on his work than the nature of the man himself so it's difficult to be sure.'

Dorothy smiled as another hand was raised. 'Yes?'

This time, the question came from the front row and Gretchen Cooper. 'Are we having a break soon? Only, I need *the loo*!' Those last words were delivered in a stage whisper, heard by everyone. There were titters of laughter.

'Just go, Gretchen!' Honoraria hissed before turning to her guest with an apologetic smile and flags of embarrassment on her already heavily-rouged cheeks. 'Sorry about that, Dorothy. Please continue. I'm finding this fascinating.'

Dorothy grinned at the audience. 'I'll take that as a sign and won't go on for too much longer. If you want more details of individual cases and trials, there are lots in my book.' She held the tome aloft. 'The 1735 Witchcraft Act repealed all the previous acts and witchcraft was no longer a capital offence. Instead, those accused were considered fraudulent and treated as such. The last person to be executed in Britain for practising witchcraft was Janet Horne in 1732. After 1735, the accused would face one year in prison per offence – a big change. Of course, the eighteenth century is known as a period of Enlightenment when many new scientific discoveries were made.

It was a time when man was considered modern, rational, scientific, as opposed to fearful and superstitious. Several famous figures of the Enlightenment took a keen interest in alchemy and the occult, including Sir Isaac Newton. Again, I write extensively about this in my book. But that, as we all know, is not the end of the story. The fascination with witchcraft continues to this day. The recent rise in popularity of Halloween is an example. Many pagan beliefs are rooted in The Witches' Creed – "If it harms none, do what you will." In other words, it's acceptable to dabble in magic, the black arts, call them what you will, as long as no one is hurt. Mediums are another example. The act of communing with the dead, often via incantations or specific rituals, is regarded by some as witchcraft. Some believe and find comfort from it, whereas many are sceptical and consider practitioners to be con artists. Attitudes today vary considerably. I will say, however, that there are some quite horrific statistics to support the fact that, worldwide, attacks on individuals and executions in the name of witchcraft are still taking place, in Africa, the Pacific, Latin America and even within immigrant communities in America and Western Europe. In 2009, a report for the United Nations High Commissioner of Refugees confirmed that the practice of persecuting and killing mainly women and children for supposed crimes of witchcraft is rife. In 2013, there was an horrific and highly-publicised case of a young woman suspected of sorcery in Papua, New Guinea who was burned alive. The atrocities of the seventeenth century witch hunts are continuing in the twenty-first century. The whole notion of witchcraft remains fascinating, fear-inducing, controversial, and a tool for persecution to this day. And that brings me back to Wickthorpe and your questions. Feel free to ask me anything … within reason, of course. Not my age … or my dress size!' She chuckled and received awkward smiles in return as people shifted in their seats.

'Me again.' Wendy Robinson raised her hand to speak as Gretchen Cooper shuffled back to her seat.

'Sorry about that,' Gretchen mumbled. 'I've got a few problems with my waterworks. Dr Holley has referred me to the hospital.'

'That's quite alright, Gretchen,' Honoraria responded, benign now the talk was nearly over. 'We understand. Carry on, Wendy.'

'I just wondered what are *your* views on curses? As Honoraria said, in Wickthorpe, much has been blamed on the curse of the Wickthorpe Witch. What are your thoughts?'

'Curses are very interesting,' Dorothy beamed back. 'My view is that the dark arts are employed by people as a means of controlling someone else to get something you want. A curse is similar in that it is used for a purpose to achieve something. In the case of Martha Lightbody, I would conjecture that her curse on the village was a punishment for the injustice meted out to her. She wanted to harm the men who were persecuting her and, in her situation, tied to a chair and about to be thrown into a lake, a curse was the only option available to her. The very fact that the curse has been believed across centuries and still resonates to this day means it worked! People continue to fear it. I suppose what I'm trying to say, in my long-winded way, is that the power of a curse lies in the belief of the person or people cursed. Without the belief, the curse loses its threat. Does that answer your question?'

'Yes, thank you. You're saying that if we all just forget about it, there is no curse?'

'Exactly. Yes?'

Valerie Hampton-Brown's arm quivered with urgency. 'That's all very well but you can't forget it when you have the proof that it exists ... when you have to live with it and the grief that it's brought ...' She rose to her full height, trembling with indignation, tears pooling in her eyes. Her husband reached to lay a restraining hand on her arm but she shook it off. Her voice rose, shrill with anguish. 'My son was killed, here in this village. He was only seventeen when his car slid off the road and into a tree near Dark Water Lake. He died instantly. It happened thirty-four years ago and, every day, the pain of it is as fresh as the day it happened. The police ... the forensic collision investigators ... *no one* could explain why it happened. There was no mechanical failure. No other vehicle was involved. It was daytime and the weather was fine and clear. My son, although young, was a careful driver. There was absolutely no reason for it ... except the curse. A neighbour saw Jonathan talking to Deborah Ryecroft, the Wickthorpe Witch, just the day before. A strange coincidence, don't you think? So do not try to tell me that the curse is not real!'

Dorothy turned panicked eyes to her right. 'Oh ... I'm sorry ... I didn't mean ... I'm so sorry for your loss.'

As she stumbled for a response, Honoraria stood and sucked in a fortifying breath. 'I think now might be an excellent time to stop for some refreshments.' She nodded to the back of the room where two ladies, drafted in for the purpose, scurried to operate the tea urn. 'Valerie, none of us can begin to imagine what you've been through. What happened to your son was a terrible tragedy. Dorothy was not trying to suggest the curse wasn't real. As you say, it's very real for you.' She left a dignified pause before adding quietly, 'We will talk more in a moment, Valerie.' Face sombre, she swung back to the guest speaker and became courteous hostess once more. 'Dorothy, on behalf of us all, I'd like to thank you for giving us that *enchanting ...*' a modest smile at the planned pun, 'and informative insight into witchcraft and witch hunters. Dorothy will remain with us for refreshments and so there will be plenty of time for you to ask her any further questions you may have. And I know many of you followed my recommendation and have bought her wonderful book. She will be very happy to sign any copies. And, if you have not yet purchased it, there are copies available to buy this evening. Now, before our tea or coffee and biscuits, I'm sure you'd all like to join with me in showing Dorothy our appreciation.'

Polite applause rang out and Honoraria muttered a few extra, gracious words of thanks to her guest while chairs were scraped back across the wooden floor. As soon as the way was clear, she hurried over to the Hampton-Browns. 'Valerie, you poor dear ...' she began.

'Don't patronise me, Honoraria,' came the harsh reply.

'I'm sorry. That wasn't my intention.' She directed a worried look at the husband, hoping there wasn't going to be a further scene. 'I can imagine that this evening has brought back very painful memories. I think ...' She chose her next words with care. 'I think that the belief in witchcraft is as relevant today as it has ever been and I know Dorothy feels the same. People have very different viewpoints, as I'm sure you appreciate.' She allowed her hand to rest briefly on Valerie's arm. 'Now, can I fetch you both a cup of tea or coffee?'

'No thank you. I think we will leave now. We wanted to hear what was being said and we have done that.' She stood and waited for her husband to do likewise. He gave a tight smile.

'Thank you for your concern,' he said. 'Come along, darling. Let's get you home.'

Thank goodness. Honoraria scampered to fetch Dorothy's coffee. *Cream and three sugars; no wonder the woman was as wide as she was tall!* She felt relieved to have contained a tricky situation with a degree of professionalism. *That had been awkward. Poor Valerie!* Honoraria had known the Hampton-Browns' only son had been killed in a car accident, but had no idea that they blamed the Wickthorpe Witch for the tragedy. No wonder she had been so frosty about Deborah Ryecroft! Honoraria shivered. You never knew what secrets people harboured. Judging by the faces, though, and the throng around Dorothy, the talk had been a success. Fingers crossed there would be no further difficult incidents. And, hopefully, attendance would be equally pleasing at the next meeting.

***

Two hours later, Honoraria locked the door of the Institute behind her and headed out into the cold crispness of the night. Everything was quiet. She walked past the Fish & Chip shop and looked across, beyond the old village pump, towards *The King's Head*, the beautiful, old coaching inn which was now, sadly, closed for good. It had once been such a hub of the village. *Shame.*

The adrenalin, which had coursed through her body all evening, was seeping away, like air from a balloon, leaving her flat and spent. Still, it had been a successful meeting and Dorothy was pleased with book sales. Post-talk discussions had reflected the diverse range of opinions in the room. Some were entrenched in their belief in the curse. Of those, the most vociferous was Enid Green. She was a bit of a witch herself, Honoraria thought, stirring up trouble and almost gleeful in her premonitions of trouble ahead. The like-minded had soon gravitated towards her – older villagers who had been in Wickthorpe when Deborah Ryecroft was a teenager. Enid had allies in Brenda Wicks, another widow who was active in the W.I. and lived down Shallow Road, and Philip Holder, a retired farmworker who lived alone in a small bungalow in Mill Lane. The latter really seemed to have it in for Deborah Ryecroft. Honoraria had overheard him saying, 'That woman is going to get what's coming to her if she ...' when someone else had interrupted him.

Then, there was the other camp who felt the Wickthorpe curse was a load of nonsense. She had cosied alongside Tom Oldridge as he was saying as much to the rector, Wendy Robinson.

'In my opinion, people often want to find someone else to blame when they suffer misfortune. Some blame God. In Wickthorpe, it's the witch. My father always liked to blame me,' he said with a wry smile. 'A curse is meaningless if you don't believe in it. And calling Deborah Ryecroft a witch because another girl had a tragic accident is just ludicrous.'

His daughter, Emma, stood beside him, nodding agreement but otherwise looking distinctly downcast. Probably something to do with that young vet, Rick Billington, now often seen out and about with Amelie Charles. *Young love*. Honoraria sighed. For her, that was a long time ago. There was no romance in her life now; her recent encounter with Jack Jones, 53, delivery driver, had been proof of that ...

First impressions were good. He was taller than her – always a bonus – and clean-shaven; reasonable-looking in a Ray Winstone kind of way. He greeted her with an enthusiastic hug.

'Wow, you're a sight for sore eyes,' he said and she was pleased she had made the effort to look her best, in a tight-fitting scarlet top with plenty of cleavage (her best asset) on show.

'Thank you,' she replied breathily, with a coy smile. 'You too.'

It went downhill from there. He told her he wasn't hungry, suggesting a drink and a packet of crisps from the bar instead of a meal. She agreed, disappointed. Dinner, the preamble for what was to come, was part of the thrill. Plus, she was always hoping she might find someone compatible, someone who might be more than a quick romp beneath the sheets ... or elsewhere, depending on how things developed. Secretly, despite the flippant wording of her advertisement, she wanted her lover to be interested in her as a person. Jack Jones was not. He downed his pint before she had taken barely a few sips of her gin and suggested they make their way upstairs. When she demurred, he looked at his watch with a frown.

'I haven't got long,' he told her. 'An hour at the most. We should be getting on with it.'

Charming! She had almost walked out there and then. But, weighing things up, she had gone along with his demands. It would be too much of a disappointment, after all those fabulous fantasies, to leave without revealing the beautiful, new lace corset she wore beneath her outer layer.

They went upstairs to a small, impersonal, double room, and she made her usual detour to the bathroom, to remove the clingy top and black pencil skirt, adjust her stockings, slip back into her stilettoes, and refresh her red lipstick. She was ready. Taking a deep breath, she walked back into the room, expecting a gasp of delight from the man on the bed. He would already be naked, she thought, erect and waiting ...

Instead, he was sitting on the bed, his back to her, phone clamped to his ear. 'Sorry, love,' he was saying. 'It's not my fault. Bloody Kev is off again and I'm having to cover. I'll be an hour ... two tops .... Yeah, see you then.' He rang off and stood to face her, wearing grey Y-fronts and one sock, both of which he hastily pulled off.

What followed took less than three minutes. Fast, furious, horribly unsatisfying.

'Thanks, love,' he said as he left. 'Sorry ... gotta rush.'

That was it. She was still in her corset, feeling as used as the single condom he had thrown carelessly in the bin. Having told Jane Holley, her neighbour whom she had asked to keep an eye on things, that she would be away for the night, she could not face returning home. Instead, she ordered a solitary dinner via room service and watched a film. By the next morning, she had chalked the whole thing up to experience and resolved, given the same situation again, she would walk away, head aloft, dignity intact. In the end, only her pride had been hurt. Jack Jones had told her he would pay the bar bill and for the room, given he was having to leave so abruptly. At the time, it was small consolation but she had graciously accepted his offer. However, when she asked the receptionist what she owed, she found she was left with the whole bill. The rat had sneaked out without paying for a thing. As she got out her credit card and paid with a smile, saying, 'Yes, everything was perfect, thank you,' she had never felt so cheap ...

She shook her head, remembering, as she clipped home in her smart, burgundy, leather boots. Perhaps she should give up on her sexual escapades. None, so far, had delivered exactly what she wanted. She thought it would be empowering but each soulless encounter left her feeling a little bit more diminished as a woman. How she missed dear Edgar! There were so many things about him and their life together she had loved: the patient way he had always listened when she described her day; the bunches of flowers with which he used to surprise her at unexpected moments; his wry humour which made her laugh out loud. Yes, he had his faults: his obsession with football and Ipswich Town FC, which took precedence over all things, including her birthdays and their anniversaries; the ridiculous amount of time he wasted, pottering in his shed in the garden; his tight-fistedness when it came to holidays. None of that really mattered though. Didn't everyone have faults? Probably, she did too, although she struggled to think of any.

It was hard on her own without his support and love bolstering her days and filling her nights with the kind of passion of which she could now only dream. Thinking about Edgar made her feel quite sentimental. Their love had been an exquisite rose, she thought, always in bud, velvet with the promise of perfection. Life without Edgar meant no flowers – not even forecourt chrysanthemums – and her own petals were fast becoming faded and jaded, her bloom well past its best. *How poetic! She really ought to write that down!*

As she unlocked her front door and slipped into the silent darkness within, unshed tears unexpectedly scorched her throat. How she longed to find him waiting, to share the success of her evening with him, to celebrate one last time in his arms! Giving herself a mental shake, she made a mug of hot chocolate, picked up a pencil and continued a crossword she had started earlier. It was not her way to indulge bouts of self-pity. And the meeting *had* been a triumph. She was sure to receive plenty of congratulation, out and about in the village, in days to come.

CHAPTER 11

Martha's diary
28th October, 1644

Praise the Lord for a beautiful late autumn day, resplendent with gold, green and orange colours! It felt quite glorious to be out in the sunshine, foraging with my new friend, Prudence. Josiah has fortunately recovered from the nasty cough which has so troubled him these past weeks, and was quite content to slumber in his sling like an angel, so we travelled further than of late, beyond the wood to the furthest edges of Mr Finch's land. There we happened across a most plentiful bounty of mint, lemon balm, mugwort and catnip. It was a sunny, sheltered spot and hence the plants have prospered beyond their usual time. I declare my basket was full to bursting when I returned.

I feel blessed to live in such charming surroundings with such a wonderful man. My love for John grows every day such as I would not have believed possible. How I thank the Lord for chancing 'pon him the day he journeyed to King's Lynn, bringing wool to market. Fate sent him my way and his eyes met mine, grey like the river. How handsome he was! I had been helping Mother that morning but the sun was shining and I liked to escape to see the boats whene'er I could. Perchance, I was there when John happened along, his cart laden with fleeces of wool, seeking directions to market. His brother was entrusted with this responsibility but was unwell that day so John was charged with the task. When he addressed me, his voice low and gruff, I could not prevent my cheeks from flaming. We exchanged barely a few words, but his lingering glance as he drove away set my pulses racing. That most fortuitous encounter turned my world quite topsy-turvy! For some days after, I made my way to that spot, praying for my beloved to return (already I considered him such). I had almost given up hope when, two weeks hence, he reappeared. Imagine! I near swooned at the sight of him. When he confessed he had dreamt of me oft since our meeting, claiming I had bewitched him with my hazel eyes, I could scarce believe the truth of it. He planned to return sooner, he said, but conflict with his father forced him out of his rightful home and he had since taken up employment in Grimston. We arranged to meet weekly after that and twas but a few months hence when I happily accepted his proposal of marriage. The wedding was a most joyful day for us both. John's father, an unpleasant man by all accounts, refused to attend but his brother, Matthew, was present with his wife, Calla. Twas the first time I had met members of John's family and I was a little shy but they were most kind toward me and it soon seemed as if we were acquaintances of longstanding. I feel sad we live so far away and cannot see them regularly, much as with my own family, but John says twill not be safe to travel for some while hence.

I am thankful for the company of a friend. Prudence is losing her natural shyness with me and, today, told me a little of her history. She has four older siblings, all brothers, and was much cosseted as a child. The marriage to her husband, a good man nigh on twenty years older than herself, and the move away from her family, have proved somewhat of an ordeal by all accounts. She misses her mother and is unused to spending much of the day alone. Her husband, Gideon, works long hours and is solitary by nature. Although she is most fond of him, she has found married life a lonely existence. Until now! She is happy to have female company nearby at last and told me she already views me as a sister. I confess, I was somewhat taken aback and most flattered. She is a sweet girl and tis delightful to share some of my knowledge with her. Always I am mindful of what I reveal though, especially to an innocent such as Prudence. After my experience in Grimston, I continue to conceal my knowledge in the art of healing, lest further accusations of witchcraft be levelled 'gainst me. John, Josiah and I are happily settled in Wickthorpe and have no desire to move in the near future. Prudence lacks guile and could inadvertently spill my secrets, were she party to them. Tis most difficult though. Today Prudence asked about Josiah's cough and I found myself telling her of my onion tea remedy! I changed the subject quickly so pray she will think no more of it.

On our way back to our respective cottages, we encountered a tall, fair-haired man riding a large, gray stallion. He was surely most striking and I noticed Prudence blushing when he stopped to converse with us. I swear I have never seen such white teeth, nor a more handsome countenance! He was polite, bid us both a good afternoon, and questioned me as to the nature of my settlement in Wickthorpe. I found him pleasant enough on the surface but there was a certain arrogance about his manner. The way his blue eyes sought mine made me uncomfortable and I confess I was eager to escape his gaze.

After he had left us, Prudence informed me we had just met Roger Holley, the eldest son of Julius Holley who owns most of the land hereabouts. Even during our short sojourn here, I have heard much of Julius Holley and the cruel way he treats his tenants. Whilst Roger was most charming, there was something about him I did not trust. I mentioned the encounter to John when he arrived home and, whilst he was most reassuring, I detected something of concern in his manner which sent shivers down my spine. I feel I would do well to avoid future meetings with that particular gentleman.

CHAPTER 12

Deborah noticed the changing patterns of the weather far more than she had when living in London. Seven weeks had passed since her return to Wickthorpe, and today the sun had a fierce bite to it. Her arms felt the heat as she weeded the border of shrubs and perennials in the rear garden. Who would have thought? She enjoyed gardening! It was all down to Kai and his ebullient enthusiasm for things horticultural. He had spent hours here, working alongside her, patiently answering questions and encouraging her, despite his lack of spare time. What a fabulous friend he had proved! And, much to her surprise, she found she loved to escape outside, to feel the soft, moist soil beneath her fingers and see the results of her labour. It was both energising and relaxing after hours spent in her home office. When she first met Kai, and he suggested she tackle the garden herself, she thought he was joking. It seemed a monumental task and she had no idea where to start. But he gradually wore down her resistance, lent her his lawn mower when she needed it, provided tools, gave advice, and generally bossed her into it. It was hard work but she had never shirked from that and it was satisfying to see order emerge from chaos. On fine days such as today, she looked forward to heading outside and pulling on gardening gloves. She had even purchased her own lawnmower.

Gardening helped take her mind off things. Not just work. Threatening notes continued to appear at regular intervals, always the same:

Witches are not welcome here. Leave before you get what you deserve.

She ripped them up and threw them away, but the words remained imprinted on her mind, a curse in themselves and a reminder of the resentment felt towards her by many in the village. Old superstitions persisted. She had heard about the History Society meeting from Ava Green, when she called into the Post Office wanting to send a parcel. They had been alone and Ava warned her then that Enid, and others, had the knives out for her. The realisation, though, that people still felt such hatred and fear as to send her menacing threats, was a shock. The words lurked, like drops of poison, in her psyche.

As time went by, and nothing more concerning happened, it became easier to dismiss the notes. Her life had fallen into an easy rhythm. During the week, she either worked at home or commuted to London. It was a straightforward trip, from nearby Elmswell station to London Liverpool Street, by train, and it was good to get back to the office for two or three days a week to keep everyone on their toes and attend meetings in person. She had set things up so the business ran smoothly without her, while she was in Wickthorpe for the year, but it was a little mortifying to discover how well everyone coped when she was not a physical presence. Sometimes, on journeys home, she even wondered about making a long-term plan to step back, take more time for herself. Quickly, she shook off such errant thoughts, as common sense reasserted itself. What would she do without work?

Every now and again, she returned to her London home, just to check everything was as it should be. Her PA, Agneta, kept an eye on things and the cleaner was in once a week, so the visits were unnecessary, but she felt she wanted to touch base, remind herself of the roots she had put down in the city. It was strange yesterday, when she visited. For the first time, she viewed her house as functional but sterile. No garden meant no outdoor space to breathe. There was no greenery, not even a houseplant. When she returned, she would have to remedy that. With her new-found passion for gardening, perhaps she would even consider moving. Having lived in the city for almost ten years, it could be time for a change. She loved the paintings in the house though – all abstract, contemporary pieces by upcoming artists. They had proved shrewd investments too. Yesterday, she had met Rafe, her art dealer friend, for lunch and it had been great to catch up on all the London news. Already she felt out of the loop. She mentioned the lack of artwork at

Greenways Farm, a situation he was keen to remedy, but she felt reluctant to enlist his help. For once, she wanted to choose her own pieces – discover some Suffolk artists for herself. Having visited various local galleries, nothing had so far inspired her, but she would find that elusive talent. It remained an ongoing project, like her gardening.

That morning, she spotted Tom Oldridge out on a self-propelled sprayer in the field next door. She had encountered him a few times, in passing, but their interactions had been brief. There had been no further invitations from him, no repeats of the night in the pub. Today, he raised an arm in greeting and she waved in return. That was it. The sight of him, as always, produced mixed feelings – a fluttering in her stomach and a bout of irritation. It now seemed absurd that, when he had initially seemed so attentive, she had suspected him of being after her money. Now, she wondered if he was deliberately avoiding her. That night in *The Lamb Inn*, she was sure she sensed something between the two of them, but it must have been her imagination, fuelled by wine. It appeared he felt no compulsion to continue whatever it was she had fancied burgeoning between them. Perhaps, in those early days, he was just being neighbourly after all. Annoying, though, as she did find him attractive. Her pride was wounded that she had been dropped so readily.

Maybe she should make the next move? It was not something she was used to – inviting someone out on a date. Men usually chased after her. But why not? Once the idea took hold, she found it difficult to push aside. She could invite him, and his daughter, Emma, for dinner – at *The Lamb Inn* as it had a good reputation for food – to thank them both for hosting a welcome party in her honour. That would be the polite thing to do. And, if he refused, that was fine too. She would know where she stood. She added Kai and Phil to her invitation list. It made her feel better to take control of the situation. She didn't know why she hadn't thought of it before.

***

That evening, she dressed with care, conscious of the effect she wanted to create – casual, not trying too hard, but sexy and appealing. A table for three was booked at *The Lamb Inn*. Kai and Phil couldn't make it so it would be just Tom and Emma for company. Tom had seemed a little wary when he answered his phone but had accepted the invitation for himself and his daughter readily enough. Obviously, with Emma in attendance, nothing would happen between them that evening, but it was an opportunity to blast him with the full force of her charm. She was under no illusions as to her power in attracting the opposite sex. If he liked her, but was a bit shy, she was happy to take the lead. A part of her brain laughed at the notion of Tom Oldridge lacking confidence with women. He must know how good-looking he was. The woman who ran the History Society had been all over him ...

At the sound of the doorbell, she glanced at her watch. Right on time. With a final glance in the mirror, she scooped up her bag and headed downstairs, eagerly anticipating the night ahead. The outline framed in the front door glass, however, gave her pause. Not Tom, nor Emma. She detoured to her study and peered out of the window. A white Porsche sat in her drive. *Bloody hell!* What was *he* doing here?

She returned to the door and opened it. 'This is a surprise,' she said drily.

'I know. Sorry. Hope that's OK.' Rupert Smytheson grinned back at her. 'I missed you and, as I had a few days off, I thought I'd surprise you.' Her ex was dressed impeccably, as always, in beige trousers and a tailored jacket. His chiselled looks drew eyes wherever he went and he knew it. 'London is boring without you, darling.' He leant forward to give her a hug which she avoided.

'How did you find me?' Her eyes skittered down the driveway. No sign yet of the Oldridges. She wondered how quickly she could get rid of Rupert. This was not the time for a reunion.

'Aren't you going to invite me in?' He ignored her question.

'No. I was just going out.' That surprised him. Typical Rupert. He always thought the world revolved around him. 'I told you things were over between us.'

'I know that.' The confident smile remained in place. 'But I thought we were friends. Friends still see each other.' *Damn.* He had her there. She was the one who had declared the termination of their relationship did not mean the end of their friendship. 'Where are we going?'

'*We're* not going anywhere. I'm having dinner with friends. Ah ... here they are now.'

Tom Oldridge strode round the corner alone. He smiled that killer smile as he approached but she could see puzzlement in his blue eyes. 'Evening, Deborah. Sorry, I'm a bit on the drag.'

'Tom, this is Rupert Smytheson, a friend of mine from London, who has just turned up unexpectedly. Rupert, this is my neighbour, Tom Oldridge. Is Emma not joining us?'

'Sorry, no. At the last minute, her mum called with some crisis or another. She's had to go over to help her. I said I'd make her apologies to you.' He turned to Rupert. 'Are you joining us this evening?'

'Yes, thank you for asking.' He shot a triumphant glance at Deborah. 'Where are we going? Who's driving? It'll be a bit of a squash for the three of us in the Porsche.'

'We'll walk.' Deborah stepped back inside to retrieve her navy cashmere cardigan and both men stepped forward to help her into it. Rupert was nearest and it was he who held it, like a trophy, as she slipped her arms into the sleeves. 'Thank you.' She pulled the door behind her. 'Shall we go?'

***

The meal was delicious but, in Deborah's eyes, the evening was a disaster. She could have throttled Rupert who took every opportunity to make Tom feel like an extra in a film where he was director and leading male. He dominated the conversation with tales of life in London, one anecdote flowing smoothly into another. Worse, he took every opportunity to caress Deborah's arm, hand or shoulder. Staking his claim. She squirmed with annoyance and spoke mainly to Tom, asking him about the farm and telling him about her efforts in the garden. But it was no use. Rupert would quickly interject with a story or a question of his own, diverting the conversation back to the two of them as a couple. It was beyond annoying. Not that Tom seemed to mind. He laughed at Rupert's stories and tucked into his steak with obvious appreciation. But this was not what Deborah had planned at all and she did not appreciate being railroaded. While she schemed how to get rid of Rupert, which was not going to be easy – the man had the stickability of superglue – she wondered how he had managed to find her. Agneta? She was the only person in London who knew her current address. But Agneta was the very model of discretion and would not have told anyone, least of all

Rupert. Her PA was aware of their break up and Deborah's subsequent relief. So, how? She decided to press the issue and ask him again.

'Ah,' Rupert twirled the stem of his wineglass between his long fingers. He gave her a wink and tapped his hawkish nose, his worst feature in an otherwise handsome face. 'That would be telling.'

She frowned. 'Was it Agneta?'

'Agneta!' he scoffed, 'I'd more likely discover the whereabouts of Van Gogh's lost *Poppy Flowers* than get anything from those sealed Swedish lips!'

'Agneta's not Swedish.'

'Isn't she? I always thought she was. Like the blonde one from Abba. Anyway, it wasn't her.'

'Who then?' she persisted.

'Who's to say it was anyone?' He took another hefty swig of wine and refilled his glass, much to her dismay. He clearly was not planning on driving back to London this evening. 'Maybe, it was down to my brilliant detective skills ...' She raised her eyebrows and said nothing, tired of the game. 'Oh, alright then,' he continued, 'if you must know, I bumped into Josie.' Damn, she had forgotten about Josie Lowe, the CEO of a cosmetics company and good friend, whom she had told she would be living in Wickthorpe for a year. 'Josie said you were staying here to sort your mother's affairs. She didn't know the exact address though. I found that out for myself.' He eased back in his seat. 'My halibut was excellent. Compliments to the chef.' He gave Freya Billington a winning smile as she cleared the plates.

'Thank you, I'll pass it on.' She smiled back as she deftly balanced all three on one arm.

'Moonlighting tonight, Freya?' Tom asked.

She pulled a face. 'We're a bit short staffed this evening so I said I'd help out. Would you like to see the dessert menu?'

'Definitely.' Rupert patted his flat, gym-toned abdomen. 'I've been saving myself.' When Freya had gone, he chuckled to himself. 'There is *one* similarity this village shares with London.'

'Oh?' Deborah was beginning to wonder if this horrible scenario was ever going to end.

'You haven't wasted any time in making yourself unpopular, have you, my love?'

'What do you mean?' she asked, instantly wary.

'Well, when I arrived, I met an old boy coming out of the fish and chip shop so I asked if he knew where I might find you. You should have seen his face when I mentioned your name! Like he'd swallowed a wasp! Obviously not a fan. Anyway, he pointed me in the right direction and then I spotted your car in a driveway. And here I am.'

'Are you staying long?' Tom asked politely.

'I've freed up a few days so as long as Deborah will have me.' He gave her a schoolboy grin. 'I know you'll be working, darling, so you won't have to bother too much about me during the day, my love. Just the evenings.' He directed another wink in her direction and picked up one of the dessert menus Freya had placed on the table. 'I think I'll have the toffee apple crumble. How about you two?'

'Nothing for me, thanks,' Deborah replied, gritting her teeth. Her irritation with Rupert was growing by the minute. When they were alone, she was going to wring his neck!

'Me neither.' Tom stifled a yawn. 'Sorry. I had an early start this morning. It's catching up on me. I hope you won't think I'm terribly rude if I leave you to it? I'm sure you'll be wanting to catch up properly with each other.'

'Not at all,' Deborah replied, her dismay at Tom's early departure tempered by relief that the intolerable situation was coming to an end. 'I'm sorry Emma couldn't join us. And that you've had to endure Rupert's reminiscing.'

'Don't be daft. I've enjoyed every minute. Thank you for inviting me. It's been good to see you again, Deborah.' They pushed back their chairs in unison and he brushed his lips against her cheek. 'See you soon.'

'Nice chap,' Rupert remarked, watching him leave. 'Good to see you've made at least one, new friend, my love.'

She scowled back at him. 'You can stop all the "my love" business. I know what you were doing.'

'What was that?' His eyes widened in mock innocence.

'Stop playing games. You were making out we were still an item. We're not.'

He shrugged. 'You can't blame me. I miss you, Debs.' He reached across the table to take hold of her hand but she quickly withdrew it. 'Now you've had a bit of time out here in the back of beyond, aren't you missing me just a little bit too?'

She sighed and tipped the remainder of the wine bottle into her glass. Rupert might have wrecked her evening but she was fond of him and it was true she normally found him good company. She could hardly tell him she had not spared him a second thought since she'd been here. Even *she* wasn't that heartless. And he had driven all the way out here just to surprise her. She could not fault his loyalty. 'I'm here for a year, Rupert. I told you that. I'm not changing my mind about us. But if you want to drop by for the weekend, every now and again, that would be lovely. Just, next time, make sure you give me some notice.'

'So I don't crash your hot date?'

'It wasn't a date but yes ... exactly.'

'And is it OK to stay for a day or so?'

'Fine, although I will be working tomorrow and I need to go into the office on Friday.'

'In London?' She nodded. 'Great. I was heading back then anyway. I could drive you.'

'Deal.' She smiled, feeling the tension in her shoulders ebb away. Having a plan, being back in control, made her feel so much more comfortable.

They spent another hour at the table, chatting amicably about mutual acquaintances, before she asked for the bill. 'Let me get this,' Rupert insisted. 'It's the least I can do after messing things up between you and Farmer Todd.'

'Tom,' she corrected. 'There is no me and him so you didn't mess things up. And I issued the invitation so I'll pay.'

After a bit more wrangling, they agreed to go halves. When Freya brought the bill, Rupert opened it with a flourish. Then he laughed. 'Looks like Farmer Giles has beaten you to it. The only things on here are your coffee and my brandy.'

'What? Oh heck, that wasn't supposed to happen! It was meant to be my treat,' she wailed. *Damn Tom Oldridge.* Now she was even more beholden to him. She would have to phone to thank him ... and repeat the invitation. The thought cheered her. His generous gesture gave her the opportunity to contact him and insist on another evening out, this time without Rupert. Maybe the night hadn't been a complete washout ...

They walked home slowly, arm in arm, enjoying the cool May night air. Deborah was laughing at something Rupert had said when a man appeared from around the corner, walking a spaniel.

'Evening,' she said pleasantly. The man said nothing, merely glowered at her before averting his head.

'Another fan?' Rupert joked. 'You're really racking them up here. What have you done to upset so many people?'

'Nothing.' She lapsed into silence, her mood instantly gloomy. She had never discussed her Wickthorpe history with anyone. She wasn't about to start now.

'Strange,' he mused. 'This is why I could never live in the country. Give me urban apathy any day.' They turned into her drive and crunched up the gravel. 'This sky though ... and these stars ... that's something you don't see in the city. It's making me feel all romantic.' He slipped his arm around her waist and nuzzled her neck while she was distracted, searching for her key. 'I don't suppose ...'

'Not a chance, Casanova,' she responded sharply, pulling away. 'In you go.'

He stepped ahead of her and then bent to pick up something from the mat. 'Hell, your post arrives late, except there's no stamp. No address either. Nothing. God, this village is weird!' He handed her a sealed, white envelope and her spirits plummeted further. She knew what it was.

CHAPTER 13

Julie Green, wife of Andrew and daughter-in-law of Enid, hurried down the road from Wickthorpe Health Centre, where she worked as a part-time receptionist, to the village primary school to pick up the girls. She was a bit late, one reason for the apprehensive knot in her stomach. Misha, her youngest, was prone to tears if she wasn't there, waiting in the playground with a big smile and a hug at the end of the school day. Her other daughter, Evaline, was two years older and much more confident and outgoing, like her dad. Misha took after Julie, shy, quiet, and often anxious.

The other reason for her own unease was Andrew himself. He was having another affair; she was sure of it. This past weekend he had been away. Fishing trip, he said. When he returned, late on Sunday evening, long after the girls had gone to bed, she detected an unfamiliar scent. She should not be surprised. It had happened before – at least twice, to her knowledge. Each time afterwards, he had sworn it would never happen again and she had looked deep into those gorgeous, blue eyes, which had melted her heart when they had first met at a company Christmas party eleven years ago, and believed him. Each time, his betrayal cut a little deeper. It wasn't just her he was hurting – it was the girls too.

In truth, he wasn't much of a father, or a husband. A tall, good-looking man like him, with plenty of charm, was used to being the centre of attention. At home, it was difficult, in the daily grind of family living, to give him the kind of adulation he craved. She did her best but, increasingly, he gravitated back to a single lifestyle, cutting her and the girls out of the equation. If she said anything, he accused her of nagging and stormed out, so it wasn't worth it. Instead, she kept quiet and suffered in silence, trying to be two parents to the girls and make up for Andrew's shortcomings.

Ava, his older sister, had warned her what he was like, back in the early days, when they had first got engaged. 'He's been spoilt all his life and he's used to getting his own way,' she said, when the two of them had a rare moment alone together. 'He's my brother and I love him dearly, but I honestly don't think he'll make you happy.' Ava's words had upset her but she dismissed them as spinsterish jealousy. She was wildly happy, caught up in the euphoria of knowing a wonderful man like Andrew wanted to marry a plain, boring girl like her.

Her parents had approved of him too. Andrew had endeared himself to mum, Isla, with attentive courtliness and beautiful, floral bouquets. Dad, Frank, had taken more warming up. A wealthy and successful businessman, he owned a chain of grocery stores offering fresh, local food at reasonable prices. Andrew worked in one of those shops and, initially, Frank viewed his daughter's suitor with a cynical eye, harbouring suspicions the golden boy was more interested in his money than his daughter. Eventually though, Andrew won the boss over with his polite, engaging manner, his enthusiasm for all things retail, and his willingness to talk about golf, Frank's other passion. He was soon considered part of the family, and marriage had sealed the deal. Now, Andrew was manager of the same store, with his eye on the job of general manager – a role currently filled by Frank's best friend and long-standing, right-hand man, Toby Trent. Toby was nearing retirement age and Andrew had been a shoe-in for the job. However, just as Julie had lost her rose-tinted glasses, Frank was also now less than enamoured with his son-in-law. Over the past few years, Andrew had proved disappointingly unreliable and lazy. It appeared he no longer felt the need to impress, confident his position within the family was sufficient to give him the reward he desired.

As Julie scurried across the playground, greeting her daughters with a cheery smile, she wondered what would happen if Frank discovered Andrew's latest infidelity. Last time, he had threatened to fire his son-in-law if it happened again. She could only hope he wouldn't find out.

***

It was not his fault women found him irresistible, Andrew Green fumed, as he headed towards *The Lamb Inn* later that day. God, his wife's nagging was enough to drive any man into the arms of another and he had exercised considerable restraint since the old man had delivered that ultimatum. 'Mess my daughter around again and you'll be out on your ear.' *What a joke!* After all he had done for the company! Frank Newman was a complete bastard and Andrew hated him, but he also knew upon which side his bread was buttered. It was not beyond Frank to tie up the company so that, even married to Julie, the sole heir to the Newman fortune, his son–in–law would not receive a penny, and Andrew was not about to miss out on his rightful inheritance. For the past two years, since his affairs had come to light, he had been the perfect husband. Well ... almost. You could not really count that quick shag round the back of the nightclub when he was on a stag do for one of his mates. The girl had been gagging for it and it would have been rude to refuse her. She wasn't even his type – too old by a long way – but needs must. His mates expected it from him and he had his reputation to consider. Apart from that, for two whole years, there had been no decent sex. You could not count marital stuff. That was just duty. Not fun, and certainly not exciting.

But eventually the compulsion to slide back into his old ways became too persistent to ignore. Frank's warning was a distant memory. If he was discreet, he decided, there would be nothing to worry about. Or so he thought. Then Julie had dropped that bombshell, tonight, after the kids were tucked up in bed. She knew he was carrying on and told him to stop before Frank found out and fired him. Her warning sounded suspiciously like a threat. *Bloody cow!*

The girl he was seeing was a local lass and had been getting a bit too clingy for his liking. He had been about to finish things anyway. But Julie's ultimatum might scupper the plans he had recently hatched. Thanks to a tip-off from someone he met on the internet, he had come to realise *exactly* what his type was. As yet, he had not taken things further, but he knew he had to. It was an itch he had to scratch. He drew in a ragged breath. God, just the thought of it was enough to bring him out in a sweat ...

The pub sign loomed ahead and he stopped for a moment, struggling to smother the fury he felt towards his wife. His carefully-cultivated reputation as an affable, easy-going lad made him popular with pub regulars. It would not do to let them see his other side – that had to remain a secret. He took another deep breath, exhaling all his frustrations. Then, he pushed the door open and headed for the bar at a lazy amble, nodding and passing the time of day with customers already in situ.

'Hello, Andy. What can I get you?' Freya Billington greeted him with a hundred-watt smile.

He gave her a suggestive wink. 'Hi, gorgeous. Pint of the usual, please.'

CHAPTER 14

Martha's diary
12th December, 1644

We are some weeks hence since I last wrote. My friendship with Prudence has grown and I have found it increasingly difficult to guard my tongue around her. Matters came to a head when Prudence suffered some blood loss and feared she was losing her child. In panic, she sought my help and I lost no time in giving the stricken girl a soup of ground ginger root and fennel to ease the cramping. When Prudence's symptoms eased, she returned to my cottage to offer her most profuse thanks. Having observed my healing powers first-hand, she pleaded with me to teach her what I knew. For the sake of her unborn child, she said. Such a plea could not be ignored! My soft heart overruled my head and I agreed. However, I took great pains to impress 'pon her the danger should such knowledge fall into the wrong hands. I recounted the sorry story of how my skills had near cost my life in Grimston when my success in healing ailments became widely-known and jealous folk accused such powers as witchcraft.

Prudence was bewildered by my tale. She told me of a woman named Mary Locksmith who lived in the village of Ixworth when she was a child. Whene'er she was ill, she was taken there. The house was dark and smelt strange, and the woman quite fierce-looking. Prudence confessed to being sore afraid of her, but her mother swore by the potions and brews Mary sold them. There had always been women such as Mary who had the means to aid the sick, she argued.

I agreed twas always so, but that witchfinders were seeking such women. Proof of guilt appeared to matter little to men such as Matthew Hopkins. I made my warning as severe as I could. Til this persecution dies down, I told her, tis best to pretend ignorance of such matters. Prudence was sufficiently chastened to promise to say nothing, not even to her husband.

Sadly though, it seems, my precautions have come to nought. Word of my knowledge has reached village ears; I know not how. Barely a few weeks passed since that conversation when a child of no more than six years came in search of me, tugging at my arm and begging me to help his sick mother. What was I to do? I scooped a sleeping Josiah into his sling and hurried after the boy. He led me to a house near the church, a narrow, two-storey dwelling built in flint. Downstairs, in a room which served as a kitchen and living room, there were three other, younger children playing on the floor with wooden skittles. Upstairs, a baby was crying and the boy headed in that direction, urging me to follow. A woman lay on a bed, bathed in sweat, pale and moaning, in extreme pain. The infant continued wailing beside her in a small crib.

Although young, the boy, whose name was Ezra, was able to answer my questions. He told me the babe was born three days hence and his mother had been sick e'er since. His father was at work, daring not to miss a day lest he be docked a week's pay. I frowned but said nought. Doubtless he worked for Julius Holley! Instead, I laid a gentle hand on the woman's head. Twas burning with fever. At my touch, the woman's eyes fluttered open and she pleaded with me to help her and her infant.

I assured her baby was fine as she clearly had a fine set of lungs. Probably the poor mite was hungry. Quietly, I asked Ezra if the doctor had been summoned, whereupon he answered in the affirmative. The doctor had come yesterday, bled the woman and said she would improve in a day or two. I then explained she needed something to reduce her fever and that I had to fetch something from home. At his panicked expression, I assured him of my swift return and instructed him to help by fetching his mother some water and making sure she drank. Also, I asked him to wring out a cloth in a bowl of cold water and lay it on her forehead. The boy listened solemnly. He was a good lad and sore worried for his ma. Finally, I said to ask at the houses nearby to see if anyone could feed the baby.

I hastened to Prudence's house and asked if she would mind Josiah, to which my young friend willingly agreed. As I left, I wondered how the boy had known to fetch me. Was my friend responsible? If so, I could scarcely blame her. The sick woman was in dire need of help and had received scant assistance from the local physician. Did the man not realise that bleeding would only worsen the condition of a woman so recently delivered of a child and likely to have suffered considerable blood loss? I could not say what had caused the woman's condition but knew I had the means to bring down her fever. The rest was in God's hands.

Now snow is 'pon the ground, my foraging days have ended for the season. Hence, I ventured into my store of dried herbs and set a pot to boil on the stove. Within two hours, I was back by the woman's side. Ezra was downstairs with the younger children. Upstairs, all was quiet and I was told a young woman along the street had taken the baby in.

The boy had done well. His mother was just as I had left her, except for the addition of a wet piece of cloth draped over her forehead. Her eyes flickered at my approach and she thanked me for my return.

I explained I had prepared a drink for her which would help to break her fever and, with my help, she struggled into an upright position. She took a cautious sip and wrinkled her nose, which I expected. It has a most bitter taste. When I was satisfied every drop had been consumed, I made the woman comfortable and left her to sleep. To Ezra, I gave a bottle of my potion, instructing him to give it to his mother when she next woke, and promised to come by tomorrow. He asked if the liquid would make her better, his face so anxious I confess I was tempted to lie to him and assure him all would be well. In truth, I was not sure. I prayed it would be so, which was what I told the boy.

The next day, I fulfilled my promise and returned to the cottage where, to my great delight, I found the woman greatly improved and nursing her child. She held out a hand to me in welcome and called me an angel. Ezra had told her of my ministrations and she was most anxious to repay me. I replied that her return to health was payment enough. I told her how her son had assisted me and why he was worthy of her praise, whereupon young

Ezra beamed with pride. When she insisted twas I who had saved her, I answered that her return to health was God's will. Twas He who had blessed me with skill in using the bounties of His creation and He who was most deserving of her gratitude.

I returned home, much relieved for the young mother but also with a great deal of disquiet. Prudence promised me she had told no one and yet news of my ability to heal has spread, I know not how. I confess I have yet to tell John of my latest adventures. He will be most displeased, but I cannot think I should have acted differently. Tis not in my nature to deny help to those who seek it. I can only pray to the Lord that he will watch over us and that I have not brought disaster 'pon myself and my family.

CHAPTER 15

'Damn!' Emma yelped as steam from the kettle burnt her hand. The morning was not going well. She had spent the last hour searching without success for a torque wrench she needed. Tom, who was out spraying when she phoned him, making the most of the calm weather conditions, was also unaware of its whereabouts. Probably, the last person to use it was Ted, the other worker on the farm and usually the sprayer operator but currently off work with a broken ankle. She wondered if it was acceptable to phone Ted while he was off sick. So far, she had held off from doing so and spent fruitless time scouring the workshop instead.

The lack of sleep had not helped her mood. She had been up at six, as usual, but hadn't got in until gone midnight, thanks to her mum's latest crisis. The end of yet another relationship. This one had lasted less than three months. Emma wouldn't mind being a shoulder to cry on but Belinda only ever called her daughter when she wanted something. She never asked how Emma was doing. Instead, the evening was spent listening to Belinda's woes and agreeing that men were scumbags. When she tried to leave at ten o'clock, she had been implored to stay a bit longer. It had taken another glass of wine (and coffee for her) before she managed to get her mum into bed and leave, with a promise of calling the following morning. She glanced up at the kitchen clock. Not nine o'clock yet. No point ringing until later. Belinda wouldn't be up.

But these annoyances paled into insignificance compared to what was really bothering her this morning. There was something wrong with Jake, her six-year-old yellow labrador. He hadn't wanted his dinner last night, nor breakfast this morning, and Jake was a typical, greedy lab who lived for his food. Currently, he was curled in his basket, watching her with doleful eyes, causing her stomach to clench with worry. A phone call to the vets for an urgent appointment was on her list but, ever pragmatic, she was waiting until opening hours to avoid being charged emergency rates. For once, she hoped Rick Billington was not the vet on duty. She could do without hearing him witter on about Amelie Charles and how wonderful she was. Emma was still wincing from their last meeting when he had waxed lyrical about the girl ad nauseum. To be honest, she did not know what he saw in Amelie, thinking her pushy and full of herself. *Sour grapes*, whispered her conscience. *No it's not*, she argued back.

The stamping of boots outside the back door heralded Tom's arrival and she slid off her stool to pour him a cup of tea. Spraying conditions had been excellent the past two mornings so thankfully the herbicide application on the March-drilled sugar beet would be up to date. Spring barley drilling was also completed. It had been a busy time without Ted who would hopefully return on Monday. *Fingers crossed.*

'Morning.' Tom appeared, looking tired and grim-faced – pretty much how she felt.

'Morning. Spraying all done?'

'Yep. Bit sticky in places, especially on Crow Hill, but that was the last load.' He drank half his tea in a few gulps and refilled his mug from the pot. 'How was your mum?' he asked as he poured a large portion of cornflakes into a bowl.

She grimaced. 'Same old. You don't want to know. Nothing major, at any rate. More importantly, how was your night out with our neighbour?'

It was his turn to pull a face. 'Fine.'

She raised her eyebrows. 'Uh-oh. What happened? Did she turn into the witch everyone's talking about?'

'Don't be daft.'

'OK, tell me what happened.'

He shrugged. 'Nothing happened. The meal was fine. My steak was ...'

'Dad!' Emma interrupted. 'I don't want a rundown of the food. How was the company? Was it just the two of you?'

'No. A friend of hers from London showed up unexpectedly. A close friend, by all accounts. I was a bit of a spare part, so I left as soon as I could.'

She frowned. 'A *male* friend?'

'Yes.'

'Oh. That was a bit awkward then.'

'Yes.'

She bit her lip and changed the subject to her concerns about Jake. Tom seemed less fussed. 'He's probably eaten something he shouldn't ... but get the vet to take a look if you're worried.' He knelt beside Jake's basket and stroked his head. 'Poor boy. Have you got a tummy ache? Have you been eating rotten rabbit carcass? Expect so.' He turned back to Emma. 'I'm sure that's all it is. How long has he been off his food?'

'Last night and this morning. I was going to ring the vet at nine and ask someone to see him today.'

'Good idea.'

Tom returned to his breakfast and the two of them chatted intermittently about plans for the day ahead. At nine, Emma phoned the vets' practice and made an appointment for Jake that afternoon. Then she tried ringing her mum but there was no reply. *Typical.* She had been up for three hours, tired and cranky, thanks to Belinda, who was now able to enjoy a long lie-in. The thought did not improve her mood. With a final pat for Jake, she made her way to the back porch where she had left her overalls hanging, pulled them on, tied the laces on her boots and headed back to work.

***

Tom watched her leave with anxious eyes. Poor Emma. She was worried sick about Jake. Hopefully, it would be nothing. Labs were all the same – far too greedy for their own good. As he finished his breakfast, he remembered the dogs he had loved over the years. Baxter, a stray rescued from the RSPCA, twice got a piece of bone stuck in his intestines. Both times, he had needed emergency surgery. That didn't stop him hunting for dead animals and crunching on their bones. Tom had needed to keep a close eye on him, not easy when you were busy and the dogs were out with you in the yard. They just had the one dog now – Emma's Jake. She'd had him since she returned to live at home after finishing her course at agricultural college.

Emma had always wanted to follow his footsteps and work the family farm. His son, Lewis, was the opposite. He had shown no interest in agriculture and was a talented artist who had studied at the Royal Academy of Art. Now aged twenty-four, he was taking a year out and backpacking with a friend. Currently, he was in Sydney, working in a bar. Tom hoped this year might help his son find his way. He worried about both his children but particularly Lewis, who took after Belinda – the same charm but also her restlessness. Hopefully, when the year was up, Lewis would settle down to something he loved. Possibly in the art world. It would not be on the farm but that did not bother Tom. He just wanted his son to be happy.

Emma shared her brother's artistic talent and enjoyed painting as a hobby. Some of her pieces adorned the walls – vibrant, colourful impressions of life on the farm. Both his children had inherited this gift from their mother. Tom had the large, work-roughened hands of a practical man and a mind more attuned to mechanics than aesthetics. Not a creative bone in his body.

His marriage to Belinda had been a mistake. He had met her at a Young Farmers' meeting. Her lithe body, blonde curls and pixie-like features had instantly captured his twenty-one-year-old heart, like an electric shock to his chest. After that, he had pursued her with the enthusiasm of a rampant bull, along with many of his compatriots, while she remained teasingly aloof from the welter of male attention she attracted. For long, agonising weeks, she flirted with all the young men vying for her notice. Tom's elation when she finally chose him – not the richest but, in his opinion, the best-looking of her suitors – was off the scale. He pictured a future together from the start, ignoring the warning signs in their early relationship. It soon became clear she had no interest in farming. She admitted she had only gone along to that first meeting when a friend told her it was a good way to meet boys. Once they were dating, she no longer wanted to attend cattle judging or ploughing competitions, instead booking tickets for shows in London and other events without checking on his availability first. They had almost broken up when the onset of harvest had caused him to cry off attending her best friend's wedding. Fear of losing her meant he often put her before his job, suffering the wrath of his father as an unavoidable consequence. And when she became pregnant with Emma, he had proposed on the spot.

They had both tried to make it work but the marriage was doomed from the start. The farming life was not for Belinda. For them both, passion ebbed away, replaced by frustration and disappointment. In hindsight, the only thing which kept them together for so long was the children. The marriage became a loveless relationship where they led separate lives. She had affairs and stayed away a lot. After his father died, he often found himself alone, looking after two school-age children and a mother suffering from early-onset dementia, whilst also trying to manage the farm. Belinda would return, without warning, butterfly wings clipped by the end of her latest affair, chastened and determined to do better. Briefly, she would become a model wife and mum, loving, caring, full of plans. But she could never sustain it and the whole exhausting cycle would begin again. Emma remained resilient but the emotional rollercoaster affected Lewis. Once, when Belinda was leaving, Tom had watched as their son clung to her leg, begging his mum to take him with her. His heart had shattered at the awful scene. From then on, he had focused all his energy on supporting his children and the farm, his own wants and needs suppressed beneath the weight of it all. It was a relief when Belinda requested a divorce, nine years ago. She had met a property developer whom she wanted to marry. He had wished her well and hoped she would be happy but, sadly, the marriage disintegrated barely two years later.

Wearily, he loaded his breakfast crockery in the dishwasher, rubbing his back as he straightened. He was feeling unusually cranky this morning and irritation from the previous evening resurfaced. Although he would never admit it, he had looked forward to spending an evening with Deborah Ryecroft. Weeks had slipped by and he had barely seen her, work on the farm keeping him busy. At least, that had been his excuse. There had been a certain amount of self-preservation involved too. When he had walked Deborah home that night from *The Lamb Inn*, she had looked so beautiful, standing there in the moonlight as they said goodnight, he had almost kissed her. How awkward *that* would have been! At the last moment, he managed to resist the temptation but the memory of it, over subsequent weeks had reminded him of that near embarrassment. Thus, her invitation to dinner had produced mixed feelings. His desire to see Deborah again was offset by the feeling he was charting dangerous waters. Certainly, she intrigued him. Having met and spent a little time with her, he refused to believe she was as heartless as her critics claimed. And, how many of the rumours about her were true anyway? With Emma there as a safety net, he had hoped to learn more of her story and get to know her better as a person. Then Emma had cancelled and he realised he was looking forward to being alone with Deborah. There was no denying he found her attractive – more than that, he was mesmerised by her. Last night, it had been difficult to take his eyes off her. By the time he left the pub, he was ready to punch that slick city friend of hers, Rupert Smytheson. The guy was all over her. Afterwards, as he lay in bed unable to sleep, he imagined the two of them, returning to Deborah's bedroom, spending the night together …

The phone rang and he glanced at the screen. Talk of the devil. 'Hello, Deborah.' His voice was curt, coloured by his recent thoughts.

'Morning, Tom. I just wanted to apologise again for last night.' She sounded bright and assured.

'No need.'

'And to thank you for settling the bill. That was kind but unnecessary. It was supposed to be my treat.'

'No problem.' He was keen for the call to end and injected a note of finality into his voice. 'It was my pleasure.'

'Anyway … I'd still like to repay your kindness. Are you free on Saturday night?' When he didn't respond instantly, she continued, her voice hesitant. 'I realise it's a bit short notice …'

'Saturday's fine for me.' Clearly, she had no idea of the sparsity of his social engagements!

'Oh good!' He could hear her relief. 'I'll sort something and let you know. Anyway, I'm sure you're busy …' The briskness was back.

'Sounds good. I'll wait to hear from you. Bye.' He ended the call, still frowning, not sure what to make of it. Was she keen to see him again or was he an obligation she felt she should fulfil? Was Smytheson still in the picture? Who knew? With a careless shrug, he headed back outside.

***

'Not eating? That doesn't sound like Jake, does it old boy?' With gentle hands, Rick Billington felt the labrador's abdomen and frowned. 'That feels normal. There's no tightness, at any rate. He hasn't been sick?'

'No.' Emma watched him with pensive eyes and nibbled on her lower lip. 'But he's definitely not himself.'

'Let's have a look in his mouth.' Carefully, he prised Jake's jaws open and peered inside. 'Oh boy, that doesn't smell too good.' He grimaced as he bent in closer.

'Sorry. He does have bad breath. I thought that was just his age.'

'You don't brush his teeth, obviously. I can see the problem. There's an infected molar giving him grief. In fact, more than one. No wonder he's not eating. He's in a lot of pain. Oops, sorry boy.' Rick released the dog and turned to Emma. 'We'll need to give him a course of antibiotics first to deal with the infection. Then we'll take another look but we may need to book him in to remove some of those teeth, and give the rest a good clean while we're at it.'

'Poor Jake!' Emma fondled his head as he turned doleful brown eyes towards her. 'I'm sorry, fella. I didn't realise.'

Rick gave her a smile. 'At least it can be easily sorted. I was worried when you brought him in. I know how much you love him.' He patted her shoulder. 'Still, all good.'

'Thanks, Rick. I've been so worried, even though I had faith you'd be able to fix him.'

'Yes. Thankfully, I'm better with dogs than I am with women.' He threw her a self-deprecating look. 'I suppose you heard that Amelie finished with me?'

Her heart leapt but she schooled her face into an expression of sympathetic concern. 'No? What happened?'

He shrugged. 'I guess I was keener on her than she was on me. Anyway, she's got a job in London so we won't be seeing her around here anymore.'

'With Deborah Ryecroft?'

Rick shook his head. 'I don't think so. I have to say, I wasn't paying much attention at that point. I was pretty gutted, to be honest.'

'Oh, poor you.' She squeezed his arm. 'I'm so sorry.'

'Yeah, I know.' His lips twisted into a grimace. 'I'll get over it.' He pulled off his gloves and sat in front of a computer screen, tapping at the keys. 'There you go. Pick the tablets up at the desk and book an appointment for one week's time. Ring me if you don't see an improvement in the next few days.'

'Thanks, Rick. Come on, Jake.'

Emma practically danced back to her car. How quickly things could change! She had arrived fifteen minutes ago, worried sick and miserable, and now her insides were zinging with happiness. Jake was going to be fine; Amelie was no longer in the picture for Rick; now, she just needed to find that torque wrench ...

CHAPTER 16

'Earth to Freya! Are you going to eat those cornflakes anytime soon? You've been sitting there just staring into space for at least five minutes. Is anything wrong, love?'

Freya jolted at her mum's question and picked up her spoon. 'Nothing's wrong. Just thinking about this weekend.' That much was true.

'You're off to Cambridge again to see Cara, right?'

'Mm.' Freya swallowed a mouthful of soggy cornflakes and put her spoon down. *Ugh. They tasted horrible.*

Sally Billington watched her daughter through narrowed eyes. Something was going on. 'You're seeing a lot of Cara at the moment,' she remarked, feigning casualness.

'Yeah.' Freya glanced at her watch and slid off her stool by the breakfast bar. 'Actually, I'd better go and pack. I'm catching the 10.43.'

'Why am I getting the feeling there's something you're not telling me?'

Freya shrugged and turned her back to her mum as she tipped the cornflakes into the bin. 'Because you're a worrier. I've told you, there's no need for you to worry. Everything is fine.'

'Is it a boy? Someone you've met recently?' Sally persisted.

'Mum, honestly, give it a rest!'

'But Freya, it's not like you to hide things from us. No wonder I'm worried!'

'Who says I'm hiding anything?' At Sally's stony-faced silence, Freya threw up her hands in defeat. 'OK, it's no big secret. I *have* met someone ...

someone very special. Now, can we leave it? I promise I'll tell you everything but, at the moment, it's too soon.'

Sally smiled, even though her anxiety had just notched up a level. 'There you go. I knew it! That explains the mooning over the cornflakes! Does he live in Cambridge?'

Freya rolled her eyes. 'Mum ... enough! No more questions.' She gave her mum a hug. 'I'll tell you when I'm ready. I promise.'

'Freya ...' Sally reached an arm to halt her daughter's exit. 'This boy ... is he ...?' She struggled to find a suitable description.

'Fantastic? Gorgeous?' her daughter supplied. 'Definitely. Now, stop fretting and let me go and pack.'

As the kitchen door closed, Sally tried to calm the worms of disquiet wriggling in her stomach. It was not like Freya to be so secretive. There was something about this boy that she was hiding, something of which she knew her mum would not approve. Doubtless, in Freya's starstruck eyes, he *was* gorgeous but was he right for her daughter?

***

At Cambridge station, Freya stayed on the train, as planned, and travelled to Kings Cross, London. It arrived on time and, with her backpack slung over her shoulder, she hurried to catch a tube train to Paddington. Once on the Circle Line, the journey took less than ten minutes. She leapt from her seat before the train had stopped moving, eager to see him. Emerging onto the street a few minutes later, she was relieved to spot the café – right where he had described – and she crossed the road. As she opened the door, her eyes searched the space, now-familiar sick feelings of excitement roiling in her gut. He wasn't there. A check of the clock on the wall told her she was a few minutes early and she suppressed her anxiety. He *would* come. Taking a corner seat, giving her a clear view of the street outside, she shrugged off her coat and checked her phone. No messages. A young lad with a shaven head, and a tattoo of a snake curling round his left ear, appeared at her side.

'What can I get you?'

She opened her mouth to order her usual cappuccino and immediately closed it again. The thought of coffee made her feel decidedly queasy. 'Tea, please,' she said as the waiter tapped his foot impatiently on the grey tiles.

'Anything else?'

'Not at the moment. I'm waiting for someone. Ah ... here he is now!' Her face lit up as the man in question caught her eye and winked.

'Tea for me too, thanks,' he said with a grin. 'Hello, gorgeous.' The waiter sidled away as he leaned towards her and pressed his full lips to hers in a lingering kiss. 'God, every time I see you, you grow more beautiful.'

Her heart melted, as it always did. 'Thanks. You're not so bad yourself, although I'm not sure about your current look!' Today he was sporting a black wig and old-fashioned glasses.

He laughed and sat beside her, taking her hand in his. 'I've been looking forward to spoiling you this weekend.'

'Can't wait.' She licked her lips and pulled her hand away to slide it along his well-muscled thigh.

He raised his eyebrows. 'Whoa. Hold your horses, young lady. Not that I'm going to object too much, but I do have other plans for us. You're going to have to wait for *that* kind of spoiling.'

'Oh.' She pretended to pout. 'What plans?'

'Aha.' He tapped the side of his nose. 'It's a surprise.' He picked up a laminated menu lying on the table. 'But first, we'll get a quick sandwich here. I'm starving.'

'Not starving for me?' she teased.

He put down the menu and transfixed her with his intense, sapphire stare. 'Always,' he murmured quietly, his deep voice full of promise. 'You don't know how much ...' He let his gaze linger on her face, his eyes brimming with sincerity, before sitting back and grinning. 'But first food. A man needs to keep his strength up.'

'Fair enough.' She smiled back, her cheeks hot with a combination of self-consciousness and desire. He really *was* all her dreams rolled into one amazing package. If only he wasn't married ...

***

The rest of the day was completely magical. In the afternoon, having dropped their bags at a sumptuous hotel, he took her to see *Les Miserables.* Afterwards, she felt breathless with the passion of the performance.

'Did you enjoy it?' he asked gently.

'It was amazing!' Her words, describing such an intense emotional experience, seemed inadequate and she lowered her head, feeling her own gaucheness.

He hugged her to him. 'I'm glad.' His voice was soft, caressing her like warm breeze. 'I've always loved it, and am so happy to share it with you. I have never enjoyed the show more ... because I was with you.' Her breath caught in her throat and her eyes filled with tears. 'Hey, why are you crying? What have I said?' He pulled a white linen handkerchief from his pocket and handed it to her.

'Nothing. They're happy tears. I love you so much.'

He smiled. 'Me too. But we'd better get going. Your next surprise awaits.'

They took a taxi to the Shard and watched the sun go down over the city as they sipped cocktails at their table. Freya had ordered a bellini mocktail and giggled at his disapproving expression. 'I don't need alcohol,' she told him. 'I'm giddy enough with all of this.' She gestured at the panoramic views. The food was as spectacular as the venue and Freya glowed with sheer happiness.

Much later, they lay wrapped in each other's arms, limbs entwined. 'I meant what I said earlier,' he murmured. 'You have never looked more beautiful. There's something indefinably different about you. You're positively glowing.' Even as he said the words, a knot of dread formed in his gut. *Oh, please God, not that!*

'It's because I'm with you,' she replied, her voice husky. She hesitated. There would never be a better moment than this. 'But, also, I have some news ...'

His face split into a broad grin. 'I knew it! You've got that job you applied for with Medimax Pharmaceuticals. Clever girl! I knew you could do it! I know that means moving away but I will be able to visit you. In a way, it will make it easier ...'

'No, that's not it!' God, how could this be going so wrong? She had forgotten all about Medimax. In fact, she had even declined their offer of an interview. That was the last thing she wanted right now!

'You didn't get the job? Sweetheart, I'm sorry. That was so insensitive of me. I know you were excited about it.' He showered her face with kisses. 'Let me make it up to you.' His hand caressed her breast before drifting lower.

'No.' She pushed his hand away and sat up. 'I need to tell you something.'

He buried his head into her breasts, savouring their firm sweetness whilst he planned his response. This was going to take careful handling. At last, he pulled away, his face a mask of frustrated concern. 'What is it?' he asked, his tone teasing and playful. 'What is so important that it keeps me from your beautiful body?'

Her eyes shone with fervour and she leaned forward to kiss him with heart–breaking tenderness. Then, she took a deep breath. 'Darling, I'm pregnant,' she said. 'We're going to have a baby!'

CHAPTER 17

That same Saturday evening saw Deborah alone with Tom, sitting at the dining table at Greenways Farm. Not what she had originally planned, but it was working out very nicely. Once Rupert was safely back in London, she had tried to reserve a table at a restaurant somewhere but had left it too late. Everywhere was fully booked. Then she noticed, in the monthly parish magazine which had been put through her door, a feature on a local woman who had set up a business delivering ready-prepared, home-cooked food to order. A possibility. She mulled over the prospect of an intimate, cosy evening at home with Tom Oldridge. The more she thought about it, the more the idea excited her. Who knew where it might lead? Sex with a fit, good-looking man was long overdue and Tom certainly fitted the bill. Tall, dark, unselfconsciously good-looking, and carelessly sexy. With that thought in mind, she was wearing lacy lingerie beneath her demure, claret, form-fitting dress, and her bedroom was ready to receive visitors. Always best to be prepared. Not that she had expectations – just desires.

And, so far, it was all going well. Tom seemed relaxed in her company and the conversation flowed easily between the two of them. The evening started with drinks and her carefully-planned questions about farming but soon branched into chat about her recent gardening exploits, films, books and even art, one of her passions.

'I have some great pieces in my house in London,' she enthused. 'Obviously, that is my opinion but they are turning out to be quite an investment. I like to look out for up-and-coming artists and some of them have now become highly sought-after. Not that I can claim much of the credit though. An art dealer friend steers me in the right direction. I bought a couple of Sally Sheerforths before she became well-known and I also have some Peter Longs.' She looked across at him but his face was blank of any recognition.

'Sorry,' he said, 'but I'm not very knowledgeable about the current art scene.'

She chuckled. 'Why would you be? But I seem to recall you have some fabulous paintings on your walls. Really striking. I've been looking for something like that to hang here but haven't found anything I liked. Who did them? They looked like they were all by the same artist. Was it someone local?'

He grinned. 'Very local. Emma did them. The ones you saw, at least. She likes to paint in her spare time. Uses one of our old outbuildings as a studio.'

'Wow!' That was a surprise. 'She's very talented. Did she have training?'

'Only at school and college art classes. Her first love was always farming and her degree is in agriculture. My son, Lewis, is the real artist of the family. He went to the Royal College of Art and even had his own small exhibition in a gallery on the outskirts of London. Sadly though, he doesn't seem to be sure what he wants at the moment. Currently, painting is on hold while he is backpacking with a mate in Australia. He's a restless soul – not ready to settle to anything. Hopefully, he'll figure out what to do with his life. I do have one painting by him, which is hanging in my office. It's one of his earlier efforts, an abstract representing man's destruction of the natural world.'

'Wow,' Deborah said again. 'I'd love to see it. Two talented children. Do they take after you?'

He pulled a face. 'Not at painting, that's for sure, although I'm pretty good with emulsion and a roller. The artistic gene comes from their mum, Belinda.'

Deborah's mind was racing ahead. 'If you wouldn't mind, can I take a proper look at Emma's work sometime? As I said, I have an art dealer friend, and Emma's paintings would be right up his street. Would she be interested in selling some pieces, do you think?'

Tom shrugged. 'You would have to ask her. Just so long as you're not thinking of luring my workforce away from the farm with visions of fame and fortune?'

It was her turn to smile. 'Emma doesn't strike me as the sort of woman who could be persuaded to do something she doesn't want. But, in the meantime, I *am* serious about offering her a commission to do some paintings for this house.' She gestured towards the blank walls. 'The sparse, modern look is all very well but I want beautiful things around me too. Then, maybe, this will feel more like home.'

'It's certainly a lot different from when your parents were here,' he said. 'I can scarcely imagine it now, how it used to be.'

'That was my intention,' she responded drily.

'Oh?'

Immediately, she was annoyed with herself. Her flippant observation had invited his question and the last thing she wanted was a conversation with him about her parents. 'Let's just say I wanted it to feel like my place, rather than theirs.'

'Fair enough.' He lay down his knife and fork. 'That was delicious, by the way.'

She nodded. 'It was, but I can't claim any credit. It was cooked by someone called Amber Jackson-Smyth and delivered to me to heat up. We've got white chocolate cheesecake for dessert with a raspberry coulis.'

'Oh, I know Amber,' he exclaimed. 'She was a schoolfriend of Emma's and married a local lad. I heard she'd started a new venture.'

'Yes, she said her business was just starting off. Before she had children, she was a sous-chef at a restaurant on the north Norfolk coast. Seemed a nice girl.'

'She is.'

There was a lull in the conversation as they both sipped at their wine, a crisp Chablis, perfect with the salmon en croute. Tom had a thoughtful expression and Deborah wondered what he was thinking. His blue eyes wore a faraway look, as if he was lost in the past, in some sad memory. The urge to touch his tanned, calloused hand, as it rested against the stem of his glass, was tantalising, and she took another gulp of wine.

When Tom did break the silence, his words were not what she was expecting. 'I spent some time with Hannah, your mum, before she died. Sometimes, I would stop for a coffee after I'd mowed the grass. She seemed lonely. Towards the end, she was confined to the house, and she was always keen for me to stop for a chat. Not that I could every time.' He toyed with his glass, rubbing the slender stem between his fingers, and avoiding eye contact. 'She was enormously proud of you, you know, and everything you'd achieved.'

His careful speech, although well-meant, lit a flare of anger in Deborah's chest. How *dare* Hannah claim maternal pride! She had no right. Resentment quickly took hold and, in the absence of a mother upon whom to vent it, her antagonism turned towards Tom. This was none of his business! Her relationship with her mother, or lack of, was not up for discussion. To cover her annoyance, she began clearing plates with an angry clatter.

'Here, let me help you.' He leapt up and ferried an empty dish to the kitchen island. In silence, they completed the task and he returned to the table, watching her with a frown. Her mouth was set in a grim line. 'Have I said something wrong?' he asked. 'If so, I apologise. I didn't mean to upset you.'

His obvious concern punctured her anger. 'It's fine,' she muttered, still not meeting his eyes. 'It's a sensitive subject.'

'I'm sorry. I just thought it was something you should know. I won't mention it again – although I guess I just have.'

His attempt to lighten the atmosphere was met with no response. Too many hideous scenarios were now playing out through Deborah's mind. 'Did my mother talk to you about me ... about what happened?' she demanded.

He hesitated. Having unwittingly touched upon a nerve, he was reluctant to say any more. 'Not really. She said you were treated badly when you were a girl and admitted she wished she had done more to protect you. You were blamed unfairly, she said, and she worried for you should you return to Wickthorpe.'

'I see.' Deborah grabbed the bottle of wine and refilled her glass. This invasion into her privacy, into a past she protected so carefully, was screamingly uncomfortable, yet now the subject was open, she could not refrain from asking another question. 'Did she speak to you about the terms of her will, the conditions attached to the house?'

He puffed out his cheeks, his face contrite. 'Yes, she did tell me,' he admitted.

A cynical snort. 'If she was so *worried* for me, didn't you think it somewhat strange that she wrote that clause in her will, saying I could only have the house if I stayed here for one whole year? *That's* not the work of someone concerned about the humiliation and nastiness her daughter might have to endure at the hands of some of the charming people of Wickthorpe ... not to mention the hate mail!'

'I'm sure that wasn't why ...' he tried to interrupt.

'No.' She held up a hand to stop him. 'Her *concern* was just a pretence. Did she tell you that she stood by and said *nothing* when my father headed up all my accusers? Did she tell you that the one time I returned, needing her help, alone and ...' An abrupt pause and a sharp intake of breath. 'She turned me away?' Chest heaving, she took another fortifying sip of wine. Her usual, iron-clad composure had disintegrated and old wounds, long sealed and hidden away, were threatening to rupture.

Tom studied her with anxious eyes. Flags of red striped her cheeks and her eyes burned with ferocity. 'Hate mail?' he asked quietly. 'Have you received some?'

At his words, her eyes widened and her face acquired a guarded look. 'Just a few notes, put through the door. Anonymous, of course. Telling me to leave. The usual witch stuff. Pathetic, actually.'

'How many notes exactly?'

She thought for a moment. 'Four ... maybe, five. All saying the same thing. Nothing to worry about.' She gave a hollow laugh. 'Nothing I'm not used to.'

Disquiet clawed at his stomach. 'Do you still have them?'

'No. Threw them away.' She frowned. He was clearly disturbed by her revelation. 'Honestly, Tom, it's nothing to bother about. I received similar back when I was sixteen, when the accident happened.' She shrugged. 'I guess people wanted someone to blame and I was convenient.'

'If you get any more notes like that, I think you should keep them and tell the police. And will you let me know? Perhaps I can help.'

She hunched her shoulders. 'I don't see how.' Her anger had ebbed away but she was still stressed and he struggled to think what to say to put things right between them. Before he mentioned Hannah, Deborah had been relaxed and charming. At times, he had felt she was flirting with him. And he had flirted right back. But now ...

'I'm sorry.' She was the first to speak. With a rueful half-smile on her lips, she heaved another sigh. 'This isn't your fault. I should not have reacted as I did. I don't know what came over me. You'd have thought, after all these years, I'd have got over this stuff.' She stood and headed for the kitchen.

'Please. No need to apologise. The fault was all mine.' He followed, gently turning her towards him and gathering her rigid body to his chest. She felt brittle and fragile in his arms, as if squeezing too hard could snap her in two. He stood there, holding her close, breathing in the heady, perfumed scent of her and feeling his body react to her nearness. 'I'm sorry my thoughtless words upset you so much. That was the opposite of my intention.' He released her and took a step back. 'Are we OK?'

'Of course.' She spun around to give herself a moment of respite. His hug had instigated a whole new set of emotions. 'You sit down and I'll get dessert.'

'Great.' He waited until she was back, seated at the table, before speaking again. 'Did you know cheesecake is my absolute favourite?'

Nodding, she cut him a generous slice. 'I did. I remembered you saying so when we were at *The Lamb Inn*. That's why I ordered it. Help yourself to the coulis.' She slid the plate towards him and cut herself a tiny sliver.

He sighed in appreciation as he took his first bite. 'Mm, delicious. Not quite as good as the one I make but ...'

'You make cheesecake?' she interrupted. 'I'm impressed. I wouldn't have a clue.'

'It's pretty simple when you have a recipe to follow,' he said airily. 'That's all cooking is – following a set of instructions and timing. I'll have to demonstrate my culinary skills sometime. I'm sure you'll be amazed.'

She raised her eyebrows. 'A bold statement! I might have to hold you to it, to see for myself.'

He pulled a face. 'Then, I may have to confess the truth. My cooking is mediocre at best. Apart from cheesecake, which has become my speciality after making one for Emma's birthday one year, I stick to plain and simple fare – meals I can rustle up quickly. Often, no actual cooking involved. Emma is aware of my limitations and cooks quite a bit, so we don't starve.' He chuckled. 'I have had some spectacular failures though. One time, I thought I'd surprise Emma and cook a roast. I should have known that kind of blind ambition was destined for disaster. I had just put a pan of oil in the oven, ready to roast potatoes, when Felix called. His tractor was stuck – it was a particularly wet year – and he needed me to pull him out. I forgot all about dinner and shot over to his place on the John Deere with some chains to rescue him. Unfortunately, it took a while and Emma returned home first to find the kitchen ablaze. The oil had caught fire and set the oven alight. It was lucky she appeared when she did, or the whole house might have burnt down! As it was, we had to have a completely new kitchen. It was some while before she trusted me to cook at all after that.'

'I'm not surprised.' Deborah's lips curved as she pictured the scene.

'But I can do a good steak and my cheesecake *is* legendary so … if you want to risk it?' He left the question hanging, staring intently at her with long-lashed, blue eyes.

'Er …' Once again, she felt flustered and her cheeks grew pink. 'That sounds lovely.'

'Well,' he cleared his throat. Best to quit while he was ahead. The atmosphere between them was still a little tense and he was wary of saying anything else which might upset her. 'Thanks very much for a great meal and a really good evening.' He pushed his chair away from the table.

'Oh, are you leaving already? Can't I offer you a coffee or maybe a brandy?' Disappointment flooded her chest, but she wasn't surprised he was making an early exit. She could hardly blame him. Her unwarranted outburst had ruined the evening. It had not been her finest hour. If only they could go back in time and do it all again. She would behave very differently.

'I …' There was a moment's hesitation when she wondered if he was about to change his mind. 'No, best not. I've had several early mornings this week and I'm pretty bushed. Ted, our other worker, is off with his broken ankle. Poor chap. He's bored silly and, in the meantime, it's left us a bit stretched.'

'Oh, I see.'

He preceded her to the front door and turned to face her. 'Thanks again for a lovely evening. I really enjoyed your company.'

'Me too.' Her voice came out slightly husky as she stared into those captivating eyes. 'See you soon.' She found her body, of its own volition, leaning towards his.

'Count on it.' With a cheery salute, he spun on his heel and stepped into the night.

Damn and blast! She had totally blown it. So much for sexy underwear! Suddenly weary, she headed back to the kitchen. Her overreaction to his innocuous comment about her mother had taken her by surprise as much as him, and left her tongue unguarded. She had almost blurted out her biggest secret. Thinking about it now, in the aftermath of an emotional evening, brought tears to her eyes and a lump to her throat ...

She was barely seventeen, scared and excited in equal measure, when she discovered she was pregnant. The temporary nannying job, for which she had fled her home, had settled into something more permanent, and she was happy living in Kensington. Her employers, the Edmontons, treated her like one of the family and her two charges, Lucille and Jenna, were adorable. Life was great. Things got even better when she bumped, literally, into a good-looking man at the local park. Early twenties; a narrow face with the intense, brown eyes of an artist or musician; black hair curling down to his shoulders. She fell for him instantly and he felt the same way. At least, that was what she thought. It was only when she told him they were expecting a baby, she discovered the truth. He was married. Instead of delight at her revelation, he erupted fury at her carelessness. 'Get rid of it,' he ordered. When she refused, he wanted nothing more to do with her.

She was left heartbroken and alone. Not completely alone, though. The one thing she knew, with a fierce, maternal possessiveness, was that she loved her unborn child with all her heart. She would do anything to keep her baby. Which was why she returned to Wickthorpe, to her parents, to ask for their help and support.

'You slut!' her father roared. 'How *dare* you bring your disgrace to my house! Again!' He raised his arm and she thought he was going to strike her. Instead, he pointed to the door. 'Get out! Get out and never come back! You are not my daughter. I never want to see you, or your brat, your *bastard,* again.'

'Mother, please?' she begged, tears coursing down her cheeks.

Hannah Ryecroft looked at her with dead, disappointed eyes and turned away. 'I'm sorry,' she said, 'but you'd better go.'

That was the last time she had seen either of her parents. She returned to London, thinking things could not get any worse ... and then she lost the baby, a girl she called Natasha. Grief consumed her and she thought she would never get over it. In a way, she never had.

Her face was wet with silent tears for the daughter she had loved so much and held for such a short time. Natasha would be thirty-two now, possibly with children of her own. She could have been a grandmother.

But she wasn't and, in the end, she had been lucky. She stayed with the Edmontons and they supported her, as her parents had not. They also encouraged her to go to night-school. She studied hard, sailed through her accountancy exams, got a job with a small firm, worked her way up ... and had a lucky break when she helped someone out. The rest of her career was a well-documented success story. In a way, her parents *had* been at the root of her achievements. Her father's constant claims, that she was useless and would never amount to anything, had made her determined to prove him wrong. She worked incredibly hard, with a single-mindedness to achieve at all costs. Her childhood had shaped her into a ruthless, uncompromising woman and she quickly built a reputation for being cold and heartless. At the time, it was the cliché description of any successful woman in business. Had she been a man, she would doubtless have been regarded as tough and decisive. But that was the world back then. She had worked with relentless resolve to further her career and, at the same time, developed a hard, protective shell to keep her safe from further hurt. She allowed men into her life, but only on her terms. Romance was fine but love was never again permitted to worm its destructive way into her heart. Did she regret those choices? Definitely not! She had everything she wanted. Almost ...

What she wanted more than anything was the one thing she could never have – the tiny girl she had lost.

CHAPTER 18

Martha's Diary
20th January, 1645

Another month has passed and winter is well and truly 'pon us. The days are short and have recently been bitterly cold. How I look forward to spring! At present, fields thick with snow, it seems so far away.

I am kept busy looking after Josiah and our home. News of my skill in assisting the sick has spread, but I am glad. I feel tis my calling to help others and I am happy to do so when I can. My services have been much in demand, especially now, with winter coughs and colds turning quickly to conditions more serious. My once bountiful supply of dried herbs is sorely depleted.

John has warned me more than once that I tread a dangerous path but it cannot be helped. Somehow, the good folk of Wickthorpe have uncovered what I sought to keep hidden and seem most thankful for it. Truly, they could not be more kind towards me. Just yesterday, Florence Merryweather insisted 'pon giving me the most beautiful shawl in return for treating a wound on her arm. It had turned bad but, after I had tended it with a poultice, is now happily healed. I cannot believe there are those in the village who would regard my arts with suspicion and tell John so. He is less certain, reminding me we both know not what Fate has in store for us. Verily tis so, and I pray every day to the Lord to protect us from harm.

I was most thankful to receive His assistance earlier today for, without Him giving me strength beyond my means, I shudder to think what may have occurred. Earlier, I wrote of a certain Roger Holley and my misgivings about him. It turns out I was right to fear him! Even now, my hand shakes, remembering his vile intent toward me. I have never been so scared in my life!

I had been summoned to Jed Finch's house to aid his granddaughter who was suffering from an eye ailment. My husband's employer is a good man and I was anxious to help in whatever small way I could. I remembered well the cure Ma had taught me. She pounded together crop-leek and garlic, mixed it with wine and the gall of a bullock, and let the concoction stand for nine nights in a brass vessel. Having prepared it so, she wrung it through a cloth, afore clarifying it, placing it in a horn and applying it to the eye with a feather. With none such potion ready to use, I was afeared I would be unable to help Mr Finch's granddaughter til I remembered Our Lady's Well in the village. Some while afore, keen to share her own knowledge, Prudence had told me of the healing properties of the water there. I could only hope she was correct as I had not tested the proof of her claim. I duly collected a small amount of the healing water in a bottle and hurried toward the Finch farmhouse. It was on this journey that I once again encountered Roger Holley. He was on horseback, as before, and seemed in jovial spirits. After bidding me a good morrow, he reined in his horse and was in a most loquacious mood, telling me he was returning from a check on two of his labourers who had been charged with repairing a fence. Some sheep had recently escaped and the men responsible had received a beating as a consequence. He had been gratified, he said, to see such punishment had improved the attitude of the idle wastrels. His words, and the cruel relish with which he spoke, made me shiver and I was most anxious to make my escape, but I did not wish to appear rude to such a man. He then asked me whence I was headed, unencumbered by the infant I usually carried. After answering his questions honestly, he allowed me to continue 'pon my way and I breathed a sigh of relief. The man's interest in me was clear to see and I resolved once more to avoid him whence I could.

Jed Finch's granddaughter, Elsie, is only two years old, or thereabouts, and was in much distress. Her eyes were red with soreness, but she allowed me to bathe them with the water sweetly enough. The child's mother and grandmother were most considerate and offered me refreshments for my trouble but I refused. Outside, I could see the sky was darkening, heralding a storm, so I was keen to return home forthwith. I promised to return the next day, and left the bottle of healing water with Mrs Finch, along with instructions to bathe the child's eyes four times a day.

Soon after midday, I made my return, having also refused Mrs Finch's gracious offer to have a man take me home by horse and cart. I enjoy walking, and do not care to put others to unnecessary trouble. Twas but a short distance to travel, less than half a mile, and I knew it would not take me long to reach Prudence's cottage, where she was minding Josiah. I confess at that time I had forgotten my meeting with Roger Holley.

I was huddled in my cloak, my head bowed 'gainst the cold wind, so I did not see him straight away. My heart catapulted in my chest as he suddenly loomed before me, on foot this time. I recalled how he had regarded me afore and was somewhat dismayed to chance 'pon him a second time, again alone. I smiled politely and stepped to one side to allow him to pass but he stayed aside me. For the first time, I realised how tall he was. He towered over me and I felt truly at a severe disadvantage.

'We meet again, Mistress Lightbody,' he said.

I recognised something evil in his smile and felt sore afraid. A quick glance over my shoulder told me we were completely alone. There was no one to come to my aid, should such be needed. I replied, trying to be pleasant and courteous, but moving to press past him, making my apologies that I was unable to tarry because of my child.

He was having none of it and caught hold of me, spinning me with ease into his strong arms. 'A kiss ... and more ... afore I allow you on your way,' he said. I fear I am much embarrassed to describe what happened next. Suffice it to say, he pressed coarse lips 'gainst mine and manhandled me towards the small copse alongside the path. I struggled desperately in his arms, trying to pull my face away. In return, he moved his head lower, chuckling at my hopeless efforts to escape him. All the while, I cried out for him to cease but he would not. I knew I was helpless 'gainst his superior strength. Thereupon, I decided 'pon a different course. I allowed my body to fall limp in his arms, even moaning a little, pretending to succumb to his abominable embrace. As he loosened his hold to push aside my clothing, I seized my chance. With all my might, I raised my knee between his legs in one hard thrust. As he yelped in pain, he released his grip and I ran, as swiftly as I could, refusing to look back to see if he followed, though I was sorely tempted.

Prudence was most astonished to see me burst into her cottage in some considerable distress. She hastened to my side and urged me to tell her what was amiss, saying I looked as if I had seen a ghost. I replied that twas a monster more like. The girl listened in horror as I recounted what had recently transpired, regarding me with great anxiety. Shaking her head, she told me Roger Holley was a dangerous man and to cross him or his family would be at my peril. She warned me most severely I had best not make an enemy of him.

Wise words indeed. Alas, I suspect they come too late. I fear I already have.

CHAPTER 19

'It's dreadful news. Just awful. Everyone liked her. She'll be sorely missed.' It was Monday morning and the village grapevine was humming.

'Who?' Honoraria stomped into the Post Office, shaking off droplets of rain, to find Enid Green and Valerie Hampton-Brown, deep in conversation. A third person, a miserable-looking, retired farmworker named Philip Holder, stood silently alongside, listening. The atmosphere was of sadness, foreboding and musty shelves. 'Who will be missed? Has someone died?' Despite her genuine concern, Honoraria could not suppress a ripple of anticipation. A death – even an expected one – brought a fillip of excitement into the mundanity of her life. Awful, she knew, but she couldn't help herself. 'Who is it?' she repeated with rather unbecoming eagerness.

Valerie turned to her with a look of imperious disapproval. 'Poor Mabel Littlebody. The ambulance was at her house this morning but she'd already gone. A carer found her cold in her bed. She must have died in her sleep.'

'Well,' said Honoraria, ever pragmatic. 'That was a nice way for her to go. And she was very old.'

'Ninety-two,' sniffed Enid, not one to be side-lined for long. 'And she did suffer terribly with her arthritis. I expect it was a happy release. Still,' she frowned at Honoraria, 'it's a very sad day.'

'Absolutely,' Honoraria agreed enthusiastically. 'Ava, can I have a book of six second-class stamps please?' Catching sight of Valerie's narrowed eyes and tight lips, she reassembled her demeanour into one more becoming to the situation, whilst Ava moved to the counter from behind the stationery shelf where she was replenishing stock. 'Awful. Thanks, Ava.'

'It's not a coincidence.' Philip Holder spoke for the first time, his sharp features pinched in a sneer.

'Of course, it's not.' Valerie spoke in a conspiratorial whisper and exchanged a meaningful look with Enid.

'What isn't?' Honoraria returned to the conversation, anxious not to miss out.

Valerie shot her a look of annoyance. 'Poor Mabel's sad passing. The timing. It's not a coincidence.'

'Really?'

'No. I saw her just last week. She had been to the hospital for a check-up and said how pleased the doctors were with her. They told her she would probably outlive them. In the best of health, she was. No reason at all for her passing except ...' A dramatic pause.

Philip nodded sagely. '*That* woman has been visiting her.'

'Exactly. The witch. The harbinger of death. I knew it would all start again when *she* came back,' Valerie added.

Honoraria frowned. 'You don't believe that Deborah Ryecroft had something to do with poor Mabel's sad death, do you?'

'What other reason could there be?' Valerie retorted. 'As I said, Mabel had just been given a clean bill of health. That woman has brought evil to this village and the sooner she goes back to where she came from, the better.'

'You're right, Valerie. Like you, I've been saying no good would come of her return. This could be just the start of it.' Enid shuddered. 'But what can we do? How can we get rid of her? I've already written to the Parish Council. So far, I've had no reply. Waste of space, all those councillors.' A glare from Valerie reminded her that the Chair of the Parish Council was none other than John Hampton-Brown himself. 'Er ... I don't mean your dear husband. I'm sure he's excellent. The rest of them though. I've tried to persuade Ava to stand but she won't.'

'Hmph, well ... I agree that *some* members of the Parish Council are less than desirable. That awful woman from Mill Close, Jocelyn Johnson, is particularly difficult. Only been in the village five minutes and thinks she knows better than people who have lived here all their lives. Poor John has a tricky task to keep them on the straight and narrow, I don't mind telling you. I will tell him to look out for your letter though, Enid. Chances are, he hasn't laid eyes on it yet. The clerk is useless and correspondence always seems to be delayed. John was remarking upon it the other day and I said ...'

Her tirade was interrupted by the jingling of the bell as the door opened. 'Why, good morning, Deborah.' Honoraria licked her lips. This was going to be interesting!

'Morning.' Deborah gave the whole group a curt nod and marched to the counter.

'Awful news about Mabel, isn't it?' Enid declared with a sly look towards Valerie.

Deborah spun around. 'Mabel? What's happened?'

'Poor Mabel passed on last night. We were just saying how *strange* it was, when she had been in excellent health for a ninety-two-year-old.'

'Oh no.' Deborah's eyes widened in dismay. 'How? I only saw her a couple of days ago.'

'Nobody knows as yet,' Valerie cut in. 'We were just saying how very ... *unexpected* it was. I suspect the coroner will be involved. They always are in cases of unexplained death.'

'Well, I suppose ... she was very old. But that's awful news.' Deborah stood at the counter, staring unseeing at the Perspex screen.

'Isn't it? A horrible way to start the week. Everyone loved Mabel. She was such a wonderful person.' Ava had appeared behind the counter. 'What can I do for you, Deborah?'

'That she was ... poor Mabel. So very sad.' Deborah stood for a few moments, composing herself, before pulling an envelope from her capacious Louis Vuitton bag and sliding it beneath the screen. 'I need to send this via recorded delivery, please.'

Silence descended as Ava set the package on the scales. 'That will be £3.49 please.'

Deborah paid with cash, received her change, nodded towards the assembled group and left the post office, clearly distressed.

'*Well!*' Enid pursed her lips and shook her head. 'What do you make of that?'

'She seemed quite upset,' Honoraria commented, feeling slightly confused.

'Don't be taken in by her, Honoraria. Mark my words, more trouble is brewing. There will be no end to it until she leaves. And I'm not the only one who thinks so.' Valerie tapped the side of her powdered patrician nose. 'Something needs to be done.'

'I've already had a few ideas,' Enid whispered with a quick glance at Philip. 'But we need to get more people involved. How about a meeting?'

'Don't you think this vendetta against Deborah Ryecroft has gone far enough?' Ava interrupted, disturbed to witness such vindictive plotting. 'There is absolutely no evidence that she had anything to do with the death of Mabel Littlebody and she was obviously very shocked by the news.'

'No evidence as *yet*.' Valerie bit back. 'The truth will out, you mark my words. Something should be done before the village has another tragedy on its hands.'

'Trust you to take her side, Ava,' Enid spat, eying her daughter with habitual contempt. 'You never show any loyalty to your poor, old mum. I don't know what I did to deserve you as a daughter.' She folded her arms and fussed at the rug around her knees. 'Always the same, that one,' she said to her cronies. 'No sense of gratitude for all I did for her.'

Ava shrugged and melted away from the counter. Best not to react to Enid's barb. She should have known better than to say anything in the first place but she could not believe what she was hearing. Someone needed to be the voice of reason in the face of such ridiculous superstition and downright spite. These women were adults; they should know better. It had been bad enough, in those awful days following Ayesha's Khan's death, seeing how the village children persecuted Deborah Ryecroft.

One such incident – Ava was just seven or eight at the time – had stayed with her into adulthood. She had been walking home with a group of other kids when Deborah was spotted, across the street, alone as usual, head averted. Someone had shrieked, 'It's the witch! Watch out everyone or she'll kill you!' There had followed a bout of screaming, during which Deborah had spun on her heel and headed in the opposite direction. The mood of the group had switched in an instant. The childish screams ceased, replaced by cunning faces. 'She's running away,' someone said. 'Let's get her.' The mob had set off after their target, some hesitant at first, but growing bolder as others broke into a run. 'Get her! Kill the witch!'

Ava winced at the memory. She had followed, spurred on by the rest as an older boy led the charge. Deborah had started to run; her pursuers accelerated, blood-curdling yells ringing through the village. The few adults they passed did nothing to stop them. 'She had it coming,' one said later.

Deborah was almost at Greenways Farm when they caught her and pulled her to the ground. She did not fight back or make a sound. Instead, she curled into a ball, arms around her head, as blows rained down on her. Older boys pushed the younger children out of the way and waded in with their feet, aiming vicious kicks at every part of her body. Ava had watched the violence and done nothing. What could she have done? Deborah had been saved by the appearance of her father and the farmworker who had fetched him. The other kids had run away, but she had watched from her hiding place behind a tree, waiting to see what happened next. Elijah Ryecroft had scowled at his daughter, still on the ground, barked at her to get up and stop making an exhibition of herself, turned on his heel, and stalked off, leaving her lying there. It was the farmworker who had helped Deborah to her feet and picked up her broken glasses. The father's behaviour was almost worse than the actual assault. She had never forgotten it. A few years later, when she was a teenager at secondary school and read *Lord of the Flies*, the awfulness of the episode returned afresh. The description in the book by William Golding, of Piggy being beaten to death by his peers, had made her physically sick.

Perhaps that was why she felt an affinity with Deborah Ryecroft. They were very different people but both had a parent who felt no affection for them. In her case, it had been her mother. Her dad was a mild-mannered man with a gentle sense of humour and a kind word for everyone. As a little girl, she had always favoured him and was resented by Enid as a result. Her mother ruled the village post office and the household with a rod of iron. Husband, Albert, was habitually scolded by his fiery wife. Only Andrew, Ava's young brother, could do no wrong. He had always been Enid's favourite. Excuses were made when he pinched money from her purse, got into trouble with the police, and even when he had a short spell in prison in his early twenties. Now, he lived in the village, barely a mile away, but rarely bothered with his invalid mother. The only time he voluntarily visited Enid was when he wanted something from her, usually money. But he was still the golden child and she, who tirelessly looked after their sole remaining parent and did her best to accommodate a never-ending stream of demands, received no gratitude. Rather, she was despised and treated like a lazy servant.

In her quiet way, though, she took pleasure in her own small acts of rebellion. She would keep an ear to the ground and warn Deborah Ryecroft if the vindictive gossip escalated into anything more concerning. The village had seen enough tragedy. She would never forgive herself if, this time, she stood by and did nothing.

***

Deborah was still reeling as she crossed the road and headed towards her car. Mabel was her rock in Wickthorpe – the person she had always been able to count on in the village. The news had set the ground shifting beneath her feet, leaving her shaken and unsteady. She had popped in to see Mabel just last Friday, only three days ago, and the older woman had seemed on good form. She had even hinted at a secret she wanted to share but said the time was not yet right. Now, the time would never be right. Mabel was gone and Deborah felt bereft.

Just as she reached her car, a male voice assailed her. 'Deborah, good to see you.'

Through the drizzle, she saw the tall figure of Dr Seb Holley striding towards her. Her heart sank. She was in no mood for conversation. Still, she gave him a polite smile. 'Hello ... Seb, isn't it?' *What was it about him which made her feel so uneasy?*

'Well remembered. I had hoped to see you before this but, it appears, the fates have been conspiring against us. How have you settled into life in Wickthorpe?' His teeth flashed white in the grey gloom.

'Fine, thank you.' The way he held her gaze so intently reminded her of a snake, mesmerising its victim before launching an attack. She gave herself a mental shake. The news about Mabel had upset her. That was why she found this meeting so disturbing.

'Well, I guess, given the weather, it's not the day to stand outside chatting. But, good to see you, all the same.'

'You too.' She smiled, relieved, as he sketched her a wave and crossed the road, away from her. Sliding behind the wheel of her Mercedes, she realised her hands were shaking. Distress at Mabel's death, she told herself.

Understandable. It had come as a terrible shock. Biting her lip, she pressed the ignition button and headed back home. She had planned a trip to Cambridge but, with the depressing weather and awful news, she no longer felt in the mood. Mabel's death had scuttled her equilibrium – no doubt about it.

Yet, as she drove the short distance back to Greenways Farm, it was the image of Seb Holley's piranha smile which lingered at the forefront of her mind.

CHAPTER 20

The following week brought sunshine and a resurgence of warmer weather which, along with her restlessness, tempted Deborah from her desk and into her garden with increasing frequency. Swathes of colour in the previously overgrown space filled her with satisfaction and she began to resent days spent travelling to London for meetings, or to catch up on things in the office. Her finger was slipping away from the pulse of her business and yet it flourished anyway. The staff were thriving under the pressure and, she suspected, probably preferred her absence. Now, when she dropped into the office, she felt more like an important visitor, someone to be cosseted and placated, rather than the person steering the helm. Still, time enough to take back full control when she was back in London permanently. In the meantime, her employees were relishing their opportunity to shine and she took a matriarchal pride in their successes. They didn't need her and, instead of feeling jealous and possessive, she realised she was happy to let go, to relinquish the burden of leadership, and let her capable team have its moment.

For Deborah, it was a chance of freedom, freedom she lacked all through her working life. It didn't matter if she played hooky. Instead of remaining chained to her desk, she often met up with Kai or Phil for coffee or lunch, took their black spaniel, Jez, for long walks when they weren't, and worked in her garden. Her passion for horticulture was an unexpected dimension to her life in Wickthorpe and, as with all things, she wanted to do it well. Slowly, with her increased knowledge of plants and how to look after them, her borders were flourishing, as was the wildlife she encouraged to her garden. She stood, surveying her handiwork with a real sense of pride, while bees hummed contentedly over purple hardy geraniums, elegant delphiniums, and delicate aquilegias. Choisya and ceanothus were among the shrubs currently flowering, but her favourite tree in the whole garden was a stately magnolia with its sumptuous, pale pink buds. The physical work provided a soothing contrast to the cerebral, business world of figures. It helped to clear her mind and to relax. Thoughts of hiring a gardener had disappeared. With the glow of hard work successfully accomplished, she packed away her gardening implements. She would miss it when she returned to the city.

As she glanced across to Mabel's bungalow, a pang of sadness settled in her chest, as it had so often this past week. She still could not believe she was gone. Mabel, although old and frail, had a mind so clear and lively that, when she visited, which she had on several occasions since living in the village, she had felt she would always be there. A sanctuary; someone who knew the real Deborah; someone to whom she could open her heart; someone who would not judge her. The news of her death had been a real shock, especially delivered as it had been, with a veneer of malevolence from her 'fan club', as she cynically termed them. She knew Enid Green and Valerie Hampton–Brown disliked her, along with most of the older population in the village, but she failed to see how blame for Mabel's death could be laid at her door. And yet it had. Some of the whispers had found their way to her ear, and there had been another note, lying on her mat, just this morning. Like the others, it was handwritten and anonymous but, this time, it contained more specific comment and a greater level of threat:

We know your evil was behind the death of Mabel Littlebody. Like the others, she was an innocent, cruelly taken from us. If you do not leave the village, you will be made to pay for your sins. You have been warned.

She sighed as she brushed dirt from her hands. So far, she had done nothing about it. Tom Oldridge had suggested informing the police when she had mentioned the notes the previous weekend but she had been reluctant to do so. Based upon her experience, interactions with the police were best avoided, she decided. Now, it was Friday evening and she was going out. It could wait until Monday. She had put it in her bag ready to show Tom later, if the opportunity arose. He had asked her round to sample the much-lauded cheesecake and she could not deny that the invitation, issued a couple of days earlier, had raised her spirits and brought on a new set of fantasies. This time, she would not mess up. The man had got under her skin and she was craving his touch. Delicious as the anticipation of physical intimacy was, she was more than ready for the real thing. Fingers crossed, it would be tonight.

She showered and dressed with care, in a flattering, red shift dress in her usual slim-fitting style and with a slightly lower neckline than she normally favoured. It revealed, what she hoped Tom Oldridge would find, an irresistibly tantalising glimpse of her cleavage. She would have loved to have paired it with her matching, red slingbacks, but the killer heels were not made for walking and, even the relatively short distance to Tom's house, not to mention the gravel drive, would be a step too far. Instead, she slipped on nude-coloured wedge sandals and grabbed the bottle of fine claret she had set aside for the occasion. She was ready.

***

Tom opened the door, wearing an apron emblazoned with the words 'Can you smell burning?' and greeted her with a light peck on the cheek. 'Come in, come in. The others are already here.'

She stepped inside, trying her best to look delighted. 'Others?' she asked.

'Jules and Felix. They can smell one of my cheesecakes from miles away. I had to invite them or I'd never have heard the end of it. You look lovely, by the way.'

'Thank you.' She shrugged off her jacket into his waiting hands and plastered on a smile. 'Jules, Felix, lovely to see you both ... and you too, Emma,' she said as she entered the kitchen where the three of them were perched on stools around the kitchen island.

They all stood as she approached. 'Great to see you too.' Jules grinned, stepping forward to give Deborah a light peck on her cheek. 'Perhaps now we can talk about something other than farming! How have you been?'

As they made polite small talk, and Tom fetched her a glass of wine, her eye was once again drawn to the three black-framed paintings adorning one wall. They were quite striking, she thought. All were farming scenes, painted in oils. The first was of grey skies, bare soil and a tractor and plough, pursued by a cloud of gulls; the second was the same scene in spring-time – vividly imagined with lush, green plants and a self-propelled sprayer; the final piece was a summer setting – harvest-time, busy with a combine, tractor and trailer, coated in a haze of dust. All three paintings were executed in a bold, simplistic style and had a gritty rawness, capturing the essence of each farming season. They told of loneliness, long hours of labour and hard-won rewards.

She turned to Emma. 'I love those paintings,' she said. 'Your dad told me they were your work. They impressed me when I was last here, and even more so now I've had a chance to see them again. You're very talented.'

Emma blushed. 'Thank you,' she replied, 'but Lewis is the real artist in the family. He even had an exhibition in London.'

'I heard. I haven't seen any of Lewis' work but I know I like yours. Would you consider a commission for some pieces for my house?'

'Really?' When Deborah nodded, Emma continued,' But I'm not properly trained or anything. I just paint for fun, when I have time, so not much recently.' She directed a pointed look at her father. 'What kind of thing are you looking for?'

'Something like those?' Deborah pointed at the trio of paintings on the wall. 'The farm. Countryside. Real life. Art which makes me feel something in here.' She clasped her fist to her chest. 'Those paintings speak to me of hardship alongside success, the wonder of nature as well as the contrariness of the weather, the joy of the work you do matched with the trials you endure.'

Emma eyes widened at Deborah's enthusiasm. 'Wow. You really *do* like them. You're not just being polite.' She shook her head in disbelief. 'I don't know what to say.'

'Say yes, you'll paint something for me.'

'I ...' she looked again at Tom, 'I'm not sure when I'll have time ...'

'No rush,' Deborah interjected smoothly. 'I'm happy to wait.'

A sharp rap had them all turning their heads as Rick Billington poked his head around the rear door. 'Oops, sorry. Didn't know you had company. Are you ready to go, Em?'

Emma scrambled off her stool and through the other kitchen doorway, which led to the stairs. 'Give me a few minutes,' she called over her shoulder.

'Can I get you a beer, Rick?' Tom asked as the younger man sat on the recently vacated seat.

'No thanks. I'm driving. On call tomorrow.'

'Going anywhere nice?' Jules asked.

'Just meeting up with a few friends in Newmarket.' He shrugged. 'Emma's idea.'

Tom gave a wry smile at that. 'How are all the family?'

Another hunch of his shoulders. 'Fine thanks. The pub has been busy so that's good. Mum and Dad have been rushed off their feet but they have managed to sort some cover to have a holiday in a few weeks. Mum is delighted about that. She's been nagging Dad for ages about a break.'

'And Freya? How's she doing?'

'God knows.' Rick frowned slightly and looked away. 'I haven't seen much of her recently. Apparently, she's got a new boyfriend she's being a bit secretive about. Poor Mum is desperate to meet him, but Freya won't play ball.' He flashed them an embarrassed grin as if realising he was talking too much. 'Anyway, how are all you guys? And ...' He glanced towards the nook in the corner where Jake the Labrador was snoozing, 'more importantly, how is the old boy doing?'

'Felix is very well thanks,' Jules giggled.

'Hey!'

'Sorry, couldn't resist.' Jules patted her husband's arm.

'Jake's much better,' Tom said as Rick crossed the room to crouch beside the old dog. 'Those antibiotics seem to have done the trick. His appetite is back at any rate.'

'Good.'

A clattering down the stairs and Emma burst back into the room. 'Ready,' she declared.

Rick stood. 'We'll be off then.'

'Enjoy your date,' Deborah smiled.

'Oh!' Bands of red blossomed on Emma's cheeks. 'It's not a date. We're just friends.' She glanced anxiously at Rick's untroubled face.

'That's right,' he agreed. 'Just good mates and always will be. Right Em?'

'Right.' Her look was slightly strained as she bid them goodbye. 'Hope you enjoy the meal. Don't let him set fire to anything.'

*****

The meal – steak, chips and the promised cheesecake – was delicious and met with unanimous approval.

'What can I say?' Tom grinned modestly. 'I'm a catch. Any woman would be mad not to snap me up.' He winked at Deborah.

'Early days,' she bantered in return. 'I would need to sample more of your cooking before I could make a judgment.' Inside, she was tingling. Judging by his appreciative looks in her direction through the meal, things were looking up.

His eyebrows raised suggestively. 'Any time ...'

There was an awkward pause and Felix coughed. 'Er ... perhaps we ought to be going.'

'Don't be daft, mate.' Tom rose from the table. 'It's early yet. I'll get some coffee. Why don't you three go through to the sitting room?'

Jules led Deborah through to the sitting room while Felix stayed behind to help Tom in the kitchen. It was a cosy room with a wood burner, two slightly battered and worn sofas in tan leather, and a large armchair. Books lined the shelves, and the floor was covered in a large, rectangular rug. A fluffy, ginger cat was sleeping on the chair so the two women faced each other on the opposite sofas. Jules grinned as she kicked off her shoes and tucked her feet up underneath her. 'This makes a nice change – Felix in the kitchen and me relaxing in here.' She sighed contentedly and took a sip from her almost empty wine glass. 'I'm the cook in our household, more's the pity. That was a mistake I made when we were first married. I took charge in the kitchen and Felix was happy to let me. Don't get me wrong, I don't mind cooking but it would be nice not to have sole responsibility for it all.'

'How long have you been married?' Deborah asked.

'Twenty-seven years.' Jules rolled her eyes. 'I know, I'm a saint. Have you ever been married?'

'No.'

'Never tempted?'

'No.'

Jules nodded. 'Probably why you're so successful – no man holding you back!'

'Possibly.' Deborah gave her a complicit grin. 'I've always liked my independence too much. It seems to me that marriage, or any serious relationship, demands making lots of compromises. I'm afraid I've never met anyone for whom I'm prepared to do that. Too selfish.'

Jules eyed her thoughtfully. 'Or, maybe, you've never met the right man.'

Deborah said nothing. She knew where this conversation was heading and did not want to give the other woman any encouragement. 'I can't believe it's been three months since I returned to live in Wickthorpe,' she said instead.

'Why? Has the time flown or has it felt like forever?'

Deborah considered the question. 'Actually, a bit of both. It's been tricky coming back and I haven't been universally welcomed ...' she pulled a face, 'but, on the whole, it's been good for me. It's given me a fresh perspective on things. And I've met some lovely people.' She smiled at the woman opposite.

Jules grinned back. 'We're not all bad. And Tom is a complete sweetheart. You and he seem to be getting on like the proverbial house on fire, although I shouldn't use that phrase in this house.' When Deborah blushed, her smile grew wider but, diplomatically, she returned to the subject of her original question. 'I'm glad you're feeling positive about living in Wickthorpe. I guess it must have been difficult coming back. I don't know what happened all those years ago, when that poor girl drowned, but it seems ridiculous that anyone would still hold a grudge against you, years later. But there,' she sighed, 'that's village folk for you, and there are some in Wickthorpe who definitely seem to have the knives out. Tom said your mother was worrying about it before she died.' She lowered her voice. 'I don't know if you know, but she asked Tom to look out for you, should you decide to return. She predicted it wouldn't be easy for you.'

'What do you mean? Look out for me?'

Jules detected the sudden tension in Deborah's tone and looked up, a little startled. 'Oh, sorry. I didn't mean any offence. Oh gosh, have I put my foot in it?'

'Not at all.' Deborah attempted a nonchalant smile. 'It's good to be honest and now it all makes sense. The drinks party when I arrived, the other times he's invited me out ... it was because my mother asked Tom to look out for me.' The bitterness of hurt pride burnt the back of her throat. She had thought he was genuinely interested in her.

'Not at all.' Jules's sapphire blue eyes beseeched her understanding. 'Tom felt sorry for your mum and tried his best to be a good neighbour. As I understand it, before she died, she talked about you and about the rough deal you had all those years ago. She hoped you would return to live at Greenways Farm but wasn't sure if you would. Tom promised, if you did, he would keep an eye out for you ... be in your corner .... you know, as we all are ...' Her voice tailed off as Tom entered, carrying a tray of coffee mugs.

'We all are ... what?' he asked as he manoeuvred the tray onto a table. 'Milk? Sugar?'

'In Deborah's corner.'

'Neither, thank you,' Deborah said stiffly.

Tom frowned. 'Are you talking about the Wickthorpe nasties who want to blame Deborah for anything bad happening? Milk gets spilt – Deborah must have cursed it – that kind of thing?'

'In a way ...' Jules answered slowly.

'Don't let the bastards get to you, that's what I say,' Felix said cheerfully as he spooned sugar into a mug. 'Some people have nothing better to do than complain about others.'

'If you don't mind me asking,' Jules said, 'why *do* they hate you? What happened when that girl drowned? I know about the superstition – the witch's curse on the village – but I don't understand what that has to do with you.'

'Jules ...' Tom began to protest but Deborah intervened.

'It's fine. There's not much to tell and it's old news, after all. The girl was Ayesha Khan, she was sixteen years old, and she was my best friend.' She paused and took a deep breath. 'Ayesha drowned in Dark Water Lake when two girls from the village dared her and me to swim across. I refused but Ayesha was determined to do it. She wanted to win their approval, you see. Unfortunately, she got into difficulties. When I realised something was wrong, I tried to save her, but I was too late. She was already dead by the time I reached her.' Her voice was flat and emotionless as she recalled that fateful summer afternoon.

The others regarded her with pitying eyes. 'That's awful!' Jules exclaimed. 'You tried to save her though. How come *you* got the blame?'

Deborah sighed, pain at the memory undiluted by the years passed. 'The other two girls insisted the dare was my idea. They also suggested Ayesha might still have been alive when I reached her. I was arrested and questioned but never charged. The accusation stuck though.'

'They lied! That's terrible! Who were they?' Jules' pixie-like features contorted in indignation.

Deborah bit her lip. The urge to let it out – all the hurt and anger caused by the injustice – was strong, but would achieve nothing other than more ill feeling. Some might believe her, like Jules, but others would not. They hadn't before. 'It doesn't matter now. Best to leave it in the past.'

'Do *you* know who it was?' Jules turned her rage towards Tom and Felix. 'You lived here; you must know.'

Tom shook his head. 'We were both away at college. We heard about the tragedy though. I remember Ayesha was the daughter of the couple who ran the shop. I think it was called Khan's Grocery Store then. I knew her by sight but that was as far as it went. She was a few years younger than us. Anyway, for us, the whole thing got overtaken by the next tragedy. Our school mate, Jonny, was killed in a car accident. That was a real shock. Jonny was so full of life. It was hard to believe he wouldn't be around anymore. We came back for the funeral and, I remember, there was nonsense going around about the curse at the time but we ignored it. Nothing was going to bring our friend back. I guess, speaking personally, that was the first time I realised none of us were immortal. It made me reflect on some of the stupid stunts we pulled and how easily it could have been one of us lying there. Poor old Jonny. And poor Ayesha Khan.'

'And poor Deborah,' Jules declared loyally, 'having to cope, not only with the grief of losing her best friend, but also with the blame for the accident unfairly heaped upon her.' Her eyes shone with compassion as she turned to Deborah. 'It must have been awful! How old were you? Just sixteen?' At the other woman's nod, she shook her head. 'Honestly, those people should be ashamed of themselves! I wish I knew who the other two girls were. I'd give them a piece of my mind. Do they still live in Wickthorpe?'

Deborah held up a hand. 'That's why it's best you don't know. It was all a long time ago. I do remember Jonny though,' she mused. 'I only spoke to him once but it was the day before he died. I didn't know who he was at the time … not until after the accident. I just remember he was kind when I needed a friend. Poor Jonny. What a waste!'

'Yes, it was.' Tom's voice was sombre and he shook his head. 'He was great – nothing like his parents. The Hampton-Browns,' he explained when Deborah looked puzzled. 'Jonny was their only son.'

'Oh, I see. I hadn't made that connection. Poor people,' she said, shaking her head.

Her sympathy gave Tom pause. Deborah was clearly unaware that the Hampton-Browns blamed her for their son's death. Telling her would only cause more grief. He decided to change the subject. 'I think I can speak for all of us, Debs, when I say we're very pleased you decided to return to Wickthorpe.'

She blushed at the warmth in his voice. 'Thank you. Now you know why I was reluctant to come back. But I am very fortunate to have people looking out for me,' she added, a sardonic note edging her voice. Jules' revelation, that Tom's attentiveness had been at the behest of her mother, had knocked her for six. He clearly had a strong sense of obligation! The best thing would be to relieve him of it straight away. Putting her mug firmly down on a side table, she stood up. 'Thank you all, but I am used to fighting my own battles. I don't need anyone doing it for me.' She turned to Tom. 'Thank you for a lovely evening and a fabulous meal but I'll make a move now.'

'What, so early?' Felix glanced at his watch. 'Oh, I guess it is gone eleven. Perhaps we'd better head home too.' He glanced towards Jules.

She nodded. 'We'll walk you home, Debs. I hope you don't mind us calling you that. Deborah seems so … so … ugh, I think I could put my foot in it again! Let's just say that Debs suits you better.'

'Debs is fine. Just don't call me the Wickthorpe Witch!' came the droll reply.

'Never that.' Jules tucked her arm companionably in Deborah's as they stepped out into the cool night air. 'Thank you for sharing your story,' she added quietly. 'It couldn't have been easy.'

'It's old news,' Deborah shrugged. 'It can't hurt me anymore.' As she uttered the words, she remembered the anonymous notes and shivered. Empty threats, she told herself ... nothing more.

CHAPTER 21

Saturday lunchtime and Honoraria Simpson-Fairchild gazed through the window of a bijou restaurant just off the High Street in Oxford. Beautiful. The perfect setting. Sadly though, not an ideal scenario. The reason for this sat opposite her – a wrinkled shrimp of a man with barely six strands of greasy white hair combed across his otherwise bald pate. She had harboured such high hopes for Harold Pinkerton, 56, bank manager and widower. His photograph had filled her with delicious expectation. Just too good to pass up. Despite the hideousness of her last experience, she had to give Harold a chance. He could be the one.

She had tried to steel herself for more disappointment, but her optimistic spirit refused to believe it could happen. Harold's picture showed a clean-shaven man with a strong jaw and smouldering brown eyes. Thick, grey hair, immaculately coiffed and swept back from his face, had sent her into a whirl of erotic anticipation. She imagined running her hands through those full locks as his lips caressed her body ...

The reality was very different. She had been unable to hide her dismay and anger when he introduced himself but he apologised so profusely she felt sorry for him.

'If I'd sent my own picture, you wouldn't have given me the time of day,' he explained. 'You looked so beautiful; I knew I wouldn't stand a chance.'

Such flattery helped to appease her. Might as well have lunch, at least. She was already booked into a hotel for the weekend, and was looking forward to exploring Oxford, a city she had never visited, whatever the outcome of this rendezvous. She had nothing to lose. And she had never been one to judge a book by its cover. Her Edgar had not exactly been an oil painting. However, having laboured through three long lunch courses, she was now mentally rehearsing her 'thanks but no thanks' speech. Poor Harold had not improved upon better acquaintance. He had a flat, monotone voice which droned on to the point of exasperation and there had been more lies. For a while, he had kept up the pretence of being a bank manager ... until it slipped out that he was actually a clerk who had worked in the same job, same place, for forty-five years. So, not fifty-six either! She sipped at her coffee and continued to stare out of the window to hide her growing irritation. He was intently studying the bill. It was taking a while. As she watched people strolling by in the sunshine, she glimpsed a couple walking in the direction of the restaurant on the other side of the street. The young woman was stunning – long, blonde hair cascading around her shoulders – reminding her of Freya Billington. She was holding the arm of an older man with dark hair, a strange-looking moustache and heavy, black-rimmed glasses, and laughing up at him. Perhaps he was her father? As they came closer, she gave a start. It *was* Freya and that was *not* Gerald Billington, the girl's father. She craned her head to see better but a couple of youths walking past obscured her view and then they were gone. Freya Billington with an older man! Who would have thought it? Her mind raced with questions. She could hardly wait to share this tasty titbit of information.

'Forty-one pounds,' Harold announced, startling her from her thoughts, 'which includes a ten per cent tip. I presume you are happy to pay half?'

'Naturally.' She could not help rolling her eyes as she presented her card to the waiter. 'That was a delicious meal. Thank you.' It had been. Shame about the company.

***

Later that evening, Freya lay between the crisp cotton sheets of a small hotel on the outskirts of Oxford, staring at the beautiful face of the man beside her. She was so lucky! In fact, she could hardly believe it. Her heart was in danger of exploding with happiness. It had been such a magical day. Since telling him of her pregnancy a week before, when his reaction had been disappointing, to say the least, she had been terrified he would finish with her. Instead, he was going to leave his wife! They were going to move away somewhere, just the two of them. Her prayers had been answered. He was her Prince Charming, the man of her dreams, her one-and-only ... and he loved her.

There had been difficult moments since she had surprised him with her announcement. They had met only twice, in secret, as usual. Both times, he had tried to persuade her to have an abortion. The second time, when she point-blank refused to consider his suggestion to get rid of the baby, he had grown angry.

'If you keep the child, you lose me. Your choice,' he pronounced, his voice cold.

She had not reacted well. 'I see,' she responded angrily. 'Because I won't do what you want, you won't give me what I want. I get it. Well, two can play at that game.' She glared at his stony countenance. 'I'll tell everyone about us – my parents, your wife, everyone – *then* where will you be?'

He had turned to look at her. The intense, blue eyes she loved so much flashed fury. He gripped her hard by the shoulders and thrust his face into hers. 'You will regret trying to blackmail me,' he ground out. 'This is not a game, little girl. These are people's lives you are threatening to destroy. How can you be so selfish?' With a muttered expletive, he pushed her away. Never before had she witnessed violence in him. For a moment, she had thought he was going to strike her!

Afterwards, she regretted her threat. 'I didn't mean it!' she sobbed. 'It's just I love you so much. I want to be with you forever. I'll do anything for you, you know that, but please don't ask me to give up my baby.' He hadn't responded, even as she wept – silly, childish tears.

Later, when those tears had dried, she was left with a cold hard nugget of disillusionment in her heart. He was not going to leave his wife; he wanted her to have an abortion. Whilst she loved him with an all-consuming passion, he viewed her as nothing more than a casual affair. *How had she got it so wrong?*

In the following days, she alternated between despair and hope. Surely, when he had a chance to think about things properly, he would come round? If only, she had not behaved so stupidly, railing at him like that! The poor man could not help but be torn between his desire for her, and loyalty towards his wife and their two children. He just needed time. She had been wrong to make those threats about going public with their relationship. That had just made him angry. If only she had handled things better ...

But it had all turned out wonderfully well after all. He had apologised and told her he had been wrong. It was the shock, he said. He had not expected it, thinking she was so young and just about to embark on a high-flying career. But her ultimatum had helped him put things in perspective. He loved her more than anything and could not bear the thought of being without her. Today, he had been achingly gentle with her, solicitous and caring. No sex, he told her sternly, until she was over the first three months. Too risky for the baby. She was dismayed at that – it was not something she had heard – but today she was content to leave it. The last thing she wanted was another argument!

The room was hot and she felt thirsty. Lovely man that he was, he had fetched her an apple juice but that was now gone. Aware of his eyes on her, she slipped out of bed and sashayed across the room to crack the window open. Voices, laughter and the clinking of bottles wafted up on the still night air. Her friends would be out partying too. She sighed. Texts and calls from them were becoming less frequent. They were tiring of her excuses. If only she could text Cara now! Her closest friend had been hurt by her abandonment, she knew. But secrecy had been paramount these past few months. He had insisted upon it, for obvious reasons, and she had been worried about letting something slip. Better to avoid contact until it was safe to reveal all. She glanced across at her brown, leather bag, slung on a chair in the corner, where her phone was secreted – switched off, of course – but knew she had to wait to share her wonderful news. He had to tell his wife first. It would be so strange to have everything out in the open at last, even though the secrecy had been exciting. It had lent a thrill to her life, which had become mundane, since she had graduated from university and been back living at home. Having a separate phone no one knew about, the clandestine meetings, even the ridiculous disguises he insisted upon wearing, had all combined to make their romance an exhilarating ride. It had been like a fairy story ... and now it was about to become real-life.

She staggered against the wall. God, she felt weird! And so thirsty. *Water*. She needed water. The room blurred and swam around her. As she stumbled, she felt his strong arms around her, steering her back to the bed.

'There you go, my darling,' he whispered.

His face loomed fuzzily before her; smiling; perfect white teeth, strangely shark-like in the greyness. A dark hair curled beneath his left nostril and, with an unsteady hand, she tried to brush it away. It stayed where it was. *Gross!*

She giggled and closed her eyes, willing the giddiness to pass. How annoying when she was so happy! She loved him; he loved her. Everything was perfect. They were going to be together ... for ever and ever ...

CHAPTER 22

The sweat-prickling heat causes the prim, navy swimsuit beneath my T-shirt and shorts to chafe my skin. School regulation swimwear, disgustingly unflattering and downright embarrassing but I have nothing else. Doubtless, Jane and Melissa will be in fashionable bikinis, showing off holiday-tanned flesh. If they show up ... I sigh as I glance at my watch. 2:15 p.m. Fifteen minutes late. Ayesha waits with me, small and dark, in a high-necked yellow top over sky-blue shorts. Her long hair is tied back in a ponytail. She looks about twelve, rather than her sixteen years, as she sits on one of the swings, gently rocking backwards and forwards, watching the road, her narrow face wearing a pensive expression.

'Do you think they're coming?' I ask. She hunches her shoulders in reply. Secretly, I hope they don't. I trust neither Jane nor Melissa. Interactions between us are sharp with their scorn. Or they ignore us altogether. This invitation to go swimming came out of the blue and, instantly suspicious, I was about to make an excuse when Ayesha accepted for the pair of us. The poor kid is desperate to get on the right side of them both. They give her a hard time during school term-time, when I'm away, and she is ostracized by others as a result of their disapproval. I can't blame her for wanting to take any opportunity to fit in.

'Here they come!'

I look up in surprise at Ayesha's exclamation and, sure enough, the unmistakeable figures of Jane Hodrick and Melissa Shipman are striding down the path towards us. Ayesha jumps off the swing and I retrieve the bag containing my towel and underwear. I see Melissa's blonde head dip towards Jane as she whispers something. Jane giggles in response but their faces are guileless as they reach us.

'Hi, Melissa .... Jane,' Ayesha greets them shyly, slinging her own bag over her shoulder.

They smile in response. 'You're both ready?' Melissa asks. We nod.

'Where are we going?' Ayesha matches her stride to theirs as we head back onto the path and past the church with its towering spire. I follow along behind, secretly envious of their casual confidence.

'Surprise!' Jane replies. I fancy I see an exchange of looks between her and Melissa. Nothing I can pinpoint but I feel increasingly anxious. I wish again Ayesha had declined the invitation.

Bees hum in honeysuckle adorning the wall as we continue along the path, past the fuel pumps on the right-hand side, and then turn right at the crossroads. We're not catching the bus to Stowmarket or Bury St Edmunds then. Melissa lives further along, in a large detached house with manicured lawns, so I wonder if we are going somewhere in her mum's car. Neither Jane nor Melissa is carrying a bag so that must be the plan. My feelings of unease recede. They can't be up to anything if Melissa's mum is involved. Perhaps they really are making a genuine effort to be nice.

However, they walk straight past Melissa's house. I stop abruptly. 'Where are we going?'

The other three turn and look at me in surprise. 'Don't you trust us?' Jane asks. 'Suit yourself if you don't want to come.' She links her arm with Ayesha's and smiles down at her. 'Ayesha does, don't you?'

Ayesha nods eagerly, thrilled at such a display of camaraderie. 'Of course,' she says. 'Come on, Debbie. Don't be a spoilsport. It's an adventure.'

'Exactly!' Melissa grabs Ayesha's other arm so she is sandwiched between them. 'If you're too scared ...' She lets the words hang in the air.

I don't care what they think but I can't abandon Ayesha. She sends me a beseeching look and I see she is apprehensive too. That settles it. 'Fine,' I say and close the distance between us. This time, they make no effort to hide the triumph in their eyes.

We continue walking, Melissa and Jane chattering about the sticky heat and how much nicer it was in Majorca, where the two families had recently holidayed together. 'It was hot and sunny all the time but there was always a breeze coming off the sea which cooled us down. And we met two gorgeous boys, didn't we Jane?'

'Tim and Steve. Complete hunks. A bit older than us. The boys around here are wimps by comparison.'

'Yeah, especially the sex. They knew a thing or two, didn't they Jane?'

'You had sex with them?' Ayesha gasps.

They give her a superior smile. 'Of course,' Jane says. 'Haven't you had sex yet, Ayesha? No.' She answers her own question and wrinkles her nose. 'I don't suppose so.' She reaches to pull Ayesha's hair loose from the ponytail. 'There, that's better. Now you don't look quite so much like a schoolgirl.'

Silence falls as we turn away from the road, up the track leading to Dark Water Lake. Now we all know what the game is. They will expect us to refuse and will taunt us even more. I'm a good swimmer, a skill learned at boarding school, but have no intention of letting these two girls bully me into doing something so foolish. People have drowned in that lake. And then there's the curse, from hundreds of years ago, when a woman was drowned as a witch. I'm not scared of that but this is a place I avoid – it gives me the creeps. I'm tempted to refuse to go further and leave them to it, but I feel Ayesha's terror as she is frogmarched forwards, so I follow.

We reach a small clearing where people sometimes bring picnics. The grass has been trampled and there is an open space leading to the edge of the water. 'Here we are!' Melissa announces with a malicious grin. She waves a hand towards the inky black surface of the lake. 'Your swimming pool, girls!' Jane joins in with the laughter as they watch to see what we will do.

'Ha ha!' I sneer with my own brand of sarcasm. 'Very funny. Come on, Ayesha. Let's go. Leave these two to their ... swim.'

Ayesha takes a step towards me but Melissa tugs her back. 'You're not scared, are you?' She leans towards her and looks into her eyes. Then she casts her off with a splutter of disgust. 'Yes, you are. You're too scared. What a baby! Well, you can forget about hanging out with us. Shame! We were hoping you might be the kind of girl who likes a challenge, like us ...'

'I am. I do,' Ayesha declares. She looks at me and shakes her head. 'I'll do it!'

'Yay! Good for you!' Jane claps her hands together, beaming approval. She looks at me and purses her lips. 'What about you, Debbie? Are you going to let your friend do this on her own or are you brave enough to join her?'

I ignore her. 'Please don't listen to them,' I beg Ayesha as, grim-faced, she removes her T-shirt and steps out of her shorts. 'Please don't do it. It's dangerous!'

'It's dangerous!' Melissa mimics, sneering at me. 'Debbie is too scared! Good for you, Ayesha. You show her!' Ayesha stands indecisively in her pale green swimsuit.

She shivers, despite the clammy heat. Fear grips my throat. She's really going to do it.

'Go on then. In you go.' Jane gives her a little push and she stumbles towards the bank. 'Show us. If you manage to swim right the way across to the far side, then you can come with us to the cinema on Saturday night.'

'Ayesha, please.' She ignores my plea and steps into the water. I admit, I am impressed by her courage. Despite the warmth of the air temperature, that lake must be freezing but she doesn't make a murmur. She walks forward until the floor drops away and she is swimming, a shaky breast stroke, head held high, away from us. I don't believe in God but, inside, I start to pray. I know she's not a strong swimmer.

'I didn't know the Paki had it in her,' Melissa says, her eyes fixed on the small, bobbing, dark head. 'Did you mean it when you said she could come out with us on Saturday?'

'Course not!' Jane laughs. 'But it shows how desperate she is to please us. Pathetic!'

'You disgust me!' I spit. My heart goes out to the girl in the water. Is it my imagination or is she slowing? I take a step forward, craning to watch her. Shadows from the trees on the other side of the lake, combined with the glare from the sun, make it difficult to see.

'Shall we leave her to it?' Jane says to her crony. 'This is boring now.'

'You can't leave!' I exclaim in horror. 'What if she gets into trouble?'

Melissa sniggers. 'That'll be your problem.'

'Please wait,' I beg as the two of them head away from the bank.

Jane turns, hands on hips. 'Stop making such a fuss! Look, she's almost reached the other side.'

I peer and see a hand waving and relief floods my body. Thank goodness! The sun vanishes behind a cloud and a sudden gust of wind whistles through the trees. A branch swings across the water, near Ayesha, and I hear a muffled cry. She's in trouble! The arm disappears. I can't see her. Bloody hell! My heart thunders in my chest as I rip off my top and plunge into the icy water. 'Get help!' I cry to the girls behind me. They are silent now and seem rooted to the spot. 'Go!' I scream. 'Run! No ... just one of you!' They both disappear.

I wade forward at pace until I can't touch the bottom. It's murky and cold, so cold. I swim as fast as I can, front crawl, smooth, steady strokes, but it isn't enough. Panic and fear clog my throat, making it hard to breathe. The water feels like treacle, tugging at my arms and legs, holding me back. The others have gone for help but it will be too late. It's down to me.

When I'm three quarters of the way across, I lift my head. The roaring in my ears ceases and the air holds its breath. I see nothing and swim on, eyes searching. The trees at the far side stand peacefully, benign now where they seemed so full of menace just a few minutes before. I head for the oak with the low-hanging branch, the one which had viciously swept across the water's surface, propelled by that gust of wind, just as Ayesha had popped up. Where is she?

I'm close enough now to see the detail of the leaves, dark green, starting to crinkle at the edges. The cloud, which had cloaked the lake in a shroud of grey, shifts and a shaft of sunlight hits the water. I stop swimming, treading water, catching my breath, desperately looking for my friend. She isn't here. She must have scrambled into the undergrowth. 'Ayesha!' I call. 'Ayesha, where are you? Are you hurt?'

Then, I catch a glimpse of white – a pale limb floating. No! I don't want to believe it. Urgent strokes take me closer. Too late. A frail, skinny, lifeless torso, in a pale green swimsuit, sagging in places; face down; long hair fanning out like a halo. 'No!' I cry again. I swim closer ... and then I stop.

Something isn't right ...

Deborah's eyes snapped open. Her fingers clutched the edge of the duvet, gripping it like a lifeline. The dream had been so vivid, so real. It was like living it all over again – the fear, the helplessness, the horror. She had been through it so often and, every time, it was just as awful.

She threw back the covers and swung her feet over to the thick, beige pile. Sunlight filtered through the blinds at the window and dust motes danced in the air. She was fine. Everything was as it should be except ...

A niggle remained ... something about the dream ... something not right.

She stepped beneath jets of hot water in the shower, determined to dismiss it. Little wonder the nightmare had returned. Talking about it the previous evening had brought it all back. Not that she could ever forget. She had been haunted by the image of Ayesha's lifeless body ever since that terrible day. Every detail of the tragedy scarred her soul. Every nightmare brought the same sense of impending doom, mingled with hope and fear. Each time, she willed a different ending, which never happened.

Yet, this time, the ending *was* different ...

As water streamed over her face, she closed her eyes and recaptured that final image. The shock, when she realised what had eluded her in sleep, made her gasp aloud. Horrified, she turned off the shower and reached for a towel, furiously trying to scrub away what she had seen. As she dried herself, her breathing calmed. *Just a dream. Not real ... or, at least, this time, it wasn't.*

The body floating head down in the water was *not* Ayesha. The long hair fanning like a halo was *blonde*. And, as she tried to haul the body out of the water, the white visage slumped against her shoulder did not belong to Ayesha either. It was the perfect, but lifeless, face of Freya Billington.

***

Rain lashed against the kitchen window as Tom Oldridge unloaded plates from the dishwasher. The heavy, charcoal sky matched the scowl on his face.

'Kitchen is still intact I see,' Emma said as she wandered into the kitchen in her dressing gown. 'What's up? Did the meal not go well?' She pulled a box of cornflakes from a cupboard and tipped some into a bowl.

'No. It was good. Everyone said so.'

'Why the face then?'

'What face? Nothing's wrong. Everything's hunky dory.' Tom gave his daughter a broad smile to prove his point and returned to his task.

'Mm ...' Emma splashed milk into the bowl and perched on a stool by the kitchen island.

'How was your night, anyway? Did the date go well?'

That got to her. Every time. And he knew it. 'It wasn't a date and stop trying to change the subject. Deborah Ryecroft looked great in that dress,' she added coyly. 'I wish I looked that good in red, but this hair ...' She flicked an irritated hand through her auburn locks before musing, 'Perhaps I should dye it? Hey Dad, didn't you think she looked gorgeous?'

'Yes, very nice,' he agreed with a non-committal shrug. In truth, she had blown his socks off. Alone in his bed, he had dreamt about peeling that garment from her delectable body, long into the night, but he was hardly about to admit *that* to his nosy daughter.

'So ... did you tell her? Did you make it clear you were interested?'

'Who says I'm interested?' he parried.

She raised her eyebrows. 'Are you telling me that you have no … er, thoughts about Deborah?' She was so close to the truth, he flushed. 'Aha, I knew it.' She shot him a look of triumph and persisted. 'So *did* you tell her? Did anything happen?'

'No, nothing happened and I don't find this conversation suitable father/daughter chat,' he said stiffly.

She laughed and spooned cornflakes into her mouth. 'Well, someone has to look after you; give you a push in the right direction. You'd be a hopeless case otherwise.'

'Are you finished with that bowl?' He took it from her outstretched hand, found a slot for it in the dishwasher and set the machine going. Emma was correct in assuming he was in a bad mood and the reason for it.   His tiredness, after a sleepless night of frustrated desire, was also responsible. He had hoped to entice Deborah to stay behind after Jules and Felix had left … or to walk her home and accept her invitation to pop in for a nightcap. There had been no opportunity for either of those possibilities. She had left in such a rush he had barely had a chance to drink his coffee! And Felix and Jules had, helpfully, offered to see her home, cutting him out of the equation.

Emma looked up from her phone at Tom's snort and sighed. 'Look, something's up. Why don't you tell me what happened? I might be able to help.'

He studied his daughter's concerned face and shrugged. Why not? Blazes if he knew what had gone amiss. 'I honestly have no idea,' he admitted. 'Everything was going well. They all enjoyed the food and Deborah fitted right in. We were having a good time, or so I thought. I made coffee. Felix stayed back to help me and Jules took Debs through to the snug.'

'Debs?' Emma queried.

'It's how I think of her. I may have used it once or twice. Deborah is a bit stuffy, in my opinion. Doesn't suit her at all. Why? Do you think that was the problem?'

She wrinkled her nose. 'I wouldn't have thought so. I'm sure if something like that offended her, she'd come right out and say so. I'd be more worried about leaving her alone with Jules. You know what Jules is like, especially after she's had a few glasses of wine. Tact isn't exactly her strong point. What happened next?'

He gave a rueful smile, remembering. 'Yes, well ... you could be right. When we turned up with the coffee, Jules was asking her about the tragedy and why half the village seem to have it in for her.'

'That sounds like a fun conversation!' Emma shook her head with a wry grimace. 'Good old Jules!'

Leaning against the sink, hands in his pockets, he nodded. 'I guess so. Debs didn't seem to mind talking about it, though. She handled the situation very well. But then she made an excuse and stood up to leave.'

'I'm not surprised. So ... are you going to tell me what happened? The tragedy? I'd love to hear Deborah's version of events.'

'Not now.' He ran a hand distractedly through his hair. 'I guess I'd better ring her ... check she's OK.' He brightened. 'It's a hellish day weather-wise. Maybe I'll invite her out for Sunday lunch. It's not a good day for doing much else.'

Emma smiled. 'Great idea. I'll leave you to it.' She sprang off her stool and headed for the door.

'Hey, before you go, how did your night pan out? With Rick?'

'A work in progress.' She shrugged as she turned back to face him. 'At least he's stopped going on about Amelie.'

'Well, I think you're a diamond. Rick doesn't know how lucky he is.'

'You know it. I know it,' she said airily. 'Pity Rick is totally oblivious.'

Tom watched her disappear through the door with the familiar ache in his heart. Emma had loved Rick since the Billingtons arrived in the village. But he had never seen her as anything more than a friend. Tom feared he never would.

With his daughter's pep talk ringing in his ears, he reached for his phone and found Deborah's number in his list of contacts. She answered almost instantly.

'Hello Tom. I was just about to ring you to thank you again for a lovely evening and a wonderful meal.'

'My pleasure. Er ... awful weather.' *God, he was behaving like a nervous schoolboy. Just get on with it.*

'Terrible. I assume you won't be out on a tractor today.'

'God, no. Much too wet for that. Anyway, Debs ... I was wondering if you fancied going out for some lunch today? I know it's a bit short notice but I'm sure I could get us in somewhere ... er ... if you fancied it, that is?' Silence stretched between them and he wondered if he had lost the connection. Then he heard her sigh.

'That's very kind of you to offer, Tom, and I really appreciate all the lengths to which you've gone to make me feel welcome living back here. But I think you've more than fulfilled whatever promise you made to my mother.' Her voice was calm but very formal. 'I don't want you to feel any further obligation towards me.'

'But ...' he was confused. 'I don't understand. What promise?'

'The one you made when my mother asked you to look out for me. Jules explained last night while you were making coffee,' she said patiently.

'Oh!' The penny dropped. *Bloody Jules!* Emma was right. 'Look, I admit your mother was concerned how you would be treated should you decide to move back here, and she *did* ask me to look out for you. I talked to Emma about it and we agreed to ask you round for drinks at ours, invite a few neighbours round, to help break the ice ...'

'You don't need to explain ...'

'But I want to. Look, Debs, I would *not* invite you for a meal and then out to lunch if I didn't like you. I enjoy spending time with you and would like to get to know you better ... if that's alright with you?'

'Oh. I see.' There was another pause and, when she spoke again, he thought he could detect a smile in her voice. 'I was going to work today ... but lunch with a good-looking man seems a much better offer. What time shall I be ready?'

'I'll pick you up at half twelve. See you then.' He ended the call feeling ridiculously pleased with himself. She had called him *good-looking*!

***

The Swan in the historic Suffolk village of Lavenham was the perfect choice for Sunday lunch. He was lucky to get a table but there had been a last-minute cancellation and they were able to take a booking for two at one o'clock. Perfect! Despite living in Suffolk throughout her childhood, Deborah had never visited Lavenham and was instantly entranced by the timbered houses lining the street.

'It's like stepping back in time,' she said, peering through the rain-spattered car window. 'I keep expecting to see horses and carts, and people dressed in medieval clothing.'

He grinned. 'I'm amazed you've never been before.'

'My parents weren't exactly ones for family outings,' she responded drily.

He parked as close as he could to the pub and they hurried inside. *The Swan* was as captivating on the inside as out. They were ushered through to a large room, beautifully preserved with oak beams, impressive open fireplaces and exposed brickwork. The restaurant was busy and yet their table felt very intimate, tucked away in one corner.

'My friends in London would love this,' Deborah said as she studied the menu.

'It's very popular with both tourists and locals,' he agreed. 'Naturally the food won't be a patch on what I served up last night, but I'm sure they'll do their best.'

She chuckled. 'You did set the bar high.'

Over lunch, they chatted amicably, finding they shared an interest in crime thrillers but that their tastes in music were very different. She named Adele, Coldplay and Ed Sheeran as her favourite artists, whilst he preferred eighties rock from the likes of Guns N' Roses and Metallica. The talk drifted round to his family and she asked about Lewis.

'He's still in Australia at the moment, with some lad he met while he was there. Originally, he was travelling with two girls but they've long since come home. I guess he'll be back eventually. As well as the bar work, I suspect he's doing plenty of partying. He always was the life and soul, very much the opposite to Emma and me.'

'He never wanted to follow on the family tradition and go into farming?'

'Not at all. When Dad was alive, it was all he went on about. Concerns about succession and keeping the land in the family. He couldn't understand why I didn't insist Lewis knuckle down, but his heart was never in it, whereas it was all Emma ever wanted. Well, that and Rick Billington.' He gave a rueful smile. 'Poor girl. Everyone knows how she feels, except Rick himself. They say love is blind, I suppose.'

'For what it's worth, I definitely think you're right to let Lewis follow his own path. He would only resent you otherwise.' She paused and took a sip of water. 'I remember your father. You're not a bit like him.'

He laughed. 'I'll take that as a compliment! He was a good man, very passionate about the farm, but very old school. Didn't believe in new-fangled machinery or modernisation. I came back from college, full of ideas, and he squashed them all. If it had been good enough for him all those years, he used to say, it would be good enough for me. We clashed over a lot of things, but I miss him still. He's been dead eight years now, and Mum died five years ago. She spent her last few years in a home which specialised in dementia. Emma and I tried our best, but we couldn't look after her when her needs became more complex. It was difficult.'

'I can imagine. I'm sorry.' She reached across the table to squeeze his hand. The contact, so casual and yet so intimate, sent heat searing through her body. She took a large swig of water while she scrambled for a less personal topic of conversation. 'What happened to the apple trees?' she asked. 'I remember picking up windfalls and your dad chasing me and other kids up the road, waving his stick, and shouting.'

'He ripped them out, just before I graduated from college.'

She was shocked by his reply. 'Why? They were his pride and joy!'

'The apples weren't making enough money. Then, we had a really bad year, and that was that. I think he always regretted it but, being Dad, he would never admit it. It was a shame. Your farm was always arable, wasn't it?'

'Yes, wheat and barley mostly. Please don't ask me any farming questions. That's the limit of my knowledge. My father believed girls had no place on the farm, other than cooking, cleaning, and bearing children, that is.' Her face became set as she spoke.

'I remember him vaguely. I know my parents had very little to do with yours, even though they were neighbours. They seemed to stay out of village life and kept themselves to themselves.'

'Apart from their church group,' she said tightly. 'My parents belonged to a small group of very strict Christians who called themselves Repentalists. As the name suggests, the focus was on repentance of sins and asking for forgiveness. They met and worshipped privately in each other's homes. The rector of the village church was far too "namby pamby" according to my father, so they formed their own community. I remember a lot of "hell and damnation" and, of course, it was led by the men. Women, like children, were supposed to keep their mouths shut.'

'That must've been difficult,' he offered carefully.

She shrugged. 'It was all I knew. Fortunately, when I was twelve, I was sent to boarding school.'

He smiled and decided to change the subject. 'Tell me about your business,' he said. 'I'm intrigued how you managed to build up such a successful operation. How did you get started?'

'Just luck, really. I trained as an accountant and was working for a firm in London. At that point, I was sharing a flat with two other girls. One of them worked for a small manufacturing company and, at her birthday party, I happened to meet her boss, Kevin. He was a nice man but I could see he was distracted, worried about something. We got talking and, when he found out I was an accountant, he asked me to look at his company's books. There was something wrong with the figures and he was worried his partner, who managed the money side, might be fiddling the business. Anyway, to cut a long story short, I discovered his suspicions were correct. He got rid of the partner, and invited me to join the business as company accountant. I accepted and soon learnt all there was to know about manufacturing coffee machines. As time went by, I made suggestions to streamline the business, and it became a lot more profitable. Kevin relied on my advice and, aged twenty-nine, I joined the board of directors. When he retired, I became MD and we expanded as technologies advanced, acquiring other small businesses along the way. And things just snowballed from there. Now, that company is just one strand of Ryecroft Industries. I invested in other manufacturing companies, usually businesses I thought had underused potential, and steered them in a more profitable direction. And that's pretty much it.'

He stared at her in admiration. 'It's an amazing story. You should write a book.'

She raised her eyebrows. 'The last thing I want is more publicity! It's one of the reasons I've been taking a step back from the company – that along with living in Wickthorpe, miles from the hub of it all. I've always preferred to let members of my team deal with PR.'

He nodded. 'Makes sense to me. And how has it been, taking a step back?'

She deliberated the question. 'Actually, quite enlightening. When I moved here, I thought this would be an opportunity to learn a bit more about myself, about what I want at this point in my life. I'm approaching my fiftieth birthday, I have all the money I could possibly want, I have no dependents other than my employees, and I've done nothing but work all my life. A friend suggested I use the time for a bit of introspection, see it as a well-earned break, and it was good advice.'

'And have you made any decisions about your life, moving forward?' he asked quietly.

'Not yet. I know now I love gardening. Definitely, I'd like to see more of the world. I travel a lot for business but then I just tend to see the insides of hotel rooms or corporate meeting rooms. There's usually very little time for anything else. But,' she shrugged her shoulders, 'obviously I can't do that at the moment, as I have to spend every night at Greenways Farm.' She paused before continuing. 'I still don't understand the rationale behind that will. If, as you say, my *dear departed mother,*' she said the words with an undertone of sarcasm, 'was concerned about the hate she knew would be vented in my direction, why on earth did she insist I return here to live? Why didn't she just leave me the house and be done with it? Or leave the house to the church, if that's what she wanted? And another thing, the money would have gone to Wickthorpe church, not the group she and my father were so much a part of. Why Wickthorpe church?'

He shook his head. 'I wish I could provide the answers to your questions but I honestly don't know. I do know that the rector, Wendy Robinson, became a frequent visitor after your dad died. She might know more. Other than that, I'm afraid I can't help. Did Hannah not leave you any indication of what she wanted? A letter left with the solicitor? Anything like that?'

'Nothing with the solicitor,' she said slowly. She remembered the box of personal effects, still untouched in one of the spare bedrooms. Perhaps it *was* time to face her past.

She lapsed into silence. Tom watched the mix of expressions flitting across her face and decided not to pry. Instead, he focused on finishing his lemon meringue pie and left her to her reflections. He did not want to spoil the atmosphere. Not again. 'That was delicious,' he declared, laying down his spoon, and patting his taut stomach. 'I won't need to eat for the rest of the day!'

'Me neither,' she smiled at him. 'This is such a fabulous place!'

His blue eyes darkened as they met hers. 'We'll come again,' he promised.

The rain was unrelenting and he drove home slowly, enjoying listening to a story she was telling about the first time she went to Japan on business. 'I was horribly underprepared,' she admitted. 'Not the business side of things ... I was very confident with all the facts and figures ... it was the cultural side. Gosh, it makes me cringe now to think about it.'

'What happened?'

She grinned. 'If I tell you, I may have to kill you. It would be so embarrassing if it ever came out.'

'You can trust me,' he said, eyes twinkling.

She gave him a sharp look. She *did* trust him, she realised; she wouldn't have embarked upon this story if she didn't. Not that it was a massive secret, in the scheme of things, but she had not joked about keeping the information to himself. 'Well, upon pain of death ... here goes. Basically, everything *not* to do in Japan, I did it. I was used to doing business in the States, where looking glamorous was a good way to get on. I went in wearing a short skirt, high heels, full make-up, lots of perfume, the works. That earned me my first black mark. The room was full of conservatively dressed men around a table. They stood as I entered and I sailed around the table, shaking hands with each one, and telling them all how happy I was to be there. Another fail. I hadn't waited for introductions, not realising that Japanese businessmen like to be greeted in order of importance. They each presented me with their business cards with a little bow. I took each one and, when I was shown my seat, slung them in a careless pile on the table to pick up later. Uh-oh! Business cards are a big thing in Japan, to be treated with respect. Worse, my pen wouldn't work when I needed to sign something and I turned the top card over to scribble on it, you know, to get the pen working. Huge mistake! That caused so much offence that the contract I had been about to sign was cancelled. I was mortified.' She shuddered. 'Tell me about your most embarrassing moment.'

He laughed. 'So many to choose from! Most of mine stem from my teenage years and some are X-rated. I think the worst, most awful, embarrassing moment of my life took place when I was fourteen and had my first proper kiss. Some of the kids in my year at school had paired up and there was lots of snogging going on behind the proverbial bike shed. That's when I realised girls could be interesting after all.'

'Ugh, a misogynist!' she exclaimed.

'Not at all. Just a typical teenager who became aware he liked girls as something other than mates. Anyway, there was this girl who had been making eyes at me. Her name was Felicia Blenkinghorn – I'll never forget that name – and she was up for a bit of snogging. Our lips met, I gave her the full works, pretty chuffed with myself. It seemed she enjoyed it, at the time. Obviously, I bragged about it to my mates, only to be told, by one of her friends, that she said I kissed like a cement mixer! The word got out and I was a laughing stock for about five minutes, although it seemed like forever at the time. It was a long while before I plucked up the courage to give it another go, with a different girl, I can tell you. You have to understand, I was a complete novice in the kissing department then, and things *have* improved a lot since.

She raised her eyebrows. 'You'll have to let me be the judge of that.'

Silence roared between them as he turned into her drive, his heart pounding. As he switched off the engine, he looked at her with a question in his eyes. 'Is that an invitation? If so, I accept.'

'Shall we go inside?' she said huskily.

CHAPTER 23

Monday morning dawned dark and forbidding. The heavy rain of the previous day had eased but hazy drizzle persisted. Honoraria threw a load of washing into the machine anyway. The forecast had said it would brighten up later and she was keen to get her laundry out on the line. Nothing like the outdoors to freshen up your linen.

Her life could do with a freshen-up too. It had been a long and difficult journey driving back from Oxford the day before. Torrential rain, and the resultant surface water on the road, considerably reduced visibility, forcing her to drive with extreme caution. By the time she reached home, her head was pounding and her nerves were in pieces. However, she prided herself on her resilience, and two strong cups of tea had been sufficient to restore her spirits. It had been a good trip, she decided, upon reflection. Apart from the disastrous date, she had enjoyed exploring some of the Oxford colleges. There was so much to see and insufficient time, arriving as she had on Friday evening and departing early afternoon on the Sunday. Next time, she would book herself in for a week, and not try to combine the visit with romance. In fact, she decided, with a twinge of regret, there would be no more SWS liaisons. At least for a while. Too many disappointments. Not worth all the effort.

And, disregarding sex and the odd spell of loneliness, there were benefits in being single. Generally, she was content with her own company, and liked being able to suit herself regarding her agenda. Edgar had always been bored by museums and historic places so such excursions had been limited during her marriage. Now she could please herself. Every cloud and all that ...

She hummed to herself as she went about her daily chores. Poor Mabel Littlebody; this time, one week earlier, her body had been discovered by one of her carers. Her death had been so sudden. You just never knew when the Grim Reaper might strike. Her thoughts centred upon those acquaintances whose age might make them vulnerable to such a visit. Gretchen Cooper, for one. The poor, old dear looked as frail as a twig in a sack. Burgeoning with Christian spirit, she resolved to phone Gretchen, and invite her round for a cup of tea and a piece of cake. It would mean a walk round to *The Pastry Parlour*, the village tearoom, to buy something delicious. Honoraria was much too busy this morning to bake. In fact, her mind spun on, she would suggest Gretchen met her there, and then she would not have to bother putting the hoover around. Not that her guest would notice. Gretchen was noticeably remiss in her own cleanliness, so was hardly likely to spot a bit of dust in Honoraria's pristine living room, but she had her standards. It would also be a chance to share her latest nugget of gossip, about young Freya Billington and her mystery man. Annoying, though, that she had been unable to identify him. From the distant and fleeting glimpse she had been afforded, she did not *think* it was anyone she knew. But there *had* been something familiar about him, a hint of recognition, which tickled the fringes of her brain like an unreachable itch. Who did he remind her of?

The wail of a siren drew her eyes to the window, just in time to see a police car race past, blue light flashing. Not the sort of thing you saw every day in Wickthorpe. It gave Honoraria pause and she wondered about its destination. She would never be surprised if it had something to do with the O'Gradys, at 22, Butchers Row. There had been trouble there before, and you only had to look at the state of their house to know what type of people they were. Drugs and all sorts! The son, who now must be in his thirties, had been arrested several times and had a spell in prison. As Honoraria turned away, a faint noise, growing ever louder, enticed her back. Another police car? No, this time, an ambulance.

'Goodness me!' she exclaimed aloud. 'I wonder what that's all about.' The noise faded and she moved away from the curtain. Hopefully, someone at *The Pastry Parlour* would know. She had better go and ring Gretchen …

***

Gretchen shuffled into the teashop with a toothy grin and wearing a shapeless print dress which hung from her bony frame like a hospital gown. At least she had remembered her false teeth today. Last time, she had forgotten and consumed a large slice of chocolate cake through a combination of inhalation, sucking and chomping, a process which quite put Honoraria off her own choice of coffee and walnut. Gretchen was a few minutes the wrong side of the appointed meeting time, and Honoraria was already ensconced at her favourite table, in the corner facing outwards so she could see everyone and everything. *She* was impeccably dressed, as usual, in a smart lemon and navy frock and matching navy shoes. Appearances were everything, after all.

'Good morning, Gretchen. Lovely to see you. Do have a seat.' She stood as her companion approached and gestured graciously to the chair opposite. 'I've not ordered yet. I said I'd *wait* for you.'

Gretchen failed to notice the pointed reference to her tardiness and nodded in response. 'Good thinking. If we both have tea, we can share a pot.'

Sally Chambers, the owner of *The Pastry Parlour*, arrived at the table wearing a red and white checked apron, bearing the logo of the establishment, and carrying a notepad. 'Hello, ladies. Isn't it lovely to see a bit of sunshine after all that rain?' she greeted them with a smile. 'You both look beautiful in your dresses. Makes me think that summer has arrived. Now, what can I get you? Today's cakes are lemon drizzle and strawberry shortcake, and we have all the usual menu available.'

'Strawberry shortcake and a pot of tea ... for two?' Honoraria raised her eyebrows.

Gretchen nodded. 'Yes please, and same for me,' she said eagerly. 'I'm famished.'

No surprise there. Honoraria kept her opinion to herself and plotted a way to steer the conversation to her Oxford news. 'So, Gretchen, what did you get up to this past weekend?' she asked casually.

Gretchen scratched her head. 'Blowed if I can remember,' she replied cheerfully. 'One day's much the same as another. What day was it yesterday? Sunday? Sunday's usually *The Antiques Roadshow*. I do like that Fiona Bruce. She always looks so elegant. And I think it was Clare who came in to do me yesterday ... or was it? No, it was a different one. Hadn't seen her before. Young girl. Sullen.' She wrinkled her nose. 'I hope I don't have her again.'

'You're talking about your carer?'

'Yes, except I don't want her. Clare is much nicer. She always brings me a little treat.' Gretchen gave a mischievous smile. 'You know ... biscuits or sweets or something. They're not supposed to, so I mustn't tell anyone. She's a good girl.'

Honoraria sighed. It really was no use trying to be subtle. 'I went to Oxford,' she announced.

'Orford? Very nice. What did you go there for?'

'Not Orford, *Oxford*,' Honoraria bellowed as Sally returned, holding a tray laden with dainty tea things.

'Oxford?' Sally asked, expertly transferring the pretty china teapot, matching cups, milk jug and sugar bowl to the table. 'I grew up in Oxford. Well, just outside actually, in a little village called ...'

She got no further as the door burst open and Valerie Hampton-Brown hastened over to their table. Her face was ashen.

'Valerie, whatever is the matter? Sit down. You look as if you've seen a ghost.' Honoraria squeezed out of her seat and steered the newcomer to the nearest chair.

Sally hovered anxiously. 'You do look pale, dear. Is everything alright?'

Valerie drew a quivering breath. 'I was on my way home,' she said, 'but then I saw you sitting there, and I thought I'd better come and tell you ... warn you.'

'Warn us about what?' Honoraria asked patiently. Honestly, she would not have expected someone like Valerie to be so dramatic! Lucky she was on hand, to instil some calm. 'Sally, would you mind fetching another cup of tea?'

'Of course.'

As the café owner returned to the kitchen, Honoraria took the liberty of laying her podgy fingers on Valerie's tweed clad arm. 'Tell us what's happened,' she said firmly, enjoying this rare moment of superiority. Momentous news was about to be revealed and she could not wait.

'I went to see Enid. We were going to plan the meeting.'

'The meeting?' Honoraria frowned. *What on earth was she going on about?*

'Yes, the meeting ...' Valerie took a quick glance over her shoulder, leant forward, and lowered her voice. 'The meeting to get people together ... to get rid of Deborah Ryecroft ... before she did any more damage. But we're too late.'

'Sandwich on two plates?' Gretchen piped up. 'I didn't catch what you said.'

'Anyway, Philip Holder came in,' Valerie continued, ignoring her. 'The police have cordoned off the path leading to the lake. There have been police cars, vans, ambulances, you name it, all parked down there.'

'Oh yes,' Honoraria chipped in, anxious to share her own intelligence. 'A police car and an ambulance sped by my house earlier this morning. I had quite forgotten. You say they went to Dark Water Lake?'

'Yes. Philip went to see what was going on but got moved back, told to go home. He asked what had happened but no one would tell him anything. Well, they wouldn't, would they?' She paused as Sally returned with Valerie's tea and the two slices of strawberry shortcake.

'Can I fetch you anything else?' she asked.

'No, thank you,' Valerie's voice was terse. 'I couldn't eat anything ... not after what's happened?'

'Oh dear. I thought you looked as if you've had a bit of a shock. Perhaps some sugar in your tea?'

Valerie shook her head and raised stricken eyes to the three expectant faces surrounding her. 'Philip hung around but there was nothing to see. Not from where he was standing. Others were there too. Naomi Clover, Rob Richards, John Davenport and that awful man ... you know, the *gay* one ... there was quite a crowd down there by the end, waiting to find out ...'

'Find out what?' Honoraria asked in frustrated tones. 'Just tell us, Valerie.'

'It's so awful.' Valerie covered her face with bejewelled fingers. 'I can hardly bear to say the words ...' They all held their breath during the tense silence which followed. At last, she withdrew her hands and spoke in a shaky whisper. 'In the lake ... they've found another *body*!'

CHAPTER 24

Martha's diary
30th April, 1645

I have much to write, both good and bad, such are the vagaries of our existence on this earth. Tis God's design for us that we suffer both sadness and joy in our lives and tis not my place to question Him. Still, tis most upsetting when woes occur.

First the joy! Prudence has been safely delivered of a baby girl. Twas a long and difficult birth and I confess to being much relieved, for both mother and babe, when the child was born. She has been named Mary Martha, after me, and indeed I am much honoured by the compliment. Dear Mary Martha is a sweet child and already full of smiles. It has taken Prudence a while to recoup her strength and I have done my best to help. Her husband, Gideon, works long hours and has had little sympathy for his wife's slow recovery, expecting his meals ready and everything at home as twas afore the birth. He has little patience with her poor health and so I do whatever I can to assist her. I confess I find Gideon a dour man but Prudence seems happy enough and she dotes on little Mary Martha.

Requests for my assistance with the sick and injured in the village have continued but I am sorry to admit not all have had a happy outcome. I was much distressed of late when a young girl I had been treating for an unknown malady passed away. The death was sudden. The girl, who had seemed improved when I last saw her, suffered a seizure from which there could be no recovery. Such things happen. I can only think that tis part of God's plan but tis difficult to take comfort from that. The child's mother was most distressed but thanked me anyway for my poor attempts at finding a cure. I was greatly humbled by her words and tried to give her solace but I fear I failed in that also. Twas a wretched day.

Then, only three days hence, there was a second death in the village, another of my patients. This time the deceased was a much older woman who had been coughing up blood. I had been treating her with the milk of sow thistle but her cough worsened and I knew not how to help her. When she died, her daughter was much distraught and accused me of poisoning her mother! I know twas her grief speaking but her words left me much disturbed. If others were persuaded that my intentions were wicked, it would not go well for us in Wickthorpe. Howe'er, since then, there have been no further deaths and folk are as eager for my help as they ever were.

I wrote afore of my fear of Roger Holley following his attempt to kiss me and worse. 'Pon that occasion, I told my husband of Holley's abominable intentions and how I had made my escape. Though I made light of the incident, laughing that Holley found me 'no easy pickings' and that he would think twice about foisting himself 'pon me in future, John was most disquieted. After such a tale, he was desirous of moving far from Wickthorpe but I was most reluctant to do so, protesting most vehemently against his proposal til he relented. In return, I swore to him I would ne'er venture out alone if it could be avoided. This I was more than willing to do to appease my husband. Howe'er, I must confess it has proved nigh impossible to keep that promise. Such an undertaking, to ne'er go out alone, is impossible for a woman with family responsibilities, to speak nothing of the requests for my help from others in the village. I said as much to my husband and he again warned me to take great care. Thus, I have taken pains to protect myself from future attacks, varying my daily routine and avoiding being alone as much as possible. Weeks passed and I had not so much as set eyes 'pon my adversary. My fear of him had grown less and I felt sure that, so long as I continued to exercise caution, he would not harm me.

Now I am convinced of it. The events of today prove tis so. This is what occurred.

Commonly, Prudence and I assist each other with our daily chores, finding companionship eases the burden of the work. However, she has been much fatigued of late, following the birth, and today I found myself alone by the river with Prudence's laundry as well as my own to wash. Josiah had stayed with Prudence and Mary Martha. The sun was shining and I was quite engrossed in my task when Roger Holley passed by. His appearance gave me quite a start and I braced myself for flight but I need not have worried. The man seemed much preoccupied and made great haste past me. Though he must have seen me, he made no acknowledgement of it. It appears Roger Holley is as anxious to avoid me as I am him!

Such knowledge has left me much relieved and I know John will feel the same when I give him such tidings this evening. My prayers have been answered. We are safe in Wickthorpe after all.

CHAPTER 25

Deborah stared through the window of the early evening train back from London, a secret smile playing on her lips, oblivious to fields and houses flashing past. Usually, she worked on the return trip. She should have been thinking about the meetings which had taken place that day, and considering the latest proposals put forward by Lainey Lewis, Strategy Director. Nothing wrong with the plans – all good ideas and she trusted in Lainey's ability to execute them – but she really could not concentrate on such matters. She had other, more interesting things to ponder ...

Tom Oldridge. Her whole body had sizzled all day. For the first time in her life, she had found herself daydreaming at inappropriate moments and having to ask for points to be repeated. Very unprofessional. But she didn't care. She was in love! Well, not love exactly – *let's not get carried away* – more the first flush of full-on lust. Feeling like a teenager, rather than a mature woman, and giddy with anticipation for nights to come.

The day before, he had closed the front door behind him and she had turned, somewhat mundanely, to ask if he would prefer tea or coffee. As her lips parted to speak, he had stepped forward and slid his arms around her waist. His head dipped; she lifted her chin. For a moment, they had stared into each other's eyes, his questioning, hers already darkening with the certainty of what was to follow. Then their mouths met, and she was lost.

The kiss started with agonising slowness; his lips caressed hers with such gentle reverence she pressed harder, demanding more. Things progressed swiftly from there and they were upstairs, naked, on her bed, urgent, desperate, out of control. That had never happened to her before. She had no idea why she had reacted to the feel of his lean, muscled body against hers with such passion and such a lack of inhibition. Even when sex with other men had been great, she was present, conscious of her actions, subtly retaining the upper hand. This time was different. She might have believed it was a one-off, but the second time, later, was just the same – an earth-shattering explosion of sensations which left her reeling. Already, she felt like an addict, counting the minutes until her next fix.

As the train pulled into Elmswell station, she grabbed her briefcase and leapt to her feet. When he left late last night, Tom said he would see her tonight but they had not set a time. She had sent him a text on the way home suggesting 7 p.m. That would give her time for a long bath to soak away travel odours and weariness. And to prepare ...

Back at Greenways Farm, she had just made herself a strong cup of tea when the doorbell rang. With a sigh, she padded through to the front door where she saw Tom's unmistakeable shape. Her pulse leapt and she rushed to let him in. 'Is it seven o'clock already?' she smiled as he stepped inside, shut the door, and gathered her into his arms. 'Mm,' she murmured against his stubbly cheek after a long, electrifying kiss. 'Déjà vu.' As she pulled his head towards her once more, already misty-eyed with arousal, his hands reached up to detach himself and give her a rueful smile.

'Much as I would like to make love to you right now, there's something I've got to tell you.' He stepped back, his face sombre, his eyes pools of sadness.

Not good news. Her heart lurched. 'What's happened?'

'Let's sit down. I could use a cup of tea myself.'

'In a minute,' she frowned, shrugging him off as he tried to steer her towards the kitchen. 'Just tell me.'

He exhaled and ran a hand through his hair. 'There is no easy way to say this. Another body has been found in Dark Water Lake. A woman.' He watched anxiously as she clutched at his arm, white-faced with shock.

'Oh God,' she breathed. 'Not again.' This time, she did not object as he sat her down. 'Who is it?'

'I'm afraid I don't know. The police haven't released details as yet. I guess there will be a formal identification and they will need to inform the family.

There are rumours flying about, of course ... typical village stuff ... awful really.'

'What are people saying?'

He shook his head. How could he tell her the biggest story doing the rounds was that she was responsible? 'Just wild guesses about the woman's identity. Nothing worth telling.'

'Who do they think it is?'

The knot in his chest, which had been there ever since he had been told, tightened. 'Best not to pre-empt the police announcement. They could be wrong.'

'Oh God,' she said again, wringing her hands as she rose from the stool and paced around the kitchen. 'It's someone I know.' He didn't deny it and, in the ensuing silence, she covered her face with her hands. 'I can't believe it's happening all over again. Perhaps I really *am* cursed.'

'Don't be daft.' He caught her hand as she stepped closer and folded her once more into his arms. 'This is nothing to do with you. You know that. I know it. Don't even think it.'

She gave a muffled snort against his shoulder. 'There are others who will think so.' In a flat, weary voice, she told him about the latest anonymous note she had received, just three days ago. With everything that had happened since, it had completely fled her mind. 'Maybe I *should* just leave.'

'Don't say that,' he said gently. 'Can I have a look at this note? It really seems to me you should tell the police.'

'I think they've got more important things to do right now, don't you?' She pulled the envelope from a kitchen drawer. 'Here it is. I was going to show you on Saturday but Felix and Jules were there. And then yesterday ... well, yesterday, there were other priorities.'

He flashed a quick grin. 'Quite right.' His face became serious as he unfolded the paper and read its contents. 'I don't like it,' he said. 'There is a clear threat here. You should tell the police.'

She shrugged. 'Maybe. Probably. Not now though. Not with what has happened today.'

He nodded and his arms tightened around her. 'Fair enough. Tomorrow though. I'll go with you if you like.'

She leaned back and gave him a tremulous smile. 'You're a kind man but I don't need anyone to hold my hand.'

'I know it.' His fingers tenderly caressed the side of her face. 'But I'd like to.'

A nugget of ice, in the centre of her heart, thawed at the tenderness in his eyes. It had been a very long time since anyone had looked out for her or wanted to protect her. For just a moment, she savoured the warm, fuzzy feeling it gave her, before the voice of logic reasserted itself. *You can't afford to rely on anyone. Remember how you've been let down in the past, how you've been hurt. You barely know this man. Don't let him get too close!* 'Thank you,' she said, pulling away from him and rubbing her arms. 'But I'll take care of it.' Her voice sounded unnecessarily harsh and she regretted the flicker of hurt she glimpsed in his eyes. But she was doing the right thing. Sex was one thing; the kind of mutual dependence he was offering was quite another.

'Fair enough,' he said again, the coolness in his voice matching hers. An awkward silence hung between them until he huffed out a sigh. 'I know you value your independence. I just wanted to help, that's all. I'll make some fresh tea. Would you like another cup?'

'Thank you.' Now she felt uncomfortable. She hadn't handled that well, but was unsure how to restore the situation. *Even more reason to keep your distance. Already, he's making you feel guilty when he doesn't get his own way.*

He placed a mug in front of her and sat down. 'Look, Debs,' he said, playing with the handle on his mug, 'I'm not very good at this stuff and, if I overstep the mark, it's fine for you to say.'

Her heart melted all over again. 'I'm not very good at it either ...' she began, when his ringtone interrupted her.

'It's Emma,' he said, looking at the screen. 'I'd better answer. Hi Em.' She watched as he listened, lines of grief carving grooves into his face. Sensing her eyes upon him, he turned away, shoulders hunched, phone clamped to his ear. At last, he spoke but his words offered no clue. 'I'm at Debs' house. I'll be back as soon as I can.'

The call ended and he swung around to face her. 'It's the worst possible news,' he said. 'The police have released the name of the dead girl.' He paused and shook his head.

'And?' she asked, the weight in her chest too heavy to bear.

He swallowed, his eyes clouded with anguish. 'It's Freya Billington.'

CHAPTER 26

The village of Wickthorpe was in mourning. Freya Billington was one of their own, a golden child. The Billingtons may have moved to the village a mere five years ago, to take over the run-down *Lamb Inn,* but they had endeared themselves to most of the population. There had been those who sneered at the Billingtons' success, particularly those who disapproved of 'newcomers' to the village. These people were now the most vocal in leading the eulogies.

'It's hard to take in.' Enid Green clucked her teeth together and dabbed at her eye with an embroidered, cotton handkerchief, rediscovered for the occasion. 'I still can't believe it. That poor, young girl. Do the police know who did it? I, for one, could point them in the right direction.'

'Mum, I'm not sure they've found any evidence of foul play. People are saying she may have taken her own life. Either way, it's incredibly sad.' Ava weighed the parcel Valerie Hampton-Brown had given her. Ordinary, mundane routines – they were keeping her going. Hearing her mother witter on, feigning sympathy for a family about whom she had always moaned, was wearing her patience to its limit. 'That will be £3.20, please.'

Valerie tipped the correct coins from her Burberry leather purse and frowned. 'Suicide? I don't believe it! Why on earth would that lovely girl want to take her own life? She had everything to live for. That's ridiculous!'

'Quite right, Valerie,' Enid chimed in. 'There are dark forces at work here. I am surprised the police haven't taken *that woman* in for questioning.'

Ava sighed. No point saying anything. People like the Hampton-Browns, Philip Holder and her mother had already made up their minds. She had heard plenty of such talk over the past few days, since the awful discovery. Fear and superstition had swamped the village and people were nervous. If something like this could happen to Freya Billington, who knew who would be next?

Lips pursed, Valerie stood by Enid. 'I phoned the Incident Room yesterday,' she muttered, her voice bitter. 'Left my number and was told someone would call me back. But no one has. If someone doesn't get in touch soon, I'll ring our good friend, Peter Allbright. He's the Chief Constable, you know.'

'Good idea, Valerie. Apparently, they have interviewed Honoraria Simpson–Fairchild,' Enid told her.

'Really? What on earth for?'

'She was here yesterday, full of the most bizarre tale. I have to say, I don't know whether to believe her or not. According to her, Freya Billington was in Oxford last Saturday with a mystery man. Apparently, Honoraria witnessed it and had passed that information to detectives assigned to the case.'

'Really?' Valerie snorted again. 'In Oxford? What on earth was she doing there?'

'No one knows, Valerie. That's what the police are trying to find out.'

'Not Freya, *Honoraria*! What was *she* doing in Oxford?' Valerie crossed her arms impatiently.

'Oh. Well, she said it was a sight–seeing trip, exploring the history of the city for the History Club. You know what she's like,' Enid told her.

'Hmph. She was probably mistaken. I can't think what Freya Billington would be doing in Oxford. I heard she had spent the weekend in Cambridge. Typical of Honoraria to want to get in on the action though,' Valerie sneered.

'No, from what I was told, Freya *wasn't* in Cambridge at all. She had told her parents that's where she was going, staying with a friend, but apparently the friend knew nothing about it. It's all a bit of a mystery. And that means she *could* have been in Oxford.'

Valerie turned back to Ava, unhappy that Enid seemed to be one step ahead of her. 'Why do you say the police think she committed suicide? What evidence do they have?'

Ava pulled a face, reluctant to be drawn into gossip but helpless in the face of such a direct question. 'They found her phone in the undergrowth at the edge of the water. Apparently, she had typed out a message saying as much. It was intended for her mum but never sent.'

'Where did you hear that?' Enid demanded, annoyed she had not been privy to such information earlier.

'I went round to see Sally and Gerald yesterday evening, after we closed, just to see if I could do anything for them and to say how sorry we were,' Ava admitted. 'They are such lovely people. And absolutely devastated, as *you* can imagine, Valerie,' she added, acknowledging the other woman's loss of a child.

'What did they tell you?' Enid demanded.

'I didn't go for information, just to offer my support,' Ava replied quietly. She was not about to tell the village's biggest gossips how she had sat and held Sally's hand, as the distraught mother had poured out her grief, shaking with disbelief. Sally Billington needed friends, not people who would tell the world the private information she had disclosed. Both she and her husband had been questioned at length about the state of their daughter's mind and they admitted Freya had not been herself in recent weeks. It had been a huge shock, though, to discover their daughter was ten weeks pregnant when she died. That was news Ava was determined to keep to herself for the moment. Doubtless, people would soon find out but not from her.

Sally had told Ava of Freya's boyfriend, about whom her daughter had been so secretive, which was why Honoraria's story, and her supposed sighting, rang true. But who knew the truth behind it all? Not the police, according to Sally.

So far, the forensic team had detected no specific evidence to suggest murder. Freya had died from drowning. A substance had been detected in the body, an antidepressant by all accounts, but an empty packet of pills had been found near Freya's phone, along with a plastic bottle of water. There was no record of such being prescribed by her doctor, Dr Singh, at Wickthorpe surgery but Freya worked at the pharmacy. She had access to the medication. Only the victim's fingerprints were found on the items and no marks were identified on Freya's body to suggest foul play. Police had informed the family there was no indication a third party was present at the time of death. Footprints, size ten, near where the phone was found, most likely belonged to a walker who had previously taken that route. The case remained under investigation and nothing had been ruled out, detectives insisted. However, Sally tearfully confided to Ava that a verdict of suicide was most likely to be the outcome of their investigations.

'I know she would never take her own life,' she sobbed. 'She had been a bit quiet the past few weeks but she was not suicidal. Not at all. I would have known. We are so close. Or we were ...'

Ava did not know what to believe. Freya had always seemed so cheerful and vibrant; it did not seem possible ... But who knew the real state of another person's mental health? Ava suspected there would be the same kind of incredulity were she to reveal that she had, in black moments of misery and despair, considered taking her own life. Everyone has secrets, she thought. Only Freya knew the truth of it and she would be forever silent.

'Hmph,' Enid grunted, dragging her back to the present. 'Well, whatever you say, I'm certain Deborah Ryecroft has got something to do with it. Strange how none of this happened when she wasn't here.'

'People still died, Mum,' Ava said before she could stop herself.

'Yes, but not in mysterious circumstances. You think about it. Before she left Wickthorpe back in the eighties, we had two deaths, both young people, including Valerie's own dear son. Now she's back and, within three months, we have two more suspicious deaths.'

'I hardly think you can include Mabel Littlebody. She was ninety-two and died in her sleep!' Ava struggled to conceal her exasperation and received a fierce glare from her mother in return.

'There was nothing wrong with Mabel until that woman visited her.' Enid snorted before turning once more to Valerie. 'The sooner we do something, the better.'

Valerie raised her eyebrows and directed a furtive glance towards the counter where Ava was still standing. 'Not now, Enid,' she said under her breath.

'What was that? Speak up, dear!'

'I said I'd better be going. John and I will pick you up at twenty to seven for the History Society meeting.' Valerie gave her another meaningful look as she left. 'You said you would appreciate a lift, as Ava wasn't going tonight.'

Ava looked up sharply. That was news to her!

'Oh ... I see. Yes, I'll be ready. Goodbye, my dear. Look after yourself and make sure you lock your doors. You can't be too careful.' Enid waved her off and immediately launched her wrath at her daughter. 'Why didn't you tell me you'd been to see the Billingtons? I would have come with you.'

Ava sighed. 'You've never liked the Billingtons, Mum. You've often said they gave themselves airs and graces and that you would not set foot in that pub while they were there. How was I to know you would want to come with me?'

'Yes, well ...' Enid huffed. 'It would be the Christian thing to do. Perhaps we should go this afternoon?'

Over my dead body, Ava thought. Aloud, she said, 'I told Sally to ring me if she wanted anything. It would be wrong to keep intruding. And why did you tell Valerie I wasn't going to the History Society meeting tonight?'

'I didn't think you were,' Enid proclaimed with startled innocence. 'I was sure you had said you didn't feel up to it.'

Ava knew she had not but allowed the lie to go unchallenged. If her mother and Valerie Hampton-Brown were going to spend the evening complaining about Deborah Ryecroft, she was quite happy to give the meeting a miss. And respite from Enid's company was always welcome. She quietly set about unpacking a delivery of stationery which had arrived that morning.

Meanwhile, Enid sat smouldering. Ava was so secretive. Fancy taking it upon herself to visit Sally Billington without even mentioning it to her own grieving mother! She was sure Ava knew more than she had revealed just now, too. She would put nothing past her. Well, Ava was not the only one with secrets ...

***

Work should have helped but the pall of shock and grief shrouding Wickthorpe Health Centre provided no respite. Julie Green smiled at patients as she dealt with appointments and enquiries until her face felt numb with the effort of it all but inside her stomach churned with misery and fear. Freya

Billington had been a colleague, someone she knew, young and full of life. And now she was dead. It was impossible to comprehend. Truly awful. Julie could not help but think of her own two girls and be terrified for them. If it could happen to Freya ...

Yet, as horrific as those thoughts were, they were not what bothered her the most. *Andrew!* Detectives had visited the family home more than once, over the past few days, to question him. And he had lied, to her at least. She did not know what to believe anymore.

Last weekend, when Freya drowned, Andrew was away. He told her he was on a stag do for an old school friend; someone she did not know. That story proved to be untrue. When the police asked his whereabouts, she overheard him stating he was on what should have been a fishing trip with his mates, Mick and Steve. The weather put paid to any fishing so they had spent the weekend at Steve's house in Basildon. Steve was unmarried so it was just the three of them, Andrew said, all smiles and overblown charm. Mick and Steve had corroborated the story and the police were satisfied ... for now.

But Julie was left fretting with anxiety. Where *had* Andrew been? She did not for one second believe he had been with Mick and Steve. In the past, his two mates had covered up for him on more than one occasion, usually when her husband was with another woman. That was why he had pretended to her he was at a stag do, a tale which would have been no use for detectives who would soon discover the lie. So far, she had not challenged Andrew about it. The truth was she was too scared of what she might find out.

How could she voice her horrible suspicion that the man everyone was talking about, Freya Billington's mystery man, could be her husband?

***

Honoraria pushed a vacuum cleaner around her cottage that same afternoon, fussing over the latest speculation about Freya Billington's death. Things did not add up. *Suicide?* She did not believe it. Having seen Freya in Oxford that fateful weekend, it made no sense. The girl had been smiling; she looked happy. Certainly not suicidal. But what had happened to her if not that? An accident? Improbable, given what she had learnt about the phone message and the empty packet of pills. *Murder* then? She shuddered.

Something to do with that mystery man she had seen in Oxford? Her image of the couple, strolling along the street, returned once more, frustratingly fuzzy in her memory. *An older man. Probably married.* But who was he? There was *definitely* something familiar about him. For a while, she was convinced it was that Richards chap, the one who had found the body. He was dark-haired and wore heavy-rimmed glasses when he was driving. She said as much to that nice, young officer who had taken her statement but he didn't seem to be too interested. Someone else later told her that the police had initially been suspicious of him but his wife had given him an alibi. Well, she would, wouldn't she? But anyway, when she saw him coming out of the village shop, she realised she was mistaken. The man she had seen in Oxford was taller and broader in the shoulders. Rob Richards was rather a puny, little man.

Her thoughts turned to the History Society meeting that evening. The resurgence of 'witch' speculation in the village had certainly sparked interest in her little club and she had high hopes it would continue. However, after the record attendance at Dorothy Fairgrove's talk, a lecture by an ex-colleague, about Catholicism after the Reformation, had not been popular. Tonight, to save precious club funds, she had decided to host the meeting at home, especially as she had been unable to secure a speaker. The agenda featured an informal follow-up to Dorothy's talk. Her plan had been to focus on the original Wickthorpe Witch, Martha Lightbody, and discuss what had happened to her. She had been able to discover no record of Martha's burial in Wickthorpe. Did that mean the theory, that Martha survived the trial by drowning and escaped, was correct? It was a fascinating mystery – one she would love to solve. She had written to several local historians and put a message on the East Anglian History Society online bulletin board, asking people to check their parish registers to see if Martha's death had been recorded elsewhere. So far, she had heard nothing back. She was hoping History Society members might have suggestions, although she rather doubted they would. The rector, Wendy Robinson, always showed plenty of interest, but the others ... well, there was not a lot of hope. This morning, Enid Green had told her the Hampton-Browns were coming to tonight's meeting. She wondered anxiously if she should have planned another talk. The last thing she wanted was Valerie getting all emotional again. But it was too late now. At least there was time to pick up some of those tasty, home-made, chocolate biscuits from the bakery. She quaked at the thought of offering the Hampton-Browns a lowly custard cream.

***

Jane Holley toyed listlessly with a magazine. Freya Billington's death had been such a shock. Since the grisly discovery of the body on Monday morning, she had been unable to face work and, after two consecutive, sleepless nights, resorted to taking tablets which knocked her out. They did not stop the dreams though, vivid and detailed. As if it had happened yesterday. Reminding her of her rotten core beneath the polished veneer. *Ayesha Khan.* She had not thought of her for years but Deborah Ryecroft's return brought it all back: the horror; the guilt; the agonising awfulness of it; the daily struggle pretending she was a good person. And now it had happened again – another drowning in Dark Water Lake. The same accusations directed at Deborah Ryecroft, the *Wickthorpe Witch*, by ignorant villagers. Her conscience, ravaged by both shame and fear, could not bear it.

Worse still, the dead girl was Freya Billington who worked in the pharmacy. A colleague. Her protegee. Whilst they had not been close, the sense of loss had struck her like a physical blow, leaving her splintered and questioning her own existence. How could it be that Freya's bright light was snuffed out while her dull, damaged soul lived on?

Seb was unaffected by it all, going about his business as usual, albeit with a demeanour of grief. His patients might be fooled but she knew better; her husband had empathy for no one. This morning, annoyed at her malingering, he ordered her to pull herself together.

'The practice pharmacy is currently short of two employees and people still need their medication,' he snapped.

She could not be bothered to argue but remained in her bed, eyes closed, until the slam of the front door signalled his departure. How could she face people when she felt like this?

Strangely, Seb had not rubbished the rumours circulating about Deborah Ryecroft as she would have thought he would. 'People are entitled to their opinions,' he said, 'and the coincidence of another drowning is hard to ignore. Perhaps there *is* something in this village curse after all.' How could her husband, a man of science, believe such a thing? But she said nothing. How *could* she without disclosing her own culpability? Seb was aware of her dislike of Deborah, mildly amused by it, but unaware of the reason for it. And she planned to keep it that way.

Jane harboured no illusions about her marriage. From the first, Seb was pathologically unfaithful. She discovered his infidelity early on and, since then, he had made no secret of it. For a time, she had bitterly wondered if Debbie Ryecroft was to be his next conquest, the way he had fawned over her at Tom Oldridge's house, but as far as she knew that had not happened. Perhaps she had turned him down and her rejection had been behind the unexpected comment he had made about her? If so, her respect for the woman would go up a notch. Not many were able to resist Seb's charm. Knowing him as she did, it amazed her how women failed to see through him. But then, neither had she, not at first. She had been too much in love. Then, she would have done anything for him, even sold her soul. And, she supposed, she had done just that. The lies she had told for him were a marriage bargain from which there was no turning back ...

In the early days, she had revelled in her acquisition of such a husband. She saw the looks they drew as a couple and knew people wondered how she had managed to snare such a gorgeous, younger man. He was eight years her junior but his youthful, good looks made the age gap seem wider. She had exulted in her triumph, smug in the knowledge he had chosen *her* to be his wife. And they were blessed with two lovely sons. How happy she had been, relishing the envy of other women! How shallow she was! Even now, she and Seb took care to present the united image of a happily-married couple. It suited them both. But, in the bitter, unforgiving light of middle age, how she regretted choices made in unscrupulous youth! And it was too late now. She and Seb were shackled together and neither of them could escape that fact.

Nothing seemed to faze Seb. He had always been unencumbered by a conscience and concerned only for himself. This morning, he had casually mentioned, should the police come calling, he expected her to tell them they spent last weekend together at home. She was not surprised by his request. Apparently, he had been with a married woman and did not want her husband finding out. *Didn't want to risk his own unsullied reputation more like!* So many times she had covered for him! Lying had become the fabric of her existence. It did not bother her before. Now, with Deborah Ryecroft back in Wickthorpe and the ancient curse echoing in each of its corners, it did.

What would people say if they knew what *really* happened in Dark Water Lake all those years ago? The fear of it consumed her. With a whimper, she huddled deeper in the chair and pulled her arms around her. Was this how Melissa felt before depression drove her to take her own life? A part of her wished she could end it all but she did not have that sort of courage and she had her sons to think about, Luke and James. They were in London, both training to become doctors, like their dad. A burst of maternal pride blossomed briefly. *Her beautiful boys ...* but they had their own lives now, rarely returning home and, when they did, accompanied by girlfriends – brash, confident women who joked with Seb and largely ignored her. Pride gave way to self-pity. She had never felt so alone.

Previously, her faith in God's mercy had brought her comfort. If she repented her sins to him, they would be forgiven. Her conscience thus remained untroubled by past mistakes. Since returning to Wickthorpe, she had been a regular attendee at St Mary's Church and had found consolation in prayers, the rituals of worship and words of the Bible. Religion and charity work gave her purpose and her life some meaning. Recently, though, she knew she had been kidding herself. Her token repentance was not enough. There would be no forgiveness for her when she faced her day of reckoning.

Wendy Robinson, concerned by the extent of Jane's grief at Freya's death, had been visiting daily and advised counselling. 'I'm here for you if you want to talk,' the rector had said. Jane had been tempted yesterday, when they had sat praying together, to confess everything but the words had stuck in her throat and the moment had passed. Now she was glad she had kept silent. The past was her cross to bear; her suffering was her penance. It was the price she had to pay to keep her secret.

CHAPTER 27

For Deborah, it was a relief to spend the day in London. The discovery of Freya Billington's body, three days earlier, had rocked her world off its axis and she had struggled to regain her equilibrium. Her nightmare, featuring the blonde-haired body in the water, assumed horrific significance in the light of the tragedy, the weight of it a huge burden. The dream felt like a premonition but how could it be? How could her subconscious know Freya would drown in Dark Water Lake? Everything she previously believed was thrown into question. There had been two deaths, two drownings, and she had a connection to both. Impossible ... yet it had happened. Her distress at the news was increased tenfold by the fear she was in some way culpable. Should she have warned Freya or her family? Only later, she realised the nightmare had occurred on Sunday morning when Freya, by all accounts, was already dead. The realisation failed to bring her comfort.

The countryside was bathed in a beautiful, golden glow as she headed on the train back towards Suffolk. It seemed wrong, somehow, that nature should revel in her splendours when others were experiencing such grief. Her heart ached for Freya's family. Tom had told her Emma was spending quite a lot of time at *The Lamb Inn*, supporting Rick, who lived there with his parents. It had been awful for the whole village and Deborah had kept a low profile, aware her presence would only anger those who believed she was responsible. How could she blame them? Yesterday, she had received a visit from two police officers, DI Honeysuckle and DS Everard. It had not been a surprise. She had suspected it would not be long before someone made accusations against her. Lulled by the rhythmic rocking of the train, her mind drifted back to the interview …

DS Everard was a portly man in his forties with a round, balding head, fleshy jowls and a bulbous nose. His superior officer, a tall woman with sharp, brown eyes, had a clipped way of speaking which put Deborah on edge. After she had invited them in and offered coffee, they questioned her regarding her whereabouts over the course of the previous weekend, particularly Saturday evening and Sunday morning. They wanted to know precise timings. When had she returned to Greenways Farm after the meal at Orchard Farm? What time had Tom Oldridge picked her up for Sunday lunch? Having determined she was alone with no alibi for the best part of twelve hours, DI Honeysuckle had moved on to Deborah's relationship with Freya Billington.

'I'd met her in passing a few times,' Deborah shrugged, 'but I didn't know her. I've only lived here for three months. I have been to *The Lamb Inn* on two separate occasions and both times she was waitressing. The only other time I saw her was at a drinks party organised by Tom Oldridge when I first arrived in the village. I spoke to her then and thought she seemed very pleasant. That is all I can tell you.'

There was a slight pause before DS Everard piped up for the first time. He spoke slowly in a broad Suffolk accent. 'It has come to our attention that you were questioned with regard to another drowning, in the same lake, thirty-four years ago.' He consulted his notebook. 'Ayesha Khan. You were there when the incident occurred.'

Deborah sighed but said nothing. Her mind flew back to the interviews which took place at Bury St Edmunds police station, with her parents in silent attendance, after Ayesha had been declared dead. The room used for her interrogation was small: no windows, whitewashed walls and an odour of stale sweat. She had told the unvarnished truth but no one seemed to believe her, including both Elijah and Hannah Ryecroft. The whole thing had seemed unreal and she had been in shock. She had just witnessed the death of her best friend and, instead of being consoled, she was accused of murder.

That was down to the other two girls involved. When they had gone for help, they concocted a story in which they were totally blameless and which cast her as the villain. Both girls came from wealthy families, well respected in the village. Deborah was considered odd, a loner, an outsider. As rumours abounded, the population of Wickthorpe made up their minds. *Guilty.* There was talk of the village curse and the original witch, Martha Lightbody. Many were convinced she must be a direct descendant of the woman who uttered those fateful words, back in 1645, condemning villagers to the curse which blighted them.

The only people to support Deborah's story, and to accuse the other girls of lying, were Ayesha's devastated parents. They knew Deborah, they said. She and their shy daughter had been friends since the Khans arrived in Wickthorpe to run the village shop in 1982. And the other girls were bullies. Ayesha had been subjected to racist abuse by many, but especially those two. No one wanted to listen. The Khans were second-generation immigrants and overwhelmed with heartache. Their views were dismissed as unreliable. Villagers felt sorry for them – of course, they did – but *they* knew the truth.

As there was no physical evidence to suggest Ayesha's death was anything other than accidental, Deborah was never charged. But the damage was done and her life became unbearable. When another teenager died in tragic circumstances near Dark Water Lake, this time in a car accident, many claimed Deborah was responsible for that also. The deaths of two young people, cut down at the cusp of adulthood, could not be a coincidence. It had been a huge relief for everyone when she had fled to London in September and had not returned. She had found a temporary nannying job when her father told her, after what had happened, he was not prepared to fork out more school fees. After the inquest, the Khans also left Wickthorpe for good. Life moved on and villagers eventually found other topics, and people, for discussion and dissection.

'Ms Ryecroft!'

Deborah's jolted at the impatient voice of the senior inquisitor and realised she had missed a question. 'Sorry, could you repeat that, please?'

'I asked why you decided to return to Wickthorpe, given your past history?' the inspector snapped. When Deborah did not answer immediately, she continued, 'Your work is in London. You didn't visit when your parents were alive. It seems a strange decision.'

Deborah lifted her chin and met the other woman's stare. 'The terms of my mother's will stated I must live here to inherit the house. I can work from home and travel to the London office when I need to. Hence, that is what I'm doing,' she replied coolly.

'Hm.' Detective Inspector Honeysuckle scrunched her lips together in a show of scepticism. 'Ms Ryecroft.' Each syllable was spat into the air like an exclamation mark. 'Your wealth is well documented. Are you seriously expecting us to believe your decision to return was driven by money?'

'That's not what I said.' Deborah's tone was equally cutting. 'The money had *nothing* to do with it.' She paused. The situation was complicated and, she realised with a jolt of self-awareness, she had shelved fully rationalising it herself. She huffed out a breath. 'It was my childhood home. It meant something to me.' Even as she said the words, she squirmed at the blatant lie. 'And it provided the opportunity for a change.' That was nearer the truth but the two detectives remained unimpressed. She caught the exchange of doubting looks between them and continued. 'Also, I guess it was a chance to set the record straight. When Ayesha drowned, people blamed me. I was sixteen years old; I had just lost my best friend and I was treated like a criminal. No surprise, I wanted to escape from the village and never return. And that's what I did. But I'm not that person anymore. Spiteful gossip can't hurt me and I'm no longer prepared to run away.' Her voice grew more impassioned. 'Greenways Farm is rightfully mine and no one is going to scare me away from it.'

'What do you mean, *scare* you away?' The detective inspector jumped on her words. 'Ms Ryecroft, during our investigation, we have become aware of a certain amount of ... er, ill-feeling ... towards you, and you must be aware of what some villagers are saying. But are you telling us that someone is trying to scare you away? Have you received threats?'

Deborah nodded. 'Several. Anonymous notes, but I threw the earlier ones away.' She had not intended to mention them but now seemed as good a time as any. Wordlessly, she rose to fetch the latest one, while the officers put on gloves.

They read without comment, before putting the note back into its envelope and into an evidence bag.

'No stamps. Were they always posted through your door in envelopes like these?' DI Honeysuckle asked.

'Yes, when I was out. I found them when I came home.'

'And how many, in total, would you say you received?'

Deborah mulled it over. 'Four, I think. Possibly five. The first one appeared the day after I arrived; then at regular intervals after that.'

'Let us know if you receive another,' the DI instructed, 'and take extra precautions to keep yourself safe. These are probably empty threats but you should be careful.'

The sudden sound of tapping at the window, where a bluetit was trying to peck his way through, made all three of them jump. Despite the strangeness of the situation, Deborah smiled. Since she had put out feeders, a variety of birds were frequent visitors to her garden. Seeing them brought unexpected pleasure.

'Little blighters,' DS Everard commented. 'My wife insists on feeding them. Spends a fortune!'

'I know what you mean,' Deborah agreed. 'It does cost a lot to feed them but as you said ...' she added with a sardonic smile, 'I have plenty of money.'

DI Honeysuckle, unimpressed by the interlude, turned attention swiftly back to Deborah. 'Just to go back to your version of events in 1988, when Ayesha Khan drowned,' she said, 'why do you think the other girls would make up a story to blame you?'

Deborah hunched her shoulders. 'I'm sure you've read the reports taken at the time. We were sixteen-year-old girls and they didn't like me. They also wanted to clear themselves of any blame. In my statement, I said the girls had invited us swimming and then tricked us, by taking us to the lake which everyone knew was dangerous. They tried to bully us into going in. I refused but Ayesha wanted to prove herself to them. She thought her life would be better if she could get them on side.' She shrugged. 'I tried to persuade her otherwise but she wouldn't listen.'

'Shouldn't you have done more to stop her?'

Deborah closed her eyes, the abrupt question slicing at the tenderest part of her. 'Yes,' she admitted quietly. 'I wish I had. But she surprised me. I didn't think she'd really go through with it. To be fair, I don't think Jane and Melissa did either. They thought we would both refuse and they could taunt us about it. Childish stuff. But Ayesha stripped down to her swimsuit and was in the water, almost before we knew what was happening. Then she was swimming ... and it was too late.' She opened her eyes to see both officers watching her with flat, expressionless stares. 'Afterwards, when the others went for help, I managed to reach Ayesha ... but I was too late. I tried to get her out of the water but the bank was too steep. In the end, I managed to climb out but I had to leave her there. And wait. It seemed to take forever before anyone arrived. The police took me home and explained to my parents what had happened.' She chose not to mention how angry her father had been. 'The next day, I was taken to the station and interviewed. Unsurprisingly, my story did not match what Jane and Melissa had claimed. They were just protecting themselves,' she said in a voice devoid of emotion, 'and throwing suspicion in my direction for good measure. People believed them, not me, and there was even talk of charging me with murder.' She shook her head. 'I didn't kill my best friend,' she said firmly, in case there was any doubt, 'and I had nothing to do with whatever happened to Freya Billington.'

A moment's silence, broken by the striking of the church clock. 'Thank you, Ms Ryecroft.' DI Honeysuckle rose in one fluid motion, leaving her sergeant scrambling to gather up his case. 'Let us know if you receive any more threats. Here is my card. We'll be in touch if we need to ask you any further questions.'

Deborah had sat for a long time, twisting the card between her fingers, mulling things over. She could not leave Wickthorpe now, even if she wanted to. There would be no running away; no allowing others to question her innocence and vilify her name. When she told the police she wasn't about to let anyone scare her away, she spoke the truth, but there was more to it than that. She thought the past could no longer hurt her but she was wrong. A reason for staying was to confront it, once and for all, so she really *could* put it behind her. Only then could she plan her future. Her thoughts strayed once more to her mother's letter. The first step was to read it. Soon, she promised herself ...

The train's arrival at Elmswell station jerked Deborah back to the present. It was early evening but still warm. Her car had been parked in full sun and seemed unbearably hot. With a sigh, she started the engine and headed homewards, remembering her giddy excitement over her burgeoning relationship with Tom Oldridge just a few days earlier. It seemed a lifetime ago. The passion they had shared no longer seemed real. She hoped the kaleidoscope would tilt back to recapture those glorious colours but, for now, Wickthorpe seemed a grim, grey place.

As Deborah pulled into her drive, she was struck by the feeling something was wrong. The house looked just the same but the sense of disquiet refused to leave her. With trepidation, she opened the front door, disarmed her alarm system and stopped dead. Another crisp, white envelope lay on the mat, unmarked, just like its predecessors. She swallowed and bent to retrieve it. Somehow, with Freya Billington fresh in her mind, it seemed even more menacing. With trembling fingers, she split the envelope and pulled out the sheet of paper. This time there were just three words:

You were warned.

Fear fizzed through her body. Something had happened ... or was going to happen. She lifted her head to survey the hallway. Everything seemed in its place, just as she had left it that morning, but the hairs on the back of her neck screamed danger. Was someone inside, waiting for her?

Heart thudding, she backed out of the door and onto the gravel. All was quiet, eerily so. The air felt dense and heavy with hazard. She broke into a run towards her car, cursing the heels impeding her progress. No one appeared. She grabbed the car door handle. Locked. The keys were in her bag, abandoned by the door. Her phone too.

'Bloody hell!' she muttered, setting off at pace down the drive. She reached Green Lane and slowed to a walk. No one was after her. No immediate threat. She crossed the road and headed for Kai and Phil's place. They were her best bet. Breathing more evenly, she rang the doorbell and Kai answered, almost instantly, wiping his hands on an orange apron bearing the slogan *One Fine Gay*.

'This is a nice surprise,' he drawled. 'Come on in. Phil's in the kitchen refusing to make me a gin.' He gave her a cheeky grin. 'Now, he'll have to relent, especially if you have one.'

She stepped inside. The normality of Kai's greeting felt warm and comforting. Releasing the tension from her shoulders with one deep exhalation, she wondered if she had over-reacted. Away from her house, her flight now seemed a bit dramatic. 'Kai, can I borrow your phone please?' Despite such thoughts, she failed to prevent the quaver in her voice.

'Is everything alright, Deborah? You look a bit pale.'

She bit her lip. 'I hope so but I'm not sure.' She passed him the note she had been clutching in her fist.'

'Hellfire,' he whistled. 'This sounds like a threat. You'll be needing a stiff drink. Phil, a large gin for Debs ... and I'll have one while you're going.' He gave her a wink as he squeezed her arm. 'Come, sit down and tell us all about it.'

'First, I need to call the police. When I saw the note, I just dropped everything and ran. That's why I need a phone.'

'The police! Good Lord, what's happened?' Phil Abbott, a tall man with tousled blond hair and muscles which told of hours in the gym, appeared clutching the gin bottle. The spaniel, Jez, scampered to greet her too, demanding attention, her tail whizzing round in delight.

'Debs has been threatened,' Kai said, handing him the note. 'She needs to call the police.' He passed her his phone.

'Thank you.' She hesitated. DI Honeysuckle's card was tucked inside her bag. Was this serious enough to dial 999? 'Do you think I should?'

'Absolutely. Anonymous threats like that should be taken seriously,' Kai nodded.

Phil frowned. 'It could be nothing, just a nasty prank,' he said. 'But it doesn't sound like it's the first threat. Have you had notes like this before?'

'Unfortunately, yes.' Quickly, she filled them in, including the advice received yesterday from the police officer. 'But I've left DI Honeysuckle's card in my bag.'

'999 it is then,' Kai said cheerfully. 'You need the police to check the house is safe for you to enter.'

'Or we could go and check.' Phil set down the bottle, and raised his eyebrows at Kai. 'Come on. Get your big boy pants on.'

'Already wearing them,' Kai replied. 'You know I need them.' He gave his partner a mischievous nudge.

Phil rolled his eyes. 'Come on then, big boy. Debs, you stay here.'

'No, I'm coming with you. It's my house. And you two need someone looking after you,' Deborah said, confidence restored at the prospect of reinforcements.

'Fair enough. Slightest sign of anything amiss, we phone the police. Right?' Phil said, picking up his cricket bat.

The others nodded, happy to follow his lead, and together they headed back to Greenways Farm. The front door was ajar, as she had left it, and Phil, armed with his bat, strode confidently into the house, Deborah and Kai close behind.

'Let me know if you see anything odd,' Phil whispered. He pushed open the doors leading to the study and the snug. Both were empty. Then he headed up the hallway leading to the open-plan kitchen and dining area. That too appeared untouched.

Heart hammering, throat taut with tension, Deborah peered around. Everything looked normal, reassuringly so, even down to her empty coffee cup standing on the kitchen island. She shook her head. 'I don't think anyone has broken in. Nothing's been disturbed ... but I guess we'd better check the other rooms and upstairs, to be sure. Then I'll not interrupt your evening any longer.' She gave her companions a grateful smile.

Phil raised his eyebrows. 'Don't think you're getting rid of us that easily!' he said. 'No way we're leaving you on your own. It's not safe. You phone the police and we'll wait with you until they get here.'

'Thank you,' she replied quietly. She glanced through the window at the rear garden and gave a shocked gasp.

'What is it?' barked Phil, raising the bat in front of him, ready to strike.

'The garden,' she spluttered. 'Look!'

A scene of devastation met their eyes. Plants had been ripped out and were strewn over the grass. Her carefully planted pots had been smashed; the bird feeders lay in pieces; and her rubbish bins had been tipped up on the lawn.

'Bastards!' Kai exclaimed. 'What a mess!' He put his arm around Deborah's shoulders. 'We'll soon get this cleared up, love, don't you worry. But first, you'd better give your friendly police officer a ring and see what she has to say.'

Deborah nodded, her throat aching at the destruction of her beautiful garden. Still, Kai was right. It could be sorted. No real harm had been done.

Not *this* time, said the voice in her head.

CHAPTER 28

It was days like this she really missed Edgar. Honoraria perched on the purple, sateen stool in front of her heart-shaped, dressing table mirror, and slowly removed the mask she showed the world. With the last vestiges of make-up gone, the sagging lines of her face looked every bit of her fifty-six years ... or even older. Where had the time gone? Inside, she was still the cherub-faced, strawberry blonde who had, after wasted months hankering after a boy who looked like Jon Bon Jovi, recognised Edgar's hidden depths. When revelation struck, she wasted no time in swapping her allegiance and exploring her future husband's assets. Her lips, thin without the bright lipstick she favoured, twitched as she remembered. What fun they'd had! What a team they had made!

There *were* disappointments though. They both desperately wanted children but it had never happened. To start with, there was no rush. They wanted to save, buy a bigger house, go on nice holidays abroad. When Honoraria hit her mid-thirties and they had been trying for children, without success, for over three years, she suppressed her anxieties and made jokes to Edgar about needing more practice. He patted her hand, each month, when it became clear she was not pregnant, and reassured her there was plenty of time. But there wasn't. When she was thirty-six, her womb had been removed in an emergency operation. She would never be able to bear a child.

With her usual stoicism, she shrugged off her maudlin moment. How many others were as fortunate as she in having enjoyed such a happy marriage? Many became soured as disappointment and disillusion set in. She could name some amongst acquaintances in Wickthorpe. At least she had her memories to sustain her. And her hobbies. The recent History Society meeting had boasted an upturn, once again, in attendance. It had been quite a squash in her small living room! She had been gratified to have the Hampton-Browns show up and was relieved they had arrived early so she could offer them the best seats. It had been a surprise they brought that weaselly, little man, Philip Holder with them, along with Enid Green, and without Enid's daughter, Ava, who usually ferried her mother everywhere. There had been an air of collusion about the quartet, right from the start, she now realised. At the time, she had more important things to think about.

The evening had started with a two-minute period of silence for Freya Billington. Honoraria thought that was only right. Then she had taken centre stage. She spent five minutes or so recapping what was known about Martha Lightbody and informing the group of steps she had taken to discover what happened after the drowning. After some initial enthusiasm from her regulars, as she liked to call them, the discussion had fizzled out. It became apparent there was an air of tension in the room, emanating especially from the newcomers. Still, she soldiered on valiantly, thinking the atmosphere was because of the recent tragedy. Little wonder they were all on edge! She had been alarmed, however, when conversation veered away from the mysterious fate of the original Wickthorpe Witch to a castigation of Deborah Ryecroft. It had been instigated by Enid Green and dominated by the Hampton-Browns. Things became particularly awkward when John Hampton-Brown produced a petition for Ms Ryecroft's eviction from the village and insisted that all present had a duty to add their signatures. Gretchen Cooper had done just that. Well, she would, poor thing. She would not have a clue what she was signing! When the document had been passed to Honoraria, she had laid it down with an embarrassed excuse.

'I'm not sure this is the time or the occasion to raise an issue like this,' she had bravely pronounced. Things got rather heated after that. The Hampton-Browns had shot daggers at her whilst Enid Green had gone on one of her rants, declaring that it was a shame they didn't live in the olden days as then they could burn witches, like Deborah, at the stake. Honoraria had been quite flustered by it all. She could not believe one of her genteel History Society meetings had descended into such a shambles.

Fortunately, Wendy Robinson had come to her rescue, saying that kind of talk smacked of the prejudice many innocent people had faced hundreds of years ago. 'We are all God's children,' she declared, 'and deserve to be treated as such. As far as I'm aware, Deborah Ryecroft had nothing to do with Freya Billington's very sad passing. If she did, I'm sure the police will act accordingly. In the meantime, I think we should all calm down and take a breath. Maybe, now would be a good time, as a group, to say a prayer for Freya and for her poor family.' She had deliberately closed her eyes and put her hands together, waiting for everyone to follow suit. Honoraria had been decidedly grateful for her intervention and fervently hoped the heat in her cheeks would disperse during the respite.

After that, she had disappeared to organise tea, coffee and cake, but kept the door open, on tenterhooks, an ear alert for subsequent exchanges. Fortunately, though, the disagreement seemed to have run its course. The Hampton-Brown posse sat smouldering in silence and made an abrupt exit after the refreshments. Only then had conversation returned to safer waters and renewed discussion about Martha Lightbody. Members agreed to conduct their own research, although Honoraria had little confidence they would do so. She hoped she would receive information from her own sources in time for the next gathering. The meeting adjourned at 9:10 p.m. and she had never been so thankful to see everyone leave. Wendy, bless her, had stayed behind to help with the clearing up, during which Honoraria had given her profuse and heartfelt thanks. Honestly, without Wendy, she shuddered to think what might have happened.

Later that night, she dreamt of a baying mob, wearing Klu Klux Klan style pointy hats, dragging Deborah Ryecroft from her bed and stringing her up from the large oak tree in front of her house. It was all most upsetting. She woke, briefly, and had a sip of water. After that, the dream morphed into a much more satisfactory, sexual fantasy, as two of the men removed masks to reveal the handsome faces of Dr Seb Holley and Tom Oldridge. Two pairs of gorgeous, blue eyes, smouldering with desire just for her. As she stood trembling before them, they removed their robes in glorious synchronicity. She reached out both hands to stroke their muscled flesh ... and woke up, much to her annoyance. Despite clamping her eyes together and willing the dream to continue, she remained steadfastly awake and rose earlier than normal, tired and frustrated.

A few days later, she had heard the news concerning the damage to Deborah Ryecroft's garden and remembered the hatred expressed at the meeting. It made her wonder. Could people like the Hampton-Browns, Philip Holder and Enid Green *really* have lowered themselves to such a mean act of vandalism? *Of course not.* The very idea was preposterous. Much more likely the culprits were to be found amongst the riff-raff element of the population, people like the O'Gradys. Many villagers had been vocal in their dislike of Deborah Ryecroft. There was no shortage of suspects.

Having dismissed it from her mind, she was both shocked and mortified to receive a very shirty phone call from Valerie earlier that day. That distinguished lady seemed convinced Honoraria had given their names to the police and suggested them as possible perpetrators of the vandalism! Apparently, she and her husband, amongst others she irritatingly failed to name, had suffered the indignity of being interviewed by officers about the matter. Honoraria had tried her best to assure Valerie this travesty had nothing to do with her but the other woman refused to listen.

'I thought you were my friend, Honoraria,' she barked. 'How *could* you suggest that John and I would be involved in anything as petty as causing malicious damage to her grubby, little garden?'

'I didn't,' Honoraria wailed but it was no use. Valerie clearly did not believe her.

'I would not be surprised if she did it herself ... to get people's sympathy. Or for the insurance. That would be typical of someone like her! But I am surprised at *you*, Honoraria. I didn't know you were on her side.'

'I'm not ...'

'Good day!'

The call ended with Valerie's typical brusqueness, and Honoraria was left clutching her phone, somewhat shell-shocked. Valerie Hampton-Brown's anger was much akin to a bomb explosion and, reeling in the aftermath, felt like post-traumatic stress.

As she wriggled between her satin sheets, which she would never replace because they reminded her of Edgar, Honoraria resolved to put the unpleasant incident behind her. Valerie was justifiably upset and would hopefully come around. If not ... she shrugged beneath the covers ... so be it. None of it was her fault and she could rest easy with a clear conscience. With a sigh, she closed her eyes and conjured up the image of Seb and Tom, once more in the throes of stripping for her pleasure. Was it too much of a self-indulgence, along with a salacious desire for revenge following that unpleasant phone confrontation, to add the older but still well-toned body of John Hampton-Brown to the fantasy? Perhaps she should punish him for disrupting her meeting? What a delightful idea!

And, with that agreeable thought, she drifted off to sleep.

CHAPTER 29

Martha's diary
13th July, 1645

Today marked the first year since the occasion of Josiah's birth. I can scarce believe tis a twelvemonth since my dearest boy was born. He is yet to take his first steps but, in all other respects, I am convinced he is advanced for a child of his age! He really is the most darling infant and much admired by many in Wickthorpe. I hope twill not be long afore he walks. He grows heavier by the day and tis most uncomfortable now to carry him in his sling (though tis not the same as the one I made when he was younger as that tiny scrap soon became outgrown). John made him a spinning top and the small toy has kept Josiah much amused. He is so fortunate to have such a kind father. I recall playing with such when I was a child and know twill give him hours of pleasure.

Now for less happy tidings – the most dreadful news. I was quite horrified to hear it. In a battle one month hence at a place named Naseby, the army of our beloved King was nigh on destroyed. Many brave men lost their lives and thousands more were captured and paraded through the streets of London like animals. I can scarce believe such a thing! Mr Cromwell and Sir Thomas Fairfax, tis said, have quite gained control of the country. Tis most worrisome. News of the King himself is uncertain but some believe he has fled south. At least, praise the Lord, we learnt he was uninjured in the fighting. Whilst he remains alive, I believe there is hope order will be restored. How I pray tis so!

If that was not bad enough, there is yet more distressing information to impart. In recent times, talk of witchcraft has become rife in the village. I have heard tell of a trial in nearby Bury St Edmunds where many women and men stand accused, including John Lowe, the man of God who was so cruelly detained in Framlingham Castle by Matthew Hopkins and his assistant, Mr Stearne. How I fear for the prisoners! I pray every night for their safe deliverance but I am afraid their fate may already be sealed. Those who discuss such matters say twill be so. Such talk has caused a deal of unrest in Wickthorpe and I have noticed how some now look at me askance as I go about my business. This very morn, an old woman crossed herself as I passed! I dare not tell John but tis most worrisome. The mood in the village has changed toward me and I fear I am not held in the regard I was before. All I can do is to keep my distance from such folk and hope that, when the trial is over, I may regain their trust.

Regarding my other concern – Mr Roger Holley – I am happy I have nothing untoward to report, though I remain much alarmed by any sighting of the man (I cannot in all conscience call him a gentleman). When I last wrote, I felt convinced he wished only to avoid me and I had nothing to fear. Howe'er, we have met twice of late, and now I am less sure. Both times, I was thankful to be accompanied by my dear friend, Prudence. He was astride his horse and bestowed 'pon me the most mocking of smiles as he stopped to wish us a good morrow. Twas as much as I could do to return his greeting and Prudence was forced to exchange pleasantries for us both. The sweet girl managed to keep her dislike of him well hidden, for which blessing I was most grateful. I would hate to see him take vile vengeance 'gainst her 'pon my account. Meantimes, I could not help but notice how oft his scornful glance came my way. His demeanour told of unfinished business yet between us. Such terrible looks of portent have led to dreams from which I wake shaking with dread. After, John holds me in his arms, offering words of comfort and asking as to the reason for such trembling. I confess to pretence, telling I know not the cause of such nightmares. My husband is no fool and I suspect he knows well enough but says naught, accepting my word. John is a kind man and would not wish to upset me further.

The fields around are growing yellow and the cutting season will soon be 'pon us. It has been a bountiful season. Prudence and I have oft been out gathering Nature's harvest. My friend is an apt pupil and I have taught her much about the herbs and plants, though I continually remind her to keep such knowledge a secret lest suspicion fall 'pon her.

I cannot help but feel we live in strange times. The war has set the world awry and I fear only God has the power to restore it as it should be. My prayers are always for our King and an end to the fighting. Meantimes, men are resorting to rooting out witches – any folk they can accuse of conspiring with the devil. Protestations of innocence seem to matter little against the word of powerful men. John Lowe is a man of the cloth and, by all accounts, long disputed the truth of the claims against him. Whereupon, tis said, he was subjected to the most abominable torture til he confessed. It cannot be Christian to treat folk in such a merciless fashion and yet the witchfinders say they are doing God's work. Tis a mystery. All I know is that there is a growing sense of mistrust around me which was not present when we first arrived in Wickthorpe. I am growing in fear for my life when all I wish is to help those who need it, as a true Christian should. I am sad to think twill not be long afore we are moving on once more but I pray twill not be so. Prudence and Mary Martha have become most dear to me. How I would hate to leave them!

CHAPTER 30

Weeks passed and life in Wickthorpe returned to some semblance of normality. Despite an exhaustive investigation, no new evidence was uncovered in relation to Freya Billington's death. The coroner recorded 'death by drowning' but whether it was by her own hand, accidental, or caused by someone else, remained a mystery.

Freya's car, a green Renault Clio, had been left in the car park area by Hundred Acre Wood with the keys still inside. DNA retrieved belonged to Freya and her mother, who occasionally used the car. Pathology from the body was inconclusive. Time of death had been recorded as between the hours of 4 a.m. and 7 a.m. Sunday morning, which meant she had lain undiscovered in the lake for more than twenty-four hours. The toxicology report revealed Freya had consumed an overdose of Silenor prior to her death. Silenor was described as a tricyclic antidepressant also used to treat insomnia. This report, along with the empty packet found by her phone and covered with her fingerprints, pointed to suicide. There was no bruising on the body, no sign of a struggle, nor evidence of recent sexual activity, the pathologist reported.

Crucially, detectives had been unable to discover the identity of Freya's lover. CCTV evidence from cameras in Oxford showed her walking with a dark-haired man wearing glasses, but none of her friends or acquaintances could identify him. The hotel where they stayed was eventually located but the CCTV camera in the entrance lobby was of no use. Only Freya had gone to the reception desk and had paid in cash for the room. The couple had registered as Mr and Mrs Taylor and staff did not recall seeing the man at all. Frustratingly, the camera in the car park was not working. Freya's best friend, Cara Minton, told detectives Freya had admitted she was seeing someone but refused to say who it was. Cara suspected he was married, and warned her of the consequences. After that, Freya became uncommunicative and failed to respond to Cara's texts. Sally Billington also confirmed she had been worried by Freya's secretiveness. It was out of character.

After several dead ends and an abundance of frustration, DI Honeysuckle's superiors and many of her colleagues concluded the most likely explanation for cause of death was suicide. Upon discovering she was pregnant, Freya had confronted her lover who subsequently wanted nothing more to do with her. An old story. In a fit of despair, the girl had drowned herself. This theory also tallied with the unsent message to her mother, found on her discarded mobile phone:

I'm sorry. Can't go on. Love you. Please forgive me xxxxxxxx

There was evidence which potentially shed doubt upon this hypothesis and questions remained unanswered. No footprints matching Freya's shoe size had been found at the scene. Had heavy rain washed them away? If so, why had they been unable to trace the source of male footprints which had been found? These had been exhaustively analysed and checked against regular walkers but the owner remained unidentified. Detectives had interviewed Freya's friends and anyone who had contact with her locally. As she worked part-time in the pharmacy and in the pub, it meant talking to a lot of people. They had particularly focused on the married men of her acquaintance and ruffled a few feathers asking for proof of whereabouts on the weekend prior to the body being discovered. Nothing had come from any of it. Most of the likelier candidates, based upon age and potential for contact, had spent the weekend at home. The weather on Sunday had meant staying indoors with their families. Anyone who had been elsewhere on that weekend had provided an acceptable alibi. The next step was to ask each man to provide a voluntary sample of DNA to match against that of the baby to rule out his paternity. This had caused a lot of anger and upset but eventually every potential suspect in the village had provided a sample. There had been no matches. The possibility that Freya had been murdered by a lover loomed large in everyone's minds, but, if someone had killed her, he or she knew what they were doing and how to hide it.

DI Beth Honeysuckle remained troubled. It seemed to her that drowning herself in a lake mired in superstitious significance was an unlikely choice of method for a young girl. Why the lake at all? If Freya was determined upon taking her life, why not choose more comfortable surroundings for her final hours and minutes? She remained of the opinion someone had killed Freya but, in terms of the investigation, they had reached a dead end. The case was left open and the investigating team were told to scale down enquiries and move on to other, more pressing matters.

Freya's body was finally released for burial and her funeral, as expected, exacted a huge turnout. Afterwards, people gathered at *The Lamb Inn* and congregated in the garden. The weather was overcast but warm and almost everyone in the village wanted to pay their respects to the family.

Deborah did not attend. Given the circumstances and the ill-feeling towards her, she knew it would be inappropriate and awkward. She sent a letter of condolence to Freya's parents and a very generous donation to the RSPCA, the chosen charity. On the day, she made sure she was in London. She felt that would be best.

Her garden had been restored and was looking better than ever. After the police had been to witness the scene of devastation, she, Kai, and Tom had wasted no time in tidying, replanting, and replacing broken pots, shrubs, and perennials. A lot of the damage had been superficial. An escalation from the notes, but no real harm done. It was designed to cause upset and fear, the police said. They urged Deborah to be on her guard and convinced her to increase the security of her home. In addition to the alarm system already installed, CCTV cameras had been placed to both the front and rear of the property. The fencing around the back garden, where the intruder had probably got in, via one of Tom's fields, had been changed from posts and rails to much higher panelling, to prevent easy access.

The first night, after the vandalism was discovered, Tom had insisted upon staying over with her and, although she protested and said she would be fine, she had been relieved. There were other benefits as well; she could not deny it. Since then, Tom had stayed most nights, whenever he could and, despite her sadness about Freya and anxiety over the threats, she had never been happier. Their relationship had grown and deepened into a joyous thing, wrapping them both in a little cocoon of pleasure. She really liked Tom. He was a good-humoured and thoughtful man, fun to be around. He never tried to crowd her and, being busy himself, running a farm, respected the unsociable hours she sometimes had to work. Life was good and Deborah was content to enjoy and accept it for what it was – an unexpected bonus to her enforced, year-long sojourn in Wickthorpe.

She was concerned though about Emma living on her own at Orchard Farm. 'The coroner recorded an open verdict on Freya's death,' she said to Tom. 'It is possible there's a killer out there, someone who preys on young girls.'

'I don't think that's likely,' he replied. 'If the police believed that, they would still be looking for the person responsible.' But her words did spark a niggle of worry and, unknown to her, he said the same to Emma.

Typically, she scoffed at his fears. 'Honestly, Dad, don't you think I can take care of myself? I'm strong, tough and have a black belt in judo, remember? I pity the man who tries to mess with me! No, you go play houses with Debs, like you know you want to. I'm perfectly fine on my own.'

Tom laughed and let the matter drop. In the end, though, another solution, very acceptable to Emma, presented itself. Rick had been finding things tough, coping with his own grief at the loss of his much-loved sister and trying to support his parents. Whilst he wanted to do what he could for them, he was finding the strain of living with their pain, as well as his own, just too much. He needed a break, he told Emma and, in a moment of lightbulb inspiration, she suggested he come and stay at her place for a while. That way, he could have a respite from some of the burden. He liked the idea but worried how his parents might respond. It felt like he was abandoning them when they needed him most. When he asked them though, they thought it was a good idea.

'It's not like you're miles away. You'll still be in the village and, hopefully, we'll see you,' Sally said. 'I know Dad and I are not much fun to be around and it will be good for you to be with someone younger, especially Emma, who has a good head on her shoulders. I've been worrying how you're coping. I think it's an excellent idea.'

Rick had given her a hug. 'I'll still pop in,' he assured her. 'Round here, though,' he waved a helpless hand at the kitchen in which they sat, drinking tea, 'I keep expecting her to walk in and ask what's for dinner.'

'I know, love.' Tears pooled once more in Sally's eyes. 'I'm the same. I guess it will always be like that.'

It was strange for both Emma and Rick to start with, especially as Tom was barely there. The first night Rick stayed over, he promised not to take advantage of her kindness.

'Ha, I'd like to see you try,' Emma laughed.

'I don't mean ... well ... you know,' Rick wrinkled his nose, his face contorting with awkwardness. 'I mean, when you've had enough of me, just say. It's only with things at home being so raw. It won't be for too long.'

'As long as you need.' Emma patted his hand, wishing it could be forever. She yawned. 'I'm heading up to bed now. Give me a shout if you need anything.'

'Will do. Thanks, Em. You're a good mate.'

'No worries.' She blew him a kiss and headed up the stairs. *A good mate.* If only he would see her as something more.

CHAPTER 31

A fine mist cast a hazy, grey hue over Greenways Farm as Deborah made her way up to the spare bedroom. It was early – barely six o'clock – but she had woken when Tom slipped from her bed. Fitful dreams had made for a restless night. Unfinished business. She could put it off no longer.

Last night, she had decided to look through the box of personal effects left for her by her mother and read her letter. For so long, it had been easy to shelve it – pretend it wasn't there – especially in the light of recent events. But it was time she knew everything, whatever pain it brought with it. Talks with Tom about his family, and particularly his strained relationship with his father, had softened the edges of her own resentment towards her parents. There were always two sides to every story; time to discover what theirs was.

Having pulled the box out from the cupboard, she sat staring at it, still reluctant to take that final step. What if she had been wrong about things all these years? Could there *really* be an explanation for everything? Probably not. With the expectation of revelation, she steeled herself for more disappointment. And hurt. Surely they could not cause her more grief than they already had, but nothing was beyond them. Was there going to be one final twist of the knife? Only one way to find out.

She pulled off the lid and peered inside. Lying on the top of a jumbled assortment of envelopes and smaller boxes was a letter addressed simply '*Deborah*' in her mother's spiky writing. She tore it open and extracted several sheets of lilac writing paper, blue-inked words covering one side of each. Taking a deep breath, she started reading:

Dearest Deborah,

Where to start? How can one write a lifetime of longings, regrets and explanations in a single letter? I confess I have no idea, but I have to try. I need to tell you things kept secret for too long. And, most of all, I need to seek your forgiveness – but I'm jumping ahead of myself. Let me start at the beginning.

I met your father when I was seventeen. My family were part of a travelling fair. I shared a caravan with Ma, Da and two older brothers. We all worked hard and money was scarce but my childhood was a happy time. Other children, from villages and towns we visited, thought our life very glamorous! It wasn't, but it wasn't bad either. Anyway, we stopped for a week on Hardwick Heath in Bury during the summer of 1969 and that's when I met Elijah. I was just seventeen. He was eight years older and very handsome. We had a secret romance. At the end of the week, he asked me to marry him and stay in Wickthorpe. His father had recently died, his mother was ill and he needed a wife to look after the home while he worked the land. Of course, I didn't realise that at the time. I thought he loved me as desperately as I loved him. My parents were unhappy and initially refused their permission. But they could see I was set on him, and he convinced them he had plenty of wealth to take care of me. He invited them to Greenways Farm to see for themselves. In the end, they gave us their blessing and set off to their next destination in Norfolk without me. They did not even come to our wedding, which saddened me, but I was madly in love and prepared to do whatever it took to be with Elijah. We were married in St Mary's Church in Wickthorpe and began our life together.

Things were fine at first. I worked hard – I was used to that. He seemed to appreciate all I did for him and Louisa, your grandmother. She was impossible to please – a hard woman and a stern taskmaster. I'm sad to say it was a relief for me when she died and there were just the two of us. Then I fell pregnant. Elijah was delighted, looking forward to fathering a son who could work the farm with him, as he had with his father. Those were joyful months. At last the time came and I did bear the son Elijah longed for. However, to my great sadness, he was stillborn. I called him Joshua and mourn him still. Whilst I was devastated, your father was overcome with disappointment. For a while, things were difficult between us. When I found I was expecting again, Elijah became very attentive, looking after me well to ensure nothing went wrong this time. Even though I fretted I might have another stillbirth, this pregnancy was a happy time in my marriage and luckily, when you were born, all was well. You were so beautiful. Big, bright eyes; a mass of dark curls.

I fell in love instantly. I was allowed to hold you for only a moment before I was taken for surgery but I will never forget my joy as you lay in my arms that first time. Unfortunately, complications during the birth meant the removal of my womb so there would be no more children. I didn't mind. You were my world and, now I had you, I was content. It was not the same for Elijah. He took the news very badly. He had set his heart on a son and was unable to resign himself to a single daughter. I'm afraid he blamed you – very unfairly, in my opinion – for the shattering of his dream and, from the first, would have nothing to do with you, or me for that matter. For a while, I was worried he would throw us both out of the family home. He distanced himself completely, even taking his meals to eat alone in his study. In the evening, he would often go out and that was when he first met members of the Repentalist Church. They convinced him what had happened was part of God's plan and that, if he prayed hard enough and followed their mantra, he would, one day, be blessed with the son he craved. He was anxious to believe them and they took to visiting us at home with increasing frequency. Elijah embraced their doctrine wholeheartedly and it also brought me comfort. For one thing, it brought Elijah back to me and I felt, as long as I did nothing to upset him or his new friends, our future would be secure.

The Repentalist Church, as you may remember, was patriarchal in the extreme. The men ruled; the woman's place was to look after the men first, the family second and her own needs last. When you were little, you accepted those rules but, as you grew older, you proved stubborn and were often openly defiant. In that, you took after your father – strong-willed and unafraid. Looking back, I see how cowardly I was. When he beat you, I dared not intervene for fear of making things worse. He was unflinchingly cruel to you but I knew that to comfort you would only increase his wrath. I did try in the early days, but I too was beaten and told that if I tried to thwart him again, he would have no choice but to throw us out. Unlike you, I lived in fear of him. I knew it was no empty threat. Also, I had no one in whom to confide. Elijah had banned contact with my own family and I was not allowed out without his express permission. I was very lonely.

But, none of that would have mattered, if you had loved me. You did in those early days. When Elijah left us alone, I cuddled you, sang to you, and treasured each gurgle you made, each smile you gave me. Then, I felt truly blessed. As time went on, I could see you resented the way I appeared to stand with your father against you. Eventually, that resentment turned to hatred. I saw it in your eyes when you visited, that final time, to ask for our help and I said nothing as Elijah heaped insults upon you, before banishing you from our lives for good. Afterwards, I wished I'd had the courage to go with you. I never knew what happened to my grandchild. As I secretly followed your career, in the newspapers and latterly, on the internet, I could find no mention of a child. I will go to my grave never knowing if I was a grandmother. It is nothing less than I deserve.

A few years ago, I received a surprise visit from Mabel Littlebody. It was after your father had died and that was the reason for her call. As I've already said, Elijah refused to allow me out for anything other than buying essentials, and I'd never met her. I had heard about her, of course – snippets when I went to the shops, that kind of thing – and knew she lived opposite. I also knew you used to visit her when you were a girl, which made me very jealous at the time. I mentioned these visits to Elijah once and he was furious. You probably remember the beating you received and his order to stay away from her. Something about her filling your head with lies and nonsense, I remember. I know you continued to visit Mabel but I never mentioned it again. You always seemed a little happier when you had seen her. Anyway, I'm rambling. Mabel turned up unexpectedly and asked if she could come in. She talked about you, to start with, and how pleased she was by your success. She asked me if you were happy and I had to say I didn't know – that we were estranged. Eventually, I admitted everything to her. She has that way about her and, once I had started, I couldn't stop. I was in floods of tears and she just sat, holding me in her arms, giving me comfort. A wonderful woman. Infinitely kind and patient.

Then she told me what she had come to tell me in the first place. She was Elijah's distant cousin. They both shared the same grandparents, Charles and Mary Littlebody. Charles and Mary had seven children, the oldest of whom was George, Mabel's father. Elijah's mother, Louisa, was a younger sister and she married Frederick Ryecroft of Greenways Farm, your grandfather and Elijah's father. Frederick was a harsh man and did not treat his wife well, by all accounts. He and George Littlebody had words over it and the two families fell out. When Frederick died, Mabel visited Elijah, to express her sympathy and to make amends for that past dispute. Elijah threw her out and told her never to return. Thus, the two relations lived opposite to each other but never spoke which caused Mabel great sadness. She said she never told you of the relationship between the two of you out of respect for Elijah's wishes.

Mabel visited often after that and we became good friends. How I wish she had been in my life sooner! Maybe, then, things would have been different. But it is too late for regrets. We often talked of you and how badly you were treated by many of the villagers when your friend drowned in the lake. I always believed your story but it was impossible for me to say anything. Since that time, I have tried to discover more about the village curse and the woman behind it. I wondered if there could be some link between you and her, some reason behind the accusations fired at you. I always suspected Enid Green knew something as she would always make a point of mentioning it, whenever I saw her, which thankfully was not often. Of course, I couldn't ask her but, being very superstitious myself, I did wonder if there was something it in. Anyway, I mentioned it to Mabel and she remembered a book she had on that very subject. Apparently, it had belonged to her father, George, and his father before that. It was written in 1845 by John Littlebody, possibly an ancestor. Mabel lent me the book and I found it fascinating. Although it is described as a work of fiction, it was based upon the life of Martha Lightbody, the original Wickthorpe Witch! Mabel lent it to me and it contained some shocking revelations, I can tell you. I will say no more about it. You need to read it for yourself. I'm sure Mabel would be happy to let you borrow it.

You have probably been wondering at the conditions of my will. I was anxious for you to return here and read this letter. Please forgive me. I also hoped Mabel's book might help to give that episode in your life some closure and I wanted you to be here long enough to read it. If you are trying to decide what you should do, please allow me to persuade you to give Wickthorpe a chance. There are some lovely people here. When your father was alive, I never realised. I was told to keep myself to myself and we only socialised with our brethren from the Repentalist Church. Since his passing, I have ventured from my shell. I have discovered a lot he told me was untrue. For example, I discovered the sale of all the farmland back in 2010, which he said was to provide much-needed finances for our Church, was a necessity after years of mismanagement and huge debts. In my final years, I've been lucky to count many Wickthorpe people as my friends. Apart from Mabel, Wendy Robinson has visited often. We have enjoyed many theological conversations which have caused me to question many of the beliefs I embraced, at your father's behest, for most of my life. I no longer have anything to do with the Repentalist Church. My neighbour, Tom Oldridge, has been very good. He is a kind man – nothing like his father. Similarly, Ava Green is nothing like her mother, thank goodness! Recently, since my illness was diagnosed, Dr Holley has been helpful and looked after me very well. The team of carers have also been lovely. I consider myself lucky to have had the chance to get to know them all. I hope that you too will want to make Wickthorpe your home. I know I have no right to demand anything from you so consider this a request.

You have been my biggest regret and my greatest pride. I always loved you but fear kept me silent. In my life, my heart has been broken into so many pieces but there has always been a special part of it kept for you.

Please forgive me.

All my love,

Your mother, Hannah x

Deborah collected the sheets, folded them carefully and slid them back into the envelope. The simple task seemed to require enormous effort. She had not known what to expect and did not know what to feel now she read her mother's words. It was like floating in nothingness. Her brain had absorbed the information but was unable to process it. The letter had been read and could not, now, be unread.

Staring out of the window, she watched two blue tits scrapping at one of the bird feeders. A light drizzle smeared the glass and imbued the garden with a Monet-like colour wash. Suddenly restless, she decided to go for a walk, despite the weather. She needed to be outdoors, expending energy.

And then, maybe, she could start to come to terms with what she had learnt.

***

Tom knew something had happened, almost as soon as he came in. He had spent a boring afternoon at a briefing about updates to government subsidy schemes and had come in earlier than usual. Deborah was tense and distracted, unwilling to engage in conversation. He went upstairs for a shower and, when he came down, suggested a meal out but she had already cooked. She wanted to keep busy, she said, and the miserable weather – it was now raining steadily – had precluded a stint in the garden. Immediately, he leapt to the wrong conclusion; there had been another threat. To reassure him, she showed him the letter.

He read it in silence and his heart ached. Poor Hannah. And poor Debs. He set the papers aside and looked across at her still form. She avoided his eyes.

'I'm sorry,' he said simply. When she said nothing, he added, 'Do you want to talk about it?'

'No,' she replied and he let the matter drop, telling her instead about the latest Government plans to replace the EU subsidies.

'I'm all for environmental schemes,' he told her. 'We have several already running on the farm. But they should not be at the expense of growing food. It will mean, if people want home-grown food, they are going to have to pay more for it. Small farms will struggle and may give up growing crops altogether.'

'Mm,' she replied. He could see she wasn't listening so he picked up one of his farming magazines. 'I keep remembering things,' she said suddenly. He looked up. Her face looked drawn and pale. He wanted to comfort her but, instinctively, knew she would shrug him off. Instead, he waited. 'Stupid things.' She gave him a strained half-smile. 'From when I was little. Like singing nursery rhymes together. She had a beautiful voice. I'd forgotten. Other things too. Like how she used to creep upstairs, after I'd gone to bed, to give me a cuddle and tell me she loved me. One day, Father caught her. He fetched his cane and punished us both – "for our disobedience," he said. The night-time visits stopped after that. One time, we caught the bus somewhere. It was a big secret. Father didn't know. We went to a fair and met some people. There was lots of hugging and kissing.' She wrinkled her nose. 'I remember I wasn't keen on all these strangers cuddling me. They all had dark, curly hair like Mother. I went on some of the rides. It was bright, colourful, noisy and lots of fun. I think there was a bit of an argument. One of the men wanted us to stay with them but Mother insisted we had to go back.' Her face clouded over. 'Of course, Father found out.' Her lips tightened. 'We never saw them again ... I guess they were Mother's family ... my family.' He nodded but remained quiet, allowing her the space to say what she needed. There was a long silence and her eyes misted. 'I always hated her ... not as much as *him*, but almost.' She sighed. 'I guess I shut out any good stuff about her. I resented her for always taking his side, never mine. She never stood up for me ... but now I know why.' She shrugged her slim shoulders. 'It should make a difference but a part of me still hates her. Why was she so weak? Why did she let him terrorise us both and treat us as if we were nothing? Why didn't she go back to her family when she could?'

She stood and began pacing the room. 'I still feel angry. That letter doesn't make it alright.'

'No,' he said gently. 'Nothing can ever right the wrongs of the past. I think Hannah knew that. She just wanted you to hear her side ... and to tell you she was sorry.' Her body slumped as she sat opposite him once more and he ached to hold her. 'Not everyone is as strong as you,' he continued. 'And, despite everything, Hannah loved your father.'

She snorted. 'Then love has a lot to answer for! From where I'm standing, it was pretty selfish and destructive.'

He smiled. 'Yes ... but it's not always like that.' He wanted to say more, but now was not the time.

'Maybe.' Her lips tightened and she gave him an accusing stare. 'Did she tell you any of this?'

'No. When we spoke of you, she told me that you were estranged. It was her fault, not yours, she said. She told me she wanted to put things right, and wanted to leave the house to you, but she was afraid you would never come back. It was the solicitor who suggested she put a clause in her will, with the condition that you had to live here for a year. I suspect she wanted you to return and show the people of Wickthorpe who you really were. Remember, she was proud of you. Also, I guess, she wanted you to read her letter. She said she had written to you before but the letters were always returned unopened.'

'That's true,' she admitted. 'I never wanted anything from her. I cut all ties.'

'And yet you did return,' he mused. 'Perhaps she knew you better than you thought ... Anyway, she was aware there would be ill-feeling towards you, from certain, long-standing village residents, and asked me to be a friend to you.' He spread his hands. 'That's all I know.'

She smiled then. 'And you have been.' Her eyes softened. 'A good friend.'

'Whatever you need.' He opened his arms out to her, his blue eyes glowing with invitation, and she readily stepped into his warm embrace.

***

Later, over a meal of coq au vin, accompanied by a bottle of red wine, they discussed the book mentioned in Hannah's letter.

'I'd like to read it,' she said. 'I grew up knowing the legend of the Wickthorpe Witch and I would like to know what happened to my namesake.' She gave a wry smile. 'Maybe I could come up with a few curses of my own.'

He grinned. 'Well, you *have* bewitched me! I'm always ready to do your bidding!'

She rolled her eyes. 'I am serious, though. I wonder where the book is. Mabel's bungalow is up for sale but I've no idea what's happened to all her possessions.'

He shook his head. 'I've no idea. Kai or Phil might know ... or the Hampton-Browns. Their house is further along Green Road. Orchard House. Big, red-bricked place.'

'I didn't know they lived there.' She wrinkled her nose. 'I'm not sure they would take too kindly to questions from me. I seem to remember the funeral directors were called Hudson & Herbert. I could ask them for the contact details of Mabel's solicitors.'

'Mm,' he said, 'good idea.' He rose from his chair to stand behind her, his workworn hands gently massaging her shoulders. 'In the meantime, there's quite a bit of tension here,' he murmured, leaning forward and dropping light kisses on her neck. 'I think we should do something about that, don't you?'

She stood and slid her hands beneath his shirt. 'I am feeling a little uptight,' she agreed, leaning into him. 'But we really should clear the dishes ...'

'Later,' he mumbled, covering her mouth with his.

***

Now, she was asleep, exhausted by the emotional toll of the day, while he lay awake, holding her tight against him, wishing he had the power to take away all her past hurt. Deborah had come into his world and found her way into his heart. He could not bear to think of life without her but, although he knew she cared for him, he had no idea if she felt the same. Whilst sleep continued to evade him, he cradled her warm body, fiercely determined to protect her from future harm and worrying that, at the end of her year in Wickthorpe, she would leave him.

CHAPTER 32

As the days rolled by, discussions in the Post Office reverted, despite Enid's best efforts, to chat about the weather rather than the recent tragedy or the Wickthorpe curse. People wanted to move on. Freya Billington's death, the police investigation and the funeral had all taken an emotional toll on even the most detached villager and the consensus was life needed to return to normal.

Ava was more than happy with that but still she remained troubled. Her brother, Andrew, had taken to visiting his mother on a regular basis which was most out of character. Not that it was a bad thing – she loved her brother, despite his faults, and the visits kept Enid in good humour; she just had to wonder at the reason. It was worrying. He was up to something. Or Enid was.

Andrew had been an unreliable, sporadic visitor in the past. They saw more of Julie and the girls. She and Enid invited the family often but Andrew rarely appeared, much to her mother's chagrin. It was lovely to see her nieces though. They were growing fast. Both were at school now and doing well, she was told. Eveline was seven, and chocolate box pretty, with long waves of silky, blonde hair which Julie liked to plait. She had inherited her dad's looks, and was clever and confident with it. Misha was small and dark, like her mum, and a little shy, especially around her grandmother. Enid made no secret of the fact she favoured the child who looked most like her son so Ava always made an extra fuss of Misha to compensate. She was fond of Julie too and feared her brother did not treat his wife well. None of her business though. She had tried to warn her sister-in-law before they married but Julie had been too starstruck by Andrew to listen at the time.

Today, Andrew had turned up at the Post Office again and, after a distracted greeting, had disappeared into his mother's cave. Something was going on. Maybe money issues, or some other trouble in which Andrew had embroiled himself. He did not always make good decisions and his mother had bailed him out, more than once, in the past. Enid had plenty of money; subsidising her son was well within her power. After all, she contributed nothing towards her own household bills. Ava scraped by on her income from the Post Office and paid for everything, too proud to ask for help. Meanwhile, Enid considered whatever Ava did for her as her due. It was her right to expect her daughter to care for her every need. Unreasonable, yes, but no point fretting. Ava had her chance to get away once and had not taken it. The old, familiar ache returned as she wondered what Patrick was doing now. Was he still in Cleveland? Still married? Children?

The tinkle, signalling the door opening, set all such thoughts aside. 'Hello, Philip. What can I do for you?' She greeted the thin, unsmiling man in her usual, pleasant manner but, in truth, she was not a fan of this customer. Something about the eyes, she thought. Philip Holder had worked in the village and she had known him all her life but would never trust him.

'Nothing today. I'm here to see Enid. Is she in her room?'

Ava struggled to keep her dismay from showing. First Andrew and now Philip Holder. What *was* her mother up to? She had a horrible suspicion she knew the answer. 'Yes. My brother's with her. Go on through.' She opened the counter to let him pass, trying not to flinch as he brushed against her, a combination of stale sweat and smoke. Listening, she heard him knock at Enid's door, the sound of her brother's voice raised in greeting, the door shutting, silence. She sighed. Enid was plotting something involving Deborah Ryecroft, she was almost certain. Despite her confidence Deborah could take care herself, she wondered if she should warn her. But she had no proof they were scheming anything. She needed more information. Should she go and listen at the door? Leaving that question hanging, she began the daily task of tidying stock away. There were only ten minutes left until closing time and it was unlikely any more customers would cross the threshold, particularly as it was another miserable day.

As she embarked on a task she could do in her sleep, the face of Patrick Velaman swam into her consciousness, as it so often did, even after all this time. He was an American who had worked, in the late nineties, at the airbase in Lakenheath. They met at a twenty-first birthday party when he spilled his beer over her best dress. She was twenty-two. He was a little older.

'Gee, I'm so sorry.' He was tall, gawky and endearing, like a leggy puppy.

'It's OK.' Her smile was pained as she surveyed the damage. The brown stain spread across her chest, staining the pale lemon cotton of the bodice like a muddy puddle.

'No, it's not. Can I … do anything?' He flapped his hands helplessly.

'It'll dry.' She shrugged and gave him a smile, noticing his long-lashed, velvet brown eyes, pools of liquid toffee.

'At least let me buy you a drink. I'm Pat, by the way.' He extended a long, bony hand.

'Ava.' She slipped her fingers into his grasp and hoped he would never let go.

They spent the evening together and, shyly, he asked if he could see her again. He was a man with old-fashioned values and reminded her of her beloved father, recently deceased. She had no idea what he saw in her but, blessedly, their admiration was mutual and blossomed into love. When he asked her to marry him, she felt she would explode with happiness. He was the man of her dreams, her saviour, her happy-ever-after.

Shortly afterwards, he was posted back to Cleveland. They had known the move was imminent and it excited her. She had long imagined escaping from her dingy life in Wickthorpe, enjoying new experiences in far-flung places. Fairy tale fantasies – and now they were happening. She could scarcely believe it. Ava Green – starring in her own romantic movie!

But then Enid became ill. After two weeks spent in hospital, she returned to the family home for her convalescence and expected Ava to look after her.

'You'll have to postpone your plans until I'm better,' she snapped when Ava protested. 'It's not much to ask … a few weeks. After all I've done for you …'

Patrick was understanding, as she had known he would be. 'It won't be for long,' he whispered as she cried in his arms. The prospect of his departure without her was almost too much to bear. 'As soon as she's better, you can jump on the first plane outta here. I'll be waiting.'

She swallowed back her tears. He was right. They would soon be together again and would have plenty of time to enjoy the rest of their lives together. If she failed in her duty now, the weight of guilt would be forever on her shoulders. With a heavy heart and a brave smile, she squashed her disappointment, waved him farewell and looked forward to their reunion.

Except Enid did not improve. Her symptoms worsened, requiring another operation. Again, she returned home but was very poorly and seemed to make little or no progress. 'I don't understand it.' Old Dr Hodder, who was treating her mother, scratched his head. 'She should've been responding by now.'

Ava wrote to Patrick every day, avidly reading and rereading the letters he sent her. At the beginning, they arrived every other day – long, rambling messages of love and devotion, interspersed with funny anecdotes about work and the people he met. They made her laugh and cry with longing for him. It was awful when he missed a few days ... and then more. He apologised. Work was super busy. She understood and shook off her fear. The letters continued but with increasing scarcity. After six long months, she was receiving barely one letter a week and, compared to his earlier correspondence, these were brief, hasty scribblings with few mentions of love. Something had changed. Ava knew it in her heart, long before her mind would let her admit it. As Enid continued to languish in her bed, she felt her beloved Patrick slipping away from her.

When the news came, it was still a huge shock. He had met someone else. Candice. He was sorry; he hadn't meant to hurt her but his feelings for Candice were too strong to ignore. He wished Ava love and happiness in her life. Forget about him. She was young and beautiful – deserved someone much better. There was no point in further correspondence. And that was it. The end of all her hopes and dreams. Ava huddled in her bed and refused to eat. She wanted to die. There was no point going on.

Except she still had to look after Enid who was short on sympathy for her heartbroken daughter. 'Pull yourself together,' she ordered. 'He's done you a favour by meeting someone else. You didn't want to be going off to America where there's all sorts going on. You're far better off here. Especially as he was never going to be faithful.' Propped up against her three pillows, she ranted at length on her new favourite topic – the failings of American airmen. 'Flighty!' she pronounced, oblivious to the unintentional pun. 'Unreliable. I always knew that man couldn't be trusted.' Amazingly, Ava's bad news seemed to spark Enid's remarkable recovery. 'I think I'd like to get up for a short spell today,' she said. 'Not for long. Don't want to overdo it ... but I *am* feeling a little better.'

Within a week, Enid was back to her cantankerous self, albeit unable to get about without some assistance. Ava's pain lasted much longer. Now, almost twenty years on, she still felt the bite of Patrick's rejection. Every day of her dreary, small life, she mourned his loss. No one knew. People regarded her as 'good, old Ava' – a permanent fixture of Wickthorpe Post Office and always ready to lend a hand to anyone who needed it. No one saw her as a woman, bursting with love, living the best life she could in her circumstances but capable of being so much more. In the beginning, she had blamed Patrick and Enid. Now, she only blamed herself. She had her chance but failed to snatch it. Other arrangements could have been made for her mother. Deep down, she confessed to herself that, whilst she called it duty, fear had also kept her tied to Wickthorpe. Her lack of courage, when it came to the crunch, contributed towards her failed relationship and there was no one to blame for that but herself.

With a slump in her shoulders, she turned the sign in the window to show the shop was closed. All was quiet and, once again, she wondered what Enid, Andrew and Philip Holder were discussing. Only one way to find out. She tiptoed along the corridor and loitered outside Enid's door. The low hum of male voices was barely audible but then she heard her mother's strident tones ring out.

'I don't care about her cameras. They shouldn't stop us from doing what needs to be done.' *Cameras?* Ava leaned a little closer, ear resting on the woodwork. She could always say she was about to offer them a cup of tea, if caught. Andrew was saying something but she struggled to make out the words. Then, Enid spoke again. 'The notes didn't work, nor the other stuff. You need to do more to get rid of her.'

'I'm not taking any more risks.' Philip's voice now, his Suffolk accent clearly distinguishable.

'But we must. Andrew,' Enid's voice was wheedling, 'I'm relying on you. Remember, it's in your best interest.'

There was a short silence. Ava strained to hear her brother's reply but his quiet voice failed to travel through the door.

'I'd best be off ...' Philip's words sent Ava scurrying towards the kitchen. Her mind spun into overdrive as she hastily assembled pans for cooking dinner and began peeling an onion. *Notes? Other stuff? Get rid of her?* Time to speak to Deborah Ryecroft – warn her. The sense of filial betrayal tasted sour in her mouth but she had to do something. If harm befell Deborah, she would never forgive herself.

And this evening's television schedule would provide her with the opportunity she needed. She would slip out later while Enid was watching *EastEnders*. Her mother would never know.

***

Ava Green's arrival at Greenways Farm that evening was a surprise. Tom answered the door, saw the harried look on her face and invited her in. Deborah offered her a drink, which she refused, and invited her to sit down.

'I'm so sorry to trouble you,' Ava began. 'I'm probably overreacting but I thought I ought to say something.'

'No trouble at all,' Deborah interrupted with a smile. Sensing Ava's anxiety, she glanced across at Tom. 'Would you prefer we chat on our own?'

'Oh no, no. I feel bad enough already about interrupting your evening.'

'Please don't worry about that.' There was a pause. Ava wrung her hands and chewed on her lip. 'Ava?' Deborah prompted gently.

She took a breath. 'I don't know if I'm doing the right thing or not but I feel I have to warn you ...'

'Warn us?' Tom snapped to attention. 'Why?'

'Not you ... Deborah.' Ava threw him an apologetic glance. 'It may be nothing but I'm worried my mother is plotting something.'

Deborah smiled at that. 'Enid? Plotting?' Her voice dripped sarcasm. 'I'm sorry, Ava, but I can't imagine your mother doing anything else!'

'You're right.' Ava's face relaxed a fraction as she acknowledged the truth of the observation. 'But this is different. I believe Mother wishes you harm.'

'Really?' Deborah knew the woman disliked her and was a strong voice behind all the witch rumours but *harm?* Immediately, she thought of the anonymous notes. Was Enid behind them?

'Yes. I know you're thinking I've been reading too many thrillers ...'

'Ava, if you are here, I'm sure you have a good reason. Tell us what you know,' Deborah reassured her.

Ava's lips wobbled in a tremulous smile. 'Well, it does sound a bit ludicrous. You know, I suppose, that Mother doesn't like you?'

'I have noticed,' Deborah replied, deadpan.

'She still blames you for Ayesha Khan. I know it's daft but she is convinced you're the Wickthorpe Witch reincarnated. I've tried telling her the curse is just superstitious nonsense but ... well ... you know my mother. She wants you gone from the village and I think she may be planning something to drive you out.'

A frown creased Tom's forehead and he leant forward. 'What makes you think that?'

'My brother, Andrew, has been visiting quite a lot recently. And Philip Holder.'

'I'm not sure I know Philip Holder.' Deborah screwed up her face, trying to recall. 'I suppose I may have seen him without knowing who he was.'

'Philip used to work for my father,' Tom supplied, 'and then for me after Dad died. Until he retired. A good worker but a bit of a trouble-maker. Not a team player. Everything is always someone else's fault. That kind of chap.'

'Yes,' Ava nodded. 'Well, today they both came round while I was working and spent some time with Mother in her room. I don't know why, exactly, but I did happen to catch the tail end of some of their conversation.' She blushed bright red and blurted out, 'I'm afraid I listened at the door.'

'Oh?' Deborah raised her eyebrows. 'And what did you hear?'

'Just snippets really but I think they were talking about you and how to "get rid of you." Those were the words Mother used.'

'That sounds a bit ominous,' Deborah chuckled, trying to make light of it. 'It sounds like she's planning to bump me off.'

'Oh no, I'm sure it's nothing like that,' Ava rushed on, unsure if Deborah's comment was serious. 'I think, though, they might be planning on scaring you, or something like that, so I wanted you to be forewarned.

They mentioned "notes and other stuff not working" so I don't know if that means anything to you?'

Deborah's eyes widened and she looked across at Tom. 'Actually, it does,' she said to Ava. 'I have received several anonymous notes, suggesting I leave Wickthorpe, and a few weeks ago, as you may have heard, someone trashed my garden. On the advice of the police, I installed additional security measures – CCTV cameras front and rear, that kind of thing. I was quite worried for my safety.'

'Oh no. I'm so sorry. That's terrible! I didn't know you'd been getting threatening mail. That *does* tie in with what I overheard. I hate to say it,' Ava shook her head, 'but I can imagine Mother being behind something like that.' She drew in a shaky breath. 'But the garden ... I can't believe ... I knew it had been vandalised, of course. Everyone was talking about it. The police even questioned the Hampton-Browns! Can you imagine? Valerie was seething when she told Mother! But I'm sure they wouldn't do anything like that ...' Ava bit her lip as she remembered something else. 'There *was* a mention of cameras ... Oh dear, what are you going to do?'

Deborah thought for a moment. 'I'm not sure. Obviously, I should tell the police.'

Ava's face crumpled. 'Oh no. I didn't think ...' The hand wringing worsened. 'Do you think they could go to prison? That would kill Mother!' Her voice was a low moan and she turned beseeching eyes towards Deborah. 'Isn't there any way ... without the police?'

'If Enid, Andrew and Philip were responsible for those notes and the criminal damage to the garden, they've caused Debs a lot of anxiety and heartache.' Tom's voice was hard. 'They should be punished.'

'Yes, I agree,' Deborah said but her face softened as she took in Ava's turmoil. 'But I don't want to cause others the same suffering they've caused me. Perhaps there is a way of stopping them without the help of the police. I realise how difficult telling them would be for you, Ava, and the only evidence we have is what you think you overheard. I'll work on it and come up with something. I would like to thank you, though, for coming to see me. That must have been a very difficult decision, given your family are involved.'

A sheen of tears coated Ava's eyes. 'I just wanted to do the right thing,' she whispered. 'I wouldn't have been able to forgive myself if something happened to you. And to find out it already has ... I don't know what to say. I know Mother can be difficult and opinionated but I still can't really believe she'd break the law.' She pulled out a tissue and blew her nose. 'I'm so sorry.'

'You have nothing to apologise for,' Deborah said firmly. She rose and stepped across the space to sit beside the other woman. After a brief hesitation, she put an arm around her and gave her a squeeze. 'Please don't cry. I won't do anything that makes the situation worse.' She directed an apologetic glance towards Tom. 'No police ... at least, not yet. Not unless it's absolutely necessary. But I will need to take *some* action. Whatever I do, I'll try to keep you out of it entirely. I don't want to cause friction in your family ... at least, any more than I already have.'

'Thank you.' Ava shuffled the used tissue back into her handbag and wriggled to her feet. 'I'd better go before Mother misses me. I left her watching *Eastenders*. I usually make her a cup of coffee afterwards. She'll be wondering what's happened.'

Deborah accompanied her to the door. 'You're a very kind woman. I want you to know how much I appreciate your friendship. It means a lot.' Ava nodded and gave her a flustered wave, before hurrying away.

'Well ...' Tom appeared behind Deborah and slipped his arm around her waist. Together they watched Ava's departure. 'That's a turn up!'

'I know,' she murmured. 'I'd never have believed someone like Enid Green would be behind those notes. She's always been spiteful and malicious but this is another level entirely.'

'Mm, I think she's quite capable of egging others on but she may not be the main perpetrator. And, thinking practically, she needs a wheelchair these days to get about. Andrew and Philip were probably the ones who destroyed the garden and delivered the notes. Hopefully, further mischief has been stymied by the cameras.'

'Yes,' Deborah heaved a sigh. 'But for how long?'

'Exactly.' Tom's arm tightened around her. 'They can't be allowed to get away with it. I know what I think but I guess it's your decision what happens next. What are you going to do?'

'I don't know yet,' she replied. 'But I do have an idea ...'

CHAPTER 33

For Deborah, walking was a newly-discovered, essential part of her day. She couldn't always get out, especially on the days she had to travel to London, but otherwise she enjoyed nothing more than stretching her legs in the fresh air. It just made her feel better. Her gym equipment continued to languish unused as she headed for the outdoors. Walking gave her a chance to think and to reflect. Its benefits were underrated. She varied the routes she took but avoided the footpath around Dark Water Lake. The last time she had ventured there was when she was sixteen and her friend had died. Someday she would go – put those ghosts to rest – but not today. Today, she had other, more pressing concerns.

Ava's information was a shock but also, in a strange way, reassuring. Knowing who was behind those anonymous threats took the sting out of them. Now, she was the one with the power. She knew something they did not; she just needed to find a way of working that to her advantage.

The morning air warmed her skin and the sun dazzled in the cloudless, cerulean canvas above. Deborah strode towards Kai and Phil's bungalow, planning on taking their energetic spaniel, Jez, with her. The sweet scent of honeysuckle welcomed her along the path. Just glorious, she thought, as she rang the doorbell. It was only when no one, human nor canine, responded she remembered they had gone away for a few days. A cottage in the Derbyshire dales. The recollection led to musings about taking a break away with Tom. It would have to be when her year's residence in Wickthorpe was up. Swiftly, she shelved the idea. She couldn't think about what would happen when her year was up.

Her steps led her towards the centre of the village and her mind closed in on itself, ruminating ideas she had discussed with Tom the previous evening. The simplest was her favourite but she wanted to let it play once more in her head, teasing out any possible issues or problems. A lively, black Labrador barked at her through a fence as she passed but she didn't notice. Deep in thought, she missed the figure of Philip Holder, watching her, eyes narrowed, through the window of his dilapidated cottage. Long strides brought her past the disused village well and in sight of the Post Office. No time like the present. The more she thought through her plan, the better she liked it. Grasping the doorknob, she stepped inside.

Enid sat, as usual, in her comfy armchair in the corner, knitting needles clacking. The noise stopped abruptly at her entrance. 'Hmph,' she jeered. 'I'm surprised you have the gall to come in here.'

Deborah flashed her a bright smile and stopped beside her, looking down, while Ava watched anxiously from behind the counter. 'Hello, Enid – just the person I was looking for!' she said.

'Oh?' The old woman's eyes crinkled with wariness and her thin lips curled in a sneer.

'Yes, I wanted to tell you about some rather unpleasant, anonymous notes I've received.' She paused. Enid continued to stare at her with cold, watery eyes but said nothing. 'I had to call the local constabulary – about the notes and the damage to my garden. They were very concerned.'

Enid shrugged and fidgeted with her knitting. 'Nothing to do with me,' she harrumphed.

'Oh?' Deborah raised her eyebrows. 'I thought you might know something. I have been doing a little investigating of my own, with the help of my friends, and we now have three suspects.'

Enid averted her eyes for the first time. 'I'm surprised someone like you has any friends.'

Deborah ignored the barb. 'Two men and a woman appear to be responsible – all residents of Wickthorpe. You would never believe it in a lovely village like this, would you?'

Enid's face contorted in anger. 'Go and crawl back to your coven!' she snarled. 'I'm not interested in anything you have to say.'

'Oh, I think you might be,' Deborah contradicted. 'You see, should I receive more nasty threats, of *any* kind, I want you to be aware, I *know* the names of the people involved and I won't hesitate to tell Detective Inspector Honeysuckle. Those people could well face prosecution … even prison.' Enid glanced up, unable to disguise a flash of panic, and Deborah saw her implied message had been received. She turned to leave, then spun around. 'Oh, just one last thing … should anything untoward happen to me, I've left all the information with someone else, along with instructions as to how it should be used. It's a shame,' she sighed, 'but a woman can't be too careful these days. Good day to you, Enid. Bye, Ava.'

With a cheery wave, she left the Post Office, head held high and a satisfied smile curving her lips. As she continued her walk, mission accomplished, she wondered how Enid would be reacting to her surprise visit. Not well, she was sure. Hopefully, it would be enough to dissuade her from further nasty schemes.

Spirits buoyant, Deborah skirted a wide arc around the outskirts of the village before heading for home. It might be petty but it felt good to have got one over that horrible woman. And, with the threat hanging over her lifted, she felt free and unfettered. Fear was an insidious thing. It had been disconcerting to discover how easily it could influence her thoughts and dreams, and affect her life. Suddenly, she could delight at the beauty of a butterfly and smile at the scent of the roses trailing along someone's garden fence, without that lurking sense of danger at the back of her neck. The world was a much brighter place and she could enjoy it in all its colour.

The hum of bees drew her attention to a stunning clump of foxgloves, just inside the gateway leading to Orchard House, the large, red-bricked building owned by the Hampton-Browns. Another couple who seemed to have taken against her. She did not remember them at all from the eighties but Tom had told her they were living in Wickthorpe when Ayesha died. Their son, Jonny, was the friend he and Felix lost in a tragic car accident. That must have been so awful for the Hampton-Browns. A wave of empathy rolled in her chest and she resolved to make a greater effort to get to know them. That was what Mabel Littlebody would have done. Deborah felt a pang of grief, remembering the old lady she had loved. If only she had known they were related. So many questions remained unanswered. She longed to learn more about Mabel's family – a family she had never had the chance to know.

As she was about to pass by, Valerie Hampton-Brown appeared at one side of her house. 'Deborah!' she called. 'Ms Ryecroft ... I need your help.' She strode down the drive, a stylish figure in a plain, navy dress and matching flat shoes. 'Please come.'

With the spirit of Mabel warming her soul, Deborah diverged from her path to meet the stricken woman. *How pale Valerie looked, how tense!* 'Is everything alright?' she asked.

'No. It's John. I think he's having a heart attack. Please help me. I don't know what to do.'

'Have you called for an ambulance?' Deborah asked, hurrying through the back door behind Valerie and through a utility room.

'Yes, they're on their way,' Valerie threw over her shoulder. 'He's in here.'

She slipped through the half-open door and into a spacious kitchen lined with wooden cabinets. Deborah followed close behind her. Puzzled, she stopped. The room appeared to be empty. 'Where is ...' She got no further. Valerie turned and her eyes darted to a spot behind Deborah's right shoulder. There was a shudder of movement at her back, two hard cracks, an explosion of pain in her head and she crumpled, unconscious, onto the tiles.

***

Tom paced, jaw set, from room to room in Greenways Farm, trying to spot something he had missed. It was 7:30 p.m. Absorbed with pre-harvest maintenance on the combine harvester, he had lost track of time and was late getting in. Usually, he would find Debs working in her office or out in the garden. Occasionally, she would surprise him and be in the kitchen, rustling something up to eat, a task she usually deferred to him. 'You're better at it than me,' she would shrug with a glint in her eye. 'It makes sense to deploy the best person for the job. I'm happy to help.' In the end, they would cook together, chatting about their respective days and enjoying each other's company.

But not today. The house was empty.

First, Tom assumed she must have gone to London. It was not something she had mentioned the night before, but something urgent may have come up. He had tried calling her but her phone was switched off. Stirrings of disquiet crept along his spine. This wasn't like Debs. She would know he'd be worried; she would have contacted him if she'd known she was going to be late in or off the grid.

He reached the door of her office and hesitated before entering. This was her private space. He felt like an intruder but these were exceptional circumstances. Debs could be in danger. The thought was chilling. In her filing cabinet, he found what he was looking for – contact details for her PA, Agneta.

She answered on the third ring. 'Hello.' Her voice sounded wary.

'Hi Agneta. Sorry to disturb you. My name is Tom Oldridge. I'm a good friend of Deborah Ryecroft's and am meant to be seeing her this evening but she hasn't turned up. Do you happen to know where she might be?'

'Ah, Tom. Deborah has mentioned you. Good to talk to you. But, to answer your question, no. I'm afraid not. It's strange because I was expecting her to ring in this afternoon. I hope everything's alright.'

'I'm sure it is,' he replied, his anxiety notching up a level, even as he sought to reassure Agneta. 'It's just I haven't been able to get in contact with her. Her phone is switched off. I was just checking she hadn't been called to the office. Nothing to worry about. Sorry to trouble you. Thank you.'

He ended the call, considering his next move. A check of the crockery loaded in the dishwasher revealed she had been at home for breakfast but not lunch. He could not help thinking about Ava Green's visit the previous evening. Was her warning too late? Or had Deborah's decision to deal with the matter in her own way reaped terrible consequences? Could Enid and her cronies be involved in Deborah's disappearance? He had no contact details for Ava other than the Post Office so he tried that number. It rang for some while and he was about to give up when the line connected. Ava's breathless voice greeted him and he quickly explained why he was ringing.

'Deborah came into the Post Office just this morning,' she told him. 'It was quite early. She came to see Mother – basically to tell her she had been making enquiries, knew what they had been up to and what would happen should they do anything else.' Her voice became a hushed whisper. 'I was worried Mother might discover my role in those enquiries but Deborah managed to do it so she doesn't suspect a thing.'

'What happened after that?'

'Mother went back to her room and got on the phone. I don't know who she called but thought it was probably my brother and Philip Holder. Hopefully, that's put an end to it all. I'm sorry, I don't know where Deborah went after that,' Ava said.

'Did your mother go out at all? Or receive any visitors?'

'No to both questions. She has been here all day and very grumpy, I might add. I can't think she's got anything to do with Deborah being missing. Gosh, it is quite late now, isn't it? I *do* hope nothing has happened to her.'

After a few more words of reassurance, Tom ended the call. He tried Deborah's phone again, with the same result as before, and then returned to the back door to put on his boots. No way could he sit and do nothing.

The sun, now a crimson orb amid swirls of pink and purple, had lost the intensity of the day's heat and a breeze had picked up, lending a nip to the air. Tom, still in shirt sleeves, was oblivious. Fists clenched, he marched towards Philip Holder's cottage. *If that man had caused Debs any harm ...* He ground his teeth, adrenalin firing through his body.

Philip Holder's home was the same small, two-storey cottage in which he had lived all his life. He had never married and had worked in agriculture since he was boy. His father had died young, and he and his mother, Jeanette, a small bustling woman who sold vegetables and jars of jam from a trestle table just inside the gate, had lived together for most of his working life. Then the house, although plain, was always well-kept, and the garden at the front neat and pretty, carefully planted with assorted flowers. That same garden had become overgrown in the years since Jeanette's departure from the world. Roses and buddleia fought for space with woody shrubs and weeds. Tom knew that Philip's heart lay in his rear garden, where he tended vegetables with a fervour bordering on obsession. Flowers were of no interest to him, nor was the appearance of his home. Curtains remained, half-hanging from the windows and ledges were thick with grime. Tom had never minded Philip – his surly manner was just his nature – but he knew his ex-employee was not popular. In recent years, before Deborah's arrival, the vitriol of the village had often centred on Philip Holder. His neighbours had complained vociferously to the Parish Council about the state of the cottage, angry that its appearance detracted from their own properties, and others were unhappy that such 'an eyesore' should be allowed in their pretty village.

Tom cared nothing for any of that. He strode up the path, the vehemence of his knock at the door causing a small shower of flaking, brown paint. It didn't take Philip long to appear. He was chewing something and his surprise, at seeing Tom standing on his doorstep, was palpable.

'Have you seen Deborah Ryecroft today?' Tom got straight to the point.

If Philip was taken aback by the abruptness of the question, he didn't show it. Instead, he just looked puzzled. 'No ...' he began, 'oh ... wait a minute, I saw her go past this morning. I was indoors and saw her through the window. She was walking. Why?'

Tom narrowed his eyes and stared at the other man's face, observing only bemusement. No indications he was concealing something. Either the man was an excellent actor or he was telling the truth. The latter seemed the most likely. 'OK, sorry to trouble you, Philip.' He took a step back, ready to make a hasty retreat.

'Hang on, what's the problem? Have you lost her?' Philip asked, his lips twisting with the first hint of ill-will.

'Sorry. No time to chat. See you around.' Tom raised an arm in farewell as he hurried away. The last thing he wanted was to discuss Debs with someone who only wished her harm. And he had other calls to make.

Andrew Green lived in a newly-built, four-bedroomed, red-bricked house just off Green Road. It formed part of an exclusive development of eight houses, all similar in style, in a small cul-de-sac. Tom's friend Felix had sold the land five years ago, and the Green family had been the first to move in when construction was complete. As Tom stormed along the brick-weave driveway, he detected the strains of a television and the pitch of young girls' voices through the open windows. It seemed unlikely he would find Debs here but he wanted to talk to Andrew, look into the man's eyes, when he asked him where she was.

Julie answered the door, looking slightly startled when she saw him. 'Hello, Tom. This is a surprise. Would you like to come in? I had just put the kettle on for a cup of tea before I start getting the girls ready for bed.'

'Is Andrew in?'

'Yes,' she gave him a tentative smile. 'Watching TV. Come on in.'

She stood aside and he stepped across the threshold, taking care to remove his dusty boots, before following her through to the sitting room. The man of the house was slouched on a sofa, staring at a massive screen on the wall opposite him, while his daughters played a board game on the floor.

'Andrew, Tom's here to see you,' Julie announced. 'Come on, girls, help me make our visitor a cup of tea.'

'Not for me, thanks all the same,' Tom said. 'I'm afraid I'm in a bit of a rush.'

While Eveline and Misha skirted shyly around the man who had interrupted their game, Andrew, dressed casually, in T-shirt and shorts, scrambled from the sofa and grabbed the remote to switch off the television. His smile was wide, revealing even, white teeth, but the blue eyes were wary as he extended his hand to Tom. 'Good to see you, Tom. Have a seat. What can I help you with?'

Tom's jaw remained set, his eyes hard, and he ignored the proffered hand. 'I'll stay standing, if you don't mind. I wanted to ask if you've seen Deborah Ryecroft today.'

A flicker of suspicion crossed Andrew's face. 'No,' he replied slowly. 'Sorry, but I've been at work all day. Is she missing?'

'She hasn't come home,' he answered. 'And I know you are someone who would wish her harm.'

'Now, wait a minute ...' Andrew's voice rose in indignation. 'I've got nothing against the woman and I haven't seen her.' He sucked in a breath. When he continued, his tone was quieter and his face wore an affronted expression. 'I'm disappointed, Tom. I can see you're worried but that's no excuse to come to my home and start throwing insults around.'

Tom remained unmoved, his reply ice-cold. 'Deborah has been receiving nasty, anonymous notes and her garden was vandalised,' he ground out, watching the nuances play across the younger man's face as he spoke. *Raised eyebrows. Feigned shock.* He paused and watched the wariness return. 'Discreet enquiries were made, and the names of those responsible have come to light.' *A flash of dislike this time, swiftly hidden.* His words were hitting home. 'So far, Deborah has been reluctant to share that information with the police but I've been trying to persuade her otherwise. She feels these *people*,' he spat out the word, 'should be spared prosecution. She's a much nicer person than me. I would hang the bastards out to dry. But, if nothing else happens, Deborah would prefer to avoid upset, especially where families are involved.' He cast a meaningful glance towards the door. 'So, I'll ask you again. Have you seen Deborah today, or do you know where I might find her? Think carefully about your answer. If I suspect you are lying, I promise, *your* name will be the first I give to the police.'

'You're very much mistaken if you think I had anything to do with anonymous notes and such.' Andrew returned to an aggressive, hands-on-hips stance, staring defiantly at the tall man opposite. 'You can't prove anything.'

'Fine.' Tom spun on his heel and stepped back into the hallway. 'Unless Deborah is at home when I get back, I'll let the police know where to find you.'

'Now wait a minute ...' Andrew stood over him, as he laced up his boots. 'If she's missing, I assure you, I have absolutely no idea where she is. As I told you, I've been at work all day, came home straight after and have been here ever since. I can prove it. You're barking up the wrong tree and I'm quite happy to tell the police the same thing.' He shrugged. 'It's up to you but I've got nothing to hide and, as you said earlier, it would be a shame to upset my wife and daughters without good reason.'

Tom stood and opened the door. 'You're right,' he said quietly. 'I have no proof that Deborah's disappearance has anything to do with you.' He waited until he spotted the beginnings of an arrogant smile. 'But I *do* have proof that *you* were one of the three people behind the notes and the damage. And I won't hesitate to use it.'

Tom had left the house and taken three strides towards the road when he heard Andrew's voice calling him. He turned to see the other man had followed and was closing the front door behind him.

'Look,' Andrew laid a placatory hand on Tom's arm as he reached him. 'Sorry, I've had a bit of a bad day and I guess I took it out on you. I genuinely have no clue where Ms Ryecroft is, I promise you.' The boyish grin didn't meet his eyes. 'I swear on my mother's life. There's no need to do anything hasty. Now, what can I do to help? Shall I call around and organise a search party?'

Tom's look was scathing. 'Go back inside to your family,' he said, shaking off the other man's hand. 'If I find out you're lying to me ...'

'I'm not, mate, I'm not!'

'I'm *not* your *mate*.' With a final glance of contempt, Tom stepped out onto the road and headed homeward, his heart heavy. He suspected Andrew Green knew nothing about Deborah's disappearance and he had run out of options.

CHAPTER 34

Her return to consciousness dragged through old nightmares. *Can't breathe ... darkness closing in ... underwater ... suffocating ... pain ... death ...*

Except death did not come and the throbbing agony continued. Someone was moaning but she could not move to help them. It was a while before she realised the voice was hers. When she blinked her eyes open, the blackness was still there, hot and musty, pressing down. She tried to open her mouth to call for help but something was clamping it closed. When she attempted to move a hand, to pull the obstruction away, she couldn't. Both arms were fixed behind her back and refused to pull free. She focused on her legs which were drawn up, knees towards her chest, so she was lying on her right-hand side in a foetal position. They too resisted all efforts to shift position. There was no room to stretch out and her feet were tied together. She was trapped.

Exhausted, she closed her eyes and willed her brain to action. The pain at the back of her head raged like a fire, spreading through her entire body. An accident ... a bang on the head which had confused her. Any moment, she would wake fully and find herself in hospital ...

Deliberately, she forced her eyelids upwards, stretching her eyes wide so vision could return. But the blackness remained. Fidgeting her body slightly brought more information. She was in some kind of box, surrounded on all four sides by solid walls. Her fingers brushed one of the surfaces, hard and rough like wood. *A wooden box ... a coffin.* Panic made her rear her head to get out. A sharp thud and the resulting pain halted her. She tried again, more cautious this time. Same result. *A coffin with a lid.* She had been buried alive!

Horror made her movements more urgent, her muffled cries for help more insistent. No one came. Her mind was now fully alert, pain ignored, as she lay and tried to plan her escape. She remembered everything – Valerie Hampton-Brown's plea for help, being lured inside the house, something cracking against her skull. It was difficult to believe. Two churchgoing members of the village community had attacked her, trussed her like a chicken and stuck her in a box. Deborah knew the Hampton-Browns belonged to the group of villagers who resented her return to Wickthorpe but ... *really?* The idea they would take her prisoner was just too preposterous. They were in their late seventies. John Hampton-Brown was a churchwarden at St Mary's. She must have got it wrong.

Another scenario presented itself. Valerie had been acting under duress. An unknown group of kidnappers had John at gunpoint, and she had been forced to act as she had. That was more likely. *Ransom money.* Deborah's wealth and success made her a kidnap risk. She relaxed a fraction at the thought. Once the kidnappers had been paid, they would release her. She had to believe that. In the meantime, she would turn her attention to getting free of the bonds which held her, specifically the rope pinning her arms behind her back. It was tied tight, her wrists fixed together. She tugged as hard as she could for thirty seconds, then rested, before repeating the process, over and over, constantly testing to see if the knot had loosened enough to slip a hand out. When that failed to work, she felt carefully around the sides of the box, as far as she could reach with her fingers, to see if there was a helpful nail or something sharp against which she could saw the rope. There was nothing.

Tears filled in her eyes as she lay for a moment, helpless and despairing. Whoever had captured her had made sure she had no chance of escape. She was completely trapped, a fly in a spider's web. Self-pity washed over her, a tide of frustration and hopelessness. She could die here alone and no one would know. There was nothing she could do. Silent, shuddering sobs shook her body.

Finally spent, she began to pull the threads of self-control back together. Tears and negative thoughts were no help. It was time to channel some positive energy and think of another plan of escape.

However, after several agonising minutes – she had no idea how many – she gave up. There really was no way out of the box without some assistance. She had come instead to the conclusion that, if escape was impossible, she would have to be patient. At some point, someone would come for her. She would stay alert and she would be ready. When the lid came off the box, then she might have a chance. If she was lucky, there would be just one captor ... and the possibility of taking him or her by surprise. At least, that was what she hoped. Wait, endure, and remain poised to attack in any way which presented itself when the time came. She was under no illusion about the likelihood of success. Tied as she was, with no weapon, facing who knew what kind of enemy, the odds were stacked against her. But she had to believe she could do it. There was no other option.

***

Her determination wavered as the hours passed, her mind drifting of its own volition. She wondered if she would ever see Tom again. He had come to mean a lot to her over the past few months and in a way she had not expected. There had been infatuations before but the rose-tinted glasses inevitably fell away and the relationships ended. The thing with Tom was different in a way she struggled to pinpoint. She liked him, she looked forward to seeing him when they were apart, she enjoyed his company, they had lots of laughs and the sex was something else.

But she was only in Wickthorpe for a year. When she left, she would leave him behind. There was no future with him ... and why would she even think there might be? Their lives were very different and it wouldn't work ... except it was working very well at the moment ... until she'd been knocked on the head and taken prisoner. Was she in love with Tom? Definitely not. She could leave him behind without a backward glance .... except that wasn't true. Already, the thought of being without him was not something she wanted to consider.

Nor did she want to think about her plight. Instead, she focused her senses on trying to discover her whereabouts. Chances were that she was still in the Hampton-Browns' house, but she may have been moved while she was unconscious. Sounds were faint but were there, if she listened hard enough. Cars passing. A distant lawnmower. The occasional bang from somewhere below her, perhaps a cupboard door being shut. The noises were reassuring. People were outside, not far away. It must be getting late in the day. Tom would return from work and wonder where she was. He would try calling her. Her phone was in her bag, she remembered, and her bag was missing. The police would know how to find her by discovering its location. Rescue could be just moments away ...

***

Tom's long strides took him back towards Greenways Farm, his fear growing by the minute. At regular intervals, he had tried Deborah's phone but the result was always the same – 'the phone you are calling is switched off.' He had also rung Emma. She and Rick were at Greenways Farm in case Debs turned up. They would let him know the second she did but he could not resist checking anyway. Desperately, he tried to think of anything else he could do. Calling the police was the obvious choice but he was aware they were likely to do nothing until she had been missing for several hours. DI Honeysuckle knew about the threats so she would be more concerned but he wanted to ensure he had tried everything he could first, just in case there was a harmless explanation.

Honoraria's sixteenth- century cottage sat, small and compact, in a tiny plot about four hundred metres from his home. As it came into view, he saw she was out front, watering hanging baskets resplendent with pink geraniums which adorned her porch. He quickened his pace, hoping to catch her before she disappeared indoors. Honoraria had a reputation for being a hopeless gossip. If anything was happening in the village, she was likely to be one of the first to know. A long shot but worth trying all the same.

'Honoraria,' he called as he approached, 'have you got a minute?'

She set down her watering can, fluffed her hair and straightened the cavernous smock she was wearing atop a pair of beige cotton trousers. 'I always have time for you, Tom Oldridge,' she simpered. 'Why don't you come and have a glass of wine with me on the decking? Watch the sun go down. It's a beautiful evening.'

'It is and another time.' He forced a smile. 'I'm afraid I have a problem and I wondered if you could help.'

'Oh?' Her plump face assumed a look of concern. 'Of course. I'll do my best.'

'I'm worried about Debs,' he said, deciding to be perfectly straight with her. 'Deborah Ryecroft. She hasn't come home and her phone is switched off. As far as I know, she had no plans to go out today and she would have contacted me if that had changed.' He threw up his hands. 'I'm at a loss. I just wondered if you might have seen her.'

'Oh dear, that seems very strange ... but she *is* a very busy woman, I'm sure. She'll turn up.' Honoraria reached across to pat his arm. 'Are you certain you won't have a glass of wine? It will help you relax while you wait.'

Tom ignored the hope and loneliness he glimpsed in those china-blue eyes and his lips tightened with impatience. 'I just need to know if you've seen her, that's all.' Her face crumpled and he immediately regretted his curt tone. 'I'm sorry, Honoraria,' he said in a gentler voice. 'I don't mean to be rude but there are people in this village who may stop at nothing to remove her from it. I'm concerned for her safety.'

'Oh yes, I heard about what happened to her garden. Oh dear, now she's missing, you say. That is a worry.' She shook her head, tutting under her breath. 'I'm so sorry I can't help you, Tom, but I haven't seen her today. *Such* an attractive woman. I often see her out walking.'

'OK. Thanks for your time and for the offer of the wine.'

As Tom stepped away, her eyes widened. 'Oh, my goodness ... you don't think ... no ... they wouldn't do anything like that ... not anything *dangerous*.'

He turned back. 'Who?'

'Enid Green and the rest.' She lowered her voice. 'They don't like Deborah. For some reason, they are convinced she's the Wickthorpe Witch, come to wreak vengeance on innocent people. They want her out of the village. Between you and me, I think they've been seriously affected by what happened to poor Freya Billington. I saw her, you know, in Oxford, with a strange man, the very weekend it happened. Awful! I know the police think it was suicide but I'm sure that man, the one she was with, had something to do with it all. If only I could have seen him better, I ...'

'How do you know about Enid Green?' he interrupted.

'Well ...' Honoraria leaned closer, encouraged by his interest. 'I've heard her spouting forth in the Post Office, of course, but I thought nothing of it. She is a bit like that, Enid is ... always got it in for somebody.'

Yes ...' Tom prompted, nodding his head, urging her to get on with it.

'But then she turned up with reinforcements at my History Society meeting last week. Enid and Ava usually attend but the others are not regulars, even if they *did* turn up at the Dorothy Fairgrove meeting. Anyway, I was delighted to see them, until I realised they had an ulterior motive. They wanted to drum up support to take serious action against Deborah ... to get her out of the village. Well, I was mortified! Luckily, my regulars are not the type of people to conduct a vendetta against someone and Enid's lot left shortly after the coffee break.'

'Who was with Enid?' he asked, suspecting he already knew the answer.

'Philip Holder.' She pursed her lips. 'Miserable, little man, he is. Always got a face like a sour grape. And the Hampton-Browns. I know they blame the curse for their son's accident but I was surprised to find *them* consorting with the likes of Enid and Philip, scheming someone's downfall. You would have thought that sort of thing was beneath them, wouldn't you?'

'Mm.' Tom was scarcely listening as she chattered on. *The Hampton-Browns?* 'Not Enid's son, Andrew?' he asked.

'No, he wasn't there. Just those four. As I said, they all came to the meeting at the Institute, when Dorothy Fairgrove gave a *most* illuminating talk on the history of witchcraft in Suffolk. Sorry, I forgot. You were there too, weren't you, Tom? I was disappointed not to see you at the next ones.' A quick glance of reproof. 'That particular meeting *was* incredibly popular,' she added proudly, 'so I would guess they thought they might find a few like-minded villagers amongst the History Society ranks. As I said, though, no one took the bait when they started their rabble-rousing talk. Well, Gretchen Cooper signed their awful petition, I suppose.' She frowned. 'But the poor soul didn't know what she was doing. It was a petition to evict Deborah from the village,' she explained as Tom's face grew increasingly bemused. 'Obviously, Wendy Robinson and I were hardly likely to tolerate such behaviour, were we?' she smiled. 'Not that we were the only other people there, of course. Usually, we have a very respectable turnout ...'

'Thank you, Honoraria. All this has been very helpful.' He gave her a nod before heading back in the direction from which he had just come.

Honoraria called after him, 'I *do* hope you find her.'

He raised an arm in response and continued. He knew where he was heading next. To Orchard House, the large, red-bricked building a little further along, just a meadow away from Honoraria's cottage, to talk to the Hampton-Browns.

***

John Hampton-Brown was astride a ride-on lawnmower, cutting verdant grass beneath a border of oak and ash, oblivious to Tom pacing up the driveway. That was good. Talking to Valerie alone would be the best option, he decided. At the front door, he rang the bell. No response. After a minute or so, he pressed the button again. Both cars were in the driveway, John's green Range Rover alongside Valerie's smaller, pale blue Ford Focus, so she must be inside. Valerie rarely walked anywhere, especially not with dusk darkening the sky. Still nothing. Tom stepped to one side and peered through a window into the sitting room. It was furnished in an old-fashioned style with high-backed sofas, frilled cushions and a mahogany sideboard. Other than the furniture, the room was empty. Huffing in frustration, Tom glanced at his watch. It was late. Possibly, Valerie had already gone to bed or was in the bath. He glanced again towards John but hesitated. If the Hampton-Browns knew anything about Deborah's disappearance, John would be a tough nut to crack. A chat with Valerie would be preferable. She had always responded favourably to a bit of charm. He decided to check around the back. Although cool, it was still a fine evening. She might be out in the garden.

He let himself through the gate on the west side and strode along the narrow path which led to a vast, manicured lawn and colourful flower beds. No sign of Valerie. Continuing around the path and back along the west side of the property, a sudden movement caught his eye in one of the windows. He stopped abruptly, just in time to see her disappear through a doorway. Furiously, he rapped on the window but she did not reappear. He stalked round to the front door and leant on the doorbell for a good thirty seconds. When there was still no answer, he shouted through the letter box. 'Valerie, I know you're in there. I want to talk to you. Please open the door!'

'Tom! What the hell do you think you're doing?'

He leapt away from the door like a naughty schoolboy caught smoking behind the bike shed. 'Hello, John.' He ignored the thunderous expression and held out his hand with an affable smile. 'I had tried the doorbell before but Valerie wasn't answering. I just wanted to have a word.'

John regarded him with cold-eyed suspicion. 'My wife is a little deaf,' he said in haughty tones. 'Maybe I can be of assistance?'

Tom tried a look of apologetic entreaty. 'I'm sorry but I really wanted to have a word with both of you, if you don't mind. May I come in?'

'It may not be convenient for my wife. It is very late.' He looked pointedly at his watch.

'I know. I'm sorry, but it can't be helped.'

John's face remained stony. 'I'll check to see if she's available. Wait there.'

Tom stood pondering while the other man disappeared back around the west side of the house. It was unfortunate he had been caught in such a fashion. John was a stickler for courtesy and old-school manners. Little wonder the yelling through the letter-box had met with a frosty reception. But was there more to it than that? And why was Valerie avoiding him? She was not so deaf she hadn't heard the racket from the doorbell, surely?

It was some while before John returned, this time with Valerie behind him. She looked pale, he thought, and apprehensive, quite unlike her usual, haughty self. However, when she spoke, her voice was as imperious as ever. 'I'm sorry I didn't hear the doorbell, Tom. I was watching the television and have it turned up quite loud. I am a little deaf, you see. Please keep that information to yourself. It's not something I'd like to become common knowledge.'

'Of course,' he gave her his most charming smile. 'And I'm very sorry to disturb your evening, especially at this late hour. I'll come straight to the point. Deborah Ryecroft is missing and I'm concerned for her safety. I wondered if either of you had seen her?' He watched their reactions closely but not one flicker of emotion crossed either countenance.

'No,' John barked. 'I haven't. Have you?' He glanced at his wife who shook her head, lips clamped in a thin line. 'I could've told you that in the first place,' he scowled. 'If that's all, we'll bid you goodnight.'

'Wait,' Tom said, as they turned to leave. 'I know about the notes and the vandalism to Deborah's garden.'

Once again, there was a noticeable lack of reaction. 'I don't know what you're talking about. Obviously, we heard about the damage to that woman's garden but what notes?' glowered John Hampton-Brown.

'Don't pretend you don't know.' Tom felt his anger simmer and struggled to keep it in check. 'You, Enid Green, Philip Holder ... you were all behind those spiteful, anonymous threats.'

'Now, you're just talking nonsense ... slander, for that matter. We have made no secret of the fact that we think Deborah Ryecroft is trouble but to suggest we would lower ourselves to send her anonymous letters is just preposterous.' There was a sardonic gleam in John's eye as he continued, 'I *was* planning to write to her, in my capacity as Chairman of the Parish Council. Her hedge along Green Road is becoming quite overgrown and is causing rather a hazard. She will shortly be in receipt of a letter from the Clerk informing her of such and asking her to get it cut back.' He glared at Tom. 'Other than that, I have had no written communication with the woman. I find your suggestion incredibly rude and would like you to leave my property.'

Tom stood his ground. 'I know you wish her harm. If you have had anything to do with her disappearance, I swear I'll ...'

'I suggest you stop right there, young man, before you force me to call the police about your threatening behaviour. Good evening.' With that, John placed a hand in the small of his wife's back and ushered her from view.

With a sigh of frustration, Tom watched their departure. He had gained no information from the couple and was no closer to finding Deborah. Maybe, he had made a mistake, accusing the Hampton-Browns like that. His disclosure of the threats to Deborah had elicited such genuine disdain he suspected they knew nothing about them. Ava had not mentioned their names the night before; he had assumed their involvement following Honoraria's comments and she was not necessarily the most reliable source. He shrugged and made a despondent way back to Green Road. If he had misjudged the Hampton-Browns, there would have to be a grovelling apology. So be it. He wished that was all he had to worry about. As he advanced through the gloom towards Greenways Farm, he withdrew his phone from his pocket once more. Time to do what he should have done at the beginning, when he first got in and realised Debs was missing. Time to call the police.

***

It was her first day at school. Funny flutterings in her tummy made her grip Mummy's hand with the might of her four years as they walked together, side by side. It had seemed exciting whilst Mummy was plaiting her hair and when she put on her brand new, shiny, black shoes, but now, she decided, school was not for her. She was scared. What would happen? Would the other children like her or would they be like Father? She was happy at home when it was just her and Mummy. Things changed when Father came in from work. Mummy got all anxious and spoke sharply to her. Father did not speak to her at all unless she was naughty when she got big smacks. Mummy said it was for her own good. She had to learn. She tried and tried to learn but she still did things wrong. Perhaps school would teach her how to get things right so Father was kind and didn't beat her. The thought cheered her as they approached the red-bricked, forbidding façade of the Victorian building. Mummy squeezed her hand and whispered in her ear but she couldn't hear what she said because of the awful noise shrieking ...

A doorbell, shrill and insistent. Realisation jolted Deborah from her doze. The box; the throbbing in her head; pain everywhere: shoulders, back, arms, legs. It all returned in a micro second. Despair ... surging hope ... senses on high alert. Someone was at the door! *The police?* Frantically, she rocked inside the box, screaming as loudly as she could through the gag. Her efforts were pitifully muffled and weak. Her parched throat rasped out cries for help, gurgling and coughing with the strain. Still, she continued. Rescue could be close at hand.

She stopped when the doorbell rang a second time. The visitor was growing impatient. She could tell by the heavy way they leant on the button, refusing to release it until their call was answered. When it finally ceased, she began her screams again, banging her feet as hard as she could against the side of the box so that it juddered and jarred. No one came.

Exhausted, broken with disappointment, she stopped. Her head roared with pain; her chest heaved as she struggled to breathe. How much air did she have left in the box? Another rush of panic. Was that the plan –

suffocation? The wooden sides seemed to close in as claustrophobia took hold. She was going to die here. There was no one to help her. Fear wracked her body. She had never felt so alone.

Eventually, the feeling of hopelessness passed. She had no idea how long it took, or how long she had been trapped there. Hours? Days? There were no clues to guide her. Straining her ears, she listened again for external noises, sounds of normality: chimes of the village clock; cars driving by; dogs barking. None of those things. All she could hear was the thudding of her heart and her own shallow breaths.

Her mind slipped once more to the past. Work, her company, achievements, triumphs. They had given her such a sense of fulfilment at the time but seemed as insignificant as dust with death looming. It was people who mattered. Her close friends; her loyal staff; Tom ... What was she going to do about Tom, assuming she survived? Could she walk away, back to her old life in London? Her chest ached at the prospect. Already he was such an important part of her life.

The situation was making her sentimental. Survival – *that* was what she should concentrate on. Plenty of time to decide what to do in the future. The horrifying present demanded her full attention. The relentless ticking of time was lulling her into drowsiness when she needed to be ready to act if – no, *when* – she had the chance.

Seconds later, the moment came.

Awareness coiled like a cobra. She was not alone! Her body tensed, fingers and toes wriggling to force blood around numb limbs. The hissing of hushed voices hovered indistinct from somewhere above. A rattle. A rush of cool air. Beneath the gag, her mouth gasping and grasping like an addict. Eyes closed despite the overwhelming need to surface from the blackness.

'Get hold of her legs.' A male voice, deep, full of authority. A man used to command. John Hampton-Brown.

Strong hands forced under her armpits. Softer hands, more tentative, gripped and fidgeted at her ankles, flexing and adjusting to get the best hold. The weak link. That was the direction to focus her attack.

'Hold on. She's bleeding. Let me put something down to protect the carpet,' Valerie hissed.

'Hurry up, then,' came the terse reply.

Another wait. When Valerie returned, she forced her body to remain limp and unresponsive while it was hauled from the box and lumped on a material which crackled beneath her. *Bubble wrap?* The urge to straighten her legs fought with the need to lull her captors into a false sense of security.

'She's still unconscious. How are we going to get her down the stairs?' Valerie Hampton-Brown's question held none of her usual, bossy hauteur. She sounded anxious.

Silence. Fingers hot on her neck. Impossible to avoid flinching. 'She's alive. I'll carry her down the stairs and we'll get her into the car. Perhaps that will wake her up.'

'Yes. She has to be conscious. I have to hear her repent her sins and renounce the devil. I need to know why she chose Jonathan.' An edge of hysteria to Valerie's voice.

'Calm yourself,' John commanded. 'There will be time enough for that down at the lake. Now, come around here and hold her up.'

Down at the lake? Renounce the devil? She had imagined many terrors but not *that*! A scream of protest built in her chest and she fought the urge to release it. *Wait!* Her upper torso was lifted from the floor and wedged against Valerie's bony frame. Still, she lay motionless, mind working overtime, as she tried to concentrate on the present rather than the fate in store for her. With panic threatening to overwhelm her, she weighed up her options. *Limited. No real chance of success. Two against one and trussed like a turkey.* But she had to try. She was younger than them. Fit and strong ... at least, she had been. Her legs were fiery with pins and needles as circulation made a painful return. Her arms had lost all feeling, secured as they were behind her back. She would only get one chance and she would give it everything she'd got. *A lucky strike. Incapacitate them both. If only ...*

Her knees were rolled off the floor. They were going to try to pull her upright so John could hoist her over his shoulder. She could hear him grunting as he bent over her. Like a rag doll, she leaned away from Valerie as if slumping forwards to the ground. Her muscles bunched in anticipation. *One deep breath. NOW!*

With all the force she could muster, she jack-knifed her body, feet aiming towards John's crotch, her head cracking back into Valerie's face with an agonising jolt. Valerie screamed and moved away so her head fell to the floor.

Another dizzying thump, but still her bound legs flailed, seeking a target. Her initial kick had made only glancing contact. *Not enough.*

'You bitch!' John spat, his voice coming from somewhere behind her. 'It's just a bruise, Valerie. Nothing to make a fuss about.'

'I thought you said she was unconscious!' Valerie's voice trembled with indignation. 'She *hit* me!'

'You said that, not me,' her husband replied calmly. 'Clearly, she was just pretending. We've learnt our lesson; she won't fool us again.'

'No one knows she's here, do they? Tom Oldridge seemed very suspicious. You're sure you dealt with her phone so it can't be traced here.'

'I've already told you ...' The air vibrated with John's irritation. 'The phone is switched off. If anyone manages to trace the location of the phone before it was turned off, they'll find it in the meadow in front of Greenways Farm, where I threw it from my car window.'

'You don't think anyone saw you, do you?'

'Valerie, for goodness sake, I'm not an idiot. Of course, no one saw me!' A vicious hand grabbed a handful of Deborah's hair, hauling her head once more away from the floor, while the other hand delivered a stinging slap to her face. With a low moan, she fell back and, as she slipped away from consciousness, she felt the breath of John Hampton-Brown against her left ear. 'There is no escape. You shall have your witch's reckoning before the night is out.'

CHAPTER 35

Martha's diary
12th August, 1645

Today has been the most disastrous of days! I have packed our things and am most anxious for John's homecoming so we can depart this village without delay. The thought fills my heart with sadness but there is naught else to be done. I pray my dear husband will forgive me.

First, I made a most grievous error. Twas naught but my own foolishness. I know well how any with knowledge in the arts of healing are in peril of falling under suspicion and I have yet another reason to fear the witch hunters. On my left forearm, I am in possession of a berry-sized mole. *The devil's mark.* Tis what folk call such blemishes. John warns me daily against the risks I take and I gave him my faithful promise to keep the mark hidden. Through my carelessness, I have failed him.

The weather has been scorching hot of late and today was no exception. The men work long hours in the fields, scything wheat and stacking sheafs, and little Josiah is happy outside whilst I do my chores. He is walking now and regularly gets into mischief so it befalls me to keep him under close watch. My dear friend Prudence and sweet Mary Martha were outside with me when a boy appeared, breathless with running. He had been sent to seek my assistance with a young woman struggling for many hours to birth her child. I have helped others in such circumstances so was unsurprised by his plea. Prudence kindly offered to mind Josiah and I hurried after the boy through the village. When we reached Holley land, chills ran down my spine despite the heat. In recent times, I have seen Roger Holley only at a distance but it made me sore nervous to be so much in his vicinity.

Howe'er, 'pon arrival at a tiny cottage, such thoughts of Holley clear fled my mind. A girl, barely more than a child herself, writhed on a narrow, wooden bed. Her face was deathly white and bathed in sweat. I feared for her life. With scarce a thought, I called for water to be boiled in readiness and rolled up my sleeves. In that moment, I confess I forgot the mark on my arm. At first, the girl's mother did not see it. She had eyes solely for her stricken daughter, asking me what was taking so long and telling me she had no such trouble birthing her seven children. An examination beneath the thin, grey blanket revealed the problem and I explained the babe was coming feet first. I was most anxious but tried to reassure the exhausted girl, telling her such an occurrence was common enough and that all would be well with a little assistance.

The girl's mother was a worn woman with the look of old age, though likely still to reach her fortieth year. Her gaze slid to the mole on my left arm, exposed through my carelessness, and her demeanour changed from one of natural concern to cold-faced suspicion. She hastened to step between me and the bed, insisting she held no truck with interference and twas time for me to leave. Better to let nature take its course, she said. That was when I knew I was done for. Howe'er, the deed was done and the girl needed my help. I tried to mask my fear and spoke kindly to the woman, suggesting she take her rest with a cup of tea. Hands on hips, she demanded I should leave, accusing me of practising the devil's work 'pon her daughter. I knew not what to do but the girl herself begged me to stay, gripping my wrist and imploring her ma to allow it. At that, I patted the girl's hand and agreed to stay, fearing that if I deserted her now, both she and her babe would surely die.

After a few hours, the child was delivered. Twas a boy but I am most sad to say he was stillborn. The girl will recover but was much distressed. I soothed her as best I could by saying there would be other babies. Her mother then uttered words which chilled me to the core.

'Not 'til she gets herself wed,' she said. 'And so long as she stays clear of the young master. Now you had best get yourself away from here. There will be those most displeased by this day's work.'

I raced toward home, mulling her words. Could the stillborn infant be the son of Roger Holley? It seemed likely, though the girl could not have been more than fourteen years. Had he taken advantage of her as he had so tried with me? Meantimes, if the woman told others of my mole, I could find myself arrested for practising witchcraft. That meant we were no longer safe in Wickhorpe.

With such thoughts filling my mind, I was lacking my usual vigilance and was horrified to find myself confronted by Roger Holley himself – quite alone and completely at his mercy. Without saying a word, he dealt me a most savage blow to the side of my head. It sent me tumbling to the ground, black spots clouding my vision. He was then swiftly 'pon me, tearing at my clothes. I screamed for help as loudly as I could but to no avail. He clamped my mouth with one hand and pinned my wrists with the other as he sat astride my hips. In response, I attempted to bite his hand, all the while struggling to escape, so he struck me again, hard across the cheek. Then he ripped my bodice clean away, baring my breasts. I have never been so terrified, knowing I was not strong enough to resist him.

Suddenly, a male voice interrupted the contemptible proceedings, urging Holley to cease his attack. Twas Malachi Smith. I confess I have never been so happy to see another soul. Holley merely smirked, telling Smith he was just having a little fun and urging him to be on his way. I managed to free my mouth sufficiently to beg for help but, in response, Holley claimed he and I were used to such games. The villain said I was lying when I protested otherwise, for fear of my husband.

Malachi Smith regarded us both, his face serious. I prayed with all my might he would believe my story. At last, he spoke, reminding Holley I was a married woman and he should leave me be. Three other men appeared behind him and my heart leapt with relief. His brothers. Surely now I would be freed?

Holley sneered that he would do as he pleased on his land, warning Smith and his brothers to leave or things would not go well for them in the future. Yet still Malachi would not back down. For a long moment, the men stared at each other, before Holley gave a careless laugh and released me. As he stood, leaving me grasping at my shredded clothes and trying to conceal my nakedness, he jeered I was not worth bothering with anyway. Then he bent again to plant a foul kiss on my lips, promising to finish his business with me, one way or another.

As he stalked away, dusting the dirt from his breeches, Malachi Smith helped me to my feet, most solicitous as to my welfare. I thanked him most profusely but he brushed away my gratitude, reminding me that I had helped his wife a few weeks back. She had just given birth and was sick with a fever. One good turn deserved another, he said.

Afterwards, I fled to Prudence's house to fetch Josiah, explaining what had occurred and saying we must leave Wickthorpe. Two terrible events had left me in great danger, both from witch hunters and from Roger Holley. I knew we could no longer stay in the village we had grown to love. The poor girl was distraught at such tidings and we bid each other a most tearful farewell. After, I returned home and set about packing up our belongings, most impatient for John to return from work.

Howe'er, tis now long after dark and still John has not appeared. I know he will be hungry and bone weary. I will tell him what has transpired and urge him to travel through the night to escape the village but my husband may well say tis best to wait til dawn. Tis unfair of me to expect anything more and most unlikely my accusers will choose the dead of night to arrest me. Verily we will be safe til morn.

I shed yet more tears as I wait for John. We were most content in Wickthorpe and I am sad to leave in such circumstances. How I will miss Prudence and dear Mary Martha! I pray that God will watch over them and keep them safe.

My prayers are also for my own family. Who knows what will befall us come the morrow? Whate'er happens, please Lord, protect my dearest husband and son.

CHAPTER 36

It was taking too long.

Tom sat, ramrod tense, opposite DI Honeysuckle in his kitchen, an untouched mug of tea on the worktop in front of him. It had been more than two hours since he had called the police and, as wasted minutes crept by, his dread increased. First, he was told it was too soon to report a missing person. He kept a tight rein on his exasperation and asked to speak to DI Honeysuckle, explaining there had been threats levelled against Deborah and DI Honeysuckle would most likely take a more serious view of the situation. She wasn't available, he was told, but someone would get back to him. Thirty minutes passed. Nothing. He had been all set to drive to Bury St Edmunds to make a fuss at the police station there until Emma checked online and told him it wasn't open to the public after 5 p.m. Instead, he dialled 999 again and received a curt response.

'Please don't call again, sir. We are aware. Someone will be in touch shortly.'

Darkness shrouded the garden outside and Tom's depression deepened. Debs was in trouble and he was powerless to help. He had never felt so utterly useless. Eleven o'clock came and went. Emma made coffee, and both she and Rick tried their best to make reassuring noises but eventually those too fell silent.

At last, car headlights swept into the drive and Tom leapt to the front door, stepping aside to allow entry to DI Honeysuckle and DS Everard. They nodded as they passed, faces serious and flagging with fatigue. 'We came as soon as we could,' the Inspector murmured, accepting both Emma's invitation to sit and the offer of coffee. 'I'm sorry for the delay. Tell me what's happened.'

Tom filled them in: Debs' failure to return home; Ava Green's revelations the night before; his own investigations and house calls that evening. He watched DI Honeysuckle's lips tighten as he outlined the visits to Philip Holder, Andrew Green, and the Hampton-Browns, but she listened without comment while DS Everard made notes. More questions followed. She was interested in his observations but also wanted to check more obvious reasons for Deborah's disappearance. Had they argued? How had Deborah seemed when they last spoke? When was that? Where had he spent the day? Could anyone verify his whereabouts? Irritation surged as he answered their questions. *They were wasting precious time.* Gritting his teeth, he detailed random tasks performed that day. Mostly, he had been in his office, catching up on paperwork and making phone calls. Other than that, work on their New Holland combine, getting it ready for harvest. He had seen Emma twice, including the half hour spent having lunch together, but otherwise he had been on his own. Their insistence on writing down the names of everyone with whom he had spoken made him splutter with annoyance. How on earth was he expected to remember them all? He had kept a note in his diary. Emma volunteered to fetch it and received a nod of approval from DI Honeysuckle who dispatched her sergeant to accompany her.

'Am I seriously under suspicion here?' he asked.

DI Honeysuckle gave him a dispassionate stare. 'We're just doing our job.'

'Look ...' He held up his hands. 'You can question me all you like but it's not going to help you find Debs. Can we save it until later? God knows what's happened to her but I'm worried sick. There are some seriously disturbed people in this village who have got it in for her. Who knows what they're capable of?'

DI Honeysuckle frowned. 'You say you went to see all the people, alleged by Ava Green, to have been behind the notes and the damage to the garden?'

'Not Enid Green, because Ava told me Enid had been at the Post Office all day. Otherwise yes, although Ava hadn't mentioned the Hampton-Browns. That was Honoraria Simpson-Fairchild, another Wickthorpe resident, who told me they were trying to whip up support for a campaign against Deborah at a History Society meeting. Of all the people I visited, the Hampton-Browns were the most suspicious. They *may* have been hiding something. For a start, they refused to allow me in, although I suppose it was getting quite late by that time ...'

'Who is Deborah's next-of-kin?' DI Honeysuckle startled him with the unexpected question.

'I honestly have no idea. Both her parents are dead and she's not mentioned any other family. Why?'

'Deborah Ryecroft is a very wealthy woman,' she replied.

Tom considered the statement. 'I suppose that would make kidnap a possibility?'

She did not respond and, when Emma and DS Everard returned with the diary, rose from her seat. 'Right. We'll be in touch. We'll take this with us, if you don't mind.'

Tom also stood. 'Please check out the villagers first. As I said, the Hampton-Browns were ...'

'We'll do our best to find Ms Ryecroft, you may be assured of that. As I said, we'll be in touch.' With a pointed glance at her colleague and a brief nod to the rest of them, DI Honeysuckle made an abrupt exit.

'She seemed .... efficient,' Emma said, with an anxious look at her dad.

'I'm sure they'll find her,' Rick added, the doubt in his pale blue eyes belying his bluff tone.

Tom shrugged and slumped back into a chair. It was going to be a long night.

'At least they took her disappearance seriously,' Emma added, perching on the arm of his chair and hugging his shoulders. 'I'm sure they'll have a team out scouring the area through the night.'

Tom wished he could believe that. He had a horrible feeling that any search would not begin in earnest until daylight ... and, by then, it could be too late.

***

'Back to the station, Ma'am?' Jack Everard yawned and turned the key in the ignition. 'It's been a long day and nothing much we can really do until morning.'

Beth Honeysuckle bit her lip and mulled over the question. He was right. It *had* been a long day and a missing person search would mean an early start. In the meantime, Deborah Ryecroft could show up. The sensible thing would be to get some sleep and hit the ground running in the morning. It was now after midnight and the Detective Chief Superintendent would want a full briefing first thing. There really was nothing the two of them could do except ... She sighed. 'Let's just drive by the three addresses Tom Oldridge has given us. You never know ...'

Jack rolled his eyes. Her response didn't surprise him. His boss was nothing if not dedicated and thorough. 'Right you are,' he murmured. 'Where to first?'

'The Hampton-Browns are closest, just down the road here.'

They drove the very short journey in silence and pulled into the drive. The house was in darkness, as they expected, and security lights flooded the driveway as they pulled in next to Valerie Hampton-Brown's Ford Focus. Curtains were drawn and there was no sign of life.

'Looks like they're fast asleep in bed, as we should be,' Jack jibed. 'Shall we move on?' He reached forward to restart the engine.

'Wait a minute.' Beth Honeysuckle's sharp, brown eyes roved the area. Something was bothering her but she could not think what it was. Blinking back fatigue, she tried to recall a mental image of the property when she, personally, had last visited. She knew the Hampton-Browns had been informally questioned about the damage to Deborah Ryecroft's garden but she had not been involved in that. Before then, they had requested an interview, saying they had information pertinent to the investigation into Freya Billington's death. As it turned out, they only wanted to point out the link between the last drowning in Wickthorpe and the latest one – Deborah Ryecroft. Beth discovered they did indeed, as Tom Oldridge claimed, subscribe to the 'Witch of Wickthorpe' version of events. But that did not make them kidnappers. Other than their peculiar superstition, which appeared to owe much to the tragic death of their teenage son back in 1988, they seemed to conform to the monied, ex-military stereotypes she was expecting.

It had been quite a cool day, overcast but dry, she remembered, processing her memory in her methodical fashion. John Hampton-Brown had been outside in his shirt sleeves, polishing his car, a green Range Rover. He was a tall, well-built man. Late seventies but clearly kept himself in shape. Valerie had appeared in the doorway – immaculate in pale blue, quite the gracious lady of the manor – and invited them inside. They had refused the offer of a drink and sat waiting for John to join them in a spacious lounge. Valerie had apologised for the slight delay and made a comment about his obsession with cleaning his car. 'It's his military background,' she twittered. 'Used to everything being shipshape and as it should be. It's supposed to rain later so I told him cleaning the car today was a waste of time but apparently it needed doing ... so there we are.' She gave an elegant shrug. 'I wouldn't mind if it went in the garage afterwards but John likes to use that space as a workshop. All his tools and benching are in there so there's no space, not even for my car.'

'Ma'am?' Jack's gruff voice disturbed her thoughts. 'You're surely not thinking about waking them up? It's the middle of the night.'

She shook her head with impatience, irritated by the interruption. Something was prickling the nape of her neck. She was missing something. If only she could think what it was ...

'Thank Christ for that!' Jack engaged the clutch and started the engine.

'No, wait. Something's not right.'

They sat listening to the murmur of the engine and the pointed drumming of Jack's stubby fingers against the steering wheel. 'This isn't your bloody female intuition working overtime again, is it?' he muttered with a wink to let her know he was joking. Her intuition had been proved right on many occasions and they both knew it.

'It's just there's something different from when we last paid a visit. But I can't put my finger on it.'

'Got it!' He grinned as she turned towards him. 'It was daylight then.'

'Ha, bloody, ha!' She rubbed her forehead. This was daft. If only she wasn't so tired ... 'The car!' She sat upright with a jerk of comprehension. 'The car. He always parks it out front. It's missing.' She opened the car door and stepped onto the gravel.

'Garage?' Jack asked as he scrambled to join her.

'He uses it as a workshop, not a garage.'

'There could be lots of other reasons. Perhaps it's gone wrong. Could be having some work done on it.'

'Maybe,' she agreed. 'But it's worth checking out.'

'Great.' He followed her towards the front door. 'This is going to go down well. I bet the Super will have a complaint in his inbox first thing in the morning.'

The doorbell shrilled a discordant note through the still night air. They both took a step back and peered upwards, waiting to see faces appear from behind curtains. Nothing happened. After a minute of inactivity, Beth tried the doorbell again and twisted at the ornate brass doorknob. It was locked.

'They're not here.' Jack's redundant statement met with raised brows.

'No kidding!'

'So?' He hunched his shoulders. 'They've gone away.'

Beth frowned. 'Tom Oldridge said it was after nine o'clock when he called. John was cutting the grass. Strange time to go out. Let's try round the back.'

More security lights lit their path and they quickly located the back door. Jack made a half-hearted attempt to try the handle and the door swung open. 'Unlocked!' he exclaimed with a whistle of surprise.

'Great detective work once again, Sergeant! I'm going to have to recommend you for a promotion. Go on then.' She gestured inside. 'What are you waiting for?'

Jack stepped carefully into the dark space and felt his way around what seemed to be a utility room. 'I left my torch in the car,' he muttered.

A flick of the light switch left him blinking. 'Luckily the Hampton-Browns have discovered electricity!' Beth retorted. 'Come on.'

She led the way through a large kitchen and into the hallway, switching on internal lights as she went. 'Police!' she called out. 'Mr and Mrs Hampton-Brown? Are you there?'

Her shouts met with silence and they headed up the stairs, checking each room in turn. All were empty; beds were made up; no one was in the house. The final room they tried was the smallest and clearly used for storage. A large wooden chest gaped open, its lid hinged and leaning against floral wallpaper. A single step forward brought Beth to an abrupt halt and her arm shot out to prevent Jack from going any further.

'Oh Jesus!' she murmured. Bloodstains were visible on the floor of the chest. 'Call for back-up and get a forensics team out here. We need an immediate alert out for the vehicle, a green Range Rover. They've got Deborah Ryecroft and are moving her somewhere else. Now, Jack!' she ordered, pulling out her own phone. 'There may not be much time!'

'We may already be too late,' Jack replied, his round, genial face grim with foreboding. 'They could be moving the body.'

***

Tom sat in Deborah's kitchen, head slumped forward in his hands. Emma and Rick, after some persuasion, had returned home, leaving him alone to his night vigil. His phone lay on the worktop in front of him, obstinately silent. From time to time, he tried Deb's number but the response was always the same. 'The phone you are calling is switched off.' He wished he had confidence in DI Honeysuckle and DS Everard – a blind belief in police infallibility – but the opposite was closer the mark. They had probably decided nothing useful could be achieved overnight and were, even now, snoring in uncaring sleep. He should be doing the same, restoring his energy for the day ahead. Sitting here, wide awake, doing nothing useful, was a pointless exercise and yet he could not bring himself to go upstairs. He had to be ready, just in case ...

His phone rattled, even before the ring sounded, and Tom snatched it to his ear. 'Yes?'

'We're at the Hampton-Browns' house.' It was DI Honeysuckle, her voice crisp, causing his heart to race. 'It looks as if Deborah Ryecroft may have been here but she's not here now, and neither are the Hampton-Browns.' A brief pause while she allowed that information to sink in. 'They've taken her elsewhere.'

Sweat beaded on his brow and the phone felt clammy in his hand. 'Is she ... is she still alive?' he gulped.

'We have no way of knowing that, sir,' she replied. 'We have a forensic team on their way and we'll know more when they've had time to investigate the scene but, in the meantime, I wondered if you might have any idea where they might be headed.'

'Me? How on earth should I know?

Another silence. 'Call it intuition,' she said, a wry note underpinning her words. 'Your local knowledge will be superior to mine. I presume their motivation must be linked to this curious village superstition about a witch's curse. Where would someone who suspected Ms Ryecroft of witchcraft take her?'

Instantly, it came to him. 'Dark Water Lake,' he replied.

CHAPTER 37

Water; cold and black.

'Ayesha! Ayesha, where are you? Are you hurt?'

A glimpse of white; a pale limb floating; a lifeless torso, face down, short blonde hair plastered to the scalp ...

That was wrong! Deborah's subconscious warred with the part of her brain which watched on, detached, knowing this was the same old nightmare. Except it wasn't. The hair was different.

... reaching under the chin; pulling the face out of the water ...

'No!' Her shout was muffled by the gag still pressed against her mouth. The alabaster face was her own death mask. It was *her* dead body floating in the lake...

Relief as she blinked into awareness. *Just a dream.* She was alive but cold, so very cold. It bit into every shivering part of her. She tugged at her arms but they would not move. They were bound behind her body and behind something else, rigid and hard.

'John, I think she's waking up.'

As her eyes blinked furiously, trying to decipher the darkness, a bright light shone in her face, blinding her and forcing her eyes closed.

'Good. About time. Let's get on with it.'

Consciousness brought renewed dread, a flare of adrenalin-fuelled fear, forcing her whole body into a futile struggle against the bonds which held her.

'I'd save your strength if I were you. You're going to need it.' John Hampton-Brown's disembodied voice came from somewhere to her right. Valerie must be in front, holding the torch shining in her face.

Grimacing, still wriggling and pulling, she continued to squeeze her eyes shut to protect them from the glare. She knew where she was. Dark Water Lake. She could sense it, smell it, even though she could not see it. An unmistakeable, earthy scent of leaf mulch and stagnant water. The Hampton-Browns had tied her to a chair, a wooden frame with a wicker seat which squeaked as she moved. She was still wearing the clothes she had dressed in that morning: a long-sleeved top and cotton trousers. Her shoes were missing and her toes brushed against damp grass and scratchy twigs. Every part of her body screamed with pain but her brain remained coldly aloof from it. It was nothing compared to the fate awaiting her. She knew what was going to happen. The Hampton-Browns were quite mad. They were going to drown her as a witch.

'Do you admit you are the Wickthorpe Witch and promise to withdraw the curse you placed on the village in 1645?' John's sonorous tones rang out, a judge about to proclaim his verdict.

Deborah shook her head and mumbled against the gag, redoubling efforts to free herself.

'Should we remove the scarf, John?' asked Valerie. 'We need to hear her repentance.'

Yes, remove the gag! Do it!

'No.' The voice of authority crushed thoughts of screaming for help. 'Too much of a risk. Someone might hear her.'

'Not at this time of night, surely?' Valerie demurred, but Deborah could detect an underlying note of acceptance and her scrap of hope withered. 'How can we determine her responses?'

'You will nod or shake your head to answer our questions. Do you understand?' John ordered. Deborah kept her head resolutely still until a hard slap to her face knocked her sideways, the force of it making it a struggle to remain upright on the chair. 'I said do you understand? Nod your head.' The voice was implacable and Deborah found herself complying. 'That's better. Now, do you admit you are the Wickthorpe Witch?' A shake of her head.

'She's denying it, John.'

'Yes, as we expected. Valerie, I believe you have a list of the charges against the defendant.'

A rustling of paper and the heat of the torch moved away from Deborah's face. Cautiously, she opened her eyes. In the moonlight, as shapes slowly took form, she detected the tall shape of John to her right. Beside him, Valerie stood, torchlight wavering over a piece of paper she held in her left hand.

'Could you hold the torch for me, John? It's difficult to read while I hold it steady.' Deborah watched his outline move behind and the torch lifted higher, so it was shining downwards. 'Thank you. That's better.' Valerie cleared her throat. 'Deborah Ryecroft, you are hereby accused of the following charges: that you are either a descendant or an incarnation of Martha Lightbody, the woman drowned as a witch in 1645; that, as said descendant or incarnation, you have sought to perpetuate the evil curse placed upon the villagers of Wickthorpe in 1645; that you knowingly caused the death by drowning of Ayesha Khan in August, 1988; that you knowingly caused the death by car accident of Jonathan Hampton-Brown later that same month, August 1988 ...' A tiny sob. A long pause. More throat clearing. 'That, since your return to Wickthorpe earlier this year, you have, knowingly and wickedly, caused the death of two more residents of Wickthorpe, namely Mabel Littlebody and Freya Billington, the latter using your preferred method of drowning. Those are the charges against you. How do you plead?'

Deborah snorted but said nothing. 'We need to hear the words, John. Can't we just remove the scarf for a few seconds?'

A beat of silence as John deliberated. 'Alright.' He loomed over her. 'How do you plead, witch?' Rough fingers tugged at the knot at the base of her skull. The gag loosened. 'How do you plead?'

Deborah screamed with every ounce of her strength but the sound emitted was a husky, broken squawk rather than the high-pitched, shrill shriek for help she had hoped. She drew in a breath to try again but the gag was forced between her teeth and pulled tight.

'There's no one to hear you,' John snarled. 'You will nod if you are guilty and shake your head for not guilty. How do you plead to the charges?' Again, she remained immobile; again, he raised his hand to strike her. 'Last chance.'

'Not guilty,' Deborah ground out through the gag, her meaning clear, despite the muffling. It was the only act of defiance she could think of. She would not follow his orders and, while she despised herself for participating in his farce, she refused to deny her innocence.

'In which case ...' A triumphant undertone to John's verdict. 'And in the face of the overwhelming evidence against you, I sentence you to trial by drowning, in the manner of witches brought to justice centuries before.'

'But what if she's innocent, John.' Valerie now sounded anxious. *Was she having second thoughts?* 'She'll drown and it will all be for nothing.'

'You and I both know that will not happen, Valerie. We are certain of her guilt. By some devilish machination, she will contrive to escape such a fate and we will be able to hand her over to the authorities, certain beyond all doubt of her pact with Satan. Or,' he mused, 'we could hang her, here in these woods. A true witch's fate. Thereby ending the curse, once and for all.'

'I'm not sure ...'

'Pull yourself together, Valerie!' Her husband's voice was sharp with command. 'This is no time to start behaving like those namby-pamby do-gooders, responsible for much of what's wrong in our society these days. We are doing this for Jonathan, remember ... and to save other Wickthorpe innocents in the future. God is on our side. Right is on our side. Evil must be rooted out. Now, help me lift the chair to the edge of the bank, just there. That's where the lake is deep enough for the trial.'

'How do you know?'

'Because I measured it, of course. Ever since we discussed this course of action ... since Freya Billington drowned and the police refused to see what was under their noses, I've been planning. These things must be done properly.'

It seemed Valerie had no further objections and the two figures approached, one either side of the chair. Deborah rocked her weight furiously, desperate to prevent them from achieving their objective, straining with every ounce of her strength to loosen the constraints which held her, but to no avail. She felt herself being precariously hoisted a few inches from the ground and manoeuvred unsteadily forwards. It took several attempts and Valerie was panting hard by the end of it but at last she was balanced precariously on the very edge of the bank. Her toes skimmed the surface of the icy water. The breeze had picked up and rushed at her cheeks. Still, she struggled. Better that than contemplate the fate awaiting her.

'Deborah Ryecroft, you are hereby ordered to undertake trial by drowning. Do you have any final words?'

Oh God. This is really going to happen.

Deborah's mind skittered in blind panic before Tom's face swam into focus, smiling, reassuring, making a promise she knew he could not keep. The image faded, replaced by the perfect features of her dead child. If there was a God, they would be reunited. The thought brought a rush of comfort and she felt her body relax.

'Deborah Ryecroft, prepare to face your judgement!'

She blotted out the voice. She could almost feel the weight of her baby in her arms. *A girl. Natasha.*

'No!'

Was that Tom, shouting, willing her to continue the fight?

'I love you, Tom,' she murmured to herself but the realisation, a starburst of regret, was too late. A violent shove from behind sent her toppling, head first, into the water.

CHAPTER 38

Letter to Matthew Lightbody
15th August, 1645

My dearest Brother,

I write with the most terrible of news. My beloved Martha has been taken from me, seized in the night and drowned as a witch. My heart is broken and I cannot go on, except I must. Our child, Josiah, barely a year old, needs my protection and that is my purpose here. But first I must explain further so you are fully comprehending of our plight.

Martha was much skilled in the use of herbs to heal the sick. Those who believe in witchcraft were suspicious of such knowledge. She also had the misfortune to bear a strawberry-sized mole on her forearm. Many consider such a blemish 'the devil's mark' although tis nought but superstitious nonsense. Martha was cautious in keeping the mark concealed from view but, in a moment of carelessness, rolled up her sleeves to aid a birthing mother. The mole was seen and Martha was, from that moment, treated with mistrust. Much afeared she would be arrested as a witch, she urged our immediate departure from Wickthorpe but circumstances prevented such action. Tis the season of harvest and I worked that night til well after dark. Much fatigued, I was unwilling to embark 'pon a journey at that late hour and we determined to leave the following dawn, a decision for which I blame myself. We were too late and my guilt is a heavy burden to bear.

When the men came, we were asleep. Martha was dragged from her bed out into the darkness. I was befuddled with slumber and overpowered by three men who seized my arms to prevent my escape, afore punching me unconscious. I caught a glimpse of one of the men. Twas a villain named Roger Holley, whom had been unsuccessful in trying to force himself 'pon Martha in recent months. I suspect he welcomed the opportunity to take his vengeance 'pon my poor girl.

Twas many hours afore I was able to free myself. I took Josiah to Martha's friend, Prudence, desperate for news. Twas she who told me, her face streaming with tears, of Martha's fate. I sank into black despair, prostrate with grief. Fortunately, Prudence took pity 'pon us and cared for my son. At such time, I was incapable of even the smallest task.

Throughout the day, we learnt more of the vile action taken 'gainst my Martha. My employer, Jed Finch, did his best to halt proceedings but the might of the rabble was too strong. Men driven by superstitious fear were incapable of listening to reason. Martha protested her innocence to the last and her courage, I am told, began to sway the crowd. Howe'er, Roger Holley would not be denied and ordered his henchman to help lift the chair to which Martha was tied and cast it into the water. No other would assist them. In a final act of defiance, Martha spoke a curse against her accusers. Such an uttering has caused much consternation in the village for Martha has not been found! When she had been under the water for some time, men leapt into the lake to pull her out. They found the chair but Martha was gone. Roger Holley ordered a search for her but, as yet, to no avail. I fear her body lies at the bottom of the lake but many are saying she is a witch and, thus, may have escaped. I pray this may be so but feel sure she would have found some way to return to us and that has not happened.

This brings me to my main reason for writing. Fear 'gainst Martha and her curse has grown in Wickthorpe to dangerous levels – dangerous for Josiah, that is. Many are calling him "the spawn of the devil" and demanding he be put to death. We can stay here no longer. By the time you read this, we will be on our way to Norfolk to beg shelter from you and your dear wife. I pray you will take pity 'pon us. I know not to whom I can turn if not to you. My mind is sick with grief and yet I must go on for the sake of my son.

Your brother,
John.

***

Letter to George & Faith Miller (parents of Prudence Harkness)
2nd September, 1645

Dear Mother and Father,

I hope this letter finds you in the best of health. I am well, as is Gideon, and our darling girl, Mary Martha, continues to thrive. She is now almost a three month and is the bonniest of infants with large, blue eyes and wisps of golden hair. Believe me when I tell you she is the most adorable creature – sunny in looks and in nature. I cannot wait for you to meet her but Gideon says we must await winter months afore we travel. He is too busy on the land to leave at present.

When I last wrote, I recounted the horrible fate of my dearest friend, Martha Lightbody. I still cannot believe it. She was the kindest of women, and the most faithful friend I could wish for. I miss her terribly, as I miss you, dearest Mother and Father. Anyway, more of Martha. Her body is still to be found! I cannot help but believe she managed to escape the clutches of those cruel men! I pray she is somewhere safe and will be reunited with her distraught husband and child. Every day I hope for good news from her.

The village of Wickthorpe has been greatly agitated this past month. The Holley family have employed many extra men in their determination to hunt Martha down. They believe she lives, as do many villagers. There is much fear of the curse and what it could mean for them. Just last week, the curdling of milk from cows belonging to Stephen Johnson was blamed on the curse! I suspect twill be so with any ill occurrences henceforth.

I hope your foot is now recovered, Father. If not, a poultice of crushed lemon balm leaves wrapped in a bandage applied to the swelling should help ease it. I am becoming quite the apothecary but keep my knowledge secret lest any should accuse me of witchcraft. I have no wish to alarm you but some folk now view me with suspicion for my association with Martha. The war is nothing in this village compared with talk of witchcraft. A man named Matthew Hopkins visited Wickthorpe just last week to root out any remaining evil. I was most relieved to see his departure.

Please convey my love and best wishes to all members of the family.

Your loving daughter,

Prudence.

***

Letter to Ralph Holder
10th September, 1645

Sir,

I will get straight to the point.

I understand you are a man of discretion, much skilled in locating the whereabouts of missing persons. I require your services to find a woman – a person of a most wicked disposition who is required to be brought to justice.

To that end, I am most desirous of a meeting between us. If you would be so kind as to present yourself at the above address at your earliest convenience, you will find it much to your advantage.

Yours in anticipation,

Roger Holley.

CHAPTER 39

Tom's dark red Land Rover hurtled into the small area reserved for cars near Dark Water Lake, just behind the police vehicle. A green Range Rover, gleaming with a polished sheen, sat ominously quiet in the darkness. *Bloody hell, he was right!* The thought made his stomach spasm with fear. *Please be in time.* The two police officers spilled from their vehicle as Tom leapt from his.

'Listen!' DI Honeysuckle held up a hand. Voices. Distant.

'This way. Hurry!' Tom blundered forwards, fumbling his phone from his pocket and flicking on the light, a pitiful beam barely showing the black, tree-covered walkway.

'Wait. Aren't the voices coming from the other side of the lake?' Beth Honeysuckle's question stopped him in his tracks and he looked through a gap in the trees to the water beyond. Sure enough, a light was shimmering on the far side of the lake. As his eyes became accustomed to the darkness and the moon slipped from behind the cloud-laden sky, he thought he could see moving shapes. A muffled scream echoed across the water.

'No!' he gasped.

His arm was gripped by DS Everard. 'Quiet!' he hissed. 'Follow me.'

They set off at a run, aided by the powerful torch wielded by Jack Everard, crashing through the undergrowth, stumbling and tripping over branches strewn by the storm a few weeks earlier. At one point, Tom fell headlong, banging his head against unyielding oak. 'Dammit!' He staggered to his feet and continued forwards, chasing the officers ahead of him, heart thundering in his ears. Panic made him careless. Something terrible was about to happen to Debs and he was unable to prevent it. 'No,' he shouted before he could stop himself.

A sudden splash splintered the cool night air. Something heavy had just gone in the water. 'No!' Tom cried again. They were still too far away. They would be too late!

All three of them were panting hard and Jack was flagging. Beth snatched the torch from him as she sped past, picking up the pace. 'Call for an ambulance!' she huffed as her colleague slowed.

Tom also pushed by him, following Beth's lead. Surely, they were almost there? It was taking too long. How many seconds since Debs went in the water? Minutes even? Time ploughed on with relentless momentum and fear robbed him of any thought other than the need to go faster. His lungs burned with effort but his feet continued to falter on the uneven surface. Another stumble sent him careering off the path and he felt his ankle give way. *Ignore it. Not much further.*

He turned a corner and, up ahead, stock-still, watching the water, stood the Hampton-Browns. Beth Honeysuckle had pulled clear of him and was already up to her waist in the lake. As Tom charged in behind her, she ducked her head below the surface. He did the same, flailing his arms, reaching into nothingness. Impossible to see anything in such a murky, weed-ridden underworld. Spluttering, he lifted his head and took another step forward, stretching out in desperation. Nothing.

'Here!' Honeysuckle's shout made his chest roar with hope. He surged towards her voice. She was tugging at something and he waded to her side to help. His fingers grasped a piece of wood, heavy and unyielding, but slender enough to clench his fist around it. The other hand reached for another piece of the object, pulling at it with all his strength, in unison with the police officer. They seemed to be like that for hours, hauling at the chair, trying to lift it above the surface, but it can only have been seconds. It yanked free in a whoosh of water droplets, Deborah Ryecroft's body along with it.

'Debs,' he cried, reaching for her.

'Leave her. Get her to the bank,' Beth ordered. Between them, they lifted her out of the water and lay her on her side. 'No pulse,' she said after checking the pale wrist. 'We're going to have to turn her onto her back. You get her free while I start CPR.'

She tipped the chair back and began chest compressions, counting as she did so. When she reached thirty, she tilted Deborah's chin, held her nose and covered her mouth with her own. After two breaths, she resumed the chest compressions. Without a word, Tom reached in his pocket, finding the penknife he always carried, and worked at the ropes. His own heart thumped a dance of dread.

'Ambulance is on its way.' Jack Everard joined them and watched in solemn silence. 'Anything?' he asked.

Beth shook her head. 'Not yet.' Her voice was grim.

'Here. Let me take over for a bit.' Jack knelt beside Deborah on the bank whilst Beth surveyed the Hampton-Browns.

'You realise, if she doesn't make it, you'll be charged with her murder,' she told them coldly.

John Hampton-Brown regarded her with disdain. 'Of course, she'll survive,' he said. 'She is a witch. *This* will be the proof. We are certain of her guilt but, when she lives, everyone will know.'

Beth shook her head in disbelief. 'You're quite mad,' she muttered under her breath.

Having finally sawn through all the ropes, Tom sat on the other side of the stricken woman, rubbing her hand, and ordering her to take a breath. 'Come on, Debs, fight,' he urged. 'Come back to us. Don't let them win. I can't lose you.'

Beth resumed the breaths and chest compressions as Jack checked his watch. 'That's five minutes,' he said.

'Where's the ambulance?' Tom muttered, fear lending anger to his voice. 'They should be here by now.'

Jack frowned. 'Give them a chance, man. It's barely been ten minutes since I phoned.'

'Ten minutes?' Tom queried. It seemed a lifetime ago. All the while, his eyes were glued to the wraith-like body lying motionless on the ground. 'Debs,' he shouted, 'don't do this! Come back to me. Debs!' He found himself sobbing her name, over and over.

Jack Everard laid a hand on his shoulder. 'Don't give up yet. There's still time.' Even as he uttered the words, Deborah's chest heaved and convulsed.

'Quick, get her onto her side,' Beth commanded. More coughs, then water – lots of it – ejected in painful explosions. In the distance, sirens sounded. 'Jack, go and meet them. Show them where we are.'

The Hampton-Browns watched Deborah's excruciating return to life with supercilious hauteur. 'I told you she would survive.' A male voice, smug in its certainty.

'She should now be tried and hung for the witch she is.' Valerie was less composed. 'You need to arrest her.' She pointed a bony finger at Beth. 'She shouldn't get away with the deaths she's caused.'

Beth stood wearily, leaving Tom to wrap Deborah in his jacket and cradle her in his arms as they waited for further medical help. 'John and Valerie Hampton-Brown, I'm arresting you on the charge of attempted murder. You do not have to say anything. But ...'

'We have done nothing,' Valerie shrieked, 'except prove to you that this woman is a witch – the Wickthorpe Witch. She is the one you should be arresting. This is a travesty. John, do something!'

John Hampton-Brown eyed DI Honeysuckle, as she cuffed his wife's hands behind her back, with cold disfavour. 'You're making a big mistake, young woman,' he barked. 'When my friend, Peter, *your* Chief Constable, gets to hear about this, I suspect you will find yourself in a great deal of trouble.'

'Look,' Valerie pleaded, 'it's not too late. If you let us go home now, we'll forget all about it, won't we, John? You can't possibly expect someone like *me* to spend a night in a police cell.'

Tom heard their voices but was conscious only of the woman beside him, the person he had so nearly lost. As her eyes flickered in bewilderment, he squeezed her to him. 'Thank God,' he gasped. 'I thought we were too late. Debs, I love you. I've been so worried.'

She gave him a half smile as her eyelids drooped once more. 'Me too,' she rasped. Another coughing fit and suddenly they were surrounded by ambulance personnel and police officers. Tom found himself pushed firmly to one side and a blanket placed around his shoulders.

'We'll take over now, sir,' he was told as another woman, dressed in green, escorted him away to be checked over.

'Please,' he called, 'take good care of her.'

'We will, sir,' came the reply.

CHAPTER 40

Honoraria awoke to sunshine streaming through a tiny gap in her purple brocade curtains and the sense that something was amiss. *What on earth was it?* Her auburn head ticked through a list: not the leak in the bathroom (that had been fixed); not the gorgeous, dark, curly-haired plumber (if only she was thirty years younger) who had been paid; not her friend, Lizzie, who had recently had the all-clear from the hospital; Tom Oldridge – that was it. Deborah Ryecroft was missing. *Oh dear.*

She slipped her feet into fluffy, pink mules, and padded through to the bathroom. Another beautiful, serene day; but this one could bring a darker turn. The thought curdled her stomach. Splashing cold water on her face helped to restore optimism. Deborah Ryecroft would surely have turned up by now, safe, and well. Honoraria crossed her plump fingers. Much as she liked a bit of drama, there had been more than enough tragedies in Wickthorpe recently and her conscience could not bear another. She may have told Tom Oldridge what she knew last night but she had since fretted that she should have spoken out sooner. Recollection of the venom with which Deborah had been discussed brought bile to her throat. She should have mentioned it to Deborah and Tom the next day, just in passing, as a casual warning. The thought *had* crossed her mind after the History Society meeting but, although the episode had made her uncomfortable, she had dismissed it as harmless. Best not rock the boat, she thought. It could upset her standing in the village.

Staring at her sagging, unadorned face in the bathroom mirror, she remembered another time, decades before ...

St Helen's School for Girls. She hated it at the beginning, but quickly learnt whom to flatter and whom to ignore, so her presence was tolerated. She knew her position was precarious, dependent upon the cruel whim of others but she survived.

There was one girl though, very clever, skinny, with thin, straggly hair and cheap, NHS glasses. Danielle Morrison. She had been bullied – name-calling, things taken, even physical abuse, from sly pinches to her arm to sticking her head in the toilet. Thinking of it still made Honoraria weep. She had not joined in with the bullying but she never stood up for Danielle either, fearful she too would become a victim. So, she had watched. Sometimes, she had even laughed at the other girls' nasty antics.

Danielle left after two terms and never returned. There were rumours, never confirmed, that she had committed suicide. The schoolmistresses afterwards interviewed every pupil, individually, asking about Danielle and how she was with the other girls. She had lied. They all had.

Shame branded her soul. Never again would she stand by, she had told herself ...

Yet, here she was, albeit a bystander to a different form of persecution. Could they *really* have harmed a successful businesswoman like Deborah Ryecroft, based purely upon centuries-old superstition? Surely not. Not people like the *Hampton-Browns*. She could not believe it. But Enid Green and Philip Holder? She grimaced. *Not so sure.*

Having dressed quickly, she applied her make-up with her usual deft touch and bustled out into the sunshine. It really was a beautiful day. Nothing bad could have happened ... could it? One thing was certain; she needed to find out.

***

Emma Oldridge watched Honoraria's approach with narrowed eyes. Bad news travelled fast, she thought, and Honoraria was obviously on the hunt for the latest gossip.

'Morning, Emma,' the older woman waved while she was still some distance away. 'I was looking for your dad. Is he about?'

'I'm afraid not. Sorry.'

'Oh.' Honoraria continued her approach nonetheless, wheezing slightly as she came to a halt at the edge of the paved area by the house, still a short distance away from where Emma was checking tractor tyre pressures. 'Do you know if Deborah has been found? I've been so worried about her since your dad told me last night she was missing.'

'Yes, thankfully she has.' Emma gave her a brief smile. 'She's currently recovering in hospital. I'll be sure to tell Dad you called round.'

'Oh, thank goodness she's been found!' Honoraria's gasp whooshed from deep in her chest. 'I'm so relieved ... but she's in hospital, you say?' Her bright pink lips quivered the question. 'Did she have an accident? Oh, I do hope she isn't badly hurt? How did it happen?'

'I'm afraid I don't know all the details, but she is expected to make a complete recovery.' Emma crossed her fingers behind her back at the evasion. No way she was going to discuss the events of the previous evening with one of the biggest gossips in the village.

'I'm so happy to hear that!' Honoraria heaved a dramatic sigh. 'As I said, I've been terribly worried. Your dad was almost beside himself when we spoke last night. Do you happen to know when he'll be back?'

'I'm afraid not. Now, if you will excuse me, Honoraria, I need to be ...'

'Yes, yes, don't let me keep you. I'm just pleased that Deborah is going to be alright after ... what happened ...' Honoraria's voice trailed off as Emma crouched behind the safety of a rear wheel.

She turned away and hurried towards the village, buzzing with the latest information. What *had* happened to Deborah Ryecroft? Why was she in *hospital*? Emma Oldridge had clearly been reluctant to discuss it but surely someone in the village would know? A quick glance at her watch. Eight-thirty. The Co-op would be open and, at nine o'clock, she could have breakfast at *The Pastry Parlour*. A little treat to herself to celebrate Deborah's Ryecroft's safe return from ... whatever. Salivating at the prospect of both food and further information, she quickened her pace.

***

The village of Wickthorpe was in turmoil throughout the morning as false claims and revelatory titbits set tongues wagging. Police vehicles and ambulances had disturbed the sleep of many a villager. Tom Oldridge's search, the previous day, for the missing Deborah Ryecroft, had already been widely reported, and many were quick to put two and two together. Claims of another dead body, this time of the missing businesswoman, were rife.

Honoraria Simpson-Fairchild breathlessly scotched that wild rumour upon her entry to the fray with the claim that said 'dead body' was recovering well in hospital. However, Honoraria was a self-confessed, deep sleeper and, as her nighttime repose had been uninterrupted, she was unable to answer questions regarding the police vehicles stationed outside the Hampton-Browns' residence. Concern was raised over the safety of the Hampton-Browns. Had something happened to them? Had Deborah Ryecroft been involved? Honoraria offered to make a visit to their house to find out. Several other villagers gallantly offered to accompany her and so it was that a veritable posse of Wickthorpe residents approached the Hampton-Brown driveway. Entry, however, was barred by a young man in police uniform who revealed that the property was 'a crime scene' and prevented them from going further. Horrified discussion followed and, by the time the group had returned to the village centre, wild postulations, such as the murder of the Hampton-Browns at the hands of the Wickthorpe Witch, were commonplace. An anxious wait for news ensued.

At last, at just after ten o'clock, there was a breakthrough. Someone had a sister who worked at the West Suffolk hospital in Bury St Edmunds, where a patient had been admitted after a near-drowning incident in Dark Water Lake. Possibly Deborah Ryecroft? But how were the Hampton-Browns involved? Questions hummed throughout the street and village shops. Villagers debated known facts and came up with their own hypotheses. Honoraria managed to make a coffee last for fifty-five minutes in *The Pastry Parlour* before having to order another. Georgia Richards, wife of the man who had discovered Freya Billington's body and thereby considered a reliable source, was the first to suggest that the Hampton-Browns had been arrested and charged with attempted murder. The police officer guarding the 'crime scene' driveway was her second cousin and had let the information slip. A collective gasp echoed through the village. That was *unthinkable*. Not the *Hampton-Browns*! And yet, people soon accustomed themselves to the idea. Some even ventured to suggest they had 'seen it coming;' the couple had never recovered from the tragic death of their son and had been quite vocal in their condemnation of Deborah Ryecroft as the 'witch' responsible. Others shook their heads.

Georgia Richards uttered the age-old wisdom, 'You never know what goes on behind closed doors.' How true, thought Honoraria, hugging her own secrets to her generous bosom, barely contained within a large, burnt orange t-shirt embroidered with yellow roses.

***

Enid Green, from the confines of her chair in the Post Office, listened to each disclosure but remained curiously tight-lipped. Her daughter, Ava, also had little to say on the subject. It was only when a fuller version of events emerged, over the course of the next few days, that Enid seemed to recover her tongue.

'Absolutely shocking!' she agreed, when Honoraria happened to pop in and make a similar comment. 'How that woman continues to get away with it is quite beyond me!'

Honoraria's forget-me-not eyes widened. 'I'm afraid you misunderstood me, Enid. I was talking of the Hampton-Browns! I know they lost their son, and that must have coloured their judgement, but I would never have believed they were so disturbed as to attempt to drown Deborah Ryecroft.'

Enid pursed her lips and shrugged. Despite her daughter's warning glance, she muttered, 'I'm just saying there's no smoke without fire. Funny how she managed to survive, despite all the odds being against it.'

'Mother ...' Ava interrupted.

'Oh, be quiet, Ava. Of course, I know that Valerie and John went too far. I would not be the one to suggest their actions were excusable but I do understand what drove them to it. And,' she raised her eyebrows in triumph, 'as I said, it *is* remarkable how that woman came through her trial relatively unscathed, just like the witches of old. As I have said many a time before, she is directly descended from the original witch, Martha Lightbody. The evil has passed through the generations. That is how the curse has continued.'

'I really don't think you should be saying such things,' Honoraria whispered with a troubled look out of the window where Wendy Robinson was hovering. 'There has been a lot of talk in the village since it happened, about how that old curse has caused nothing but trouble. Time it was forgotten. As Dorothy Fairgrove said, when she gave that fascinating talk on the history of witchcraft at one of my History Society meetings, such curses only have power if they are believed. Best to forget about it.'

'You can believe what you like, Honoraria,' Enid sniffed, 'but I know the truth. I tell you this – more harm will come to people in this village if that woman remains here.'

'Enough, Mother!' Ava interjected as the door opened. 'Honoraria's right. Such talk will get you into trouble.'

As usual, Enid had to have the last word. 'I'm entitled to my opinion, thank you,' she scowled, 'and you mark my words ... there will be more deaths to come.'

CHAPTER 41

It took a few weeks for Deborah to recover from her physical injuries. The mental scars would take much longer. Her sleep was haunted by dreams of drowning, sinking deeper, chest bursting with lack of air and that final, awful moment when she had to succumb to the burning pain of water seeping into her lungs. Things blurred after that but, as the nightmare revisited, night after night, she remembered something else. A woman. Dark hair tied back from her face. A long, white nightdress billowing. A pale hand extended, guiding her. Then blackness.

When she first woke in the hospital. Tom was slumped asleep in a chair by her bed and she watched him for a while, drinking in features she thought she would never see again. His eyes snapped open, crinkling with joy.

'You're awake!' He shot from the chair and placed his lips against her forehead. 'I was so worried about you. How are you feeling?'

She considered the question. Mostly she felt numb. Painkillers had worked their magic. 'Lucky to be alive,' she answered.

He took her hand in his calloused palm and squeezed it. 'I know. I honestly thought we'd lost you.'

'A woman saved me,' she told him. 'A woman with dark hair.'

He nodded. 'Beth Honeysuckle. She was the one who found you under the water.'

She closed her eyes, remembering. 'Beth,' she breathed. 'Is that her name? I didn't know. Please pass on my thanks.'

'I'm sure you'll be able to tell her yourself. She's keen to interview you.' Another squeeze of her hand. 'But not yet. You need to rest.'

She nodded and drifted off once more.

Beth Honeysuckle visited the next morning, dressed in her usual jacket and trousers, Jack Everard by her side. They recorded the details of her imprisonment by the Hampton-Browns, nodding at her responses which matched the forensic evidence. She, in turn, asked about her captors. Having had visions of them kidnapping her from her bed in the dead of night, she was reassured to learn they were both being held in a secure psychiatric hospital. Deborah was told they had pleaded not guilty to the charge of attempted murder, insisting they had acted according to ancient laws regarding witchcraft.

Before the police officers left, Deborah thanked them both profusely for their part in her rescue. 'Strange question,' she said to Beth, 'but, if you're a detective, why were you dressed in a nightie that night?'

'I wasn't,' Beth frowned. 'What on earth made you think I was?'

'Oh!' Deborah shook her head, confused by the denial. 'My memory must be playing tricks. Take no notice.'

Beth smiled. 'That's not at all surprising. You've been through a terrible trauma and it will take a while for you to recover. Have the hospital staff talked to you about counselling?'

'Yes.' She had refused outright, to begin with, but had been persuaded to consider it. The logical part of her brain accepted it would be a good idea but the private part, which had kept secrets for so long, cringed at the prospect.

'Right, we'll be off then. You take care of yourself.'

The two detectives departed, leaving her pondering. Beth Honeysuckle may have been the person who dragged her from the depths of Dark Water Lake, along with Tom, she had since learnt, but she was not the woman whose guiding hand helped her, night after night, in her dreams. That woman had been by her side, silently urging her to fight, to survive, to break free from the ropes which bound her. Whilst she was unable to recall details of her face, she retained a clear picture of the white, cotton nightdress the woman was wearing. That made no sense unless …

No! Her mind rejected the idea immediately. She was becoming as fanciful as those superstitious villagers who believed in the Wickthorpe Witch and her curse. As Beth Honeysuckle suggested, she had been through a terrible ordeal. Her mind was superimposing details, long imagined, about the awful drowning of Martha Lightbody, onto her own experience. Perhaps counselling would be a good idea after all.

***

Deborah had been back home at Greenways Farm for three weeks, enjoying lazy afternoons reading in her garden and making plans for her future. Her enforced hospital stay meant she had unwittingly broken the terms of her mother's will. Strangely, the thought did not upset her as much as she would have expected. She resolved to begin the year again. It would be annoying to have to postpone thoughts of travel but otherwise ...

Her incarceration and brush with death, at the hands of the Hampton-Browns, had led her to reflect on her life and what she considered important, things which made her happy. Some were in London: friends, art galleries, theatres ... but, in all honesty, she could no longer include her work. With the grip of death upon her, there had been no regrets for that. Where once, she had felt driven to succeed, to prove herself, over and over, ambitions to expand the company further held little appeal. With that realisation, she decided it was time to take a further step back from work. Life was too short to spend time on things which failed to make her heart sing. She discussed it with Paul, her finance director, and invited him to consider the position of CEO. She would remain a director but he would be at the helm. He was shocked, as she knew he would be, and claimed he was incapable of stepping into her shoes. The image of her short, squat, bald colleague in her red high-heels had set her chuckling ever since. Once he realised she was serious, he was unable to conceal his excitement and she was content. *Ryecroft Industries* had a strong team. She had no doubt the company would continue to flourish with less involvement from her.

She also decided to sell her London home. For the time being, she would remain in Wickthorpe, fulfil the terms of the will and enjoy her garden. One evening, as her mind's eye framed a perfect sunset, she resolved to embark upon a painting course. She had no idea whether she possessed any artistic talent but she had always longed to have a go herself. No time like the present.

Other plans were rather more tenuous. Since she had been home, she had been through the entire contents of the box left by her mother, hoping to discover more about her. In that, she had been disappointed. Hannah Ryecroft had kept no diary. There were no photographs, other than the ones she had already found of Hannah as a child with her siblings. The letters, bundled together and secured by a rubber band, which she had hoped may provide further insights, were all addressed to her father. No personal correspondence kept by her mother. In fact, all the remaining contents belonged to her father: his letters; bank statements; papers detailing the sale of the farm land – some to Felix Goode and some to Tom Oldridge. One day, she would perhaps go through it all properly but Elijah Ryecroft's business affairs currently held no interest for her. Her regrets were all for Hannah, that her own pride and hurt had kept her away from Wickthorpe, even after the death of her father. In doing so, she had lost the opportunity to know the woman who had always secretly loved her daughter and who had herself been a victim.

There was also nothing in the box which shed more light on the nineteenth century book, based upon the life of Martha Lightbody, which Mabel had lent her mother. Deborah had contacted Mabel's solicitors and enquired as to its whereabouts – a long-shot, she knew. So far, she had heard nothing back. She was told by Kai Melandri that Mabel had left the proceeds of her bungalow to a charity which supported work in Malawi. A house-clearing company had been used to dispose of the contents. Deborah was anxiously awaiting the name of that company so she could make further enquiries. The prospect of reading the book was tantalising; the possibility that such a significant document may elude her was devastating. She had history with the Witch of Wickthorpe; she needed to find out more about her. She had even phoned Honoraria Simpson-Fairchild, to see what Wickthorpe's self-proclaimed local history expert could tell her. Unfortunately, not much beyond the facts Deborah already knew, but Honoraria had begun her own enquiries and hoped to have more information soon. The call had ended with an entreaty for Deborah to join the Wickthorpe History Society. Perhaps she would, if it meant finding out more. The mystery of Martha Lightbody haunted her dreams and she needed answers.

Her future regarding Tom Oldridge was more difficult to resolve. Things between them had somehow become complicated. As she convalesced, he continued to live in her house but slept in one of the spare rooms. He was attentive and caring towards her, as he had always been, but a distance now strained between them and she was not sure why. The passion, which had always flared hot in their relationship, had been snuffed out, leaving her feeling frustrated and confused. To compensate, she withdrew from him, remaining cool and polite. Having recognised that she loved him, she had wondered, in hospital, what the future held for them both. Marriage was not important to her. Being with him, loving him, and having her love reciprocated, were all that mattered. But now, having returned home, he was clearly having second thoughts about their relationship. The realisation had torn her hopeful heart into shattered pieces. Not that she would admit it or show it, of course. If he did not want her, she would deal with it, pride and self-respect intact.

The onset of harvest meant Tom was working long hours. Some evenings, she found herself joined by Rick Billington, probably at the behest of Emma, who was busy alongside her dad. He really was a lovely lad. She could see why Emma was so smitten. Sadly though, he still regarded Emma only as a good mate and Deborah foresaw another broken heart when Rick met someone else. He often spoke to her of his sister, and his family's anger and frustration that they still had no answers. How could they come to terms with Freya's death when they were no closer to understanding the manner of it? They were adamant she had not committed suicide and that someone had killed her. None of them would rest until they discovered the identity of Freya's mystery man and had brought him to account. Even if he was not responsible for her death, they wanted to know what had happened. Rick told her his parents had recently hired a private investigator and were pinning their hopes on his ability to provide answers where detectives had failed. Deborah prayed this strategy would garner success. Not knowing had to be the worst.

Throughout the day, clouds had been building and fat droplets of rain spattering the window quickly merged into a heavier shower, enough to halt the progress of the combine harvester for the rest of the day. Tom would be in soon and it was time for them to have a talk. She knew what she had to do; she had a plan.

She hoped the execution of it did not destroy her.

***

'Annoying about the rain.' She gave Tom a sympathetic smile as she handed him a bowl of pasta bolognese.

He thanked her politely and shrugged. 'Yes, but the forecast is good for the next few days. Depending upon how quickly it dries out, we should get the wheat done before the next band of rain, forecast for the weekend.'

An awkward pause.

'Look, I ...'

'I've been ...'

They both stopped and looked at each other.

'You go first,' Tom said, laying down his fork and watching her intently.

She did the same, sick with dread. 'It's just ...' She steeled her shoulders and swallowed. 'I've really appreciated all that you've done for me and everything ... and the fact that you've stayed here while I've been recovering ...' She stopped. Impossible to say the words.

'You want me to move out,' Tom said stiffly. 'It's fine. I understand.'

Her heart plummeted. She had been hoping, against hope, this conversation would take a happier turn. At almost fifty, she had at last found the love of her life but he was not for her. Another disappointment in a string of disappointments. He did not return her feelings.

Tom pushed away from the table. 'I'll get my things together and get out of your hair.'

'No, please ... finish your meal first.' She gestured helplessly at the discarded pasta.

'I'm afraid I have no appetite.' He stood and walked away.

'Wait!'

When he stopped and turned, she rose and walked to face him. She was not prepared to let things finish between them in this mediocre fashion. She wanted answers. Why hadn't it worked? Why had his feelings cooled so readily? He was not getting off the hook this easily.

His eyebrows raised at her approach. 'Look,' he said through gritted teeth. 'It's been clear for some while that you no longer ... care ... for me as I care for you. I guess you're planning on returning to London. I can't say I blame you, after all that's happened. I suppose I was expecting it.'

His words stopped her planned speech in its tracks. 'What do you mean – I don't care for you? It's *you* who has been distant since I returned from hospital.'

'I beg to differ. *You* have grown increasingly cold towards *me*. Even Emma and Rick have noticed.'

She stared at him in confusion. 'But that's because it was clear you were having second thoughts about us.'

It was his turn to look puzzled. 'What on earth made you think that?'

'The way you behaved towards me. The odd, light peck on the cheek but nothing more. I want to know why. What happened to make you feel so awkward around me?'

He shook his head. 'You'd been through something horrendous and I was just giving you time and space to get over it.' He frowned. 'Of course, I wanted to kiss you senseless when I finally got you home, but you had suffered a serious head trauma, quite apart from nearly drowning! I was so desperate for you, it nearly killed me to act with such restraint. But I would never have forgiven myself if I'd hurt you. And then it became clear you were detaching yourself from *me*. I guessed that was because you were making plans to leave.'

Hope surged in her chest. 'I'm not leaving,' she murmured, her eyes locked with his. 'I'm staying in Wickthorpe.'

'Then why ...?'

'I didn't know why you were being so ... polite around me. It was like we were strangers. I thought it was because ...'

'Ssh.' He placed a finger against her lips and closed the gap between them, pulling her into his arms. 'I love you, Debs. I've been completely crazy about you since the moment we met. I've dreamt of marrying you and spending the rest of my life with you. Never ever think otherwise. The big question is ... how do you feel about me?'

'Oh.' She stared up at him, drowning in the passion she saw in the tortured lines of his face, as he awaited her reply. 'I'm not sure about marriage ...' Instantly, she felt him begin to pull away and tightened her grip on his arms. 'But the rest of it ... I feel the same ... spending the rest of my life with you ... everything ... I ...' She got no further as he covered her mouth with his own and her whole body ignited in response.

Much later, as she lay cradled in his arms, listening to the strong, steady beat of his heart, she told him of her teenage pregnancy and the daughter she had lost. 'I love you,' she told him as he held her close and kissed away her tears. 'Apart from my employers at the time, who were like the family I never had, no one knows about Natasha. But I wanted you to know. I've made mistakes in my life. I'm not perfect.'

He pulled away, just enough so she could see the intense love burning in his eyes. 'To me, you are,' he said.

CHAPTER 42

Two months passed and colours of autumn graced the trees and hedgerows of Wickthorpe. Memories of the scandalous events of the summer cooled, along with the weather, and village life returned to normal.

Enid Green, unrepentant after a visit from the police, continued to spout poison about Deborah Ryecroft whenever she got the chance, but most of it had to be directed at her long-suffering daughter, Ava, as her previous allies avoided her. Several weeks had crawled by without a visit from Andrew. Ava seemed to know more of his whereabouts than she, his poor, invalid mother! Disgraceful! According to Ava, he had recently taken his family on a holiday to Cornwall. Interestingly, she also discovered he no longer spent evenings at *The Lamb Inn*. Enid would never admit it to another living soul but she strongly suspected Andrew was the man involved with Freya Billington before she died. Nothing got past her, and she knew her son had been a regular at the pub in the weeks leading up to the girl's death. Despite what her stupid daughter thought, she was aware of her son's nature. Certainly, she did not blame him for the affairs since his marriage to that insipid wife of his. If Julie was unable to keep him satisfied, it was little wonder her boy had to seek solace elsewhere. Still, in all other respects, he had married well and, when Frank Newman died, he would inherit, via his wife, a thriving and profitable business. Andrew had apologised for his absence and told his mother he had to keep Julie sweet for a bit. Whilst Enid didn't like it, she accepted he had to do what was necessary. She could be patient.

That weasel, Philip Holder, was another story! He had crawled into his hole and she had not seen hide nor hair of him since. Doubtless, he had been frightened off after that visit from the police. He always was a spineless wretch.

Despite what both men might think, Enid had not ceased her plotting against Deborah Ryecroft. Far from it. Her family had history with the Wickthorpe Witch. Her father had often talked of it when she was a child and fragments from those long-forgotten conversations had recently resurfaced. In particular, Enid had recalled her father mentioning a book, one she had never read. It told the story of the original Wickthorpe Witch and revealed how Deborah Ryecroft's family were involved. Enid's family too. She had always known, but the book could provide the proof to get rid of the witch and her curse, once and for all.

She just needed to find it ...

***

Ava was thrilled to see her brother, at long last, taking a proper interest in his family. When she had last seen them, after their return from two weeks in a beautiful cottage in Looe, Julie and the girls had seemed happier than she had ever seen them. It would be wonderful if recent events had cured Andrew of his wandering eye but, privately, she had her doubts. Her brother was a chameleon, excelled at playing whichever role he chose. It was difficult to imagine this latest incarnation enduring but perhaps that was her own cynicism at work. Love never lasted. She knew it. She was the living proof. Men (her beloved father excluded) were faithless creatures whose heads were soon turned by a pretty face.

Yet, her hopeless heart still yearned for Patrick Velaman, her first and only love. It had been autumn or 'fall' (as he called it) when she kissed him that last time before he left for Cleveland, and the changing colour of the leaves never failed to bring her heartache back to full focus. Sometimes, her silly imagination would conjure up his return. *He had always loved her; he had never forgotten her. Could she ever forgive him?* And she would fall gladly into his open arms ...

Foolish woman to even think such thoughts. It was the nostalgia of a warm afternoon in mid-October, and the gentle shift of golden sunlight glinting through reddish orange foliage of the beech tree in their back garden, making her feel so stupidly romantic. An impatient brush of the hand was sufficient to disperse the unwanted tears. Time to prepare the evening meal. Cottage pie. Her mother would complain about mince but too bad! She had given up trying to please her.

***

As Ava bustled about her tiny kitchen, Honoraria prepared for the latest meeting of the Wickthorpe History Society. The membership had shown a gratifying increase in recent months. Even Deborah Ryecroft had started coming along, although so far, and rather disappointingly in Honoraria's opinion, she had failed to persuade gorgeous Tom Oldridge to do the same. The two of them seemed to be very much an item, another dash to her own romantic hopes, but she wished them well. She liked to think it was the timely information she shared with Tom, on that fateful night, which led to Deborah's rescue. Certainly, the couple had thanked her and even extended an invitation to a dinner gathering. Her social life had taken an upward turn and for that she was grateful.

For tonight's History Society gathering, she had booked the Village Institute. Colleagues from other local history groups were expected and the focus was once again on seventeenth century witchcraft in East Anglia. A large attendance was anticipated. One gentleman, who ran a history group in Little Horseshoes, a village on the Norfolk coast, had told Honoraria he may have discovered further information about the legendary Martha Lightbody. He had refused to be drawn upon the nature of that discovery, tantalising Honoraria with the promise of revelation on the night of the meeting. His name was Marcus Monk and, after they had spoken on the phone, she could not wait to meet him in person. Marcus had a deep, cultured voice, which conjured images of oysters, caviar and a Regency style romp between the sheets. He would be tall with a fine head of hair and dark eyes. A widower. With a thing for redheads. A salivating prospect.

***

Julie Green tiptoed upstairs to bestow a goodnight kiss upon each of her sleeping daughters. It was something she did every night, even though she repeated the ritual later when she went to bed. A superstition. Her kiss would keep them safe. Andrew thought she was daft but, if they were going out together for the evening, she refused to leave before the girls had fallen asleep and she had kissed them. They were everything to her.

She and Andrew had been going out more as a couple recently. 'Date nights,' Andrew called them. He had certainly been making an effort since she challenged him about his lies – the ones he told both her and the police – concerning his whereabouts on the weekend Freya Billington died. It had taken all her courage to confront him. She had been shaking with anxiety, fearing the worst. But she had been determined. The worry over it all was making her ill. She had threatened to throw him out of the house and tell her father why. He would lose everything ... unless he told her the truth.

Of course, to start with, Andrew denied it all, growing angry and storming out of the house. When he returned, a day later, he was a chastened man, pleading with her to forgive him and to give him another chance. 'For the sake of the girls,' he begged. Oh yes, he knew her weak spot.

She had insisted on answers. Finally, he confessed he had been unfaithful. 'It meant nothing,' he sobbed. 'I was weak. It was a terrible mistake. I promise it won't happen again. You and the girls are everything to me.'

'Was it Freya Billington?' she demanded.

He swore it was not.

Had he told her the truth? Did she believe him? She had to; she could not bear the alternative. Eventually, she had relented and let him off the hook, as he had known she would. She had to admit, things between them had been good since then. A family holiday; date nights; board games with the girls on rainy weekends; trips to the coast when the weather was fine. They even cuddled up together on the sofa most evenings after the girls had gone to bed. Life was good. As Julie bent to kiss Misha's dark head, she prayed it would last.

***

Jane Holley stared sightlessly at her phone. The screen showed a text from Honoraria, a reminder about the History Society meeting that evening.

She would not be attending. Whilst she had, after a leave of absence of several weeks, returned to work, she was seldom seen out within society. She just could not face it.

The villagers of Wickthorpe had remarked upon the change in her. When she did put in a rare appearance at a village function, it was as if she was there under sufferance, they said. Acquaintances commented privately upon her listless manner, wondering if she had suffered some kind of breakdown. Her husband, Seb, however, seemed unperturbed by his wife's malaise. He remained his jovial, good-humoured self as he conducted check-ups, diagnosed ailments and made hospital referrals, as usual. But that was insufficient to stop people talking. *All was not well in the Holley household.* It was widely considered that the handsome doctor had made a poor match in the first place. 'Whatever did he see in that miserable woman?' villagers asked with a degree of malicious relish. 'He could surely have had his pick.' Some single women of a certain age hoped the marriage was finished, making the gorgeous doctor available for their advances. There were even those, inconveniently encumbered by marriage, who harboured the same fantasy. Dr Holley was universally popular amongst Wickthorpe's female population.

Jane was not privy to the gossip but guessed what people were saying. She retained few illusions, especially where her husband was concerned. Shortly after the body was discovered, her statement to the local constabulary claimed, on the weekend Freya drowned, she and Seb spent the whole time in the house together. She was busy with household tasks and Seb was embroiled in a never-ending pile of paperwork. It was such a filthy weekend, neither of them had ventured at all. *A lie.* Seb was away on that Saturday, as he so often was at the weekends, gallivanting with his latest conquest. He returned unexpectedly, early Sunday morning, while she was still asleep. When she awoke, she discovered him showering in their guest bathroom. Downstairs, clothes circled in the washing machine. She remembered making some acidic comment about both activities and being told to mind her own business. Seb was preoccupied and short-tempered, and she knew better than to question him further. A little later, she was required to drive him to a supermarket in Ipswich where his car was parked.

Clearly, his love life had not gone to plan that weekend, she thought, with a certain amount of glee.

When the awful revelation of Freya's death emerged, Seb had given her strict instructions about the alibi she was expected to give him, should the police come asking. It was not the first time. Trouble seemed to follow Seb around. Naturally, she did as he asked. For her own sake, it was important to protect her husband's untarnished reputation. It would be humiliating to have his sexual shenanigans investigated and, even worse, given a public airing.

However, much later, as further information about Freya's private life emerged, specifically the suspicion she had been involved with a married man, she began to wonder. A detail she had forgotten at the time fell into place. That Sunday, the day before the body was discovered, Seb had driven off, despite the rain, and been gone for a couple of hours. He refused to say where he had been. On Monday morning, when he drove them both to work, she noticed the interior of his Lexus was immaculate. On the previous Friday, she had nagged him about its filthy state. When she commented, he snapped that the car had been valeted on Saturday, to stop her whining. Yet, two weeks later, when she checked the pockets of his jacket before sending it to the dry cleaner's, she found the receipt. The car had been valeted not on Saturday but on *Sunday*. In torrential rain. Why had Seb lied about it? Was it a genuine mistake or did her husband have something to hide?

It was then that the possibility first occurred to her. Was *Seb* Freya Billington's mystery man? *He couldn't be.* She did not believe it ...

But if he *was*, what did that mean? Surely, he could not have been involved in Freya's death? *Definitely not.* But the more she thought about it, the more she worried. And what about all those other times she had covered for him?

The worst of it was, she could not speak to Seb of her latest suspicions. If she were a stronger woman, she would ask him outright. Demand answers. She never would though. Not now. That time was long past ... and meanwhile the face of Freya Billington haunted her nights.

EPILOGUE

Letter addressed to Roger Holley Esq
11ʰ November, 1645

Sir,

I have been most industrious 'pon your behalf.

You asked me to make enquiries as to the whereabouts of one Martha Lightbody. In the course of said enquiries, I thought it desirous to discover something of her background. She was born Martha Sturry in 1622 to parents, Solomon and Mary. She was one of seven children and lived in the town of Kings Lynn where her father and brothers work as wool merchants. Thereupon, I travelled to Kings Lynn to learn whether she had mayhaps sought solace there. You may rest assured as to my discretion with regard to those questioned. In all instances, I was informed there have been no sightings of the woman you seek. Should she make an appearance, I have bribed several in her neighbourhood to notify me post haste.

Meantimes, her husband, John Lightbody, has also travelled to Norfolk, to the village of Little Horseshoes, where his brother works a small piece of land. A child journeyed with him. Sources say the man is much downcast, convinced of his wife's death. Again, I have informants in place should she arrive thence.

Despite my extensive searches, I regret to report I have been unable to detect the whereabouts of Martha Lightbody. Are you sure she lives? Myself, I can only conclude she may have perished afore now.

Do you wish me to continue in the service your employ and continue my investigations? I await your instruction.

Your servant,

Ralph Holder.

Roger Holley tossed the missive carelessly aside. The nerve of the man! Holder clearly thought his time was being wasted but, despite the grovelling claim, his 'servant' had failed him. Martha Lightbody was alive. He was sure of it. The knowledge seeped through his blood and vexed his skin like an itch he could not scratch. He would not rest until he had found her.

And then he would take great delight in destroying both her and her curse, once and for all.

***

ACKNOWLEDGEMENTS

Writing a novel, in my experience, is a journey beset with difficulty and self-doubt. I am thankful for many people who have given me support and encouragement throughout the process. Special thanks must go to Sue, Sara, Mark, Sandra, Jan, Lily and Kerry, who agreed to critique *The Lightbody Legacy*. I fully appreciate your insights, advice, comments and encouragement. My book would be a lesser novel without them. I am also grateful to my friends on social media for their advice, morale-boosts, support and humour, which have kept me going through the tough spots.

Thank you, Rob and Derek, for designing the cover, and especially to Alex, my editor, proofreader and a complete star.

Most importantly, I would like to thank **you** for choosing to read *The Lightbody Legacy*. If you enjoyed it, I would appreciate a review, however brief. Reviews are invaluable in helping other readers to find my books.

I really hope you are now itching to read *The Lightbody Bequest*, the second part of *The Lightbody Mystery* duology.

BOOKS BY CAROLYN RUFFLES

The Lightbody Bequest.
The second and final book in *The Lightbody Mystery series.*

What happened to Martha Lightbody?
Was Freya Billington murdered?
Who else is scheming against Deborah Ryecroft?

The Suffolk village of Wickthorpe is slowly recovering its equilibrium after the dramatic events of the summer, but problems remain. Ava Green finds living with her mother increasingly difficult, and dreams of Patrick Velaman, her long lost love. Emma Oldridge's unrequited passion for her best friend, Rick Billington, seems as hopeless as ever, especially when Rick's ex, Amelie Charles, reappears on the scene. Honoraria Simpson-Fairchild continues to seek new ways to spice up her love life, while Jane Holley's world unravels around her.

Meanwhile, the legend of the Wickthorpe Witch continues to haunt many in the village. After her horrific experience, Deborah is convinced her fate is somehow linked to that of the original witch. She wants to find Mabel Littlebody's book, *The Life and Times of Martha Lightbody*, to discover more. Honoraria is also determined that Wickthorpe's History Society should find out what happened to Martha Lightbody. Enid Green has her own secrets concerning the village curse, and seeks further information about the witch to use for her own ends.

And the body of another woman is found in Dark Water Lake ...

Discover more secrets, intrigue, and romance in *The Lightbody Bequest.*

Other titles by Carolyn Ruffles.

The Girl in the Scrapbook.
Who to Trust.
The Vanishing Encore.

https://carolynrufflesauthor.com.

ABOUT THE AUTHOR

Carolyn Ruffles writes both contemporary and historical fiction, laced with mystery, romance and suspense. She loves reading books which tell a compelling story: books with drama and emotional depth; books with characters who stay with her, long after their tale has ended; books about ordinary people embroiled in extraordinary situations and learning about themselves in the process. This is what she strives to write.

Having retired from teaching, Carolyn wrote her first novel, *The Girl in the Scrapbook*, which was published in November, 2018. *Who To Trust*, followed in March 2020 and *The Vanishing Encore*, her third book, in 2021. If you wish to find out more about Carolyn, visit her website https://carolynrufflesauthor.com. By signing up to her readers' list, you will receive the link to a free short story, *Memories Forgotten*, about a subject close to her heart.

Carolyn lives in Norfolk with her husband Mark. When she is not reading or writing, she loves visiting interesting places, walking, gardening, and looking after her two beautiful grandsons. She also loves spending time with family and friends, especially if there's a glass of wine involved!

Printed in Great Britain
by Amazon